THE VEILED DESCENDANTS

Book 2 of The Veiled Duchess Series

Sophia Menesini

Copyright © 2020 Sophia Menesini

All rights reserved

The characters and events portrayed in this book are fictitious. Any similarity to real persons, living or dead, is coincidental and not intended by the author.

No part of this book may be reproduced, or stored in a retrieval system, or transmitted in any form or by any means, electronic, mechanical, photocopying, recording, or otherwise, without express written permission of the publisher.

ISBN-13: 9798652739317

Cover design by: Despina Panoutsou
Printed in the United States of America

*To [insert name here], thanks for the encouragement
to a twenty-year-old turning her fanfiction
into a tragically conceived indie book.*

CONTENTS

Title Page
Copyright
Dedication
Chapter 1: Prologue — 1
Chapter 2: Beginnings — 11
Chapter 3: At Game's End — 27
Chapter 4: Red-Handed — 45
Chapter 5: Governor — 57
Chapter 6: Father's Daughter — 68
Chapter 7: All the Empress's Horses, All the Priest's Men — 77
Chapter 8: The New Crew — 83
Chapter 9: I Think I'm in Trouble — 94
Chapter 10: The Queen's Pirates — 102
Chapter 11: Setting Sail — 111
Chapter 12: The Sins of the Father — 124
Chapter 13: I'd Fight for You — 135
Chapter 14: Get to Know Me — 146
Chapter 15: Whose Side Are You On? — 152
Chapter 16: Strange Bedfellows — 163
Chapter 17: Trial by Boiling Water — 170
Chapter 18: The Cost of Power — 181

Chapter 19: Kindred	191
Chapter 20: The Bond that Binds	207
Chapter 21: The More You Know	213
Chapter 22: Back to the Island	223
Chapter 23: The Family Thicker than Blood	233
Chapter 24: Close to Me	243
Chapter 25: Forever Isn't Long Enough	254
Chapter 26: I See You	260
Chapter 27: Keep the Faith	269
Chapter 28: Brother's Keeper	283
Chapter 29: Mercy	295
Chapter 30: I Failed You	305
Chapter 31: The Wedding	319
Chapter 32: The Last Dance	336
Chapter 33: First Night	344
Chapter 34: Warm by the Firelight	355
Chapter 35: Last Night	373
Chapter 36: Last Rites	376
Chapter 37: Don't Tell	394
Chapter 38: One Last Hope	417
Chapter 39: Darkest Edge	427
Chapter 40: The Focal Point	456
Chapter 41: Dawn	465
Chapter 42: Hades's Bargain	467
Chapter 43: Too Late	471
Chapter 44: Inheritance	481
Chapter 45: Epilogue One	500
Chapter 46: Epilogue Two	505

Glossary	509
Acknowledgement	519
About The Author	521
Books By This Author	523

MAP OF NEREID

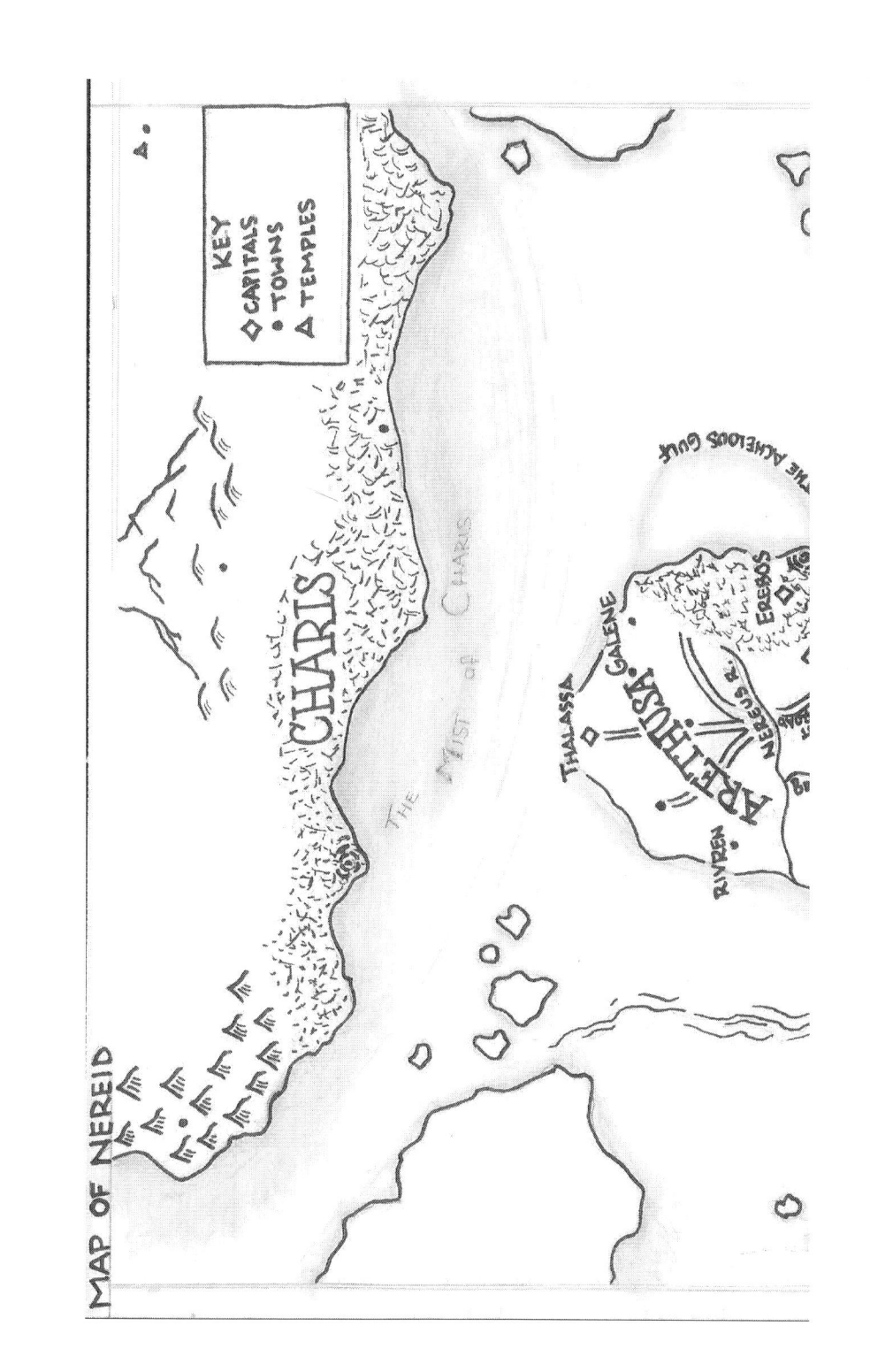

KEY
◇ CAPITALS
● TOWNS
▲ TEMPLES

CHARIS

THE MIST OF CHARIS

THE ACHELOUS GULF

THALASSA
GALENE
NEREUS R.
RIVREN
ARETHUSA
EREBOS

TENARO ISLANDS
PORT TOWN
ORENA
THE OLD SEA
THE AIOLOS REEF
MÉTIS
OCEANUS
TRIDENT FORK
THE EASTLANDS
MELINOE R.
LYCOS
COCYTUS
SLAVER'S BAY
HYPHUS
ACHERON
THE NEREIDAN OCEAN
HELIOS
KNOWMAN'S CANYON
PIERIA ISLANDS
N
S

CHAPTER 1: PROLOGUE

Ceto

The wind filters through the palms, shaking the leaves and casting shadows on the black sand in the palace courtyard.

Empress Ceto sighs, admiring her beautiful garden from where she sits on a delicately carved stone bench. Black thorny bushes with ruby-red roses spring from what should be unfertile sand.

The sky overhead is dark and dreary in Acheron, the capital of Lycos, and enslaved elves stand at each end of the courtyard holding a large canopy over Her Majesty and the imperial court.

Large pillows are scattered around the garden where she waits with her royal cabinet, keeping the serpent-like courtiers close.

In particular, a dark-haired vision with sharp pointed ears and a razor smile stretches contentedly on her pillow closest to the throne. Thetis.

Ceto withholds a growl at Thetis's cavalier attitude. She wishes she could accuse her of treason, but the elf has too many allies and too many talents.

The empress's spies can't even confirm Thetis's involvement in the poisoning last month.

If only Ceto had stopped the marriage between Thetis and Count Aegis four years ago. How the siren weaseled her way into that spiteful old count's heart, no one truly knows.

She merely appeared in the empress's court one day on Aegis's arm. Furthermore, when he died a year later with no proof of foul play, the law was clear.

Thetis would receive his position in court.

Every assassin she sent after Thetis failed, and after a while, she gave up trying and decided to make use of the elf when she could.

None of them have any idea why they've been called to the garden today, but until she knows for sure who helped that whore of an elf escape, she plans to keep them all on their toes.

Several new faces appear at the entrance to the courtyard following a frail elven woman with a limp.

Ceto glances to Thetis, searching for a reaction to the other elf's pain, but the countess simply ignores the slave, and instead her brown eyes narrow on the strangers' faces.

The empress observes the dark-haired men walking down the courtyard aisle with the foreign tattoos obscuring most of their facial characteristics. They all have long hair of varying shades, braided back into tight buns, and they remain behind the servant with proper etiquette.

Once they're a fair distance from Ceto, each one kneels, waiting for her acknowledgment.

"My lady, they refused to give their individual names," the slave explains gesturing to the men kneeling behind her with a frightened scowl.

The elf's hands are laced together in front of her and her eyes are downcast. With difficulty, she also kneels at her mistress's feet.

"They wished to simply be announced as the Hunters."

Ceto's eyes scan each man. She gestures for the elderly elf to come closer. Again, with difficulty, the slave stands and limps over to Ceto carefully.

The empress smiles sweetly and, once they're face-to-face, backhands her.

The woman cries as her bad leg gives out from under her and she falls to the ground. Whimpering, she looks up at Ceto, cradling her cheek in pain.

"That'll be all. Leave now," Ceto commands.

The slave scurries up—but she's careful not to move too quickly and bring attention to herself.

A moment of silence passes as Ceto allows members of her court to examine the Hunters, and she grins especially at Thetis.

They're a guild of some of the finest bounty hunters in the known world. Native to Helios and faithful to the god of sunlight, Apollo. They're ruthless, intelligent, and above all, never stop searching for their marks.

"Hunters? Are you?" Ceto inquires mockingly.

She crosses her legs in a seductive manner. Her dress glimmers, opaque at the top and falling translucent just about mid-thigh, trailing behind her in a long train of see-through material.

Her feet are bare and the one still touching the ground draws circles in the black sand.

The leader makes himself known with a slight nod, answering her flippant question. He kneels at the forefront and Ceto notices he has the most tattoos.

His tan skin looks rough, wrinkled like leather, and his hair is as black as Ceto's.

He looks up, remaining in a kneeling position on the ground in front of her, but she can feel his eyes raking over her body with obvious lust.

She watches his every move as his gaze lands on her bare midriff and his tongue darts out of his mouth, wetting his bottom lip. He takes in her velvet black top and the blood-red beads falling like droplets over her breasts, her green dupatta scarf draping over her bosom to portray a semblance of modesty against the skintight top piece.

When he's done examining her, his black eyes meet her golden-brown ones.

"Aye, Your Majesty."

His voice is gravelly, experienced, and Ceto leans forward, resting her weight with her arm on her crossed knee.

"And your real names," she commands.

"I don't have one. None of us do. An identity makes it impossible for anyone to disappear. I am simply a Hunter," he tells her plainly, and she can see he isn't being coy.

She lets the answer go for now.

There's seven of them. Two blonds, a redhead, and three brunets not counting their black-haired leader. They're all varying ages and their hair is done up in the same bun style. They wear the same outfit, too, all black leather: pants, boots, and long-sleeved shirts with an embroidered golden sun over their left breast pocket.

"Did your guild tell you why I sent for you?"

The lead Hunter shakes his head.

Ceto gestures with her hands for him—for all of them—to stand, straightening up her posture as they do.

They're quite tall but far enough away from Ceto so it doesn't look like they're looking down at her.

Thetis has been watching their every move, her face smiling, carefree, but Ceto can see the gears turning in her mind as she considers every word.

"Why is he here?"

Ceto grins and turns to Thetis, happily acknowledging her outburst.

"I have a job for them."

The music in the courtyard stumbles. Barely enough that only a trained ear would pick up on it. And the voices turn to a whisper.

Now she has everyone's attention.

"Nereid is infested," Ceto continues. "I've hired you to exterminate the infestation. For the good of all."

"And this infestation?"

The lead Hunter's eyes flicker briefly to where Thetis is lounging.

Ceto smirks as the countess tenses, waiting for her empress's response and surely expecting a different answer than the one she gives.

"Pirates."

Thetis and the Hunters seem to visibly relax. It's then that she notices the redheaded Hunter is an elf.

How typical, she chuckles to herself.

"They have terrorized the countries of Nereid for long enough, and as a woman of law, it's time I put an end to it," Ceto grandstands.

There's an applause from the imperial court and she nods, taking a bow for her theatrics.

"Noble effort." Thetis claps alongside the rest of the serpents. "But pirates are practically their own civilization, with numbers equivalent to the elves in Erebos. They are but seven men."

"No. They're not," Ceto challenges Thetis and stands.

Her hair falls in ringlets down her back, and her crown of obsidian shards twinkles off the green firelight burning in the lamps at each corner of the courtyard.

"They are the Hunters of Apollo."

The room's whispers extinguish.

The Hunters of Apollo are known throughout Lycos, but to actually acquire their services is as dangerous as being one of their marks.

Thetis looks like a gaping fish trying to find her wits as she finally recognizes the sigils on their suits. Ceto hums in pleasure at the elf's expression.

"We work with many pirates," the lead Hunter drawls. "Some are great allies of the Hunters. What you're asking would cost a steep price."

"I am well aware."

The lead Hunter sighs. "So what do you offer?"

"Something your guild has been desperate to reach for years. Access to the Lycon Vault of Secrets."

The court bursts into outrage, counts and countesses standing with shouts of objection. She is well aware that most members of her court are probably marks of the Hunters, and presumably what's keeping them alive today is the information hidden in her vault.

The Hunter is silent; it's obvious he's thinking the offer over.

"All of it?"

"Not all. But you won't be disappointed," Ceto states.

"You don't strike me as the charitable type, Empress. Why do you want to kill pirates?"

"Oh, I don't really, some can be quite useful. But you see, there's one in particular and I plan on taking everything she holds dear. Starting with her whole bloody race."

She has a moment where she imagines Shea vividly in the Hunter's place. Kneeling before the empress in chains, glaring with every bit of her rebellious fire.

"So, you want us to kill her? This pirate?"

The image of Shea fades at the Hunter's question.

"No."

"No?"

The question comes from Thetis, who is now sitting up straight in her seat, fully invested in the conversation.

"No. I want you to make her wish you had. I want you to take everything from her. Her crew, her ship, her allies, and her boy. And then I want you to bring her to me at any cost necessary. You will be compensated."

"Just who is this pirate?"

Ceto revels as the name leaves her lips, "Captain Shea Lara of the *Veiled Duchess*."

The Hunter doesn't respond.

In fact, his expression sours, and he frowns deeply. His fellow Hunters fidget but draw back into their solid forms.

Ceto's smile disappears, her friendly facade turning cold. "Is there a problem?"

"I'm afraid we can't help you."

"And why not?"

"Let's just say she's…protected. Still, we can take down every other pirate if that's what you wish?"

Ceto's voice turns shrill. "You know what I wish, and you will do as I say!"

The soldiers stationed at the garden walls draw their weapons and the two closest lunge toward the seven men.

The first is skewered with his own blade by the red-haired elf, and the other is held down by the first blond while the second snaps his neck in a choke hold.

Ceto doesn't move.

Her other soldiers hesitate, waiting for her orders. The garden is taut with nerves, and the royals anxiously await the Hunters' next moves.

The leader casually steps over the impaled soldier and walks closer until he's standing before the empress.

"Her protection has been bought by someone more powerful than you. One not of this world. I'd let go of this fixation; you never know, you could find your vault doesn't offer you quite the protection you presume."

Ceto slips her silver dagger from her dress and almost manages to slit the man's throat, but he catches it. A small nick is all she gets.

He looks at her, impressed, running his eyes over her body one last time.

"We'll let ourselves out. Oh. And thanks for the tip. About the vault and all. We'll have to look into it."

He throws the dagger past her head, and it lands somewhere in the garden behind her stone bench.

The black-haired Hunter whistles and the other six turn to leave.

Ceto's breath comes faster.

He turns back to give her a mocking salute, but his

image wavers and instead she sees Shea standing in his place.

She salutes the empress as well and smiles in a gloating manner.

Ceto growls loudly as the image disappears. She feels as enraged as she did when she received the news that Shea helped that Arethusian bitch take back her queendom.

She'd killed as many red-haired elven slaves as she could find in her fury, including her favorite, Lyle.

Lost in her thoughts, Ceto almost stomps her foot in frustration when one of her courtiers screams.

The sounds of grunts and harsh breaths fill the air, and she looks up in time to see the Hunters fighting a new player.

From the look of him, he's another elf. There's something about him that she finds familiar.

He kills every one of the Hunters, leaving six mangled corpses behind him. All of them except the leader.

The elf's face is speckled with gore blending in with his freckles. He manages to pin the Hunter to the ground, hitting him until his face is a battered mess.

Finally, the stranger intertwines his bruised hand into the Hunter's braided hair and drags him across the floor until he's standing in front of Ceto.

The elf drops the Hunter before her, placing his foot on top of the other man's chest, pinning him in place.

She's quite impressed with this new player, but she doesn't want to seem overly eager.

Ceto ignores him, childishly, and sticks her feet into the sand, squishing her toes under the cold ground with a giggle.

She hears the elderly slave attendant she slapped before come running as fast as she can into the gardens, trying to avoid the twisted bodies along the walkway.

The guards stationed around the courtyard remain wary, ready to strike.

Ceto smiles as the slave falls to her knees before her, babbling apologies for allowing someone into the court unannounced.

Ceto pays no attention to the woman's words. Instead she imagines Shea in her place, wearing her iron collar and the same pitiful dress. But the slave's pleas quickly drown out the illusion and Shea disappears before her eyes.

"If you don't quit your incessant chattering, I'll have your tongue!"

The old elf sobs but forces her hands over her mouth to stifle the cries.

Ceto tries not to laugh; she'll have the woman's tongue anyway for allowing this break in protocol, but it's better to let them think they have a chance.

"Go," Ceto commands and the slave does.

She steps closer to her new guest and places her bare foot on the pinned Hunter's face. She wipes her sandy foot over his eyes and mouth, rubbing the dirt into his open wounds.

He groans in pain.

She practically squeals in delight, stepping away so she can look at the elf in front of her fully.

His eyes are stunning, a teal, neither green nor blue. His hair is dark red. He's tall, very tall, and there really is no blood on the elven robes he wears.

Ceto realizes the material's color is actually blue, but it's so dark that to an untrained eye it would look black. His hair is cropped, and his freckles span every inch of his features.

There's a large conch shell attached to a rope belt on his hip. He can't be more than thirty, late twenties perhaps, and he carries himself with the confidence of royalty.

"I must thank you, stranger, for righting the wrong this man insulted me with. But answer me this. Who are you?" Ceto demands, her guards seem to finally find their courage and surround the two of them, drawing their weapons to protect their empress.

The elf doesn't respond.

Ceto bristles at the insolence but asks her next question.

"Why weren't you arrested at the gates?"

"Because I'm not a threat." The man's voice is soft; it sounds as if he's whispering the words.

But Ceto can hear him clearly, she can hear the power behind every syllable.

"These men would say differently, as would the trail of corpses behind you. Now I'll ask once more. Who are you?" Ceto commands.

She snaps her fingers for the other guards in the courtyard to clear the area.

The imperial court is ushered out, until only Ceto, her guards, the mysterious elf, and the pinned Hunter remain.

The elf bows and looks Ceto directly in the eyes. He's mesmerizing, and something about him reminds her of the woman who haunts her every dream.

"My name is Perses. I'm here to talk about the future of Nereid. And I think you can help me."

CHAPTER 2: BEGINNINGS

Beck

Seagulls coo overhead as the large Oceanan ship known as the *Iron Serpent* slices through the gray morning waters with a strong breeze filling its sails.

Naval men mosey about the deck, staying relatively ready against Lycon attack, but they're so far up north everyone is pretty much at ease.

The governor's son clutches onto the rope ladder of the vessel at about half distance to the crow's nest, staring out as the sun rises over the horizon. Fixated on the line where the sky and ocean meet.

The wind pushes his mid-length dark brown hair away from his face, leaving his deep brown eyes exposed to the wide-open sea. The breeze is harsh and it makes his eyes water as the ship pushes against the invisible force, sailing its way toward the peace summit at the palace of Arethusa, where the young man's father will ally himself with the new queen, Joana.

It's been a year since she came into power, after the nasty political uprising led by her own father, which almost destroyed the royal matriarchy. But if rumors were to be believed, she defeated him with the help of a pirate lover, who disappeared just before the new queen took the throne.

Since then she's been putting her queendom back together and helping Oceanus against the growing attacks from Lycos, attempting to take back the free state and rejoin them with the empire.

The young man tries to push any thoughts of his father's—and soon to be his—state away; all he wants is to enjoy the sun on his face and wind off the sea.

"Beck!"

A voice shouts from below, and the young man groans at hearing the irritated tone of his father's advisor echo across the air.

"You're wanted on the afterdeck. Get your head out of the clouds, boy! We're just about crossing the borders of Oceanus into Arethusa."

Beck glares down at his father's old friend, Caius, taking in his solemn features.

From all his years of frowning, first at Beck's father, Orion, and Orion's impulsive behavior, and now at the wild youngling his best friend had produced, it seems the man's blond hair has gone prematurely gray, beginning to stain his beard as well.

Beck grins obnoxiously. "I'll be down in a minute."

He begins his climb reluctantly down, uneager to leave his post, mumbling the whole way under his breath.

"With how far out we've sailed from the mainland, it's not like we'll arrive at Thalassa anytime soon."

Beck's feet hit the upper deck, and Caius walks over and smacks him on the head.

"What was that for?" Beck groans, rubbing the back of his skull. "I came down."

"You shouldn't have been up there in the first place. You're twenty-four years old, three years from inheriting your father's position as leader of Oceanus. You need to stop gallivanting about and start paying attention to the politics ahead of you."

Beck opens his mouth to respond, but he's cut off by a voice from across the deck.

"Caius, cut the boy some slack; Beck get over here now," Orion, governor of Oceanus, shouts before returning to his duties at the map desk.

Chuckling can be heard from the navy men surrounding the two nobles, and Caius, with his everlasting grimace, turns toward the helm with a blushing Beck following behind.

The young leader-to-be admires the harpoon launchers as they walk briskly toward the afterdeck. They're stationed at varying points along the gunwale on either side, a recent invention by Oceanans. They need only aim and load the harpoon and the giant spears would do the rest of the damage.

They jog up the remaining steps to the helm, and Beck straightens his white peasant shirt, tucking any stray material into his dark brown lace-up pants that are also tucked into his black boots. He looks like a crown prince should, though Oceanans don't use words like that, not after escaping the chains of the empire and gaining their struggling independence.

Instead he is Master Beck, the governor's son, who will one day become the governor of Oceanus and rule beside the elected officials of the Oceanus Senate.

But that won't be for another three years; he still has much to learn under his father's teachings—and unfortunately Caius's, who will serve as his advisor as well.

Beck approaches the table in front of the helm.

His father stands at the center with his advisors and the admiral of the navy overlooking the map nailed to the surface.

Beck can't help but glance over his father's strong frame. He wishes he could have inherited his father's stout figure, but instead his muscles are leaner. He figures he must have inherited that from his mother's side.

Lady Elizabetta of Oceanus. She'd been an incredible woman. Fierce where Beck's father was gentle, kind when he was strong, Orion used to tell Beck that she was his perfect match.

Beck was sixteen when she died, killed by Lycon soldiers after she was abducted in an outlying village and then murdered when she tried to escape. Since then, he's begun to feel guilty for his appearance, his light skin compared to his father's tan, his almost black hair compared to his father's light brown, which has highlights of blond and gray running through it.

He even confessed to his father his guilt, but Orion merely laughed and said because of Beck it was like being able to see Elizabetta still, every day, and it made him proud.

Orion looks up from the map he's pointing to, his eyes landing on his son, and his happy grin shakes Beck out of his reminiscing.

"There's my son. Daydreaming, were we?"

Orion teases and gestures Beck closer to the table.

Caius's frown deepens, obviously disapproving of Orion's reaction to the boy's disappearance, but Beck merely scoots around him, grinning back at his father.

They clasp hands in the traditional Oceanan greeting, but Orion also ruffles Beck's hair like he's a child again.

"Dad..." Beck sighs, fixing his hair and pushing the longer strands behind his ears.

"Orion, the boy needs to be more aware of his duties. He will be governor soon." Caius sniffs, his hands clasping behind his back.

Orion shoos the other advisors away, leaving Beck, Caius, the helmsman, and the admiral alone with him.

"Not too soon. He's fine, Caius. You need to relax, honestly you create more wrinkles every day."

"I wouldn't say I'm the one creating them, sir." Caius's eyes narrow at Orion and Beck, but the governor merely laughs a dismissal.

"Admiral, tell my son what we've been discussing."

The Oceanan admiral nods. "Certainly, sir. Well, Master Beck, you're probably wondering why we're sailing so far out from the mainland?"

"It had crossed my mind, yes," Beck answers, and Orion claps him on the back.

"See, Caius, the boy is learning already. Very observant."

Beck stifles a smile and he can practically hear Caius's eyes roll.

"Most *terrific*, sir," Caius drawls.

The admiral doesn't hold back his amusement and chuckles at Caius's sarcasm before continuing, "We received reports that Lycon scouts have been seen all over Nereid, some as bold as to be entering Arethusa regardless of the closed borders to the empire."

Beck shakes his head. "But why?"

"We don't know," Orion responds, looking over the map that Beck now realizes displays all of Nereid.

There are purple crosses all over the chart in every corner of the continent except of course the Eastlands, symbols of sighted Lycon scouts.

Beck's hands tighten on the table's edge and he leans carefully, examining the map more closely.

"It started about a year ago. After the Arethusian coronation. Small teams of Lycon soldiers expanded across the map and then stopped at random points. It's as if they're waiting for something," the admiral explains.

Waiting for what? Beck wonders.

"So that's why we're sailing so far from the edge. You're worried about the scouts along the coast."

"We don't need them reporting back to Ceto any information until we understand why she has so many men stationed across Nereid," Orion states, brushing his fingers over Acheron, Lycos's capital.

"It's an act of war," Caius mutters.

"Perhaps," Orion agrees, "but this is not a war we can fight alone."

"Still, we shouldn't be going to Arethusa, we know nothing of this new queen. She could demand Oceanus become a part of the queendom."

Caius sounds as if he's reminding Beck's father, like they've already had this conversation.

Orion's expression grows tired and his hand rubs his temple in irritation. "Even so, our sources are depleted. Oceanus can't hold Lycos back forever. They're making it over the mountains and we are suffering innocent casualties."

Deep sorrow etches over the lines of his face, and Beck reaches out and grabs his father's hand in comfort, thinking of his mother.

Orion smiles sadly. "I don't care about my title or position. We are fading and we need help. The fact that this new queen has closed her borders to the Lycon Empire is enough for me to believe that she may help us without demanding our freedom in return."

"For our people," Beck states and Orion nods.

"For our people," the older man repeats.

The wind picks up and the admiral has to grab some of the papers from flying off the helm table. The breeze takes on a stronger gust, and Beck sees the helmsman turn the wheel ever so slightly.

The ship shifts perhaps two notches farther out and suddenly the world goes still.

It's as if Zeus, god of the sky, snapped his fingers and the wind melted away. The early morning sun that was shining before, Beck notices, is now covered in clouds. The sky is gray and turning darker. Which should mean more wind, but the sails have fallen flat and the ship slows to a coasting speed.

"Strange," Orion mutters.

Beck turns toward Caius, surprised not to hear him complaining, but finds the old advisor at the edge of the ship looking over the rail toward the bow.

The admiral salutes to Orion and takes off down the steps to see if anything can be done to pick up their speed again.

The air is still, and the men below have gone eerily quiet as if they feel something too, a presence that shouldn't be here.

"Caius?" Beck calls to the older man, taking a step toward him.

"Orion? I—could you come here?" Caius beckons the governor closer, and Orion does as he's asked, stepping around the table and past his son to the helm's rail.

"What is it?" Beck questions.

Caius points out to the horizon, and Beck walks away from them both to the head of the afterdeck, looking out over the bow.

"Do you see what I'm seeing?"

Beck searches for anything out of the ordinary, but he sees nothing. There's nothing out there.

Except, suddenly, something catches Beck's eye. A rippling in the water ahead of the ship—and not a small ripple, because if it were there'd be no way Beck could see it from the helm.

No, a large rippling of the water disturbs the morning waves. And it's heading straight for the ship.

"What in Atlantis—" Orion begins as he sees the ripple too, but he's cut off from finishing his thought.

The beast breaks through the water with a thundering cry. Water explodes over the vessel's deck from the massive splash, carrying some of the men overboard.

Beck holds on to the rail looking over the upper deck, now completely soaked as he stares down a massive, towering serpent.

"Dear gods," Beck whispers, gasping at the size of the creature.

He glances up to the state flag, flying from the crow's

nest, and can't help but be reminded of their symbol and patron god Ladon, a hundred-headed sea serpent from the childish tales of heroes of old, who guarded the eastern reaches of the sea and the island and golden apples of Eris.

But this snake only has one head and it's easily the size of half the ship itself.

Its body is strange, silver with fins that flare out from behind the sea serpent's eyes. There are thin sparkling fins all the way down the creature's long form. It screeches a high-pitched roar and slams its body into the side of the ship.

The ship lurches to the right. There's a crack down below, and men and women scramble, shouting to check the damage.

"To your positions!" Orion bellows, grabbing his son by the arm. "Get down below before you get yourself killed," Orion commands, but Beck shakes himself free.

"I'm not going anywhere."

Water bursts over the upper deck as the sea serpent rises from behind the ship; it screams again and then strikes its head, quick, to crash into the helm.

"Run!" Orion hollers and throws his son over the ship's railing.

Caius jumps from the top of the steps.

Beck can hear the helmsman screaming as he hits the main deck. He gasps for air and watches his dad jump from the upper deck just as the snake's head collides into it and rips the ship's steering off.

Orion lands next to his son with a groan, and water splashes over them both as the helm crashes into the water and the snake submerges once more.

The ship groans at the loss of the back, and Beck knows the *Iron Serpent* won't stay above water long with this much damage.

"Dad?" Beck worries, turning his father over.

Orion's eyes are open, and he looks to Beck with a nod.

"Sir, we need to abandon ship." Caius reaches them

both and pulls them to their feet.

Orion is clutching his ribs, but they all look okay for now.

Beck sees the navy men and women lowering the longboats into the water, but they'll never make it with the serpent out there.

Orion knows it too.

"We can't outrun that thing. We need to take it down."

"Sir, it just took out half our ship—"

"And it's coming back," Beck states, pointing at the rippling water past the wrecked back of the ship.

"The harpoons, how many are left?" Orion grunts, as they all turn back, scanning the remaining parts of the ship.

"Six," Caius sighs.

"Admiral!" Orion shouts.

"The admiral is dead, sir," a young woman calls back as she runs toward the three men.

The ship is teetering, and they all try to adjust their balance as the ship sways.

They're sinking.

"Well, you've just become a navy captain, ma'am," Orion states, slapping the newly named captain on the back, and she grunts from the strength.

"Aye, sir." The woman nods. "What do you need?"

"Officers at the harpoons, we have to take this thing down if we're going to give the rest of the people a shot at escaping."

The female captain nods. "Right, sir, I'll gather the soldiers."

She takes off, shouting orders.

A screech echoes through the air. It's like it's toying with them. The senators and advisors are being loaded onto the lifeboats and lowered to the sea. The sailors shout for Caius, Beck, and the governor to board.

"Go on then, I've got a snake to slay." Orion grins as he reaches out to hug Beck, but Beck steps back.

"I'm not going anywhere without you; if you're manning the harpoons, I am too."

"Beck, you're my heir. I need you on the lifeboats."

"No!"

"Beck, listen to your father—" Caius tries, but Beck cuts him off.

"I'm not leaving you."

Orion sighs and pinches the bridge of his nose. There isn't any time.

"Fine, fine but you do as I say," Orion commands.

"Sir—" Caius objects.

The ship is shaking and Beck can feel the slow descent toward the depths.

"I'll take the center harpoon," Beck says and starts to take off for the launcher when his father stops him.

"Beck?"

"Yeah?" He turns back to his father only to be met with a right hook. The punch lands with enough force that it knocks the young man off his feet.

His back is on the deck and he can't keep his focus, his mind swimming.

"I'm sorry, I love you, I'm sorry, and I love you."

Beck hears his father's muttering and then he's being hoisted off the deck and into someone's arms.

"No," Beck tries to stand, but he can't quite get his legs to stay under him.

"Caius, take him, now," Orion commands, and Beck feels a long kiss on his forehead. Hands hold his face and words are whispered against his cheek: "May you rule with peace and unity."

The coronation promise of a new governor.

And then Caius is dragging Beck toward the lifeboats and he can just barely make out his father heading for the center harpoon on the bow.

Beck struggles, but his vision swims. There are more hands throwing him into a boat and the creature of the damned is screeching into the air. The boat drops with velocity, and as the lifeboat hits the water, Beck's vision begins to clear.

He jerks himself out of Caius's grip as he's rowed farther away from the sinking *Iron Serpent*. He can see the snake leaning onto the ship, and an arm wraps around Beck's waist as he's hoisted back in case he tries to jump overboard.

They're rowing farther away, until they're at a safe enough distance that the sinking ship won't drag them down with it, then it's as if they cross a magical barrier because the wind returns sharply.

Beck shouts for the soldiers to stop rowing and they do, just as confused by the sudden change.

"Row back."

"No, don't," Caius demands.

"I said row back," Beck growls and the soldiers listen.

They row toward the ship, crossing the invisible barrier once more—the wind stops. It disappears like the snap of someone's fingers, and Beck commands them to keep rowing.

And like magic, as soon as they pass whatever line is in the middle of the sea, the wind reappears, whipping harsh and strong.

Shouting brings Beck's attention back to the ship; he can hear the distant release of the harpoons launching, and each one hits the serpent with penetrating speed.

The creature screams in agonizing pain, and Beck can just make out his father at the center launcher in the bow of the ship. He's waiting for the creature to hit the deck—and it does, hard enough that the wood splinters and the men and women on the lifeboats cover themselves from falling debris.

Beck watches as his father releases his harpoon and it lands right in between the serpent's eyes.

It falls.

The rest of its deadweight slams through the main deck and cleaves the ship.

The men and women who manned the launchers are

jumping into the sea, but Beck loses his father's figure in the chaos of the snake taking down the ship.

"The governor!"

Someone shouts from one of the nearby lifeboats, pointing toward the front of the ship, and Beck sees a figure jumping from the bow. He hits the water and that's all Beck needs.

He elbows Caius in the face and dives into the cold water of the sea.

"Beck! You get back here right this instant!"

But Beck ignores him and swims as fast as he can to where he saw the figure fall.

There's a strong current as the ship and serpent sink; his lean muscled arms slice through the water, pulling him closer to where he'll hopefully find his father.

"Dad," Beck calls as he nears the area where he saw his father jump. There's debris everywhere, and Beck pushes his hair out of his eyes as he scans the water for Orion.

Finally he sees a body hung over a piece of floating wood, and he takes off toward it, kicking his legs as fast as they'll go.

"Dad!"

Beck reaches the figure.

"Beck," Orion coughs, blood dripping from his mouth and down his bottom lip.

"Dad, my gods."

Beck feels his father's body, searching for the cause of the pain radiating on Orion's face—and finds it, a large piece of wood sticking out of his father's left side.

"It's okay, I've got you," Beck whispers as his father groans.

"We've got to get to the lifeboats," Orion commands weakly.

Beck adjusts himself so he has a hold on the wooden raft supporting his father from sinking below.

"Yes, little prince, you should swim back beyond my

border before another monster happens by."

Beck startles as a new voice joins his father's, and he looks up to find a man—no, an elf, standing on the water in pristine black robes.

His short red hair is slicked back, and it makes his freckles stand out against the morning light. But what Beck can't shake is that the elf is walking on water.

"Swim, little prince, I'll meet you there."

The man vanishes into thin air and Beck feels something lurch inside himself; he begins to kick, carrying his wounded father on the plank of wood back to the lifeboats. He paddles as hard as he can, and he can feel the moment he passes the invisible border once again.

A wave of water splashes against the force as if there really was something waiting for them, hoping it'd catch Beck and Orion before they crossed.

Beck makes it back to the boat with Caius, and a few of the soldiers jump in to help get Orion into the boat.

Caius sets up a makeshift bed using some of the padding left in the longboats for emergencies, laying Orion on top of it, and he cries out.

They pull Beck in while he tries to catch his breath.

"Caius, there's something else out there—"

Caius turns to look at Beck, but his eyes go wide at something behind him.

Gasps can be heard from the varying lifeboats and Beck begins to shake. He doubts it's from the vicious wind.

People are murmuring and the soldiers stand at attention, drawing their swords.

Beck finally turns.

There he is, standing on the water barefoot. The elf is tall but not abnormally so, perhaps a few inches taller than Beck, who's five foot nine.

The wind whips the strands of his robes around, making him look like death personified. And to Beck, listening to his father's ailing breaths, the piece of wood still stuck in his side, that's exactly what he is.

"Well done, little prince." The elf smiles, and it's taunting.

Beck growls, unsheathing a sword from the soldier's scabbard in front of him and standing to point it at the elf. "Who the Underdeep are you?"

"Ah, forgive me, I'm Perses. Commander of the seas as you've now seen. You shouldn't have crossed my border."

Beck doesn't like the sound of that, and he can hear his father's breath shudder.

"You did this? The serpent?"

"I've given the seas back to the monsters that once ruled them, yes, you would have been safe had you not sailed so far out. The people of Nereid have forgotten that the sea has not always belonged to them. You should thank me for the lesson, it's not one you're likely to forget."

Perses gestures to Orion, and Beck doesn't look back.

His skin feels like it is burning despite the cold.

"How are you here? What do you want?"

"I have a message for the queen of Arethusa. And you're going to tell her for me."

"And why would I do that?"

"Because your father will surely die out here—don't you want to at least give him a chance, little prince?"

Beck bristles at the nickname.

"What are you?"

"*I* am the new ruler of Nereid. And I have the power to help you try and save your father. So, what will it be? Time is wasting."

Beck wants to ask how—why? How can this elf have the power to summon sea monsters, and why did he unleash it upon them? But instead he keeps his grip steady and the sword pointed at the dark elf.

"What's the message?"

"Good choice." Perses grins.

He disappears before their eyes and then reappears just

as quickly, directly in front of Beck. The sword falls from his grip, and in a mocking gesture of the kiss Orion gave his son earlier, Perses kisses Beck's forehead.

Beck gasps as images and words flood his mind. The information is overwhelming, and he falls to his knees on the longboat.

"Beck!" Caius shouts, alarmed. "Get away from him."

His voice trembles as he holds his dying best friend, watching his pseudo-nephew clutch his head weakly.

"You'll tell her?" Perses asks.

Beck breathes heavily and looks up at Perses with angry tears in his eyes. "Yes."

"Very good, little prince, very good."

And then Perses is gone, reappearing back where he began. He pulls a conch shell from his robes. It pulses with black, bubbling power.

"Good luck." Perses smiles and puts the shell to his lips.

Before Beck can object, Perses blows.

Sound fills his senses—including the screams from various members of the survivors.

Beck's eyes close, and when they do, the loud screaming stops. He opens his eyes and finds himself, all of them, all of the lifeboats, on a shore.

And not just any shore.

Beck looks up at the cliffs and sees the palace of Thalassa.

They're in Arethusa. So much is swirling in his head. He can hear people begin to scream again while others are throwing up, sick with vertigo.

Beck listens to his heart beating wildly in his chest, Perses's words echoing in his head.

His father's cries bring him back.

"Get him to the castle! We need to move. I need to see her," Beck shouts, and soldiers scurry to their governor's side.

People climb out of the boats, falling, and Beck can see Arethusian soldiers marching toward them in the distance.

Caius clutches his chest, his eyes wide, as if he's seen Hades himself.

But Beck can't think about that now.

"I have a message for the queen."

CHAPTER 3: AT GAME'S END

Jo

The light is peeking over the sill when Jo awakes. Her eyes adjust to the sunrise glow, and the open arches allow the morning breeze to filter in past the waterfall running over the windows.

She sighs. Relishing just a few more minutes in the warmth of her cream silk and bear fur blankets trapping her own body heat.

They'll be here any minute, she thinks.

Her eyes flicker over the queen's bedchamber, which so long ago belonged to her mother, Queen Triteia.

And now they're hers.

She turns in bed, lying on her back, and looks to her left, imagining vibrant red hair lying over the pillows beside her.

A lithe muscular frame covered in freckles, tan from the sun. Her back faces Jo and it feels so real, like the queen could reach out and touch her. But her fingers grace the empty pillow instead and Jo lets them fall down to the comfortable surface.

One year.

One year since Jo murdered her father, became queen,

and proposed to the woman she loves.

Killing Mariner felt easy in comparison to ruling Arethusa alone.

Jo misses Shea with all of her being.

She gave Lieutenant Soren—well, now her general—instructions to keep an eye on the captain and report her movements to Jo.

The queen made plans in the early months to capture the elf in person, but reports came back that changed her mind.

Shea has been looking for the Lycon Vault of Secrets. The thing that started their entire journey together and the treasure Shea gave up on to save Jo's country.

Jo couldn't stop her after everything, and so after a year, according to the reports, Shea is now close to finding the map, and once she has that, all she'll need is the key.

Jo figures letting her have her last score is the least she can do, but gods, she misses her.

Caeruleus arrives every once in a while with letters and small gifts tucked within his claws.

With every letter Jo feels as if she can last another month, and then a fortnight passes, and she feels alone all over again.

A knock raps at the door, drawing Jo out of her thoughts. She sits up in bed, pushing her blond hair behind her shoulders and straightening her posture.

"Enter."

The double doors open and in storm Rhea and Gaea in their fabulous morning moods with maids following behind.

Jo's two ladies-in-waiting, Beroe and Eione, also enter.

The maids quickly get to work tidying up, and one heads to the enormous white marble fireplace to get it started.

Jo laughs as she notices Rhea and Gaea cling to each other upon entering.

"My dear, it's freezing in here. Did no one keep the

queen's fire roaring all night?" Rhea screeches, rubbing her nearly translucent, white fingers up and down her wife Gaea's arms.

"And what—what are the—the bloody windows doing open?" Gaea shivers.

Beroe, Jo's old schoolmate and friend, signals for the maids to close the arches with a heavy drapery. The fabric closes over the arches, previously displaying the gorgeous falling water over the windows and the sun reflecting off the shower, leaving the room darkened.

"I'd actually prefer the windows open, I like the breeze in the morning, and I asked them not to light the fire until morning. It makes the chambers too warm," Jo explains.

Eione, a noble lady from court who was quickly becoming a close friend, folds back the covers for Jo to get out of bed.

Her hair is red but not the same shade as Shea's—more of a coppery blond, really, and it makes Jo nostalgic every time she sees it.

It's tied up in a tightly braided bun. Her dress is a light purple with a sheer material bunched under the sleeves and above her bodice, giving her chest the appearance of feminine modesty. It falls to floor length and a blue gem sits at the bottom of the corset just as the dress flares out at her hips. The color gives her light skin a creamy look, complementing her brown eyes.

Beroe, her other lady-in-waiting, is in the same style dress. But hers is a light orange color, like the sunset. It makes her dark skin glow, and the red gem at the bottom of her bodice complements her tightly curled brown hair.

Beroe steps forward, offering her hand to Jo, who takes it and stands, smoothing out her white nightgown while Eione folds the covers back over the bed.

"Good morning, Your Majesty." Eione smiles, taking a deep blue, heavy robe from one of the maids, who Jo recognizes as Miranda.

She holds it so Jo can put her arms through.

Once the robe is on, Jo ties the silver rope belt around her waist. She adjusts her hair and murmurs to Eione and Beroe a good morning in return.

"Gaea, Rhea, what are you doing here so early?" Jo questions, eyeing her two advisors.

Beroe and Eione take seats at a table that has been quickly set up by the staff for the queen's breakfast.

Jo walks the rest of the way to them but doesn't take a seat just yet.

After becoming queen, she made her two escorts her advisors, knowing that she couldn't have them watching her every move anymore.

So, like any new queen, she chose her new attendants. Lady Beroe and Lady Eione, esteemed women and daughters of prominent noble council members, and now her friends.

"We thought it might be prudent to discuss the peace summit. The governor will be arriving this afternoon—"

Jo cuts Rhea off, "This isn't anything I don't already know."

"Dear, something like this event hasn't happened since Oceanus's first year of independence a century ago." Gaea frowns, disliking the disregard given to her wife.

"And?" Jo asks, keeping her gaze on both the older women, trying to dissect their expressions.

"They're dying," Rhea sighs. "Their country is on their last breath, and they can't stand against Lycos any longer. They're flailing."

"And you suggest I tell them that?"

"Yes," Gaea agrees, surprising Jo.

"And then you tell them that we'll help," Rhea continues, and Gaea finishes, "By having them give Oceanus to Arethusa, and becoming citizens of the queendom."

There's a moment of silence by every member in the room.

"You're suggesting that the queen uses the peace summit she called, in order to take their country just as Lycos is trying to do, by force?" Beroe says, standing and going to her queen's side.

Rhea and Gaea look at each other and nod.

"Yes," they state together.

"No."

The room returns to the deathly quiet state it had been in a second ago, the staff, Jo's ladies-in-waiting, and her old escorts noting the ice in Jo's voice.

"Joana," Gaea begins.

"Lady Gaea, I am your queen, and while I will always love you"—Jo nods to Rhea—"both of you, you have overstepped your bounds. I have called this summit to offer aid, not threats. You're both excused. And"—Jo takes a breath but keeps her voice firm—"I think it best if you don't attend the welcome rites."

Rhea opens her mouth to object, but Gaea stops her. "We see. As you wish, Your Majesty."

Jo keeps her posture and gaze steady. She waits until the heavy doors have shut behind them and then reaches for Beroe's hand, which is already waiting for her.

"Damn them," Jo whispers.

Eione is also standing, and she helps Beroe urge Jo toward her seat at the breakfast table.

"They are old, Your Majesty, burdened by a time less merciful than today," Eione tries politely to comfort her, but Beroe merely snorts.

"They're two salty old women stuck in the past. But they love you. They need to understand that you are the queen, not their child."

Jo smiles at both of their comments, and as her two ladies take a seat, she can't help but laugh.

"They are quite salty, aren't they," Jo chuckles.

"Must be all the sea air," Eione mutters and then goes silent.

Her eyes widen and her cheeks turn bright red due to

her comment.

Beroe and Jo stare at her wide-eyed as well before breaking into laughter.

"Why, Lady Eione, I don't think I've ever heard you speak ill of anyone before." Jo snorts, thanking her lady's maid Miranda, who smiles as she pours Jo a glass of juice.

"I don't think she ever has," Beroe teases, and Eione smiles.

"Anything for you, my lady." Eione grins and lifts her glass of juice in salute to Jo.

"Well I appreciate it. Now." The table takes a moment to sober and then it's time to get back to their regal duties. "The peace summit."

"Your dress has been chosen," Beroe confirms, "and the royal guard awaits at the port to escort the governor, his son, and the dignitaries to the palace."

"His son?"

"Aye. I mean yes," Eione corrects herself, but it makes Jo smile.

Eione is from an outer estate on the eastern coast of Arethusa, closest to the elven Eastlands. The language is laxer. In fact, life is more casual there in general.

Jo has expressed her wishes to visit someday, as Eione's accent reminds the queen of her red-haired elf.

"Yes," Eione continues, "Master Beck of Oceanus, next in line to become the governor. He rises to power in three years; it wouldn't be a bad idea to speak more directly to him. He'll be the one you'll be dealing with soon enough."

"I see, very good, Eione."

"If I may, ma'am," Beroe begins, and Jo sees Eione subtly shake her head, but of course Beroe doesn't listen.

"I hear that the heir is quite fair to look at."

Eione rolls her eyes and Jo chuckles.

"You have, have you?"

"Yes, perhaps a more permanent alliance would not be unwise to consider," Beroe expresses delicately.

"Marriage," Jo clarifies.

The two ladies nod and Jo realizes Eione agrees.

"No." Jo shakes her head gently but firmly.

Eione sighs. "My lady? It's been a year, and while you are strong to rule by yourself, surely, a consort at your side might, perhaps, alleviate some of your…stress?"

"You've had no one share your bed, and I know you've had offers," Beroe points out.

Jo waves the comments away, eating the bits of fruit and toast on her plate brought by Miranda.

"Beroe, as I appreciate your candor about my stress, I am an engaged woman."

"But are you?" Eione asks.

Jo looks up, shocked, as if she's been slapped.

Eione must see the surprise in her queen's expression because she at least has the decency to look guilty.

"Yes, I am. Arethusa has a consort and her name is Shea Lara."

"Okay then. We are all with you and will support Mistress Shea, but, ma'am, I fear that if you do not bring her in soon, the council will no longer be able to approve your choice and will ask you to find another."

"Soon, Beroe, Eione. She's close. She gave up everything for me to give me my everything back. I have to give her a chance to go after what she wants."

"But why can't she do that here?" Eione questions once more.

"Because as queen I can't support what she's after unless I want war," Jo explains.

Eione's face turns white at the implication.

"But as her fiancée, I can give her time."

"I don't know how much time you two have left," Beroe tells her in all honesty.

Jo places her hand on her friend's in acknowledgment.

Soon the maids are clearing the plates, the table is taken away, and her ladies help her dress for the occasion.

They've chosen a deep blue gown with quarter-length sleeves that fit her every curve. Shimmering, glossy material fans out, and the stiff tulle makes it look almost like ethereal tentacles. They place white metal armor on her shoulders and white plate metal around her neck, more decorative than for actual battle use. A belt made of pearls is placed on her hips, and Eione gets to work on her hair as Beroe helps her into her flat blue velvet shoes.

"And so it's a great honor to have—"

"To receive," Eione corrects as she finishes the many braids on the top of Jo's head, leading to a small bun before the rest of her white-blond hair falls freely down her back. Eione places a silver spiked crown in front of the high bun at the back of the braiding.

"To receive, yes thank you." Joana smiles before going back to practicing her welcome speech. "It is a great honor to receive—"

Beroe begins to stand from helping Joana into her shoes when the heavy double doors to her chambers fly open with tremendous force.

Eione and Beroe step in front of their queen protectively until they see who it is.

Rhea leads a small battalion of men and marches into the room. Jo pats Beroe and Eione to move aside and meets Rhea halfway.

"What's happening?"

"They were attacked," Rhea tells her.

Suddenly Shea's face, bloody and lax, flashes across Jo's mind, and her throat closes up.

"Who?" Jo chokes out.

"The governor and his party," Rhea clarifies and she doesn't comment on the release of breath from Jo as she relaxes ever so slightly.

"Where are they?"

"They're here."

Jo's eyebrows knit together in confusion. "How is that

possible? They're hours off our shores."

"Your Majesty, you need to come immediately. One minute, the entire Oceanus party was at sea and the next they appeared on our shores. I can't explain, but there's someone who can and he needs to see you."

"Who?"

"The governor's son," Rhea tells her.

Jo is already pushing past her, the battalion following their queen's lead as she marches down the halls.

"Where are they, Captain?" Jo demands.

The captain of the castle guard tells her he'll take her to them.

"Joana!"

Jo stops and turns back to Rhea, standing at the door to her chambers.

"He says he has a message for you."

"That's fine," Jo waves her off, but Rhea shakes her head.

"Dear, he says *he* has a message for you."

Jo nods for her to continue.

"He says it's from the god that attacked them."

Jo blanches. "The god?"

"You didn't see him, Jo." Rhea shivers. "There's something out there."

The words put a chill in Jo's spine. She's never seen her escort look so terrified.

Jo nods firmly and snaps for the captain to lead her on.

But she wonders what message a god could possibly have for her?

***

Jo arrives in the ballroom, stepping through the doors, and she can't help but remember all the eyes that fell upon her a year ago when she entered the room on her father's arm.

Wild and worried eyes fly to her presence as she marches down the blue carpet aisle, looking every bit the queen she is.

At the end of the aisle, in front of the thrones, she sees a man that looks to be about her age and an older gentleman with graying blond hair and a thick beard, his frame lean.

As she marches closer to them, the young man tries to speak, "Queen Joana—"

But Jo keeps her gaze ahead on her throne and passes him without a word.

Out of the corner of her eye, before she steps too far and he's out of sight, she sees his arm reach out to stop her, but his attendant restrains him.

Smart man, Jo thinks and finally arrives at her throne. She turns and scans the room, taking in all the scared and sobbing faces, and she knows that Rhea was right.

But what exactly is out there, Jo intends to find out.

She takes her seat on the throne. Five guards take their posts on either side of the dais and another waits at the bottom of the steps to oversee the young man and his escort.

She eyes the young man, memorizing his features. His lithe muscled frame, his dark brown hair and caramel eyes—he's handsome for a boy, she thinks, and then assumes this must be Beck, the governor's son.

The older man with him holds no familial appearance to Master Beck and so Jo wonders, where is the governor?

"What happened?"

Jo waits for a response and finds confirmation in her assumption of Master Beck's identity.

The younger man pulls his arm out of his attendant's grip and stands at the bottom of the steps leading to the thrones.

His escort moves behind him, off to the side, and the Arethusian guard places his hand on his sword gently.

"We were attacked," Beck states.

His eyes are hard and red around the edges, as if he's been crying, or holding tears at bay.

"Where is your father?" Joana demands, letting him

know she knows who he is.

Beck's eyes drop to the floor and there's a tick in his jaw before he speaks. "Fighting for his life in one of your guest chambers, ma'am. He was injured in the attack; a length of wood pierced his abdomen."

Jo closes her eyes. So much for the peace talks.

She opens them again and meets Beck's gaze. "So then, this all falls to you."

Beck straightens up and nods.

"Who attacked you?"

Beck laughs and Jo's eyebrow rises.

"I thought they told you," Beck responds.

"Forgive me if my belief wavers," Jo scoffs.

The anger on Beck's face from her response doesn't affect her nearly as much as it should.

"The only information I was given is that a god gave you a message for me. Spare me the metaphoric speeches, was it another ship that destroyed the *Iron Serpent*?"

"Actually it was another serpent," Beck spits, and Jo can tell the niceties are over. "A sea serpent like nothing I've ever seen. And then a god, he looked like an elven man, but I say god because I've never encountered a mortal who could summon monsters from the depths, and walk on water. Nor one with the ability to transport six longboats full of people from one part of the ocean to the next. Have you?"

"No," Jo breathes, and she doesn't have to question Beck to know he's telling the truth; she can see it in his people's eyes.

Suddenly she remembers a conversation she had so long ago with a blond-haired boy in a brig.

"Then why wouldn't the monsters be real as well?"

But Jo knows that the monsters are real, she's fought them, after all. Now there's another question, one she wonders if Aster would answer so quickly like the one before.

If the monsters are real, then why wouldn't the gods that made them be real too?

Jo shakes herself out of her reverie. Whispers rumble through the crowd of Arethusian nobles, Oceanan delegates, and soldiers.

"I've seen powerful magic before, there are fewer rules than one can imagine. Let's hope for everyone's sake this god is mortal," Jo grits out, and she can see in Beck's eyes that he's not so sure.

"The serpent? Is it dead?"

"Yes," Beck tells her. "But that's not Nereid's problem."

"And what is? What's this message that he gave you?"

Beck smiles, though it's empty of emotion, and the chill Rhea gave her grows.

"He's taking it back."

"What?"

"The elf or god. He's taking Nereid back."

"I don't understand."

"He showed me images in my head." Beck turns his back on Joana and speaks to the crowd. "The dark city of Lycos falling, creatures overrunning the roads, Oceanus"—there Beck's voice trembles—"burning, and Arethusa…"

He stops and turns back, staring down the queen of Arethusa.

"Arethusa falling from its cliffs to the sea, erased. All of us as we've done to his people. And the best part?"

"What could be better than that," Jo answers wryly, devoid of humor.

"We can't leave. He's put a barrier around Nereid, a barrier the *Iron Serpent* crossed. He's given the seas back to the monsters, and as long as we stay inside the barrier, they can't reach us."

"But as long as we stay inside the barrier, he destroys us anyway. Interesting message," Jo mutters.

Beck laughs, either from exhaustion and or his frustration finally getting to him. "That's not the message. That's the situation."

He takes a step forward, and the guard at the bottom of

the steps draws his sword, but Jo holds her hand up in a halting gesture.

She allows Beck to walk up the rest of the steps, and then he kneels down in front of her, so their eyes meet.

"You have a month."

"A month," Jo whispers.

"And then he's coming, he's coming for us all."

"Who?"

"Perses."

The doors to the ballroom fly open, and a trembling squire squeaks as all eyes turn to him.

"Your Majesty?"

He calls and Jo shakes her head. Beck is still kneeling at her feet.

"A young woman and a man are here to see you; the mistress says it's very important."

"Now isn't the best time," Jo growls.

"She says it can't wait."

Jo wipes her hand down her face.

"Joana."

The mistress's voice echoes through the room.

Jo looks up and sees the woman who haunts her nightmares standing at the end of the aisle beside a man she's never seen before.

"Venus," Jo says.

She doesn't stand.

Venus and the older man make their way down the aisle.

Beck straightens from his position but stays close to Joana's side.

Venus stops at the steps and bows, the older man behind her doing the same.

She's still beautiful, but her clothes look weathered and worn and the cloak suggests she's been traveling for some time.

The man is also gorgeous.

Jo holds no attraction, but she cannot deny his beauty, and his eyes are a color she can't place, blueish green, constantly changing, almost swirling. His hair is gray with scattered strands of auburn. But his face is smooth, lacking the wrinkles that should match the gray.

"It's been a while," Venus says as she straightens from her bow.

"A year," Jo agrees, but all she can see is the love of her life kissing those perfect lips, and it makes Jo want to throw her out a window. "Why are you here?"

"Perses," Venus states and in that moment that's all she needs to explain.

"How the Underdeep do you know about him?"

Venus sighs and looks up to the heavens.

"We know everything, Joana, and we're the only ones who know how to stop him."

"He's a god." Beck snorts, staring both of the newcomers down. "What can you do?"

There's a chuckle from the man. "I like this one," he mutters to Venus and his voice, gods, it gives Jo a different kind of shiver.

She notices that Beck uncrosses his arms, turning an interesting shade of red.

"Don't worry," Venus smirks, noticing the two leaders' discomfort. "He affects everyone that way. Oh, and Perses is not a god."

"He's mortal. Powerful but mortal. He's a demigod," the man speaks again.

Jo forces herself to hear what he's saying.

"He's my son. And the only being that can kill him is his brother. Only a child of Poseidon can kill another child of Poseidon. They're the only ones powerful enough to do it."

"Child of Poseidon?" Jo repeats, mystified.

"We're back. The gods, that is," V murmurs, gesturing to Poseidon and herself. "We apologize for disappearing, but it seemed like you guys had it handled. Except, now there's a bit of a mess, so we're back. To help fix the problem."

"Clear the room," Jo commands.

The guards, the people, all of them are still standing slack-jawed, and Jo has to repeat herself.

They finally move out and the palace soldiers clear the ballroom; one of them tries to take off with Beck, but Jo orders him to be left. Finally it's just Joana, Beck, and the two supposed gods.

"And why should we believe either of you?"

Beck is pacing back and forth, still trying to comprehend the entire dilemma.

"Because we don't have any time left," V growls. "We have to find Triton, he's the only one who can take back control of his conch shell."

"The god? Triton?"

"I've seen it." Beck pauses in his pacing. "He used it to transport us all here."

"It has many gifts, transport, enhancing abilities, sirening," the man, Poseidon, explains.

"And where is he?"

"Aphrodite and I—I mean Venus," Poseidon amends when Venus glares at him, and Jo just about faints.

Her fiancée's ex is the goddess of love, way to give a girl an inferiority complex.

"We've been together for the past year to confirm his location and preparing for war," Poseidon finishes.

"Wait," Jo bites out. "You've known about Perses for a year?"

Venus and Poseidon look at each other.

"Longer," Beck murmurs, outraged. "How long have you known your son was a murdering psycho?"

Poseidon's eyes narrow at Beck, and suddenly Jo doesn't think he likes the young man so much.

"Three years. He trained with his brother Triton, he wanted to become immortal, and I rejected the proposal. He tried to kill me and Triton prevented it. That's when I sent

Triton away. I assumed he killed Perses and that he lost his conch shell in the process, when Perses fell to the deepest depths of the Underdeep. But then a year ago, Perses surfaced. I had to close the gates of Atlantis to prevent him from stealing my trident, closing off my power. I barely escaped. The boy rose in Erebos and was forced out by the council. The elves put a barrier around the Eastlands preventing anyone access in, especially Perses."

"The Underdeep? As in the realm of the sea gods?"

"The elves have access to it. Do try to keep up," Venus explains.

"But how did he get to the Underdeep in the first place?" Beck asks.

"It's a tradition among the elves to send their people who present with magic into the pit as a sort of initiation. Some come out and some don't. Perses had presented with powerful magic before he could even be tested. They sentenced him to life in the Underdeep."

"So, he was put there by his own people because of fear?" Beck growls.

"Fear can make people do terrible things," Jo mutters. "So Triton? Where is he?"

"Tenaro. I sent him there on a pilgrimage to prove himself to me."

Beck growls, "Past the boundary into monster-filled waters. How in Hades do you suggest we get to him?"

"That is where our solution comes in," Venus tells them.

"What solution?"

"There's another child of mine," Poseidon states.

Pieces are starting to come together, and Jo finally stands. She walks down the steps to stand directly in front of what she's coming to believe really is a god.

"Then why can't this other child defeat Perses?"

"She's not strong enough, not yet, and she won't be before the deadline," Venus explains.

Jo's stomach is twisted in knots—she has a bad feeling about all of this.

"Who is she? This girl we need?" Jo demands.

Poseidon smiles, and she sees now that he's examining her.

"You remind me of my wife," he tells her. "No wonder she likes you."

There's a creeping realization on the horizon of Jo's mind, and she's already shaking her head as if that will stop the inevitable truth.

"Who is it?" Beck snarls, tired of all the games.

"Her name is Shea," V announces, "Captain Shea Lara of the *Veiled Duchess*. And she is the only demigod daughter of Poseidon alive today."

Jo shuts her eyes tight as if it will turn all of this into a dream. A hand grasps hers and it makes Jo's eyes snap open.

She's staring into her lover's father's eyes, and she sees it, she sees the truth. She pulls her hand from his grip.

"And she's the only one who can take us to Tenaro safely," Poseidon states.

Venus opens her mouth to continue, but Jo turns from Poseidon to glare at her.

"You knew. All this time. And you never told her what she was."

"I couldn't," Venus tries to explain, but Jo refuses to listen.

"Guards!"

"You know who they're talking about?" Beck investigates, looking mildly confused.

The guards usher in and await Jo's command.

"Yes," Jo responds before giving her orders to the soldiers. "Contact General Soren. Tell him it's time to bring Shea home. Before it's too late."

Jo looks at V. "She won't come easily."

V produces a pouch from her cloak and hands it to one of the guards before giving her instructions.

"Here, take this. Tell the general to use it as a last resort. This will work."

The guards rush off to contact General Soren.

Jo sits back heavily in her throne, staring off into the distance toward the garden, toward the Lover's Fountain.

She clears her throat and speaks to the remaining beings in the room, "Gather supplies. We leave for Tenaro as soon as she arrives."

CHAPTER 4: RED-HANDED

Shea

"I told you we shouldn't have stopped in Lycos!"

"You really want to have this conversation now?" Shea growls, ducking as another arrow flies over her head, piercing straight through her captain's hat.

The arrow hits a barrel and her hat drops to the ground in front of her. She picks it up as they continue running through the Lycon port.

A screech echoes from above and Shea scans the sky, spotting a blue blur shoot past Aster, Caen, and herself.

"A key? I thought we were here for the map," Aster shouts, diving out of the way as an arrow almost pierces his back.

He manages to roll, but loses some of the supplies he's carrying.

Caeruleus screeches again through the air.

Shea turns around to see her familiar catch a flying arrow headed for the small of her back.

She whistles up to her faithful Lionbird and hears a yowl in response.

The strange Hunter of Apollo shouts in frustration and pushes past a group of elven slaves to keep up with the three pirates. She still can't believe a Hunter of Apollo is hunting alone, normally there's at least seven of them in a group.

She's come to the assumption that he's no longer with the order because he's missing their signature long hair that is normally tied up in a braided bun. It's obvious his black hair was cropped at the shoulders, forcibly from the look of his ragged ends. A disgraced Hunter, perhaps?

Whatever the reason, he seems to hold a personal grudge; the older man has been after them for months. His scarred and tattooed face showing up at the worst of times.

"Well, now we have the key." Shea grins, answering Aster.

She places her hat back on top of her head and briefly looks down at the small black key dangling from her neck.

For a year they've been searching for the Lycon Vault of Secrets. Shea thought this stop was going to lead them to the map but instead it had led them to a small temple in the slums of Acheron dedicated to the worship of Queen Amphitrite. Not exactly popular considering the patron goddess of Lycos is Scylla, the treacherous cliff side sea monster.

Expecting to be turned away, Shea was shocked when the priestess had taken one look at her and felt compelled to help.

The priestess explained that she had stolen the key from the high priestess of the royal temple of Scylla in the heart of Acheron when she had been an acolyte. She'd kept it hidden ever since she escaped and became a follower of the queen of the sea.

She gave it to Shea and told her that when the time was right, she'd know what to do with it.

And Shea definitely knows; all she needs is the map and this slave port will become just a port.

Freedom for her kind.

Another arrow flies past her and she's brought back to the trouble at hand.

Not only does she seem to have her own personal

bounty hunter, Shea has heard rumors of at least six sinkings of famed pirate ships all over Nereid. Good men that she had allied with on more than one run.

But they had to risk coming to Lycos, especially with the lead they had for the vault. At least now they have the key to it.

After obtaining the piece, Caen, Aster, and Shea headed down to the market to gather other supplies the ship was seriously lacking. They hadn't thought to bring a large party, not with the amount of people after them. They needed to sneak in quietly and sneak out. Unfortunately, the Hunter had followed them to Lycos, and he caught sight of them almost immediately. Not a lot of places for Shea to hide in Lycos.

"A key!" Caen shouts angrily, drawing Shea out of her thoughts. "It's *a* key. For all we know, it's a fake! Now we have no map and a fake key. Why do we follow you again?"

Shea ignores Caen in favor of glancing back toward their assailant, her red hair braided away from her face, as she can't let any loose strands fly in front of her one good eye.

Caeruleus screeches through the air as an arrow flies past her precious companion and Shea almost stops running, shocked by the close call.

"Caeruleus! Back to the ship!"

Caeruleus yowls but listens to Shea as he flies off in the direction of the *Duchess*.

She swiftly uncaps the waterskin that is hooked to her belt where her gold sword used to be.

After everything that happened, Mariner using her own sword to cut things away from her, Shea couldn't find the resolve to continue using it. She tried when she first got back, but every use only brought her unease. Instead it now sits in her quarters collecting dust.

She stares at it sometimes after waking up to her or Aster's screaming from the nightmares, but she doesn't dare touch it.

She pulls the water from the flask using her magic. She's cultivated it over the past year and become quite the impressive Aquarian: elves who can manipulate water, Aquarius magic, and use it to their will. Apparently, it's an extremely rare elemental gift to develop without being claimed by a god, like those who go through the Underdeep initiation in Erebos. Which has only given her more questions as to who she is—as her ability with water isn't the only thing that has developed.

After her miraculous recovery from her duel with Prince Mariner, her healing became magically quick, cuts closing after a few hours of receiving them.

If she washes her wounds with water, the liquid will knit the skin back together in minutes. It's terrifying, which is why she hasn't told anyone—not even Caen—about her new gift.

She pushes the water from the flask back toward the ex-Hunter of Apollo and imagines razors in the water's place. It shapes the liquid, changing the form until it's thin like knives. As soon as it reaches the enemy, she slices the water down on his release arm where he's holding the string and arrow, causing him to cry out in pain.

He loses his hold on his bow, slowing him down.

That's all they need.

"This guy just doesn't give up," Aster complains, trying to hold on to the four bags of supplies he managed to grab before the Hunter showed up.

"Less whining, more running," Caen orders.

Shea laughs when she sees Aster shoot him a glare.

She draws the water toward her using a summoning position with her hands, while also collecting some seawater from the harbor, pulling all of it back into the waterskin.

She caps the top of the bag and they keep to their course, running away from the port to the black beaches leading up the coast.

They shouldn't have stopped for supplies on their way

back from retrieving the key, but the *Duchess* was dangerously low.

The seas have changed. Monsters of old now guard the horizons and the crew has luckily survived more attacks than they'd probably care to admit, thanks to Shea's growing abilities.

On top of her powers as an Aquarian and her new and improved healing skills, her charms and barrier spells are also more effective. Now she can simply enchant the ship and sail past enemies unnoticed. The masking spells are harder to pass by the monsters, but to mortal eyes they're invisible.

It's incredible and extremely draining.

The first time Shea did it, it'd been an accident. She saw the *Banshee*, a rival pirate ship, and something had ripped from inside her. She hit the deck unconscious before she could see the mist she'd created veiling them from the threat.

Shea's built a tolerance since then and can stay conscious after using that much magic, but there's still a long way for her to go. Most of her magic is self-taught charms and forms. In whatever this is, she's merely a novice, but it's at least enough to keep them moving.

When they got the message about Lycos and the priestess, there'd been some debate, but their goal was clear and so the crew, with some reluctance, dropped anchor along the upper coast away from the port.

The former Hunter of Apollo isn't the only one hunting them.

Lieutenant Soren, who helped them all defeat the prince, has been after them under Jo's orders just like they agreed to since day one.

He's been trailing their every move, and he's attacked more than once to make it interesting. But overall, Shea can't help but think her princess, now queen, is letting her get away. And each time it happens, she wonders whether she's elated or disappointed.

"Where is he?"

Shea shakes herself out of her musings as they drop off the wooden planks and hit the ground with a smooth landing. She looks back toward the port but sees no sign of their assailant.

"I don't know."

Shea answers Aster, who's bent over his knees trying to catch his breath.

She examines the blond boy—no, young man—with a fond expression. He turned sixteen two weeks ago and he's finally grown into his ears.

Shea winces at the thought as her green eye catches the blue scarf wrapped through Aster's hair, over his forehead and the tips of his scarred ears, tied at the base of his neck. His chest has broadened out a little and his pale green eyes are just a tad more serious than they used to be. They're the same height, and it makes her groan every time he brings it up.

Their eyes meet and he smiles, but she still notices the flickering of his gaze to her owns scars.

He scans her damaged left eye before averting his gaze.

Shea smiles back at him like she didn't notice.

It never changed back to its green color, still pure white. Caen bothers her about wearing a patch, but she wears her scar and white eye with pride; she won't hide because she fears that's what *he* would have wanted.

The port's expanse is finally behind them, and Caen, who's carrying six bags of food on his shoulders, is panting slightly.

"We should continue on to the ship, we have enough to last us a week here, it'll at least get us to Oceanus."

Shea thinks it over and then nods. She wonders if she cut the Hunter deeper than she thought, although she's seen him fight through worse. He may have gone for a healer and if so, they could be able to gain some ground between them.

"Let's move."

They take off at a jog down the beach, scanning for

hidden figures or oncoming attacks along the tree line border inland, but they don't see any.

After about an hour, they believe they're finally in the clear and slow to a walk. They're close enough to the *Duchess* anyway.

Shea takes the opportunity to walk beside Aster.

"Something on your mind?" Shea inquires as she steps into place next to her cabin boy.

She can't help but smile as he steps into the surf, the seawater lapping at his boots.

It's been a long year for the both of them.

"The usual," he answers, finally meeting her gaze.

Shea sighs.

It's time she gave him the talk.

"Aster. It happens when it happens, it's not something that can be forced and you shouldn't want to force it either."

Aster stops and Shea does as well. He meets her eyes, his eyebrows wrinkled, and his mouth turns downward.

"But it should have happened by now and you know it. I'm getting too old."

"There isn't a time limit. There have been cases where it's taken elves into their adult life to receive."

"You don't know that!"

"Look, Dari says—"

"Dari?"

Shea inwardly groans.

She should have kept her big mouth shut. Shea tries walking farther along the black sandy beach to catch up with Caen, but Aster jogs up to her, falling into place beside her once again.

"You've been talking to Dari? So you are worried?"

"Aster." Shea smiles, looking at the teen as they keep walking. "I'm not worried. She's more knowledgeable with these things and I wanted to get all the information I could. It's not the end of the world if it doesn't happen."

Aster kicks a bit of sand toward the water and growls

in frustration.

"It's just one more thing to make me less of an elf! Face it! You came into your magic at what? Eight? I'm never getting magic, I don't even have my tips, which is probably why —"

Aster cuts himself off, and Shea stops him, placing her hand on his shoulder and turning him to face her.

"Is why? Is why you don't have magic?"

Aster nods, his bottom lip a ghost of a quiver.

He's grown so much from the trauma.

Shea examines his almost adult face. Sixteen

It's only been a year, but she can't remember the last time he cried.

Prince Mariner affected them both; he left permanent scars that will always keep him in their lives, but he took more than just the tips of Aster's ears, Shea realizes. He took Aster's security as an elf, and Shea wishes she had spotted it sooner.

She pulls his hard-muscled frame close to her and wraps her arms around his broadening shoulders.

"Now you listen to me," Shea whispers into his ear. "Losing your tips had nothing to do with your claiming. For one, we're not in Erebos, we can't go through the initiation, and who wants to be tethered to some old god anyway. Besides, some elves don't even receive magic, but that doesn't make them any less elven. Nor does losing your tips. Being elven, it's just a race. It doesn't define who you are as a being. Is Dari less of an elf because she doesn't have her left arm?"

Aster hugs Shea closer and shakes his head no.

"Am I less of an elf because of my eye?"

At that Aster pulls back, looking to Shea's eyes with a shocked expression.

"No! You're amazing, you're stronger than that."

"And you"—Shea grasps his face between her palms, smiling—"are stronger than this. You don't need magic, Aster, to be a part of our culture. You're a fighter. You're a pirate, and you're my kid regardless of matching ears or matching magic, or matching eyes!"

Shea laughs and it makes Aster chuckle too. She pushes up onto her toes and kisses the top of his forehead, which he protests, playfully pushing her away.

"We should probably catch up."

"Yeah," Aster agrees with a grin.

He looks up ahead and cocks his head. "I don't see Caen."

Shea scans ahead as well. "He's probably turned the corner waiting for our lazy asses. Come on, we don't need a grumpy Caen on our hands."

Shea breaks into a jog and Aster follows her lead. They round the corner of the beach and come face-to-face with Caen on his knees.

His hands are bound behind his back and four Arethusian soldiers are holding on to him with a gag in his mouth. Among the four soldiers are about twelve other men, but the one who catches her attention is the general, standing at the forefront of the ambush.

"Soren."

The former Lieutenant Soren, and now General Soren, as Shea had been apprised from Jo's letters, stands before her, sword drawn along with his other men.

A screech echoes nearby and Shea sees Caeruleus imprisoned within a gilded birdcage, his large paws slashing at the bars. One of the navy men near the cage is clutching his wounded arm, covered with deep scratches; he must have had the pleasure of catching her Lionbird.

Shea turns toward the shoreline to find the *Duchess* tied to an Arethusian navy vessel, and two longboats beached.

She curses in elvish.

It's too bloody soon.

"Captain Lara, pleasure to see you again."

Aster draws his sword, but Shea grabs his hand, ordering him to lower his weapon with a shake of her head. He knows the rules; they don't kill Arethusians, which means it's time for some heavy persuasion.

Caeruleus yowls from his prison and Shea finds herself having trouble concentrating.

She tries not to think about the fact Soren wouldn't be here without Jo's orders. She thought she and the queen had come to an agreement, the vault then marriage—perhaps not.

Shea subtly uncorks the top of her waterskin and steps toward Soren with her hands in the air and an easy smile on her face.

"General, what a surprise," she says, sending a glare in Caen's direction, who grunts at the accusation with wide eyes, showing her his bound hands.

"Yes. Unfortunately our queen has had to move up the timeline of your return due to unforeseen circumstances," Soren explains, but he doesn't sheathe his sword.

"I just received a letter from her a few days ago, she mentioned nothing."

"This development is extremely recent and she orders your immediate return, so let's make this quick. We accept your surrender, yada, yada, all hail the future queen consort." Soren chuckles, giving her a teasing bow, but Shea is in no laughing mood.

She's not ready for this. She can feel her heart beating faster and the palms of her hands bleeding sweat.

"Soren, I can't come to Arethusa now. I'm too close to the vault. You'll have to tell the queen to wait a little longer."

Soren stares as if he wasn't expecting Shea to resist. Shea laughs inwardly at his awkward expression, but Soren quickly recovers with a grin and begins to chuckle again.

"Right, yes. Hilarious, Your Highness, but really, we must go. We're expected in Arethusa no later than tomorrow."

"You'll be going alone." Aster steps up beside Shea

with a growl.

Shea notices Caen's eyes roll and Caeruleus seems to be in agreement with the giant as he huffs, slouching to the bottom of the cage.

Okay sure, the odds aren't great, but Shea can't lose, not yet. She takes another step toward Soren.

"Just give me a couple of weeks, a month at most, that's all I need."

"Shea, this is an order from your betrothed and queen. I cannot disobey and neither can you. I've taken your ship, and I suppose to make sure there isn't any funny business you will ride on the *Hippokampos* with me"—he gestures to the Arethusian ship—"Caen will sail behind on the *Duchess*. There's no choice here. You're coming home."

Shea snaps instinctively, "Arethusa is not my home!"

The beach is silent.

Soren frowns.

"Well. That is something to discuss with your future wife, but I, *Captain*, am a general. I serve the Arethusian queen, and right now my orders are to take you in. Don't make me do this the hard way."

"You won't win in combat; we're holding back. Let us go, Soren, let me go and I'll return to her in no time. I promise."

Soren sighs.

She's right in front of him, his sword inches from her chest, and she watches a battle wage within his brown eyes.

He turns away, sheathing his sword, and Shea breathes out a sigh of relief.

"Thank you, Soren, really. After all these months I think we could call each other friend—"

Soren turns back toward her and before she can react, he throws some sort of dust out of a pouch, hitting her directly in the face.

She can't help the gasp of surprise, but she inadvertently breathes in the mysterious dust. Her vision goes awry, black spots dance with every blink, and she can feel her right leg give out as she lands kneeling on the sand.

She can hear Aster shouting and vaguely sees Soren order the guards to restrain him, which they do easily.

Before she can fall any farther, Soren rushes forward, catching her. She can't move, every muscle in her body has gone limp and her vision is almost black.

"Cheater," Shea tries to mumble, but it comes out more like a jumble of sounds.

Soren sighs. "I do consider you a friend, Captain. But there are much bigger things on the horizon and Nereid needs you to fix them."

Shea's not sure she understands the last bit of what he says, but then, she's falling. Falling into a dreamless sleep.

CHAPTER 5: GOVERNOR

Beck

The world should be dark. The clouds should be tumultuous, full of thunder and crashing lightning. The seas should be terrible, gnawing away at the shores, attempting to sink Nereid below its harsh waves. The world should be ending, and yet, the sea has never been calmer. The sun shines brightly on Beck's shoulders, casting a warm glow upon the Arethusian balcony overlooking the white cliffs. The air is sweet, and the breeze softly caresses his dark brown locks. The world should cease, but everything still goes on even now after Governor Orion has drawn his last breath.

Tears wretchedly make their way down Beck's cheeks no matter how hard he tells himself to stop crying and be strong. Every time he closes his eyes, bloody bandages fill his vision and wet rasps echo through his ears.

Orion's final words offer shallow comfort.

"You have to go on. You have to protect your people. Queen Joana is a good woman."

"Dad, you can't leave. Not yet."

"You're the governor now, son. As leaders, we do whatever it takes to protect our own. Be strong, Beck. To save Oceanus, you must become more, and save Nereid. I'm so proud of you."

Orion's chest gave one last effort and then fell still, only two days after arriving on the Arethusian shores.

Beck can't tell whether it's been minutes or hours since he stumbled out onto the balcony and threw up over the rail. No one followed him, and he preferred it that way.

His father's words repeat over and over inside his mind.

But he *can't* do this.

He's not like his father. He can barely take care of himself and now he has a whole country to run.

Just before his father's death, he'd received news that the captain of the *Veiled Duchess* would be arriving today.

Tears begin to gather once again at the corners of his eyes. His shoulders shake and before he knows it, he's crying again. It's like his body is ripping at the seams and all he wants to do is ask his father for help, but he can't.

"Beck."

He startles, turning quickly at the sound of his name, and finds Caius in the doorway to the balcony. He furiously wipes at his eyes, glancing behind Caius to look for the other advisors. He doesn't want them seeing him cry. But Caius gestures calmly, shaking his head.

"I've sent them away. It's just us."

Beck turns his back on him. He has no desire to see anyone.

"Beck, we need to discuss our next step."

Beck bites his tongue. He shakes his head, his eyes scrunching closed.

"I can't."

"You must. Time is growing short. The captain will be here any hour and we must decide on what is to happen—"

The words are overwhelming and he can't shut them out. He growls his frustration and cuts Caius off as he slams his fist into the nearest pillar. He feels the skin break on impact but he doesn't care. He merely pulls it to his chest, cradling his hand as he slides his back down, leaning against the railing until he's seated.

Caius lets out an appalled shout at the scene of aggression and kneels on the ground, reaching for Beck's hand, but Beck pulls away, glaring at his advisor.

"I can't do this right now."

Caius stares at him, examining the tears still inching down his face, and sighs.

"I'm sorry, Beck. But you don't have a choice."

Beck looks away, then objects as Caius reaches for his hand again, but Caius grumbles a soft command and Beck reluctantly gives it to him.

Caius studies the cuts, there will be bruising, but for now he removes his handkerchief and wraps it around the split knuckles.

"It's not fair. He wasn't ready."

"I don't think death cares much for convenience. Hades orders and Thanatos obeys. The fairness of mortals a mere trifle on their mind. Orion lived a good life, and now he can rest with your mother, Elizabetta, in Elysium."

"I feel like I just lost her. I can't lose him too," Beck whispers, the sea breeze messing his hair.

"His body may be gone, Beck, but you'll never lose him. He raised you to be who you are, and in doing so he instilled a part of himself within you. As long as you are true to the man your father raised you to be, Orion will always be with you, as is your mother."

Caius leans forward and runs a hand through Beck's hair. He pulls him closer and they embrace.

As Caius squeezes him lightly, he closes his eyes, leaning his head against his advisor's shoulder.

"You're the governor now, Beck. You're the leader of Oceanus. And we need you," Caius whispers into his ear.

Beck nods and pulls away reluctantly, giving the man he grew up with a small smile.

He stands from their kneeling position and takes a deep breath. He doesn't wait for Caius to follow; he gets up from the ground and walks back into the room.

There's a strange decaying smell to the air, but he tries to ignore it as he approaches the bed. They've pulled a sheet over Orion's face.

Beck comes to the bed until he's right beside his father's still body.

He hesitates a moment. Caius reenters the room, and Beck shakily lets out the breath he's been holding on to. He pulls back the sheet, but this time the tears don't fall even as he stares at his father's pale face. He reaches forward, his fingers going to the collar of Orion's shirt, and he clasps the chain he knew he'd find there.

He pulls it out and removes the necklace from around his father's neck, careful not to break it. He finds his mother's wedding band still attached. Opening the clasp, he sets it on the bedside table and then reaches for his father's left hand. He slips Orion's ring off his finger with a small gasp.

He can't help how his eyes flicker up to his father's face, hoping he might awake from the loss of his ring, but his eyes stay closed and Beck takes a shuddering breath. He slips the large ring on the necklace with the smaller one and re-clasps the metal before slipping it over his head.

Caius has come around the large wooden frame and he does what Beck doesn't have the strength to do—he replaces the sheet back over Orion's face.

Caius leads Beck away from the bed and sets him down at a table in the corner of the guest quarters. The advisor sits down across from him.

"So?"

Beck's hands clasp around the two wedding rings and he clears his throat, keeping his eyes on Caius.

"My father's body will need to be returned to Oceanus. It'd be best to leave in the morning with everyone else."

Caius nods. "I'll arrange our transport. I think it would be best for us all to return to Oceanus so that we can prepare our borders against the coming assault."

Caius moves to stand, but Beck grabs his arm.

"I'm going with the queen, her captain, and the gods. I need to see this through."

Caius blinks. "I don't understand."

"I will not be returning to Oceanus with you."

Caius sits. "Are you out of your mind? We just lost your father, we can't lose you as well."

"Oceanus needs an emissary on this mission—"

"Fine then, send a guard, a lord, someone disposable. You are not."

"No one is disposable," Beck snaps, his eyes narrowing. "You will never say anything like that in my presence again."

Caius's eyes widen. "Yes, Governor. I apologize. But still, Beck, I can't allow you to go on this mission."

"I make the rules around here, isn't that what you said?"

"Yes, but not stupid ones!"

"Caius. Father would have gone. He would have stayed with this every step of the way to make sure his people are safe. They need help finding Triton; I'm going to help them. It's my decision. It's what he would do."

"And look where that got him."

Caius points over to the bed. Beck reels back as if he's been slapped. He refuses to look. He gets up from the seat, moving to step past the older man, but Caius grabs him.

They struggle, but Caius manages to turn Beck toward the bed, pushing him, and he stumbles to the footboard, looking down at Orion's dead body.

"You need to return home. Protocol must ensue, and you must take your place as ruler. You are not some ruffian prince climbing a rope ladder anymore. You have other people to worry about."

Beck straightens. He turns, growling at Caius, "You think I don't know that? I'm doing this for my people. You will return home, you will bury my father while I find this god, and you will then wait for my instructions! And if you ever lay a hand on me again, I will have you arrested. Do you understand me?"

Beck stalks forward to stand inches from the other man, glaring into his eyes.

Caius runs a frustrated hand through his hair and looks about to argue when a knock at the door interrupts them.

"Yes," Beck answers.

He's still glaring and he holds his ground even as the guard at the door enters the room.

"Sir, your presence is required in the throne room. The captain has arrived."

"Beck—"

"I'll be right there," Beck cuts off Caius.

He moves toward the guard and feels Caius begin to follow, but he stops him, speaking over his shoulder, "I'm going alone. You will inform the other senators of my decisions. Is that clear?"

Caius opens his mouth, frustration clearly written across his face, but then shuts it.

He nods stiffly. "Yes, sir."

Beck leaves Caius alone in the guest quarters with his dead father and follows the guard to the throne room.

He's too busy thinking about everything that's happened to realize they've arrived at the doors a few minutes later.

The soldier begins to open the door, but Beck stops him.

"Wait. Please, could you give me a moment?"

The guard salutes him and walks away from the door, leaving Beck alone.

"Just breathe," he murmurs to himself.

You can do this. You just have to walk through those doors.

Beck steadies himself, his breath coming too quickly. He thinks he might pass out as black dots litter his vision. He's swaying on his feet, but a hand steadies him.

It's warm on his back, firm, and when he turns around, he finds himself face-to-face with a pair of gorgeous eyes, one almost completely white and the other the prettiest shade of green he's ever seen.

The black dots recede, and bright red fills his vision, framing the illustrious green and phantom white eyes.

It's a woman.

He notes her ears through her hair—an elven woman.

"You're panicking. Drawing the air in too quickly. You'll pass out."

The woman lifts Beck's hand and places it on her chest over her sternum. Other people surround them, but they're a blur in comparison to her; all that remains is the woman.

"Copy my breath," she murmurs.

As she takes a deep breath, Beck feels drawn to follow her. Every breath she draws, he takes as well, his chest slowly rising in the same rhythm as hers.

"Better?"

Beck nods, but he doesn't trust himself to speak.

The tunnel disappears and they're not alone. A giant of a man stands behind the redheaded elf, along with a blond teen. Soldiers stand at her side and to the back of their little group. And a decorated officer is next to Beck, examining him.

"Are you alright, sir?" the general, from the looks of his medals, asks, placing a hand on Beck's shoulder.

"Fine, thank you. Must be the heat," Beck stutters, but his gaze returns to the smiling redhead.

"Hey, I know you." Red grins.

She removes Beck's hand from her chest; he didn't realize he hadn't removed it yet. His cheeks warm and he knows he's blushing.

"Yeah?"

"You're Orion's kid, of Oceanus. Right? The governor? I make a point to recognize royalty nowadays."

Beck feels a pang in his chest, but he nods a confirmation.

Red seems to notice his wince and her features turn concerned, but before she can speak again, the general corrects her.

"That's Governor Orion, Captain."

"Oh."

Beck figures Red believes that's the mistake that caused him to wince, but when he meets her gaze again, she's still watching him.

Suddenly Beck realizes the title the general gave this mysterious woman.

"Captain?" Beck asks.

"That's right." She grins. "Captain Shea Lara of the *Veiled Duchess*. Your father has always been a sort of friend to piracy."

"Yes, well, I think your fiancée has waited long enough," the general states. "Don't you think, Shea?"

Fiancée.

The word stops Beck's heart.

The general nods for his soldiers to get the doors and the grand entrance opens to the awaiting members inside the throne room.

The general and his guards pass by Beck, but before Shea continues, she reaches for Beck's hand and gives it a light squeeze.

"Thank him for me." She winks.

Beck nods and Shea passes into the room. The giant and the teen follow her in, and he vaguely hears the giant whisper to Shea, "What is it with you and these royals?"

Beck suddenly realizes his mouth is hanging open. He shuts it, and adjusts his peasant shirt, tucking in a stray piece of material in the back before running a hand through his hair to tame it.

The doors slam behind Beck as he enters.

Queen Joana is seated on her throne, but he doesn't see Venus or Poseidon yet. There's a frown on Joana's face and it brings a slight buzz of happiness to Beck's core; he can't say he's her biggest fan.

He appears to be late to the party as he approaches and finds the conversation has distinctly turned into an argument.

"You won, Jo. I'm here. Don't try to turn this around."

"This was your idea! I don't understand why you're angry with me when all I did was finish the bargain!"

"Because I thought you understood! You had plenty of opportunities before and you let me go, and I thought it was because you knew what I was going after but clearly it doesn't matter."

"There are larger things at play here, Shea, that's why I called you back. And for your information, I've been incredibly lenient with your activities. In fact, I've had to send plenty of nice gifts and apologies to your run-ins."

"I never asked you to do that," Shea snaps.

"You didn't have to! It's my job to clean up your messes. You are my future queen consort, and it's time you started acting the part," Jo shouts.

The room goes silent.

Shea is scowling at Jo and Jo is glaring at her. It seems to take the queen a moment until she finally notices Beck standing solemnly in the back.

"Master Beck. My apologies, welcome. How is your father doing?"

The group parts and he briefly meets Shea's gaze as he steps to the front.

"He's dead, ma'am. I'm the governor now. And while I'm sure the captain would love to continue being berated by you, I would like to make sure his death doesn't go unavenged. So? Would you like to tell her or should I?"

The giant man with Shea barks a laugh while the blond teen glares at him.

Shea turns to look at him with a crooked smile. He glances at her and instead of anger and pity, like he finds in

Jo's eyes, in Shea's there is a small amount of amusement and understanding.

"I'm sorry for your loss," Jo replies stiffly. "But I don't think either of us are qualified to relay the news."

She turns to the guard by her throne. "Bring them in."

Beck steps aside, allowing Shea to take the center of the aisle once again, and watches as the guard heads for the side door.

"What is all of this about?"

Shea looks to Jo with a raised brow.

The queen stands from her throne and walks toward Shea with a neutral expression.

"Things have happened while you've been away."

Shea cocks her head as the queen arrives in front of her, and Jo pushes a strand of hair behind the pirate's ear.

A sharp pang erupts in the pit of Beck's stomach and he has to look away.

The blond teen rushes forward before the guards can stop him and gives Jo a hug.

"Missed you," the boy says.

"Missed you too, Aster," the queen replies, hugging him back.

Shea smiles fondly at the two of them.

Beck can't help but think it's a very pretty smile.

"Your Majesty."

Beck and Jo turn at the address to find Poseidon and Venus walking behind a guard entering the room.

"Venus?"

Shea hurries toward the goddess but stops short of hugging her; she looks back at Jo, who gives her a tight nod, before embracing the woman.

Venus pulls away first.

"Shea, it's so good to see you."

Shea unknowingly side-eyes her father, looking at him curiously before turning her attention back to the goddess of love.

"What are you doing here?"

"We're here for you," Venus responds.

Shea looks back at Jo.

"I don't understand."

"Shea," Jo tells her, "we need to talk."

CHAPTER 6: FATHER'S DAUGHTER

Jo

"Okay. Hold on. Let me just sum all this up. An evil elf, who happens to be your son, is attempting to take over Nereid with an army of fish people. He also has your other son's magic shell, which gives him a ton of power. In order to stop your first son, we need your other godly son to restore control of the shell back to him so he can kill Perses. Am I missing anything?"

Caen finishes his rant with a snarl. He's got his hands on his hips and he's glaring at Jo like it's all her fault.

Because of course when it comes to Caen, it's always her fault.

"Besides the fact you need me to navigate the waters to Tenaro in order to find Triton because the elf has unleashed the monsters from Hades back into the oceans," Shea finishes the summary.

"Didn't we just make this trip last year?" Aster grumbles.

He's taken a seat on the stairs leading up to the throne and his comment makes Jo smile.

"That's not the only reason we need you," Beck speaks up.

And Jo doesn't like the way Shea's and Beck's eyes light up when they meet.

"That's not for you to tell," Jo snaps, cutting off Beck, who glares at her.

"She deserves to know."

"There's something more?" Caen groans, his head falling into the palm of his hand.

"Why didn't you tell me who you were?" Shea turns on Venus, who looks ashamed.

"I wanted to, but it's not who I was anymore. I was merely Venus of the Slippery Serpent, just a mortal."

"But you're not mortal, are you?"

V winces at Shea's question.

"Shea, she came here to help you," Poseidon speaks.

"You stay out of it. I still don't know what to think. I'm just supposed to believe you're Poseidon, god of the seas and creator of Nereid? If you're really him, why haven't you stopped this? Why not call on the seas and wash your son from our shores back to the depths," Shea states, crossing her arms over her chest.

"We're not as powerful as we once were. Without my trident, and with the gates of Atlantis closed, I don't have the power to defeat him. Triton doesn't draw his power from Atlantis like I do, he draws it from me, and as long as I'm on the mainland, all of my children are more powerful than I."

"Fine, then...where were you when your son went evil? Why didn't you stop him then?" Shea accuses.

Poseidon frowns.

"I try not to interfere with my children's lives, he was banished to the Underdeep by the elven council in Erebos and consequently found by Triton. I thought he was dead after he tried to kill me three years ago."

"So because you were an absentee parent, we've got a demented elf who wants to take over our world."

"Not all of my children turned out so bad," Poseidon mutters.

Jo can see the anger storming over his features; it reminds her of a certain redhead she knows.

"Poseidon," Venus objects.

Shea gets up in the old god's face.

"Oh yeah, like your other son who's hiding from you. Who supposedly killed his brother. Father of the year."

"Actually I was thinking of my daughter, who is a fearsome captain and engaged to be wed to a queen."

Jo watches Shea's eyes widen.

The captain takes a stumbling step away from Poseidon, but she manages to right herself as she continues to back away.

"What?"

Caen steps forward.

"Shea? You're talking about Shea? Shea is your daughter?"

Poseidon smiles bitterly. "Yes, she's mine."

Caen takes a seat on the step beside Aster with a choked breath.

Jo swiftly goes to Shea. She places her hands on her shoulders.

"Leave us," Jo orders.

Caen stands and starts to argue, but Jo directs her order to Soren.

"I want everyone out."

Soren salutes and orders the men. They grab Caen and Aster, who struggle. Beck doesn't move either.

"Leave us," Shea repeats.

Reluctantly, the three men leave. The guard by Poseidon and Venus begins to usher them away, but Shea stops them.

"You two will stay."

Despite the heaviness of the situation, Jo can't help the satisfactory chill that runs down her spine at Shea giving the guards orders, like she belongs here.

It takes a few moments but finally the room is empty

except for the two gods, Shea, and Jo.

"Did you know?"

The question is directed at V, and she takes a placating step toward Shea.

"That isn't why—"

"Did you know?"

V nods sadly. "I did. He asked me to look after you."

"Thank you, you can go."

"Shea, don't take it out on her," Poseidon commands, but Shea holds up her hand.

"You will not speak. V, you can leave, I need to speak with...Poseidon."

"Do you want me to go too?" Jo asks, but Shea shakes her head, grabbing her hand.

"I'd prefer if you didn't."

Jo nods and the remaining guard escorts V out, leaving the three of them to talk.

"I don't believe you," Shea states.

"It's the truth. How else did you think you could do what you can do?" Poseidon tells her.

Shea opens her mouth, but he cuts her off, "I've been watching you. I know you know about your abilities. Well, at least some of them."

"What abilities?" Jo asks.

"It doesn't matter," Shea whispers, but Poseidon answers.

"Her abilities that mark her as my daughter."

Poseidon looks her over, and his eyes widen briefly like he finds what he's looking for.

"I see you haven't had a chance to heal that cut above your brow. Here, let me help you."

Shea frowns, reaching up, and Jo notices the cut she'd missed upon her first inspection. It looks old and scabbed over.

"You do that this morning?" Poseidon questions as his body moves into a strange stance.

It reminds Jo of sword footwork, his body positioned more solidly.

His hands come up and he uses a series of gestures. Water splashes from the Amphitrite fountain behind them and then a large column of water is being manipulated straight toward Shea and Jo.

Jo yelps in surprise, but Shea turns. She pushes her own feet into the same stance and with a similar set of gestures catches the water with her hands extended, stopping the liquid from slamming into them both.

Poseidon surprises her by sneaking up behind her.

Her focus wavers and the water inches closer, but she regains her power and keeps it in the air. Half the fountain's water is suspended above them.

Jo knows this move is different and more powerful than when Shea made the whiskey bottle float above the bed in her captain's quarters last year.

"Still don't believe?"

Poseidon siphons a bit of water from Shea's hold and presses it to her forehead. The water glows as it stitches the cut back together, the scab disappearing, and Shea's forehead looks as if it was never marred.

The water absorbs into her skin, and with some difficulty, Shea places it back into the fountain. Once that's done, she thrusts her elbow back into her father's gut, causing him to stumble with a grunt.

"How dare you," she accuses, storming toward him.

She grasps the lapels of his jacket so they're face-to-face.

"If that display of power doesn't prove you're my daughter, your temper certainly does," Poseidon groans, pushing Shea off of him and staring her down.

"So then, this elf?" Shea croaks.

"He's your brother. Yes. Half. His mother was an elf from Erebos."

"Like mine." Shea laughs but it's hollow.

Poseidon looks as if he might say something but he simply nods.

Jo steps closer to the love of her life, turning her around so they can look at each other.

"I know this is a lot. And trust me, I know a thing about fathers turning out to be something they're not. You're a...demigod." Jo looks over to Poseidon, making sure she's said it right, and he gestures for her to carry on. "We can deal with that."

Shea shakes her head. "No."

"Yes. Yes we can. We find Triton, he's your brother too, and then the two of you take on Perses with your father. I will be there every step of the way to help you, to support you."

"But why me?" Shea asks, eyes wide, staring into Jo's for the answer.

Jo leans her forehead closer to Shea's so that they're touching.

"Because the Fates knew you could do this. Trust me."

"I was supposed to get the vault. I was supposed to get the vault and marry you," Shea whispers.

"Well, that was before we found out you're the daughter of a god and that your half brother is trying to wipe out humanity. And you said my family was crazy."

Shea laughs, and presses a soft kiss to Jo's lips. It warms Jo's soul and if she could, she'd take Shea on the throne room floor right at this moment, but a small cough from Poseidon halts her desires.

They break apart and Shea takes a breath.

"Alright. So I guess we're going back to Tenaro. It's my ship; that means the queen of Arethusa and the king of the sea follow my rules. Got it?"

"Whatever you say," Poseidon answers with a short bow. "Just let me know when we're leaving."

He exits the throne room, leaving the two of them alone.

Shea collapses, stumbling over to the steps in front of

the throne, and Jo sits down with her.

"I was so mad at you."

"Yes. Soren warned me," Jo chuckles.

"Of course he did."

"I had planned on waiting until you found the vault. Do you believe me?"

Shea looks over and stares into her eyes. It gives Jo a chance to really look at the scar over Shea's left eye, and the white film that covers her iris.

"I believe you. Though with the world ending, I don't think the vault will be of much use. When I thought of reasons for why you were bringing me back, this certainly didn't cross my mind."

"Why didn't you tell me? About the water magic, the healing?" Jo asks without any heat.

"I didn't want anyone to know," Shea replies with a shrug. "I was just figuring it out on my own, I wasn't ready to let anyone else in on it. Not you or Caen."

That makes Jo smile. "So Caen doesn't know?"

Shea laughs. "Aye. You guys need to get over this competition you've got going on."

"There's no competition. But if there was, when you decide to tell him about the water magic, will you be sure to also inform him that I already know?"

Shea laughs, and Jo grins. She's missed this.

"I missed you," Shea tells her and Jo realizes she said the last bit aloud.

"Where did you go? The first half of the year, it's like you fell off the world maps. Soren searched everywhere and then one day you popped up in Oceanus," Jo jokes, waiting for Shea's explanation, but an uneasy look crosses Shea's face.

"Aye. I did just that. I found something. Did some meddling in something I shouldn't have. Found that the world is a lot bigger than we think it is," Shea whispers, looking down at her clothes and fiddling with the metal clip on her belt.

Jo decides to leave it there.

"Well, I'm glad you found your way back onto the map."

Shea grins. "Me too, sort of. So, the young governor? Beck. What's his story?"

Jo sighs.

"Your half brother sent him here. Well him, a few senators, and their families. His father was mortally injured in a battle with, believe it or not, a sea serpent. Then they magically appeared on our shores. I have a feeling he's going to try to come with us."

"Understandable. He probably wants to see things through for his people. Honor his father by taking down... Perses." Shea hesitates before saying her half brother's name.

"But he'll probably just get in the way," Jo complains.

Shea studies her a moment and then bursts out laughing, much to Jo's displeasure.

"What?" Jo questions.

"He doesn't like you."

"No! I didn't say that!"

"You didn't have to. He wasn't shy about it, and I can see your distaste for the man clear on your face."

"Oh please. That's not why I don't want him around."

"Oh yeah, sure. Not the fact that you're miss sunshine and everyone who meets you loves you immediately. And now someone doesn't, and you don't like it."

"Quiet you," Jo mutters, pushing Shea over.

But Shea pulls her over too and Jo falls on top of the sea captain with a laugh.

"Did you try using your healing on your eye?" Jo wonders aloud.

Shea cocks her head. "Yes. This is as far as it would heal. Does it bother you?"

Jo stares at the blemished skin and then runs her thumb over the deep scar that starts above Shea's brow and ends below her damaged eye on her cheek.

"No. I just wish I could have killed him before he hurt you. You're beautiful no matter what. Even if you begin to sprout gills and a tail," Jo laughs, kissing Shea on the nose as she looks up in horror.

"You don't think that's possible right?" Shea mock gasps.

"Maybe," Jo teases and Shea jokingly growls.

She pulls Jo closer, down into a deep kiss, and the many months apart make them more aware of how much they've missed each other's touch.

Jo's hands slide down Shea's body, grasping her hips.

"I wore this dress to remind you of the first time we met. I changed three times," Jo tells her.

Shea's eyes roam over the glossy white material and the gold shoulder plates.

"And you look great! But do you think you could both stop the little love session that's about to begin and focus on me?"

Jo and Shea startle, looking up from their precarious position to find Countess Thetis of Lycos at the end of the aisle, marching toward them with a small boy on her hip and two Lycon guards at her side.

CHAPTER 7: ALL THE EMPRESS'S HORSES, ALL THE PRIEST'S MEN

Shea

After being kidnapped on the shores of Lycos and shipped to Arethusa, Shea thought she avoided a reunion with the elven countess, but apparently fate has other plans.

After getting over the shock of seeing Thetis, with a child no less, Jo quickly took action, leading them all to her private chambers to speak.

"Perhaps I should go update Caen and Aster, let them know what's going on."

"If you wish," Jo tells Shea as they arrive at the doors to her chambers.

"Shea, wait," Thetis stops her. "Joana, thank you for agreeing to see me. Would you mind going ahead? My guards will apprise you with the details of my journey. I just would like a quick, private word with Shea."

With Thetis's back turned to her, Shea waves her

hands at Jo in alarm.

She shakes her head, mouthing the word *no*, over and over. While she's doing her mime act, the nosy little child on Thetis's hip looks toward her, giggling at her movements.

Thetis turns to see the cause of the giggling, but Shea stops before the other elf can see, making quick work of examining her nails.

Jo huffs at the display. "That'll be fine."

Shea glares, feeling totally betrayed, and Jo chuckles.

When Thetis turns to face Shea, Jo mouths, *You'll be fine*, behind her back and continues into her private chambers.

Shea plasters a fake smile onto her face, hoping to fool the countess.

Thetis rolls her eyes at the attempt.

"Relax, I'm not going to bite," Thetis drawls, and the child on her hip smiles at her voice.

Shea grunts in acknowledgment, but as the child faces her, she finally takes in his features.

The deep black color of his hair and his pointed ears are just like his mother's, but the curls remind Shea of her own, and his eyes—his eyes remind of her of her old reflection. They're bright green, almost the exact shade as Shea's.

Before Thetis can tell Shea what she needs, Shea steps closer, examining the child's face.

He looks like his mother, yes, but there are small features, the sharpness of his chin and his cheekbones. He can't be more than three years old. The boy reaches out with his hands, touching Shea's face.

Shea flinches back, but Thetis murmurs to her that it's alright. Shea returns her face close to the child, and he babbles in his small unintelligible language, periodically getting a few words right.

A thought echoes through her mind, from a conversation a year ago in the black tower while they studied a painting of the Underdeep together.

"A blessing you said? From Triton, when you were claimed?" Shea mutters, and when she looks up into Thetis's eyes, she sees the confirmation.

"I can see that you finally know who you are," Thetis tells her, adjusting the child on her hip.

"You knew," Shea gasps, but she can't quite take her eyes off the small boy.

"Of course, if the family resemblance wasn't enough, the power emanating off of you was. Well, it's clear to anyone with magic, especially to a fae like me, who practices dark magic, that you're a demigod."

"Why didn't you tell me?"

"It wasn't time. The Fates were still sewing the tapestry, but now we're in the thick of it. The storm is here."

The voice in her head from last year, she finally places it. It was Poseidon. All of this has been building for the last year while she was off chasing the impossible.

"This is insane," Shea whispers.

"Indeed," Thetis responds.

The little boy babbles again, drawing Shea's attention.

"Was it...? Were you in love?"

Thetis laughs coldly. "I thought we were, or I thought he loved me, but he took what he wanted. I was too naive to understand. But he gave me Proteus, so I try not to regret."

Shea looks up to the ceiling, heaving a sigh. "So, one half brother wants to take over the world and the other is a heartless romancer and absentee father. I think I was happier just knowing my adopted family, and now I have to find them both."

Thetis startles. "You're going after Triton?"

"He is apparently the only one who can defeat Perses. After we find him, hopefully, he'll stand with us against him." A thought crosses Shea's mind. "You wouldn't happen to know where he is, would you?"

"No. Last I heard he was in the Underdeep. You should stay away from him. He's dangerous, maybe more so than

Perses. Although now that I've seen the fae in action, I wonder."

Shea's eyes widen. "You've seen Perses?"

"It's why I'm here. Ceto has joined with Perses. He came to her just under a year ago with promises of making her his consort. Those of us smart enough to see through his power know it's a lie. He talks about the freedom of elves and putting the humans back in their place, at least when Ceto isn't around. Not only does he have a small army of Merrow, elves who were lost in the Underdeep and transformed into lesser fish beings— twisted and gnarled—he now has Lycon fae elementals and Ceto's army at his back. He's coming here."

"Here?"

Jo is standing behind Thetis; she must have come out to check on them when she heard the last of Thetis's message.

"Yes. Counts and countesses have been escaping from the Lycon court, not all were lucky, but I managed to get my son and myself out. I came to warn you. Time is growing short. Perses plans to march on Oceanus and then take Arethusa. He knows Poseidon is here; he knows about you, Shea."

Jo comes to stand next to her. "Then we need to leave, now. We can't wait any longer, how much time do we have?"

Thetis thinks. "I—well, the last thing I remember before escaping the court…They said a month. A month until they reach Arethusa."

"Can we do it?" Jo turns to Shea.

Shea thinks it over, charting the course in her mind. "Yes. Maybe. But you're right, we need to leave now."

Jo nods. "Okay. I'll finish packing. Thetis, you of course are welcome here, you have Arethusa's protection."

Thetis opens her mouth to object, but Shea stops her.

"Poseidon's coming with us, he won't be here with you and Proteus. You'll be safe."

Thetis sighs, kissing the top of her son's hair, and nods, thanking Jo.

"Let Caen and Aster know the plan," Jo tells Shea.

"I'll speak to Master Beck as well, he deserves to know," Shea responds, though Jo rolls her eyes.

"Very well. We'll meet at the docks."

Jo orders a guard to take Thetis to a guest chamber, giving the countess a quick hug before returning to her own chambers.

Shea goes to leave as well, intent on finding Caen, Aster, and Governor Beck, when Thetis stops her.

"Shea."

Shea turns back to the countess, and her nephew.

"I don't want him to know about Proteus."

Triton—the message is clear and Shea nods her understanding.

"Promise me. You won't tell him about my son," Thetis presses, her gaze intense.

Taken aback, Shea replies, "Okay, I promise."

Thetis goes ahead with the guard and just as they're about to round the corner, they run into Poseidon, who looks rather hurried.

Thetis freezes in front of the god, staring at him with recognition, and Shea walks toward the group, glaring Poseidon down.

"I could have sworn I felt Triton's presence," Poseidon murmurs and then sees Proteus.

The toddler babbles and reaches for the old god. Understanding seems to dawn on him and he reaches for the baby, but Thetis pulls away.

"The boy is his?"

"No," Thetis spits. "He's mine."

And with that she continues on down the hall with the guard; they turn a corner and disappear from sight.

Shea makes to leave as well, but Poseidon speaks, causing her to stop again.

"Your brother deserves to know he's fathered a child."

Shea looks back at him and chuckles.

"No. He doesn't. We leave in an hour, be at the docks or you'll be left behind."

Shea leaves him in the hall.

CHAPTER 8: THE NEW CREW

Shea

After wandering the halls for at least an hour, Shea finally sucks up her pride and asks a servant where her crewmen might be. With a giggle and a blush the servant tells her that they're in the kitchens within the servants' quarters. She ends her answer with a Your Highness, which makes Shea's skin crawl. She's surprised she already knows who Shea is.

She ventures down to the servants' quarters and thinks about how she's finally come to terms with wanting to marry Joana—and yet. The thought of what she'll become when she does scares her. It's more than a title; she'd be a queen, queen consort, to be exact.

When she had written to Dari and Phoebus to tell them the news, they were happy, thrilled in fact, but completely unbothered by Shea's new title and not any help with coming to terms with it.

A hallway with a rope blocking off the steps leading up shakes her out of her thoughts; she recognizes the stone walls and the tapestries pinned up. Mariner's chambers lie at the top. No wonder it's blocked off. The tips of her ears burn and she scurries past and into the kitchens as quickly and gracefully as she can.

She bursts through the doors, and yelps from surprised servants and cooks echo as the door slams open.

"Oops, sorry," she murmurs, closing the door softly behind her.

The kitchen is huge. Rows of hot stoves, vegetables hanging on the walls, there's an ice room in the far back at least twenty feet long, and large cured meats hang from the ceiling. The cooks and servants smile at her as she steps farther inside, some even bow.

A booming laugh catches her off guard. She spots Caen talking to a female elf, whose staining blush appears to be becoming permanent.

The servant laughs back at whatever Caen tells her and Shea notices a pile of potatoes at the table where they're sitting.

Aster is next to the giant, but he's facing the other way talking to Master Beck as they peel potatoes together.

Aster is talking animatedly with the Oceanan, but Beck seems to be taking it in stride, chuckling at whatever Aster says.

A cook tells her to look out as he steps around her and she dodges him, side-stepping around the big cast-iron pot he's carrying.

When she turns around, her eyes meet Beck's from across the room.

She studies his face.

His jaw is square but not overly so, soft still from youth. His dark brown hair shoots up in all directions; she thinks she can even see some shadows of black running through the waves. His eyes are warm, a caramel brown that she finds herself sinking into…no.

She pulls herself out of her trance, coughing. Her ears tinge pink in embarrassment.

When she looks up this time, it seems her cough garners the attention of Aster and Caen, who wave her over. Beck is smiling at her with a charming grin, but she can't bring herself to look at him again, feeling guilty.

"Captain, there you are, I'd like to introduce you to someone." Caen grins, his gold eyes bright, and his permanent worry line has even softened slightly.

Shea comes around the table, nodding at Beck in acknowledgment. He murmurs a hello.

She quickly steps away from him, though, and ruffles Aster's hair as he complains, before finally standing next to Caen and the elven servant.

The young woman, she realizes, isn't so young. She's probably closer to Caen's age, in fact. Her skin is a nice tan, and she has hazel eyes and curly black hair, with a little gray, that has been pinned up in a bun. The woman smiles and even curtsies to Shea, who groans softly, while Caen chuckles.

"Shea, this is Miranda, she's a servant here at the castle. Apparently, she's one of Joana's personal handmaidens."

Shea looks at Caen with an arched brow at his enthusiasm but instead catches how he's looking at Miss Miranda. She's never seen him look at anyone like that besides Paetre maybe. She smiles at Miranda and extends her hand out to the other elf, who takes it tentatively.

"It's good to meet you, miss," Shea quips with a smile to put Miranda at ease.

"You as well, Your Highness, we've been waiting for your return. We're so happy for Her Majesty Joana, and if it's not too bold to say, the elves are especially thrilled with the match."

The comment catches Shea off guard, but she doesn't let her surprise show. She finds herself biting her lip. "Really? Well thank you. I'm still trying to come to terms with my eventual title."

"Queen," Aster repeats, eavesdropping on the conversation, as if it has finally dawned on him, "but then how will you be able to run the ship?"

Shea opens her mouth to respond, but Beck answers instead, "I'm sure your captain will figure it out, why don't you run these potatoes over to the cooks. I think that's enough."

Aster looks like he's about to object, but one look at Beck, and Aster is blushing instead. He nods and picks up the first peeled basket of potatoes. He tries to grab the second one but all of the adults in the room protest and he stops.

Miranda grins, placing a hand on Caen, who Shea notices smiles encouragingly, and walks over to pick up the second basket.

"I'll go with you."

Aster thanks her and they continue off to one of the cooks at the long row of stoves.

"You fancy her," Shea states, surprised, and Caen turns to her with a frown.

"I—I do not," he stutters, but his eyes are drawn back to the older elf laughing as Aster torments one of the cooks.

But there's something about the gaze. It's not like how Shea looks at Jo, or even this new male character she's been introduced to, though she tries not to think about Beck. Caen's eyes have a bit of hope, and strangely, resignation. She can't quite pin his emotions down like she normally can.

"Right," she murmurs and takes a step back only to bump into another body.

Shea freezes, feeling the warmth from the other person radiating into her back, and turns, finding Beck's smirking features.

"You alright?"

She realizes she's still frozen in place against his chest.

Shea coughs, "I'm fine," and scoots away as quickly as possible until she has Caen in between them.

Caen looks at her with a quirked brow.

"So." Shea clears her throat again. "I came down here to tell you we're leaving."

"Oh," Caen breathes, his eyes dancing over Miranda's

form before returning to Shea. "Good, the sooner we're back on the hunt for the vault, the sooner we can return."

Shea opens her mouth to correct him, but Beck beats her to it, "Wait, you're not going to help us find Triton?"

"Actually. We are."

"We're what?"

"Caen—" Shea can see the wheels spinning in his head, but he's off before she can explain.

"Did you not learn anything from last time?" Caen seethes, shoving his chair back so fast it falls over to clatter on the stone floor, drawing attention from the others in the kitchen.

"Caen—"

"We should stick to the original plan, find the vault. They don't need you for this. For all we know, it's all bullshit anyway," Caen rants.

He turns on Beck. "I mean can you even say for certain what you saw?"

"Yes, sir, I can. We need her. She can't run away from this," Beck growls, standing his ground against Caen's impressive height.

"And I don't intend to," Shea commands, drawing Caen's attention back to her.

"Shea—"

"Caen!" she repeats, finally getting him to listen. "Like it or not, this is my fight, I really am his daughter. There are things, signs, I ignored. This fight is real and I'm a part of it. I can't leave, because if I do, there won't be anything to come back to. Perses will win; forget pirates, and royals, and that Hunter who's been chasing us for months. Perses will end it all and it will be my fault because he's my brother and I chose not to do anything about it. So? Are you with me or not?"

The kitchen is quiet around them; all of the servants are watching the conversation, waiting for Caen's response.

Shea can feel eyes burning into the side of her face, and when she turns to meet them, her mouth goes dry as she's caught in Beck's trance again.

He's smiling at her, only this time it's much brighter; she can see pride in his eyes.

Caen huffs.

"I'm with you, Captain!"

Aster comes running to her side, and it makes her break Beck's gaze as the blond teen slams into her. He puts an arm around her shoulders and she finally has to admit the kid is taller than her.

Miranda giggles at the display and Caen gazes at her. There's a wistful look on his face, and for a moment Shea wonders. She wonders if maybe it's time for her to let him go.

Maybe it's time for Caen to retire.

"Caen."

Caen turns back to Shea; she can see his eyes flick over her face as if he's studying her before he nods.

"Alright. We find Triton then. I'll tell the crew, give them their outs, but they'd follow you anywhere, Captain. You know that."

"I won't begrudge any who wish to stay," Shea emphasizes, noticing the hesitation in Caen's eyes, but he smiles and shakes it off.

"I'm with you till the end, kid. Raised by two pirates"—as Caen mentions Paetre, the light in his eyes when he looks at Miranda fades, and he clears his throat to cover it with a smirk—"and somehow, we ingrained this stubborn sense of responsibility in you. Go figure." Caen chuckles. "Right, well. We best get to the ship."

"You guys go ahead. I'll meet you down at the docks, I need to speak with Master Beck," Shea tells them.

Caen shoots a glance in Beck's direction and nods. He pushes Aster toward the door as he protests at the manhandling, and Miranda offers to walk with them.

Caen starts to hold out his arm but then rescinds it. He declines Miranda's offer and walks out the kitchen doors with Aster in tow, leaving a surprised Miranda behind.

"Captain," Beck murmurs with a soft smile.

There's a strange pull toward him and she can't put her finger on why it's there, but she offers to walk him back to his guest quarters.

He accepts.

They leave the kitchens together and walk through the winding halls of the palace. Lavish carpets soon replace stone floors and bare walls turn to arched windows with water falling over the open air like a curtain.

For a time, they walk together quietly, Beck occasionally murmuring a "turn here or head straight," until finally they're heading down one long hallway. They're almost to the guest rooms when she recognizes the path from last year, where she escaped the dungeons and was taken to Lady Catherine's room.

Shea realizes she hasn't seen the old woman yet.

Shea stops farther down the hall as they come across an open balcony, the water falling around it and the moon shining on the clear liquid, making the balcony glow white like starlight.

"Stunning," Shea whispers, stepping into the encased balcony.

They can see the city from here, and farther out the ocean's horizon. The water blurs the shapes slightly but for the most part it's fairly clear. Stone benches are placed around the balcony and Shea takes a seat, groaning as she does.

Beck sits down next to her. He looks over at her and laughs.

She turns to him, startled. "What's so funny?"

Beck shakes his head. "I'm sorry. It's just you look so out of place here and yet you don't. Your clothes point you out as common and yet the ease of your expression, it seems as if you were meant to live in a castle."

Shea snorts at his evaluation and leans her back against the stone railing, not minding the little drops of water hitting her jacket. They hadn't changed clothes, thank Triton, on their way to Arethusa.

Her mind cringes at the casual use of his name now that she knows he's her brother.

She'd stayed in her dark brown pants, black boots, a purple peasant shirt, and her black doublet coat.

Though her new captain's hat has suspiciously gone missing.

She looks like a pirate, and yet she does find herself strangely at home here in this palace. She supposes it's because it reminds her of Jo.

A warmth blooms in her chest at the thought of her fiancée.

"You must love her very much to give up your life for all this," Beck tells her, and it shakes her out of her thoughts.

Shea chuckles. "Oh yeah, a life of piracy for the leisure of a palace?"

"It's still your life," Beck responds.

She shrugs, relaxing against the railing and bench, while Beck rests his arms on his knees, looking back at the elven pirate.

"Aye, I do love her," Shea whispers.

They lapse into silence, enjoying the warm evening air.

"I'm sorry about your father."

Beck turns to her, surprised, then acknowledges her sympathy. "Yes, I believe you are. I—did you know him?"

"No." Shea smiles. "Not personally. But Mister Caen served on your father's first command ship, many years ago. He remembers him fondly, and I've always admired your father's stance on free trade. Oceanus's sanctuary was somewhere we could always go when the *Duchess* came under fire from Arethusa or Lycos. To my understanding, your father created the Sanctuary law."

"He did," Beck confirms proudly. "He believed everyone needed a safe haven. And after my mom died, he really reinforced the law so future generations and the Senate would have a hard time disbanding it...after he was gone."

"He was a good man," Shea agrees. "I'm sure Caen would be able to tell you more about his time in service to your dad, he doesn't talk about it often, but from my understanding your father was about your age when Caen was in service to him."

"So does that mean I can go with you?" Beck asks with a grin.

"Who am I to stop a leader of a country from coming on a mission to save Nereid?"

"Your fiancée would prefer I stay behind," Beck grumbles, and Shea chuckles.

"Yes she would."

"I'd like to go. I need to see this through," Beck explains.

Shea sits up and leans forward onto her knees as well; she looks over at him and their eyes meet.

"I know. When I lost my father"—Shea stops, and reluctantly corrects herself—"my adopted father, Paetre, I did everything in my power to honor his legacy. I stepped up and eventually in his name I completed his final score. It didn't make the pain go away, but it made me feel like I had at least brought him peace. If you believe killing Perses will bring your father peace, will bring *you* peace, I won't stop you and I can't. Because no one could stop me in my quest for the Pearl."

"Wait, you're the pirate who stole the Pearl of Lycos?"

"Impressed?" Shea grins.

"Maybe a little," Beck chuckles but then sobers. "Thank you. My dad always had all the answers; I just feel like I don't know what I'm supposed to do."

Shea nods. "I remember the feeling. Of course, I had a crew of fifty, not an entire country. But you do what they did; you lead and pretend to know all the answers because that's how they did it. And at least if you come with me, I have a shot of making sure Arethusa and Oceanus both have good leaders to rule after we destroy my…Perses."

Beck catches her correction and reaches out his hand, placing it on hers; she almost jerks away but instead remains calm, not wanting to cause a scene.

"Paetre?" Beck says, asking if he'd said it correctly, and Shea nods. "Paetre was your father, Shea. Just because Poseidon helped create you, that doesn't replace Paetre. He raised you and if you ask me, that means more than any blood source."

Shea smiles at the comment. "Thank you, I guess I needed to hear that."

Beck leans forward and Shea finds herself leaning in too.

"You're welcome," he murmurs.

They've scooted closer together, their lips inches apart. His eyes are like melted chocolate and she can feel herself falling into them. There's something familiar about him, something that she connects with more so than with Jo, as if they've walked similar paths.

Jo.

Her name pushes the wind out of Shea and she jerks back. Shea stands as quickly and gracefully as she can.

Beck stands with her, a red blush staining his features.

"So, I'll meet you at the docks then." Beck shrugs, trying to play off their almost kiss.

Shea coughs, clearing her throat. "Yes, right, of course."

They stand there a moment longer, neither of them moving.

"Right I should—"

"Yeah we better—"

Their words crash together as they head for the entrance of the balcony. They stop in the hall again, staring at one another.

"Well I should—"

"I'll head out—"

Shea's ears are as red as his, and she feels the need to jump from a very high distance, but instead she waves and walks away. She goes left and Beck goes right toward the guest rooms.

Shea wants to curse—she can't help looking over her shoulder as he walks away. She tells herself it's not disappointment she feels when he doesn't look back. She faces the hall ahead and makes her way to the docks.

CHAPTER 9: I THINK I'M IN TROUBLE

Beck

What was he thinking? He'd almost kissed the queen's fiancée. But she almost kissed you too, a wicked voice whispers from the back of his mind. He mutters a curse as he can't help but look back as Shea walks away; he waits a moment and tries to suppress the disappointment when she doesn't do the same. He turns back around and heads for the guest quarters.

He doesn't have much to pack; his clothes and things went down with the ship. Including his flute his mother gave him years ago. She always loved music and so he learned to play just for her. When she died, it brought him the most comfort to play her old favorite lullabies and sea tunes—it made it seem like she was still here.

He arrives in front of the door to the guest quarters, takes a breath, and places his hand on the handle, but he can't bring himself to turn the knob.

He gave his orders to Caius before he left earlier today. His hand reaches up and clutches his mother's and father's wedding bands on the chain around his neck. He can't see his father's corpse again. He drops his hand from the knob and heads back down the hall but at a leisurely pace—he's not ready to see Shea again just yet.

It's more than her beauty that has caught his attention: she's smart, funny, and he feels as if they're kindred spirits. Something in his soul recognizes her on a deep level and now that he's met her, he wants to know her fully.

But she's engaged, to the queen of Arethusa, Oceanus's allying queendom.

Who cares, that voice whispers again, and it sounds surprisingly like his father. *If you want her, fight for her...She's not married—yet.*

After asking a couple of servants, he finally finds his way to the stables. He arrives at the end of his path through the gardens and enters the royal courtyard. Looking up ahead, he finds Captain Shea Lara once again.

She's petting a midnight black horse, speaking in what Beck recognizes as elvish as he walks closer.

He catches the end of what one of the stable hands is saying to her: "Please, Your Highness, I would prefer to get you a calmer horse, or perhaps you could wait for Her Majesty and ride with her in the carriage?"

Shea is still speaking in elvish to the midnight stallion. "Chaláróste tin omorfiá mou, xekouráste ton fílo mou. Proféro ti dýnamí sas. Sas zitó voítheia. Íremos agapitós, vres eiríni mazí mou. Chaláróste ton fílo mou. Eímaste éna gia aftó to taxídi méchri na to xanasynthésoume."

Her voice is enchanting, and Beck's own eyes feel as if they're growing heavier.

The elven stable hand clutches his chest as he almost falls over.

The stallion neighs, rearing back a little, but Shea repeats her last phrase, "Chaláróste ton fílo mou. Eímaste éna gia aftó to taxídi méchri na to xanasynthésoume."

The horse's breathing seems to even out and the stallion taps his hoof on the ground a couple times before kneeling down. Shea climbs onto his back much to the young man's objection, and the horse rises from its position on the ground back to standing.

"Oh, Your Highness, please, I beg you. Remus is dreadfully temperamental," the stable hand begs.

"Then why did you bring her this horse?" Beck asks, chuckling.

He looks up to Shea and finds himself asking permission to pet the horse. She smiles and nods, whispering into the horse's ear as he whinnies back at her.

"I did no such thing! She arrived at the stables as I was taking Remus back to his stall and asked for a horse. I told her I'd get her one and she insisted on riding Remus," the stable hand protests, glaring at the black beast.

"He's as good a horse as any." Shea shrugs. "Besides, you told me I couldn't get a saddle or reins on him, and I did."

"Yes, well, that was very unusual as he nips anyone who usually tries," the man mutters—he still has his hands outstretched as if he's worried she'll fall.

"I'd like a horse as well, please, I'm riding down to the docks too."

"It'd be no trouble to get a carriage, sir," the stable hand tries, but Beck shakes his head.

"A horse will be fine. Mind if I ride down with you?"

Beck looks up at Shea, still petting Remus, and he can't tell in the dark, but he thinks she might be blushing.

Her pale eye almost glows against the torch's firelight in the courtyard.

"Sure. I don't mind."

The stable hand sullenly sighs as Beck smiles.

"Just stay with her until I get back. I don't trust that bloody beast," the elven man gripes.

"I'm sure she can handle it, but I'll wait."

Shea laughs as the stable hand scurries off.

"Thank you, that's one thing I don't think I'll ever get used to. The worry for my safety. These poor people look at me as if I might break," Shea huffs and the horse neighs in what sounds like agreement.

"Trust me, I remember. Growing up as a royal, stubbing your toe around a servant was the equivalent of losing a limb." Beck chuckles, stepping away from Remus so he can look up at Shea better.

"I'm sure my appearance with all my scars doesn't help," Shea murmurs, and she pushes her braided hair farther away from her damaged eye.

"I don't think so. Scars are badges of honor where I come from. To Oceanus, your appearance tells us you're a great warrior. Someone who can take care of herself, someone who should be respected, not protected."

Shea grins down at him—and yes, she's definitely blushing now. It brings him a small amount of satisfaction.

"May I ask," Beck begins but stops himself.

"What?" Shea inquires.

"Can I ask what you were saying to the horse in elvish?"

"I'm surprised you recognize the language," Shea tells him.

"I grew up around a lot of elves. Many, many free elves live in Oceanus. Sanctuary," Beck explains with an easy smile.

"Sanctuary," Shea repeats with a grin. "All I said was to be calm, to rest easy, my friend, and that we would aid each other in our journey to come before we part again."

"And that worked?" Beck chuckles.

"Aye. I've always been good with horses. A mystery my adopted father could never figure out since I lived on a ship and I didn't spend much time around them," Shea explains.

"A trait you inherited from me," a deep voice interrupts.

The stable hand brings out Beck's horse just as Beck and Shea turn to see Poseidon walking toward them. Venus is standing in the doorway from the palace to the courtyard, speaking to a naval officer.

Shea's smile disappears.

"Why would I have inherited it from you?" she growls.

Beck expects Remus to become unsteady at her turn of mood, but it's as if she and the stallion are one.

"Well, I created them. Horses I mean," Poseidon tells her.

Beck hops up onto his mare quickly. It takes him a moment to register what Poseidon says, and then—right, lord of the sea and horses, well that's not intimidating.

Shea doesn't respond, continuing to glare at him.

"We'll see you at the docks."

Then she takes off into the night. Shea and Remus fly through the Arethusian gates, and Beck quickly rides after them.

He follows her as she weaves through the cobblestone streets, the stone homes and wooden houses a blur as they ride. The homes go from large to small and shrink smaller the farther down the loop they go, until finally they arrive at the city gate and take a right, heading toward the docks instead of turning left and straight down the Trident road that crosses all over Nereid.

They trot along the wooden planks that cover the sand and extend out into the plains where scattered hamlets lay around the countryside.

Farther into the docks the midnight market has opened. Strange glowing fish are hung from booths; men and women in capes and hoods visit sketchy shops for things they can't buy in the daylight. The underworld is awake and suddenly Shea seems much more in her element.

"You kept up." Shea laughs from atop Remus, and Beck trots toward her so that the mare and stallion can walk beside each other.

"With great difficulty—you weren't kidding, you can ride," Beck tells her and it causes her to lose her smile again.

"I guess there's a reason for everything I can do." Shea shrugs.

Beck isn't quite sure what to say so he offers silent

support and rides along beside her as they pass through the Arethusian dock market. Ships can finally be seen off to the right as the market fades and the ship dock takes over.

Beck gasps when he sees it. It looks harrowing in all the torchlight. The *Veiled Duchess* lies at the end; the moon highlights the three masts and their burgundy sails. It casts a ghostly shadow over the dark-wooded vessel. The figurehead causes a sharp ache in Beck's chest, and it feels like she can see inside of him, past the wooden veil obscuring her face. He feels vulnerable.

"You coming?"

Beck forces himself out of his reverie and finds that Shea has already dismounted her stallion and has tied the reins to the horse post on the dock. She's striding away toward the massive vessel, and he scrambles to climb down and do the same. He ties the beautiful gray mare to the post and gives her one last pet before heading after the captain.

She marches up the gangplank, shouting orders to this and that crewman. As he scans the entirety of the ship, Beck's eyes land on the steering deck, and he can vaguely make out the blond teen from before, who seems to be caught between the wheel and a brown-haired young man who looks a little older. The brown-haired lad has got him pressed against the steering, leaning forward to kiss him—but they jump apart quickly as Caen arrives on the navigation deck.

Beck smiles and heads farther down the dock. He's not really paying attention and he apologizes as he bumps into someone. He grabs the man to keep him from falling over into the water. When their eyes meet, Beck groans.

Caius brushes Beck's hands off of him and adjusts his suit.

"I see your head is still up in the clouds," Caius drawls, glaring at him.

Beck rolls his eyes. "I'm fine. We're heading out soon."

"So are we, Queen Joana has informed us that Perses is attacking Oceanus, and soon."

Beck's eyes widen and he crosses his arms over his chest.

"What, why wasn't I told?"

"You didn't return after your meeting; she came to find you after getting information from a Lycon informant. Apparently Perses is coming for Oceanus first, and Lycos has allied with him. Arethusa only has a month before he finishes us all off. She came to tell you, but you were gone. So she informed the Senate and I, and offered the people of Oceanus sanctuary. Perses will find the city empty upon arrival and we can only hope it will make him think twice before invading a city with two armies."

Beck takes in the information the best he can. Looking past Caius, he can see the Senate boarding the next ship over. He sees soldiers carrying his father's body on board.

"Father would have hated us abandoning the city." Beck sighs, running a hand over his face.

Caius chuckles bitterly. "Yes, but we don't have the manpower to beat Perses, let alone the entire Lycon army; we barely have the means to withstand small battalions anymore. Oceanus has fallen, which is why we'll need you to rebuild. So don't die out there, hmm?"

Beck laughs, but he can hear the sincerity beneath the sarcasm. He pulls Caius forward into a hug and ignores the advisor's objections.

"I'll try not to," Beck whispers.

And for a moment, Caius hugs him back, whispering into his ear, "Find the fish boy, get what you need, and then come back and kill this elf for your father."

Beck pulls away and nods. "You got it."

Caius returns the gesture and bows to Beck.

He walks away after that, and Beck continues to the gangplank to finally board the *Veiled Duchess*. As he nears the ship, he notices the two guards who were standing with Caius are now following him.

"Um, soldiers, what are you doing?"

The female soldier, who Beck recognizes from the *Iron Serpent*, the woman who fired one of the killing blows into the sea serpent, steps forward.

"Senator Caius gave the orders, sir; we are to protect you with our lives."

Beck starts to object, but when he looks past them, he can see Caius standing at the end of the dock with two more soldiers. He points at both of them.

Beck sighs and nods.

"Alright. Just, you're not going to be following me around all the time, are you?"

The woman grins. "We'll try not to, Governor."

Governor. Now that's going to take some getting used to, he thinks, and he allows them to follow him up onto the *Veiled Duchess*.

CHAPTER 10: THE QUEEN'S PIRATES

Jo

After speaking with Thetis for a more in-depth, first-hand account of her knowledge of the elf Perses, Jo finishes packing her things.

She ponders everything Thetis relayed, and for the first time since she took the throne, she feels a small flare of despair.

Perses has Ceto and the entire Lycon army behind him, not to mention supernatural creatures from the realm of the gods. He may not be an immortal, but his power rivals one.

Jo has to take a seat as her breath leaves her. She can't help but wonder if she's leaving her people to die. That when she returns from this far-fetched journey Arethusa will be no more than ash and smoke. But then she's reminded of Shea, the woman she loves, connected to everything. She'd bet on her any day.

She pushes her dark fears down and places her last piece of clothing in the chest.

She's just about ready, dressed in an Arethusian naval suit, when a knock sounds at the door to her personal chambers.

She assumes it might be Thetis again, perhaps she has

more to say, but after Jo cinches the buckles on her trunk, she answers the door only to find Rhea and Gaea on the other side.

"My ladies, what is it?"

Rhea and Gaea exchange sharp glances with each other, when finally Gaea sighs.

"Your Majesty, we should be coming with you."

Jo laughs, stepping away from the door and leaving it open as she walks back to the trunk. She calls out to the guards stationed at the door to her chambers, and the two men venture in to pick up the large chest.

"Take it to my carriage immediately, I'll be down in a few moments," Jo orders before finally turning back to face her old escorts.

The two women are clutching each other, their arms linked, staring at the woman they raised with solemn expressions.

"I'll be taking some soldiers with me, but that's it. Shea's ship is already at capacity; I can't ask her to accommodate two non-working hands."

"Then perhaps you should stay here; there is no reason you should go and risk your life on some fool errand. Perhaps we can find a compromise with Perses, find a way for Arethusa to survive diplomatically."

Jo shakes her head. "That's not possible."

"How do you know?" Rhea cries.

She takes a step toward Jo, and Gaea tries to stop her, but the old woman shakes her wife off, approaching the queen she considers her child.

"Why should you risk your life? You're the one who matters, not some street urchin—"

"You will not speak of her in that way anymore!" Jo roars.

She storms toward the pale old woman, staring down at her with blazing eyes. "Shea is to be my wife, and I will not have you speak of her in such a manner. I am going because my life is no more important than anyone else's, if I die then another young daughter of the court will replace me! But I will not sit here, behind high walls, as my country, as Nereid, crumbles around me."

"But I don't want you to die, you stupid girl," Rhea shouts back with a choked gasp.

Gaea goes to her, and Rhea collapses against her wife weakly. Jo wants to reach out to her, but she needs to make a point. She's not their little girl anymore; she's their queen and they have no right to question her judgments.

"It doesn't matter. It's my decision. I am the queen, not you. I have no plan on dying anytime soon. But you must hear me—you raised me, but I am not your daughter. And Shea will be my wife and your queen consort, and you will give her the same respect you give me."

Jo turns on her heel, almost out the door, but Gaea's frail voice calls after her.

"She doesn't deserve you."

Jo laughs harshly, a hand going to the door for support. "You're wrong. It's quite the opposite. And if you don't like it? Get out."

She walks away, leaving behind the only two women she ever truly considered family.

As she passes through the halls, an ache in her chest makes her stop suddenly. She leans against one of the many portraits scattered along the palace walls and takes a deep breath, her hands shaking after the confrontation. But as she pushes off the wall, she recognizes the portrait behind her.

Queen Triteia's gray eyes are staring down at her. Jo smiles, taking in one of her favorite portraits, admiring how the painter somehow managed to capture the laughter and light that used to be within those silver orbs.

There's a smirk hidden behind the regal smile, and Jo places a hand over her mother's painted hands, folded on her dress.

"What would you say? What would you do if you were

here and in my place? Would you stay?"

There's no answer.

There never is.

Water trickles in the background over the open arch and moonlight streams through the waterfall, casting a glow over her mother's beautiful face.

"She's amazing, Mom. I think you would have loved her. She's got this smile like yours and her hair is like fire. Her eyes are so green, I feel like I'm lost in the forest when I gaze into them, but then there's this spark of gold and it feels like actual sunlight. She's so strong..." Jo is rambling, she knows this, and yet she can't stop talking.

Water frays at the edges of her eyes, small sobs cause her to tremble, and her throat falters like it's closing.

"She's stronger than me." Jo laughs, tears falling freely. "I'm scared. I'm scared of how much I love her. I'd give her the world if I could. I'd give her armies, a family if it would make her happy."

Her voice breaks off and her knees are trembling.

"I miss you so much."

"She misses you too."

A voice speaks from down the hall, and Jo jumps. Instinctively, she pulls free the concealed dagger at the back of her waistline, pointing it at the stranger. But as Jo's tear-filled eyes investigate the end of the hall, she recognizes the figure.

"Venus," Jo gasps.

She sighs and puts the dagger away as the goddess approaches, her hands held up in surrender as she nods to the dagger.

Her blond hair is in a high bun on her head and she's wearing a flowing purple gown.

"Well, you've certainly changed in the past year," Venus jokes, but Jo doesn't laugh.

Instead she wipes her eyes and squares her shoulders against the goddess of love.

"I'm marrying a pirate, I figured I should learn to be

more prepared and able to protect the ones I love," Jo responds curtly.

She curtsies to the goddess and attempts to move past her, but Venus stops her with a hand to her shoulder.

"She does miss you, you know."

Jo stops, mostly out of confusion, and turns back to the other blonde until they're facing each other.

"I'm sorry?"

Venus steps closer to Triteia's portrait, leaving Jo in the middle of the hallway. She looks up at the regal queen with a soft smile, folding her hands in front of her much like Jo's mother.

"Your mother," Venus tells her. "She does miss you."

"How could you possibly know that?" Jo scoffs.

She turns to leave again until she remembers who she's talking to. Sheepishly she walks back over to Venus and stands beside her in front of her mother's portrait.

"I can remember the day the match was made. The day your mother was born, the love from Lady Catherine, well… I could feel it all the way in low town. She loved Triteia with the very essence of her being."

Jo chokes on her breath. "Wait. You're saying you were here, in Arethusa? When my mother was born?"

Venus laughs. "Darling, I was here when Doris was born. Under different names of course, and different looks, but the Slippery Serpent has always been owned by a lady. I briefly became a man, the son of a previous disguise, for about ten years, but frankly I prefer my feminine form."

Jo attempts to absorb the information as Venus continues.

"Before that, though, I lived on Olympus. But times changed. Gods fell, my husband." Venus's voice cracks, but she pushes through the obvious emotion. "Hephaestus was killed by another god after Zeus disappeared. After that, I left and maintained a human form for the past one hundred and fifty years. Lost a few of my abilities, but sensing love? I've always kept that one. And Catherine loved her child. Just as Triteia loved you when you were born."

Jo smiles at that, the tension in her shoulders releasing.

"It was a different feeling compared to your father's birth."

The smile falls away and Jo bristles. "I don't want to talk about him."

Venus frowns. "No, I suppose you wouldn't. But, Jo—"

Jo glares at her for the use of her nickname, and V quickly corrects herself, "Joana. I just thought you'd like to know that the day you were born…When he saw you for the first time, before the hate whispered in his ear, before the darkness edged into his heart—he loved you. He looked at you and he felt it because I could feel it."

Jo shakes her head. She doesn't want to hear this.

A memory surfaces in her mind from a year ago.

"Did you ever love me?"

"If things had been different," he had answered, *"maybe I could have."*

Jo pulls away from Venus, a hand gripping her forehead.

"Why are you telling me this?"

"This isn't what I wanted to say. I just, I'm the goddess of love—"

Jo laughs angrily. "Yes, I know!"

V stops.

She takes a deep breath before continuing. "Your mother misses you too. That's what I wanted to say. And you're right, she would have loved Shea."

V takes a step past Jo, intending to leave her behind, but Jo grabs her arm this time and the goddess allows herself to be stopped.

"What's your game here?"

"What?" Venus gives her a confused look.

"Are you trying to hurt me, distract me? So you can get

Shea back?" Jo snarls.

V scoffs, pulling her arm firmly from Jo's grasp.

"Forget it."

V takes off down the hall but Jo can't stop, all the emotions she's feeling turning into one—anger.

Jo goes after her, but V keeps walking, and Jo hurries to keep up.

"No! Why are you here?"

"I'm here to stop Perses, same as you. I just wanted to offer you some comfort. You seemed to be having some trouble back there, but it was my mistake."

Venus turns the corner and Jo realizes they're at the door to the courtyard. She stops the goddess before she can leave.

"We don't need you anymore; we have Poseidon and Shea. You've said yourself you're the goddess of love, what can you do?"

V looks at her sharply, glaring.

"Love and war have gone hand in hand for ages; trust me, if it comes to a fight, I can hold my own. You need to learn to trust me."

"You're a liar. You lied to Shea for years, why should I trust anything you say? You don't know anything about my mother or my father."

"Gods, Joana, can you even hear yourself? You're yelling at the goddess of love, and your father-in-law to be is the king of the sea! I think you can safely assume that the rest of your religion is real too. Love doesn't end in death; it's the one true immortal thing in this universe. So when I say your mother misses you, I can feel how proud she is all the way from Elysium, and yes, you murdered your father, so maybe you don't want to hear how he forgives you as he's tortured in eternal punishment for his crimes—"

The red anger has faded, and the tears have returned. Jo can feel the truth spilling from those words, and she can't listen to it anymore.

But Venus steps in front of the door, blocking her exit, and grabs the queen of Arethusa by her arms.

"No! You will listen to me. Your Majesty, you are strong, just like Shea, but that temper of yours…You need to learn to trust and listen, or you'll never be as effective as you want to be. I am not here to take Shea from you. Because, Jo, your romance has been written in the tapestries for centuries!"

V relaxes, dropping her body back against the closed door, and when she releases her, Jo falls to the floor.

"I am scared we are going to lose," Jo whispers, kneeling.

V laughs and it makes Jo look up at the lavender-eyed beauty. "We could. We could lose everything, but we're going to try."

V pushes off the door, but as her hand lands on the wood, she turns to face it. Her brow furrows, and Jo can just make out a soft pink glow emanating from her fingertips.

A throat clearing catches them both off guard, and Jo can only imagine how they look. V standing in front of the door and Jo kneeling before her. Jo scrambles to get up and comes face-to-face with Poseidon.

Poseidon walks down the hallway, stopping in front of the two of them.

"Hello."

"Hi," Jo murmurs, and V repeats the sentiment.

"Everything alright?" Poseidon asks, taking in both of their appearances.

V is still staring at the door with a frown, so Jo answers.

"Fine, we were just heading out into the courtyard to ride down to the ship."

"As was I," Poseidon responds, and then leans toward Venus. "Really? My daughter's fiancée?"

Venus turns sharply back to Poseidon with a glare. "That's not what this was, you simpleton."

Jo stutters an objection, but Poseidon simply brushes past them both with a chuckle and opens the palace courtyard door to walk out.

V shakes her head and Jo bites her lip.

"Don't worry, Shea wouldn't believe it anyway if he said anything."

"Right," Jo answers.

V takes a step out the door.

Jo thinks she can hear Shea outside talking to Poseidon.

"Venus!" Jo calls.

V stops and turns back to the queen.

"Thank you. I—I want to be great. I want to be a good ruler, and I need to learn to trust. I just haven't had a good track record with the people I was supposed to rely on."

"I understand that." V chuckles, probably thinking of her own family. "I'm not the one you have to worry about."

V walks out the door entirely and Jo's brow furrows at her last comment.

She follows the goddess outside just in time to see Shea and Beck ride off through the palace gate together, leaving Poseidon in the dust.

Jo stands beside Venus, who is looking fixedly after them.

"You're saying I have reason to be worried?" Jo says, looking in the same direction.

"I'm saying your romance has been written for centuries, but you're not the only choice her path could take. Learn to trust, Jo, because you may need to make some very important compromises to get what you want."

V gestures after Beck and Shea, leaving Jo's side as the carriage pulls up in front of them.

Suddenly, Jo has the urge to take off running after them on foot. But that's ridiculous because Shea is hers.

Isn't she?

CHAPTER 11: SETTING SAIL

Shea

Shea leaves Beck behind for the main deck. She'll be seeing him quite a lot on the voyage anyway, and with all the feelings he seems to be causing, she needs to clear her head and put some distance between them.

Her feelings haven't changed. She knows she loves Jo, more than anything, but as she looks over at Beck and sees his handsome face, a strange fluttering fills the pit of her stomach.

Since she'd fallen for Jo a year ago, she hasn't been with another. Sure, she's looked at both men and women, but her feelings for Jo overpowered any sexual desire for some one-night stand. But this feels different; when Shea looks at Beck, she feels something she felt a year ago on a beautiful night such as this as she attended a grand Arethusian ball.

She almost laughed when Beck had gasped upon seeing the *Duchess*. It never fails to impress, and as she boards her fine vessel, she can't quite contain her own awe at the magnificence of the dark-wooded ship.

A yowl erupts from above and Shea spots Caeruleus flying over the *Duchess*, making sure everything's in tip-top shape.

She's sure he's relieved to be out of that cage.

The deck crew are scattered along the quarterdeck preparing for launch. Mister Tero is barking orders to release the sails and double-check everything's tied down.

"Mister Tero?" Shea calls, inspecting the deck cannons.

"Aye, Captain," the old sea dog greets.

"I see some sloppy cannon knots over here, I want these cannons tied down properly."

"You heard her, you mangy deck rats. Herron, get over there and redo those knots! Nothing but the best, I want this ship spotless; we have guests, boys."

Shea chuckles to herself.

Caen probably mentioned the extra navy men who will be joining them on the voyage. She smirks as Tero readies the ship with the intention to impress, as he was once an Arethusian naval officer himself. He'd finally admitted that little secret to Shea on their last voyage north.

Shea strides across the deck confidently, catching Caen speaking with Strom, the blind cook, who seems to have a messily written list of supplies. He's shouting at Caen quite loudly and Shea is just about to interrupt when her eyes catch James pinning Aster to the steering wheel on the upper deck.

Her ears turn bright red and her eyes narrow. It's not that she doesn't approve of the relationship; she'd been ecstatic when they had apprised her. She just didn't realize that would mean touching…and kissing…and well, that's her little boy up there.

She hurries over to where Strom and Caen are arguing and interrupts with a sweet smile.

"What seems to be the problem, Mister Strom?"

Strom turns his milky white eyes in her direction, and she can see her giant quartermaster is just about at his wit's end.

"Captain, I gave Mister Caen the list needed for this voyage of necessary supplies and he forgot three items! Potatoes, onions, and the most crucial. A spice for my secret sauce."

"Strom, you have potatoes and onions!" Caen barks.

He rubs a hand over his face and Shea stifles a laugh.

"But not Arethusian potatoes and onions, nor my spice! Captain, these are necessary items, especially with Miss Joana coming to stay with us."

Shea grins, glancing at Caen, who looks as if he's going to strangle the cook.

"Well then, we'll get them, Mister Strom. Mister Caen, there's urgent business on the afterdeck I need you to deal with immediately. Strom, I'll get you an errand boy to get the supplies as soon as possible."

"But he has—" Caen objects.

"Afterdeck, Caen," Shea orders, and Caen growls, stomping away up the stairs.

Shea places her hand on Strom's shoulder, and he smiles warmly at his young captain.

"Thank ye, kindly, Captain. And might I say you're looking radiant today," Strom tells her and she laughs as he bows.

"How would you know? You old blind dog." Shea lightly slugs him on the arm, and he chuckles and shrugs.

"Eh, it always worked with Paetre."

The cook heads back down to the galley, leaving Shea with the list.

Above she can hear Caen berating James and Aster for the public display of affection, and Aster comes running down the stairs away from Caen, leaving poor Mister James to suffer his wrath.

Aster catches sight of Shea and his eyes narrow on his surrogate mother.

"You sicced Caen on us," he accuses, his arms crossing.

Shea looks around and then points at her chest innocently. "Who, me? Of course not!"

"Yeah right. I'm sixteen years old, I'm not a kid anymore."

"I know! You're a very adult man, and as a very adult man I need you to run to port and collect these extremely important supplies."

Shea thrusts the list out to Aster, who takes it. She whistles and Caeruleus meows before landing on Aster's shoulder.

The teen looks down at the listed supplies and rolls his eyes.

"The grocery list? Really?"

He adjusts his shoulder under the weight of the Azulean Lionbird.

Shea nods. "Yup and you best get going. Caeruleus will help. You wouldn't want the two of you to get left in Arethusa."

"This is so not fair," Aster grumbles.

He yelps when Caeruleus nips his neck for complaining.

Shea rolls her eyes as he glares at the creature but then reluctantly takes off toward the gangplank leading onto the dock.

As he leaves, Beck arrives on the quarterdeck with two Oceanan soldiers behind him. He stops Aster briefly, and Aster smirks, pointing back to Shea, who's standing in front of the deck doors.

Caeruleus ruffles his feathers, and then her cabin boy disappears down the gangplank, out of sight.

Shea withholds the groan and waves back when Beck hails her. But before he can take a step toward her, she edges back to the afterdeck stairs, pointing over her shoulder, turning tail, and running up the steps.

When she glances over her shoulder, Beck is still grinning at her, and a small flip splashes in the pit of her stomach.

She quickly prays to the gods he won't come after her and then stops, because for all she knows her father can hear her prayers.

And has never answered one.

Luckily Beck seems to catch the view of the bow and takes off in Mister Tero's direction.

Shea turns her focus to James and Caen at the helm's desk, talking about the charted course.

"ETA?" Shea questions as she comes to stand in front of the railing surveying the quarterdeck.

She tries to avoid looking at Beck as he moves to the bow for launch.

"If we can avoid enough encounters and perhaps keep the wind on our side, we can get there within a week as usual. Maybe more though if the monster attacks are more frequent," James speaks up.

Caen clears his throat behind Shea and she turns to face her young helmsman, who seems to be blushing as Caen glares at him.

"Also, I apologize for my lapse in position, Captain, such a public display will not happen again," James explains, staring at the ground instead of meeting her eyes.

Caen huffs and Shea smiles softly at James. She steps away from the railing and approaches the desk, standing across from him and placing a hand on his shoulder.

"James," Shea murmurs, and the he looks up to meet her kind eyes.

"You'll always be kids to me, understand? I'm happy for you both."

James smiles brightly.

He salutes. "Aye, Captain. I understand."

"Why don't you head down and see if you can help Mister Tero with anything, while I finish up here with Caen? He'd quite like this launch to be our best."

The three of them chuckle and James nods. "Aye, ma'am."

Shea replaces him behind the desk, looking down at the charted maps next to Caen as James hops down the steps to the quarterdeck.

Caen pulls a hidden chart from his vest and places it on the desk, using the compass on the table to flatten it out.

Shea examines the updated diagram of the ship, noting the new cannons, and the addition of two harpoon launchers on the quarterdeck.

"With the navy officers joining us on the voyage, I recommend recruiting them to gunner positions," Caen voices.

"I agree. Are we stocked weapon wise?"

"That's where our foreign potato budget went," Caen snorts.

"Great," Shea murmurs. "We need to be prepared for a fight."

"You think it'll be worse than before? I mean, from my understanding, the border has been up for a while. We've come face-to-face with sea monsters for months now."

"But at a smaller rate, one maybe two a month…But if Perses catches wind of us, we could be encountering more attacks than before," Shea declares.

Clapping sounds from the deck, along with hoots and hollers, catch Shea's attention and she walks to the railing, smiling as she sees Joana come aboard with four Arethusian naval officers, including Soren, who she seems to be in deep discussion with.

Poseidon and Venus appear after her. Shea's gaze lingers on her father for a moment, and she jumps back when his eyes catch hers.

Caen walks up to the railing and notices Poseidon staring at her. He places a protective arm around his surrogate daughter.

Shea can't help but smirk when she sees Poseidon's eyes narrow at Caen's arm.

Jo finally looks up from her argument with Soren and spots Shea at the afterdeck rail. Two of the soldiers bring a heavy chest up the gangway, and Jo gestures to the double doors.

The crew continues working around them.

Venus and Poseidon head off to the bow where Beck is talking to Mister Tero, and Aster arrives on the ship, back from the market carrying three bags of supplies. Caeruleus takes two of them, flying off down the side of the ship through the galley window.

Catching the position of the moon, Shea would guess it's past midnight, and they need to be getting underway.

"Where would you be taking that extremely heavy chest?" Shea shouts to the naval guards carrying it toward the deck doors.

They freeze, looking up at the pirate captain.

"To our quarters, of course, Captain," Jo calls back with a challenge, and the poor soldiers look between the two women, unsure whether to continue to the room or not.

Shea grins down at the queen, satisfied, and nods. "Aye, of course. If I can see you a moment, Your Majesty."

Shea notices that the request seems to catch the others' attention as they too make their way to the afterdeck steps.

The soldiers take the chest down below, and Soren follows sullenly behind Joana as she climbs the steps to the helm with Beck, Poseidon, and Venus close behind.

Shea strolls back over to the navigation table, Caen at her side, and waits as the group files onto the afterdeck.

Jo leads the party as she comes to stand directly across from Shea on the other side of the table.

Soren stands beside her, with Poseidon and Venus close behind, and Shea finds herself, unconsciously, looking for Beck. She turns to see if he's come up the steps and jumps when she finds him directly to her right.

"Sorry, didn't mean to scare you," Beck murmurs with a soft grin.

Shea can feel the tips of her ears heating in embarrassment and she quickly clears her throat in acknowledgment.

She turns back to the table, facing Joana, and notices the queen's sharp expression as she looks between Shea and

Beck.

The captain groans inwardly; the last thing she needs is her fiancée noticing the awkward tension between the neighboring leader and herself.

She pushes the thoughts away and straightens up, smoothing out the world map that now covers the ship's weapons chart.

"Good to see we have everyone here. Now we've had various sources confirm Thetis's information. We have a month before Perses hits Arethusa with the Lycon army as well as his own. It'll take us just about two weeks to reach the Tenaro Islands, a week to resupply at Orena, and a two week return home. Which means we unfortunately won't be able to make it back in time to take a stand in Oceanus," Shea acknowledges, regretfully glancing at Beck.

Beck's features harden, but he nods. "We know. With coordination from General Soren, one of my advisors, Senator Caius, will be leading an evacuation of Oceanus to Arethusa."

"We'll make sure everyone gets out before the invasion, you have my word, sir," Soren declares, giving the young governor a small smile. "Although while we're on the subject, I think it's prudent to reiterate my concerns."

"What concerns?" Shea asks, and Jo sighs.

"Soren, the decision is made," Jo orders, turning a glare to the former naval man.

"Your Majesty, with all due respect, Arethusa is about to descend into panic and chaos. An entire nation will be entering our borders because of a larger threat. I can't believe that you leaving is in the best interest of the queendom."

"The noble council will be able to take on the weight of my absence. Lady Catherine will be returning soon from her leave, and I've put Countess Thetis in charge of the palace affairs while I'm gone."

Shea's eyes widen in surprise.

Soren's do the same.

"A Lycon?" he gasps.

A sultry laugh cuts off Jo's response, and the group parts as Countess Thetis arrives on the afterdeck.

"Don't worry, General, I promise to be on my best behavior." Thetis grins, curtsying to Beck and Jo. "Majesty, Governor."

"Thetis, what are you doing here?" Jo inquires.

Poseidon finally breaks his silence as his eyes look around the Lycon elf. "Where's the child?"

"He's safe," Thetis replies, and Shea can practically hear the *from you* she withholds.

"I figured there'd be a game plan meeting before you all left, and I thought I'd attend. As well as see you off. As I was saying, General, if Oceanus can spare their governor, surely Arethusa can spare their queen."

Soren shakes his head, caught at an impasse. "Very well. If I can't convince you to stay, then I must insist upon two naval ships to follow."

This time Shea speaks up. "Won't work. We're going to need to be fast, and I can't be worrying about two ships off the *Duchess*'s flank."

"Considering that the queen and her future wife are setting sail into monster-infested waters and to the ends of the world, I think two ships is a happy compromise for a worried general," Soren snaps, glaring at the captain.

Looks like the stand-off at the beach hasn't been forgotten yet. Shea grumbles to herself, looking down at the maps to avoid Soren's gaze.

"I won't take abled men who have a better chance of protecting my people than dying at sea. One ship has a better chance of sneaking through the barrier and sailing to Tenaro. We've supplied men for Shea's crew; they'll be enough protection. That's final."

"But, Your Majesty," Soren growls, and then he does something even more surprising. "Lady Shea, please understand—"

Jo slams her fist onto the navigation table, making everyone but the gods jump.

"General. I've given my orders, and my fiancée will one day be queen consort, but you will speak to me until then, as I have final say. Understood?"

Soren apologizes, "Yes, my queen."

"Dismissed."

Soren nods. He salutes, but not before catching Shea's eyes. She can see within his gaze the message clear as day, *Bring her back.* Shea nods subtly—she will.

Soren marches down the steps toward the dock.

"Well...Glad that was all settled. I do have another reason for being here though," Thetis comments, breaking the silence after Soren's departure.

"What is it?" Shea murmurs.

"Venus."

V looks over at the countess and steps closer, leaving Poseidon at the ship's rail.

"Countess?"

"I know you had plans to sail with the *Duchess*, but if I might, I think it'd be best if you stay in Arethusa. People will be agitated and confused. Some will know of the coming threat while others will have a harder time accepting the truth. A woman of your talents might be useful. I've known claimed elves of Aphrodite before and their effect on crowds can be quite an advantage."

Shea blanches, reluctantly imagining an orgy happening within the Arethusian palace gates.

As if Thetis can sense what Shea is thinking, she clarifies with a chuckle, "Charm speak, Captain, of course. In fact, I had a personal friend who was claimed by you back in Erebos. She proved most useful as a mediator."

Venus looks back to Poseidon.

"It's a good idea," Venus muses.

Poseidon straightens, a sickly expression falling across his features.

"No. He'll listen to you."

"You're his father, and I have a feeling a lot has changed. I need to stay, part of fixing our errors is helping the people we had a hand in creating. Perhaps I can do that best in Arethusa; maybe it was the reason I chose to stay there all along. The Fates are funny that way." As V voices her last comment, she winks at Shea, reminding her of their conversation in the tavern so long ago.

The Fates are cruel mistresses indeed.

Poseidon sighs but nods.

He pulls V toward him, and for a cringing moment Shea thinks they might kiss, but they merely hug. It's hard to look, but eventually they break away and V rejoins Thetis.

"Caen, alert the crew. We leave as soon as possible," Shea orders.

Caen steps away without a word, passing James on his way up to the afterdeck. The teen's eyes widen slightly as he sees everyone on his deck, but he passes through silently and readies himself at the helm.

Caen's orders on the quarterdeck can be heard from above, and Shea notices that the vessel headed for Oceanus has set sail.

Beck is watching the ship sailing back toward his homeland.

"We best be off," V notes, and Thetis bows to Beck and Jo once again.

V does the same, but before she follows Thetis down the steps, she glances back over her shoulder.

"Shea, good luck." V blows a kiss in her direction, and the elf can't stop the soft smile that spreads across her features.

Then before V leaves, she turns to Jo and says, "Remember what I told you. The heart, much like a rose, can wither if it's not properly cared for and then bloom when a new sun hits."

She's gone before anyone can respond.

Shea steps up to the rail, avoiding Poseidon as she watches the two beautiful women depart from her ship. The men pull the gangplank up from the dock.

Caen calls from below the railing on the quarterdeck, "We'll need an hour or so, Captain. Tero ordered repairs to the hull."

"Very well."

The crew make the final arrangements and it's another hour or two before they're able to sail.

Shea's eyes wander over her crew. She spots men she recognizes and then the new Arethusians she doesn't. She observes her comrades-in-arms as they go about their duties, warily watching the soldiers that have infiltrated their ranks.

If only Paetre was here.

How would he react to seeing pirates and lawmen working together to save their world? Somehow she doesn't think he'd be impressed.

She closes her eyes, breathing in. The feel of a hand on her back makes her jump, and she leans into the hand, assuming it's Jo's, but the palm feels much bigger now.

Her eyes shoot open and she shrugs off her father's touch, recoiling.

There's sorrow in his eyes, frown lines around his mouth, as she jumps away, but she has no intention of bonding with a god, particularly one who has been deaf and blind to the pain of his people.

Poseidon stalks toward the steps, leaving Beck, Jo, Shea, and James on the afterdeck.

"My lieges," Shea teases, ignoring her father's abrupt exit.

Jo comes to her right side as Beck steps to her left, the two of them closing her in.

She can feel their warmth on either shoulder, Beck's strength and Jo's power. But somehow instead of feeling trapped, she feels safe placed between these two leaders.

"Are we ready to launch the ship?" Shea inquires to

James.

He confirms they're ready.

She nods to the two royals who remained on the afterdeck with her during the final preparations.

Beck grins at her before turning his gaze to the bow, and when Shea meets Jo's eyes for approval, she finds a question there, as if she'd been examining their exchange. It disappears quickly, but Shea takes note of it anyway.

"Aye, Captain," Jo concedes.

"Well then. Weigh anchor," Shea announces, and she listens as Tero's bos'n call fills the deck.

She hasn't heard that whistle since Paetre, and it looks like the old sea dog really is pulling out all the stops for the new naval crew.

She laughs as it takes some of the men a moment to remember which tune means what order. As she's surveying the crew, she notices Poseidon down among the deck crew checking the belay pins. Caen walks toward him, and she can hear just over the wind as he tells Poseidon that if he's going to check the crew's work he might as well lend a hand and help with what needs to be done.

Caen orders Aster to the crow's nest, and a yowl echoes across the deck. Shea looks up in time to see Caeruleus flying through the air back from the galley. He soars around the crow's nest and lands on the edge, cooing at Aster as he waits for him to climb the ladder.

It's not long before the ship cuts through the tides and is sailing away from Arethusa on the open sea.

The world ahead, Shea can almost forget what she's really doing out here and who's on her ship. But she can't forget, not for the sake of Nereid. This is the trial she's been waiting for and it's only just begun.

CHAPTER 12: THE SINS OF THE FATHER

Shea

"We have some time before we reach the boundary. The men have been assigned bunks in the crew's sleeping quarters. So I figure I should point out where you two will be sleeping," Shea explains as she leads Poseidon, Beck, and Jo below deck.

The launch went off without a hitch, and Shea remained on the deck for a while until she felt Caen could manage. Now it's time to make everyone comfortable for the two-week journey ahead. Night has almost ended, and the morning sun should be rising any moment. Shea leads them down the winding halls and looks back to see Beck catch himself against the wall.

His cheeks bloat slightly before he manages to swallow, and she stifles her chuckle.

"Don't worry, Mister Beck, you'll get used to the swaying."

Beck groans in response but trudges along behind the three ahead of him. They pass an open door on the way to Beck and Poseidon's shared quarters, not that they know that yet.

Shea doesn't bother to glance in but is stopped when

she hears Jo shout.

"Nol!"

Shea turns just in time to see her queen go running into the open doorway, and she swears she can hear a grunt as papers go flying into the hall. Shea pushes back past her father as best she can without touching him and looks into the doctor's quarters. In the hall, Beck is leaning against the back wall with his face pointed skyward and his eyes closed as if he's still trying to catch his breath.

"I thought you were a sailor, Governor," Shea teases.

"I was," Beck murmurs. "Until my ship sank at the destruction of a giant snake and my father died."

Shea's ears burn, the tips a bright red and barely distinguishable from her hair.

She realizes this isn't seasickness but anxiety.

"I'm sorry."

It doesn't feel like enough, but Beck opens his eyes anyway and gives her a reassuring smile. His hand reaches out and brushes hers.

"I'll be okay."

Shea reluctantly turns away, picking up the papers that scattered into the hall when Jo ran into quarters of the ship's doctor.

"It's wonderful to see you again, my dear."

"How have you been?" Jo asks, practically bouncing with joy. "I hope Caeruleus brought you my letters, the court physician's post is still available, you know."

Nol is standing in front of his desk, his cot in the corner, with a large examination table in the center. It's enough space that he can get by but certainly not as extravagant as a court doctor's position could get him.

Shea feels a small sliver of jealousy in her stomach at the idea that her own fiancée is trying to poach the best doctor the *Duchess* has ever had.

Nol gratefully takes his research from Shea. Ever since the monsters appeared in Nereidan waters, any creatures—or pieces of them—left on board have been brought to Nol. He's taken to researching and documenting their existence.

His whole cabin now smells like fish, but he doesn't seem to mind, and Jo definitely doesn't appear to care.

"I did get your messages. I apologize for not writing back, but these past few months have been long. I've been studying our new friends, the creatures that I hear this elven priest has conjured."

"Have you found anything new?" Shea interrupts, and Jo jumps as if she'd forgotten she was there.

Nol grins, holding up a finger and walking to the cabinet in the back of the cabin. He fishes through papers and vials until he finds a silver flask, which he grabs and brings back to the group standing in his doorway.

He hands the flask to Shea. "Poison taken from that water wyvern that we encountered off the coast of—"

Shea coughs, stopping Nol from finishing that sentence; the last thing she needs is for Jo to really know where she's been the last year.

"Well, anyway, it could have taken down your elephant in under a minute. I've made enough that you can coat the tips of the harpoons with it, at least ten of them. If we want any more, we'd need to go back to where we encountered it."

"And where was that?" Jo inquires.

Nol looks to Shea for the answer, and just as the captain is about to open her mouth to respond, her father speaks instead.

"I know." Poseidon grins.

Shea turns sharply toward him with a frown, silently warning him not to say anything, but he simply smiles and shrugs.

"They are creatures of my kingdom," he explains.

Shea smiles sweetly. "Then perhaps you should have kept it from killing people, it did a lot of harm before we came along."

She expects Poseidon to look ashamed, but instead he

looks wistful. "My dear, it's their nature. The merfolk would say the same about you."

Shea doesn't have a response, so she curses absently to herself as she realizes it's not a bad argument.

Instead she turns back to the doctor, who is staring at her father with vivid interest.

"Doctor," Shea continues, and Nol looks to her, "that'll be all. Like before, I'll be assigning Jo to work beside you. With the extra men, we'll need an extra healer for the wounded we'll surely have."

"Well I hope our services won't be needed, but I'll be happy to work with you again, Nol," Jo exclaims, hugging the physician once more.

Nol pulls away and takes her hand in his, kissing the back. "An honor, my lady. And I'm sure when the captain retires, and if the position is still open, then I'd love to join the court, but my allegiances are first and foremost to Shea and the *Duchess*."

Pride fills Shea's chest and she nods in gratitude for the kind words. Nol salutes back, and Jo watches the exchange with a grin and shrugs.

"Worth a try, and at least you won't have to wait long. Why perhaps we'll have this whole mess sorted by the end of the month and be married by the next." Jo laughs and Nol chuckles along with her.

Poseidon is quiet, and Shea's not sure Beck heard, but she can merely force a smile. Married. She'd forgotten about all that. Of course, she loves Jo, none of that has changed, but the deal has come to a close. She's been caught, which means the vault isn't next after all this, but a wedding. Her wedding to the queen of Arethusa, after which she will become queen consort.

Her brain starts to shut down when a thought crosses her mind. Ceto has joined with Perses. Lycos has chosen a side and the wrong one at that, which means the empress has committed a crime *against* Nereid. Forget the vault; this could be her chance to bring Ceto's reign to an end once and for all. If they get this right, the slave trade in Lycos could fall, and Shea will finally have the power to change things. Maybe times will be changing for the better after all.

"I'm sorry, Captain, but might we continue on. I think I'd like to lie down," Beck's quiet voice mutters from behind her, and when she turns, his pale handsome face causes her heart to flutter.

She steps closer to him, positioning his arm over her shoulders, as he doesn't look quite well.

"Are you alright?" Shea offers, and he's so close to her it makes everything she was thinking before harder to comprehend.

"With your support, I'm great," he murmurs back, and it makes her heart beat firmly in her chest.

"What's this? A sick passenger?"

Nol steps forward, taking Beck from Shea, though the governor tries to wave him off.

"I'm fine. Really, I probably just need some air. Assign me a job too, and I'll get to it," Beck objects.

He tries pushing away from Nol again, but the doctor has dealt with Caen and Shea on many occasions when they've been past the point of needing sleep, and so he holds on to the young man.

"No. I think he could do with a rest. He's had a rough go of it, what with the world trying to end. Maybe you could give him some valerian root mixed with—"

Shea can't say what came over her, but there's something about his pain that she wants to fix, and so she reaches inside to where her magic lies and pulls.

"Shea, your eyes," Jo starts to say, but Shea cuts her off.

"Ýpnos," Shea commands, and then Beck is falling.

His eyes roll back in his head, and Nol shouts, catching the young man in his arms—a difficult task considering he's about four inches shorter than the governor.

Shea shudders out a breath and Jo is at her side.

She feels a large body press past her to the doctor and watches as her father lifts Beck into his arms.

"Shea, are you okay?" Jo asks, looking her over.

She places her hands on each side of Shea's face, but Shea's eyes dart past her toward Beck.

"I'm okay. I didn't mean to—I don't know what happened."

"Your magic is getting stronger. That's good, you'll need it," Poseidon tells her.

Nol tells the god to bring Beck back into the doctor's cabin, instructing Poseidon to lay him on the table. Nol even grabs the pillow on his cot to place under his head.

Nol checks Beck's pulse and sighs in relief.

"He's fine. I'll take care of him. You go, I hear we'll be hitting the boundary soon."

Shea nods and steps away, Jo and Poseidon do the same as Nol closes the door on him.

Shea shakes off the guilt she feels for using her magic on Beck and gestures for Jo and her father to follow behind.

"Let's get you to your quarters."

"Shea, wait," Jo protests, but the captain is already walking ahead.

Jo calls her name a few more times until finally she goes silent. Shea focuses on the hall and the wood under her feet as she finally makes it to the room she's assigned to Beck and Poseidon.

"You'll have to share, it was this or the main crew quarters. Caen felt it'd be better if you and Beck were separate, so he gave up his private cabin," Shea recites as she walks into the familiar room and turns only to wince as she sees Jo is no longer there, just Poseidon.

"Where's Jo?"

"I told her you'd meet her at your cabin," Poseidon states, and he closes the door behind him as he steps in. "I think we need to talk."

"I don't think so," Shea replies, shoving past him, but

he grabs her and before she can react, he has her pressed up against the wall.

Caen's desk has been pushed up against the far back to make room for a second cot, his bed moved off to the side as well. Otherwise the room is pretty bare. Many of Caen's documents and maps were moved to Aster's old room for storage as her boy heartbreakingly announced to her six months ago that he was too old to sleep in the captain's quarters and that he'd prefer to be with the crew. So she had let him go.

"You may be grown, but I'm still your father and you're going to listen to me."

Poseidon's growl brings her back to the present and she tries to shove him off but is surprised by the strength holding her back.

"How are you—?"

"Holding you? Benefit of being around my children, it strengthens me as well, although not nearly enough as my trident or Atlantis would."

Shea starts to struggle, if his being around her makes him stronger, then that's the last thing she wants.

"Shea, would you stop. Stop it!"

"No! I won't, you are not my father. You're simply the dick that helped give me life. I had a father and he's dead, I don't need you!"

"You bloody well do," Poseidon snarls, and his anger pins Shea in place.

Her chest is heaving and so is his as she glares Poseidon down. He glares right back.

The worst part is that, looking at him, she sees herself. The eyes, his mouth, she can see Proteus's cheekbones within those storming features. She'd been an orphan when she met Paetre, no family to speak of; she'd made the family she has now.

But now there's blood. A father, two half brothers, and a nephew. She has blood family and the little elven girl in her wants to rejoice; now she knows where she comes from. The only problem is the truth behind her origins is a nightmare and she's looking at the monster who started it all.

"I'm sorry," he finally says.

"What?" Shea growls.

"I'm sorry."

"For what?"

"For not being what you expected," Poseidon sighs.

He releases Shea and she has a mind to walk out the door, but for some reason she stays leaning back against the wall, rubbing her wrists.

"I've never been father of the year," Poseidon chuckles, sitting down on the cot. "Underdeep. My younger brother is a dick and yet somehow he always managed to have some form of relationship with his mortal children."

Zeus, Shea's mind helpfully supplies, the name of the king of the skies.

He's not favorably worshipped on Nereid, as the creation story stems from Poseidon and all Nereidans believe the king of the sea to be their creator.

Shea tries not to think about the implications of being related to the rest of the pantheon. Just because Nereid is an ocean culture doesn't mean the other gods aren't visibly worshipped, it's just not common. Small clans within the Eastlands pray to the female goddess Artemis for good hunts, and outlander farmers in Lycos pray to one they call Ceres, or in the north of Arethusa, Demeter.

But according to religion, those other gods are not the Nereidans' creators, and so their temples and talismans are few and far in between on the ocean continent of Nereid. But if Shea's father is real, then that must mean the others are too, and the world is a lot bigger than anyone has realized.

Shea learned this very lesson over the past year. Shaking away the memories of how far she wandered, Shea brings her attention back to her father.

"But I do love you. All of you. Triton, even Perses. I was blinded with immortality; each of your lives is so fleeting in the grand scheme. It's hard to get attached and always painful when your time here ends."

Shea spits out a bitter laugh, crossing her arms over her chest. "Can you not hear how that sounds? We're not your pets, we're people, direct descendants of you. Screw your immortality; that is not an excuse for absent parenting. I was stolen by slavers. Taken from my mother, and my home, and you let them. You could have stopped them."

Poseidon shakes his head as he stands from the bed. "No. I cannot see all from the Underdeep, and by the time I knew, you were on the *Duchess* with...Paetre."

"And so what? You thought piracy was better for me than being with my mother?"

"No—"

"They took me from her! I'm lucky I found people who cared for me and loved me, but she didn't know that. Did you even tell her? How many times did that sad mortal woman pray to you for the return of her child?"

"She asked me to leave you there!"

Shea's mouth audibly shuts. Her eyes are wide and her face pales, as if he struck her in the gut.

Poseidon doesn't look much better. His own handsome features darken. He tucks a strand of his jaw-length hair behind his ear and wipes a hand down his face with a sigh.

"What?"

"It's not what you think," Poseidon explains.

He tries to step closer to Shea, but the captain flinches back, her shoulders hitting the wall as she forgets she was leaning up against it.

"She didn't want me?"

"No! She loved you, but after Perses was exiled because of his power, she was afraid that when the time came for your claiming, they would do the same to you."

"She couldn't have known that," Shea growls, pushing off the wall and heading for the door.

Her father races past her and blocks her exit; she stops

and looks up into his pleading face.

"Yes, she could."

"No—"

"Yes! Because she was on the council who voted Perses's exile. Ami sentenced him herself. And then she got pregnant. She realized what she'd been part of."

Shea can't believe this, any of this. Her mother banished her half brother and left her with pirates and her father just let it happen. Her eyes burn as she uses all of her strength to hold back her tears; instead she keeps her eyes on Poseidon, glaring at him as if a simple look could rip him apart.

"Ami?" Shea mutters, and the name resonates to her very being.

"Yes, your mother. Ami," Poseidon says with a ghost of a smile.

"And here I thought I only had you to blame for the end of Nereid. Looks like I can blame Mom too."

Shea shoves past Poseidon, and he stumbles. His back hits the wall and Shea stalks away, hoping he won't go after her, but she's not fast enough. He catches her arm and pulls her back toward him. Her fist flies on instinct, but his other hand catches that too.

"We're done," Shea barks, trying to pull away.

"No," Poseidon growls back. "We're not. Like it or not, you need me. Your powers are only going to grow. If you think that little trick you did with the Oceanan boy surprised you, wait until you force someone to sleep and they don't wake up at all because you can't control your powers."

"What do you want from me?"

"I want to help you, but I need your permission to do so."

Poseidon releases her from his grip and she almost falls back from the force of trying to escape, but she manages to catch herself on the hallway wall.

Shea wants to kill him, but something inside her knows she's scared of these growing powers and the only one capable of understanding what's happening to her is, unfortunately, him.

"How? How can you help me?

"We train, every day. A couple hours each morning on the deck, early so that most of the crew is below in case things get out of hand. Give me a chance to teach you and then maybe we'll have a chance against Triton."

Shea's eyebrow rises. "You mean Perses?"

"Him too."

"Are you saying we might be in for an unfriendly welcome from Triton when we get to him?" Shea inquires with a frown.

"I don't know. That's the truth."

Shea nods. Guess immortality wasn't the problem after all.

"What do you say?"

Shea wants to tell him to walk the plank and get eaten by a hydra, but instead she says, "Fine. Right before first light. We've been up all night. Morning sun should be coming up soon, so we'll start tomorrow. I'll meet you on the deck. But if I don't think it's worth it, then I don't want to see you until we reach Triton. Got it?"

Poseidon chuckles darkly. "Got it."

And Shea leaves him at that. She stalks away down the darkened hall and doesn't stop until she hits the steps leading to the quarterdeck. She's about to go up when she remembers that Jo is waiting for her in her quarters. She thinks about going up anyway, but with everything that's happened, she hasn't really gotten a chance to properly see her fiancée.

Shea turns around and heads to her quarters. Besides, Caen will let her know when they hit the boundary. They've both got some time to spare.

CHAPTER 13: I'D FIGHT FOR YOU

Jo

As Shea storms off toward the quartermaster's room, ignoring Jo's shouts, Jo starts after her once again but is stopped by Poseidon, who puts a finger over his lips in a gesture of silence. Jo closes her mouth, Shea's name dying in her throat.

"I'll take care of her. I should talk to her about this alone anyway. Why don't you head off to your cabin? I'll send her your way after."

"I don't think—" Jo tries to object, but Poseidon has already turned her around and is pushing her in the opposite direction before going after his daughter.

Jo sighs, sending a silent prayer up to Amphitrite for strength, then freezes. She's sending a silent prayer to Poseidon's wife about his demigod daughter, probably not the best course of action.

But overall, she thinks it would be best if Shea talks to Poseidon alone. At the very least Jo knows her fiancée can handle herself.

Jo pauses as she passes Nol's closed door and thinks about the young man lying on the exam table inside. It didn't take a genius to see how Shea looked at him, the concern in her eyes, and yet, Jo doesn't doubt the captain's love for her.

Sure, the jealousy rises in the pit of her stomach, but she doesn't for one second believe that Shea doesn't love her. She's just not ignorant of the connection that's sparked between the two.

They've been apart a year from each other. A lot can change—in fact a lot has changed. Shea's powers have grown, she's the daughter of a god, and Jo is no longer a dutiful princess but the governing queen of her own country.

Time didn't just stop for a year.

Jo isn't guiltless, with the countless balls and the many governing functions, she's looked even if she hasn't touched. She came close once, but she couldn't bring herself to do it. All she could think about was her captain, and if she ever found out, she would ruin everything. It wasn't worth the risk.

Events have altered Jo's perceptions of the world; she shouldn't ignore the idea that the same hasn't happened to Shea.

Jo nearly runs into the door at the captain's quarters, so completely lost in her thoughts she hadn't even realized she kept walking. She shakes her head, trying to clear her mind, and pushes the door open.

It's like going back in time as soon as she passes the threshold. There are small differences, the fabrics on the bed have changed, there's more items scattered along the floor. But the mirrors have remained, in fact there's definitely more than before. The standing mirror is still off in the corner covered in silk scarves and dazzling jewelry.

Light is starting to stream in through the stained glass in the back of the cabin, spreading beautiful colors throughout the quarters and over the centered bed pressed up against the windows.

Shea's desk still sits in the center of the room with various maps strewn all over it.

One of the windows is open and a meow draws her

attention.

Jo closes the door behind her, and when she turns back to face the room, Caeruleus is perched on the back of Shea's intricately carved wooden chair behind her desk.

Jo smiles as he jumps from the chair to the table, pulling his wings against his back, and drops, spreading out across the maps and other important paperwork.

His blue fur looks absolutely brilliant in the colored light, and as she walks the rest of the way to the desk, she notices bits of gray scattered through his Azulean bright green wings. His silver-blue eyes open and close as he relaxes on the desk, his massive paws kneading the hard surface.

Jo grins down at him and pets the top of his head all the way down toward his feathered tail. She laughs when his nails puncture through one of Shea's documents. Carefully, she extracts it from his paw and places it out of the way. Knowing how sturdy the desk is—a flash of a memory streaks through her mind's eye of lazy kisses and warm cuddles from a year ago on a life-changing voyage—she hops onto the edge and scratches Caeruleus's belly as he purrs louder in approval.

"Hello, Caeruleus. I was worried about you, you know. I hadn't heard from you in a while before everything happened."

Caeruleus swivels his body so he's lying on his back and unfurls his wings to make himself more comfortable. The gray is more noticeable on this side of his wings; Jo absently wonders what the average life span of a Lionbird is. She also notes a few of his feathers seem to be missing.

"I'm worried, Caeruleus," Jo murmurs and Caeruleus's eyes open. He seems to meow in acknowledgment.

"We were apart for so long, Shea and I. And together for so short a time. Perhaps things have changed. I look at her and my heart beats faster. She takes my breath away and my mind sings but...we're not the same people we were a year ago."

Caeruleus mewls, turning back onto his front. He lazily stretches and gets up, walking closer to Jo. He presses the top of his head against her petting hand and places a paw on her thigh.

"She's not saying it, but I can tell. She found something this year, and it affected her. She's wiser now, more experienced than the young captain I once knew. When we met, it was like I found the other half to who I was. I still feel that way when I look at her. But so much has happened."

Jo hisses in pain when Caeruleus's razor-sharp talons cut into her thigh as he kneads against her pants. She hears the naval uniform rip slightly.

"Caeruleus," Jo chuckles and the Lionbird meows, releasing Jo's thigh and dropping back onto the desk. His tail flicks every so often.

"I'm sorry. I'm complaining, aren't I?" Jo sighs, and the answering tail flick says it all.

"I think I need to let her go."

Caeruleus growls, his bright silver eyes staring at the queen. Jo shakes her head with a smirk.

"Not like that. I don't want to leave her, but we've been apart a year. I know what I want; every written letter was enough for me, to keep me going, but I won't judge if it wasn't enough for her. I love her, I want her. But I need her to choose me."

Caeruleus sneezes, then brings his paw up to his face, licking the pad.

"I need her to choose me," Jo repeats, standing from the desk.

"Caeruleus, you're a genius." Jo laughs, straightening out her naval uniform.

Caeruleus yowls in objection of her standing from the desk and goes back to cleaning himself.

"Don't you see? I can't expect her to just go back to the way things were because things aren't the way they were. We're different, the both of us. I need to show her that's okay.

Well, take that, Governor Beck. I romanced her once, I think I can do it again."

"There you are."

Jo jumps as the door to the cabin opens behind her and Shea saunters in.

Jo's gaze wanders over the redhead's gorgeous form. From her dark boots to her loose pants held up by a scarf belt, the flowing material of her peasant blouse and black doublet obscuring her luscious bust to her braided red hair complementing her golden skin.

Their eyes meet as Jo studies Shea's one green and one white eye, and the more she stares the more entrancingly beautiful she finds them. They're a mark of her strength and that's gorgeous in itself.

"I was wondering where you could have gone when I found myself alone with Poseidon," Shea remarks, closing the door.

She leans back against the wood, crossing her arms over her chest.

Jo's face heats and she has to look down to compose herself before meeting her fiancée's heated gaze again.

"I'm sorry. You both needed to talk eventually, and he caught me off guard. I shouldn't have left you."

Shea tries to keep her tough exterior, but a small smile breaks the illusion. She pushes off the door, walking straight toward the queen, surprising Jo by wrapping her arms around the back of Jo's neck and pulling her in for a hug.

She smiles and pulls the elf closer, putting her arms around Shea's middle. She decides not to mention that she can see that Shea is on her tip toes from one of the mirrors, instead she just enjoys the feeling of having her close.

"It's okay. You were right, as usual. I needed to hear what he had to say." Shea sighs, pulling away.

Jo resists the urge to tighten her hold and releases the captain.

"Do you want to talk about it?" Jo asks, clearing her

throat.

Shea opens her mouth to answer but stops and instead groans when she notices Caeruleus lying on her desk.

"Caeruleus, how many times have I told you? Not on the desk, you mangy Lionbird. Go help Aster with watch."

Caeruleus yowls and continues to lie on the desk.

"Caeruleus," Shea warns.

The Lionbird looks up and Jo swears he glares at his mistress, mewls, and then stretches slowly.

She laughs as he kicks three rolled-up maps off the desk behind him.

"Don't encourage him, Jo!"

Shea grumbles and picks up the maps.

Caeruleus finally takes flight, flying once around the room. He lands on Jo's shoulder and nuzzles the side of her jaw with his face, before he's off and gone through the window.

Shea's still mumbling to herself as she puts the maps back on the table.

Jo smiles and walks up behind the elf, wrapping her arms back around Shea's middle and then pulling Shea against her chest.

She buries her face into Shea's braided hair.

"I missed you," Jo tells her.

Shea chuckles. "I missed you too."

She turns in Jo's arms. The blonde can feel the captain's stare, but she keeps her expression open, allowing the examination.

"It's going to work," she says.

Jo smirks. "I know."

Her eyes flicker down to Jo's lips.

"Do you want to, uh," Jo stutters, "talk about anything? Catch up?"

Shea grins. "Not exactly."

The captain is leaning in, and Jo closes the last of the distance between them. A shiver runs down to the base of her spine as their lips touch.

She moans at the feel of Shea's plump lips, and it gives the redhead the opportunity to press her tongue inside, deepening the kiss.

Jo's hands fall to Shea's waist, working at the fisherman's knot on her hip. It takes some coordination, but soon she unties the scarf and Shea's pants fall to her ankles.

She's vaguely aware of the elf kicking off her shoes and undergarments, until she's naked from the waist down, her peasant blouse falling over her firm bottom.

"Should we be doing—" Jo huffs as her hands run up and down Shea's muscled sides.

"Gods yes," Shea interrupts, breaking the kiss so she can focus on getting Jo's leather belt undone.

Jo toes off her own shoes while Shea whoops in success at getting Jo's belt off, dropping it to the floor.

Jo pulls Shea back in for a kiss, moaning as their bodies press together, basking in their warmth.

The captain's fingers make quick work of Jo's last fastenings on her pants, and Jo helps her push her trousers down to the floor before kicking them off.

She undoes the buttons on Jo's naval uniform and grins when she finds only a white corset underneath.

She offers her hand and Jo takes it as she's led to the bed.

They stop with Jo's back to the bed, and Shea takes off her blouse, exposing her beautiful body, her breasts bandaged down like usual.

Jo licks her lips, wanting to hold that beautiful form as she makes love to her over and over again.

Even after a year, it's nice to know the attraction is still there.

She gasps as she's pushed back against the bed and falls on top of the firm mattress. Grabbing one of the pillows, Jo presses it under her head as Shea climbs on top of her.

"Look at you take charge," Jo murmurs huskily, letting

her eyes roam over Shea's muscled physique until they land on strange markings peeking over the top of Shea's shoulders.

"Don't I always?" Shea teases, holding herself up as she leans down to kiss Jo again, but the queen stops her.

Her thumb brushes over the marking.

"What is that?" Jo murmurs.

Shea cocks her head, confused, and looks to her shoulder before understanding lights her eyes.

"Ah. That."

"That?"

Shea laughs and gets up; she takes her braided hair and brings it over the front of her shoulder exposing her back fully. She turns so Jo can see.

Jo gasps and sits up to examine the tattoo.

It's a huge Lionbird covering almost Shea's entire back, detailed, the mouth open in a roar. His wings peek over the top of her shoulders and his tail drops to her hip. Greens, blues, and black run through the entire tattoo. Her freckles stand out on her shoulders from the ink and along her arms.

Shea turns back to Jo with a sultry smile.

"Do you like it?"

"It's stunning," Jo tells her and runs her fingers down the side of Shea's arm. "You're beautiful," Jo breathes and laughs when Shea's pointed ears turn red.

"Oh hush," Shea groans, pushing Jo down and climbing back on top of her.

Jo grins and sighs as Shea runs her hand through her hair.

"Where'd you get it?" Jo asks, but Shea merely kisses her.

In a mysterious adventure it would seem, Jo wonders, but pushes the thoughts away so she can focus on the task at hand.

She brings her hands up, squeezing Shea's firm backside, pulling her closer.

Shea moans at the touch and breaks the kiss, instead pressing her lips to the side of Jo's jaw, trailing down to her neck.

Her breath comes quicker, and she moans as she feels Shea slipping lower and lower until the captain spreads her legs.

Jo can barely believe this is happening; after months of waiting, she finally has this gorgeous creature back in her bed.

Shea's breath on her sex causes shivers down her pale body, Jo's stomach clenching in her gut. She huffs a laugh, remembering how a month ago she'd been self-conscious about her body after the little bit of royal weight she'd gained. When there's a country to run, she's stuck behind a desk with little time to keep up on her sword training.

But with Shea, she feels wanted and beautiful.

That's how it's supposed to be, right?

Jo will deny the squeak that flies from her mouth later as a creaky floorboard, but for now, she can't hold back the high-pitched noise that escapes as the captain's tongue presses against her.

Jo's hands fly to the rich material covering the bed, the muscles in her legs flexing as Shea's hands grip her inner thighs.

The pleasure is mind numbing. Jo can feel her toes curling and gasps as Shea's tongue delves deeper inside.

Her eyes flutter over Shea's gorgeous red hair, gods, she's been dreaming about that hair for the past year.

She feels Shea's hand start to move closer and Jo almost inwardly sighs, ready to tell her that she doesn't like penetration, when she feels that coarse hand pause and instead slide up.

She doesn't remove her mouth, just stays fixated on Jo's building pleasure center and instead tweaks a nipple.

Jo moans and has to tell herself not to cry in the middle of sex.

Shea remembered.

She's close. Jo can feel her orgasm building in the pit of her stomach, and as Shea abuses her nipple, she starts babbling.

"Shea! Yes, you're so good, baby, oh! Poseidon, yes!"

Jo shouts as she comes, her mind going blank in ecstasy.

And then she recounts everything she just said.

She looks down at Shea with a sheepish smile.

Shea sits up, purses her lips, eyebrows furrowing, and then frowns.

"Oh gods," Shea groans.

She flops down beside Jo, wiping her mouth with the back of her hand and then throwing it over her eyes.

"I'm sorry…it just kind of…slipped out."

Shea hums in acknowledgment, but she doesn't remove her hand from her eyes.

"I could still take care of you," Jo consoles, trying to salvage the moment.

"No, I'm good. Something about you screaming my father's name in the middle of sex was akin to a cold-water bath," Shea gripes, removing her hand only to glare at Jo.

"Well, I've said it before during sex."

"That was before!"

"I know, love, I'm sorry. I promise I'll try not to say it again," Jo tells her, kissing Shea's naked shoulder.

She smiles softly at Jo, turning her head to look at her.

"Yeah?"

"Whatever you want, darling," Jo murmurs.

She grins, noticing her captain's ears blushing from the pet name.

She files that away for future use.

A knock sounds at the door, and without waiting for an answer, the person pushes into the room.

"Caen wanted me to tell you that we've reached the border," Aster informs.

He freezes when he catches sight of Shea and Jo naked on the bed together.

"Oh Poseidon!" Aster shrieks.

"Aster!" Jo shouts, grabbing the pillow under her head to cover up her half-naked form.

"Aster, what have I told you about barging in?"

"I knocked," Aster yells, turning his back on the two of them as they each scramble for their respective clothes.

"Knocking is only half of it, then you wait to be invited in. Tell Caen I'll be there in a moment," Shea orders, pulling her peasant blouse off the ground and over her head.

"But—"

"Now!" Shea and Jo both shout at the same time.

The door slams behind him on his way out.

Jo's eyes meet Shea's; they're both breathing heavily, hearts pounding, but as soon as their eyes meet, Jo feels the first snort of a giggle. Soon they're laughing as they clumsily pull on their clothes.

Shea finishes tucking in her blouse and then ties her belt off on the side of her hip; her boots are on and she grabs her hat off her desk and places it on her head.

She strolls closer to Jo as the queen finishes buttoning up her blue naval uniform.

Shea waves Jo's hands away and buttons the last three. She looks up at her, and Jo smiles down at her elf.

She places a chaste kiss on those sweet lips and laughs when Shea deepens it.

They break apart.

"I'm still in this," Shea whispers to her.

And before Jo can ask her if she heard everything from before, the redhead is gone and out the cabin door.

CHAPTER 14: GET TO KNOW ME

Beck

Voices and colors swirl behind Beck's eyes. He can hear his father's voice screaming as the wooden shard that killed him collides with his abdomen.

His mother's tortured cries fill his ears and a fractured outline of her still, lifeless form in her pretty yellow dress fills his sight.

He can barely feel his lungs filling with air until he gasps as he sees black gates and dark swirling water rushing toward him. He cries out as the water crashes into him, drowning him. His head is in agony as the pressure builds and he tries not to breathe in the bubbling water, until he can't do it anymore. It invades his lungs and he's choking on it.

A distant voice calls his name.

He turns his head in the direction of the sound.

His eyes open, and he gasps, jack-knifing on the medical table as he sits up, coming out of the excruciating dream. Except not all of it was a dream—his parent's deaths, those were real.

Beck groans, falling back to his forearms, lying on the table. He hears his name again and turns to see a vaguely familiar man with spectacles and blond-grayish hair tied back in a ponytail. His face choppily shaven.

"You're," Beck croaks, then clears his throat and tries again, "you're the doctor?"

The man nods with a soft smile and helps Beck sit up and swing his legs around so he's sitting on the edge of the table.

"I'm Dr. Nol. How are you feeling?"

"Like someone hit me over the head with the hilt of a sword."

"Yes, I'm afraid you'll have to thank the captain on that one. She wanted you to get some rest."

"So she knocked me out?" Beck asks, reaching to touch the back of his head, searching for the bump.

"More like willed you asleep, her magic sort of intervened," Nol explains.

It's then Beck notices Nol observing him before writing in a journal.

"She knocked me out with magic?" Beck asks, searching for clarification.

"Pretty much."

So much for a doctor's perspective.

Beck pushes off the table, attempting to stand, but he almost falls over as his legs buckle underneath him.

Nol rushes to his aid, helping him back onto the table.

"Easy there, it may take you a moment to get your sea legs back."

Beck eases down, closing his eyes. He manages to take a shallow breath as sweat drips down the back of his neck.

"How long was I out?"

Nol smiles.

"Not long. Fifteen, twenty minutes or so, she brought you down, but whatever happened didn't keep you out too long. We should be coming up on the boundary pretty soon."

As Nol finishes his comment, Aster bursts into the medical bay with a quick knock on the door.

He sees Beck on the table and his eyes seem to widen with horror before he sighs, taking in Beck's appearance with relief.

"Good, you're dressed," Aster comments with a wide grin.

Nol's eyebrow quirks and Beck chuckles.

"Should I not be?" Beck inquires.

He tries to push off the table once again and is happy to find he can stand.

Beck's question catches the teen off guard, and he feels the young man's eyes rake over his lean frame, resulting in Aster's cheeks staining a light pink.

"Mister Caen," Aster squeaks, but clears his throat to avoid his voice cracking, "Mister Caen wanted me to alert you, Dr. Nol, that we've arrived at the boundary. The captain has been notified and has given orders to make sure the medicines are locked down and safe."

"I'll get it done now, thank you," Nol replies and quickly gets to work crating the various glass vials around his cabin.

Aster turns to leave, but Beck stops him.

"I'll accompany you up, something tells me I'd prefer to be above deck anyway," he mutters and Aster nods in acknowledgment, leading the young governor back up to the top deck.

They pass naval officers and crew members along their way. Right before the steps leading above, Beck spots an Arethusian naval officer. Her blond hair is tied in a braid with what looks to be some kind of ribbon.

He mutters to Aster to go ahead, hoping to talk to the officer and see if she needs any help.

He comes up right behind her and places a soft hand on her shoulder, and when she turns, Beck finds himself face-to-face with Queen Joana.

"Oh Triton," Beck curses quietly, but Joana's smirk makes him think it wasn't quietly enough.

"Careful, Shea has a new thing about her family members being used as passionate curse words," Joana warns him.

And if he actually liked her, he might've laughed, but instead he simply hums with a nod.

Her light smile disappears from her features and she crosses her arms over her chest.

"Something you need, Governor?"

"No, Your Majesty. I was just looking for Shea," Beck tells her, avoiding her gaze.

"She's up above on the afterdeck, I needed to finish... fixing myself, so I let her go ahead. Apparently we've stopped short of the boundary, they're preparing the battle stations before we cross."

Beck tries not to think about what "fixing herself" means and instead turns to start up the steps.

"Beck!"

He stops but doesn't turn back to Joana. Instead he waits for her to come up the couple of steps until she's across from him.

He looks up and meets her eyes.

"I feel as if we've gotten off on the wrong foot," she tries, and Beck chuckles at her attempt.

"Is that so?"

"Yes. I think it is. We're allies, our countries. And I think we could even be friends."

Beck goes silent and he can see Joana is really trying.

Her face is so earnest, but there's this little dark voice that whispers from the back of his mind.

He listens to it.

"No," Beck states and then takes another few steps until he's right at the double doors leading out onto the quarterdeck.

He feels Joana's hand wrap around his upper arm to pull him back toward her.

She's on the step below and he looks down into her fiery gaze.

"No?"

"No." Beck shrugs.

"Could we at least try having a conversation?"

"There's nothing you could say."

"What is your problem?" Jo accuses, and she tightens her grip on his arm.

"I don't like you." He shrugs. "I think you're arrogant and righteous and definitely one of those people who always thinks they're right. So no, I don't see us being friends."

Beck dismisses her hand and reaches for the door handle.

"That's not it. You don't like me because I have something you want."

Beck freezes. He knows he shouldn't have because he's inadvertently proven her right, not that he'd admit it.

"I don't know what you're talking about."

"Oh, come on, I see the way you look at her," Joana growls.

Beck smirks and turns back to the queen. "Then you've also seen the way she looks at me."

She takes a sudden deep breath but composes herself with a cold smile.

"Yes. I have, but I also trust her and what we have. So knowing how she feels about you, I thought maybe we could find some common ground and be friends. We're both rulers. We have things in common, like ruling young."

"No, I became governor because of circumstances I couldn't control. My father died!"

"I lost my father too," Jo exclaims. "He died last year."

"My father was taken from me, you murdered yours! I'd say that's a big difference," Beck shouts, seething with pain.

Joana's mouth clamps shut. Her eyes gloss over, but she doesn't allow any tears to fall. She swallows hard and looks up into Beck's eyes.

"I killed him to save Shea, and it was the hardest and

easiest decision I have ever had to make. But don't think it didn't affect me, not for one second. Because I still dream of plunging that sword through his back *every night*. You don't know me. But maybe if you could get over yourself, you could get to."

Jo pushes past Beck, and he lets her.

He watches her stride ahead past the crewmen on deck and feels his own eyes start to burn.

Two crew members push past him down the steps, and he takes a deep breath before following the wounded queen to the afterdeck.

CHAPTER 15: WHOSE SIDE ARE YOU ON?

Shea

The boundary is straight ahead, and Shea doesn't need her spyglass to see. The sheer amount of power is visible even to a mortal eye. The first light of the morning shines brightly on the barrier. The presence ripples and cracks with energy, a glistening screen cutting straight down into the water and clear up past the clouds. Every bird that flies through the shimmering mist screeches as if in pain before continuing on.

Shea finishes the letter to Phoebus on the helm's desk and makes quick work of attaching it to Caeruleus's paw. She doesn't want him losing it, and she doesn't want her familiar anywhere near the ship when they cross.

Caeruleus will make it through and she'd rather Phoebus and Dari were apprised of their upcoming arrival so they could collect the supplies quickly and then head on to Tenaro.

Shea can feel the unease of the crew. She watches as some of them stop what they're doing to glance at the magnificent display of raw magic.

The horizon looks more like a mirage through the boundary, wavy, like looking through heat rising off the ground. The clouds above are dark, but the sunrays are still fighting to shine through, casting a strange aura on the dark ocean water.

Caen is next to her, and unfortunately Poseidon is on her other side as she finishes her message to be carried by Caeruleus; they're double-checking the charts.

The harpoon launchers are primed, and gunners have been placed at every cannon, whatever is coming their way won't know what hit them.

Once the letter is attached, she picks Caeruleus up and brings him to the ship's rail.

"Okay, old man, you get there in one piece, you hear, no catching fish on your way or getting eaten by sea serpents," Shea murmurs into his ear.

Caeruleus growls at the *old man* comment but ultimately purrs as Shea flinches when he kneads her hand, causing puncture wounds.

"I'll see you there," Shea tells him and throws him into the air.

Caeruleus spreads his wings and catches the wind with a yowl. He flies toward the boundary and Shea's fists clench as he crosses. He yowls once more but besides a brief falter, he keeps flying to Orena.

They wait another moment, and nothing happens, so Shea figures they can proceed.

Aster shouts down to Tero from the crow's nest, confirming a clear view, and then Tero shouts orders to James.

James nods, awaiting his captain's orders.

Shea looks down to the steps and finds Jo coming up them; she smiles but then frowns when she notices Jo's sullen expression.

Beck is behind her, but instead of following her up, he takes off toward the two Oceanan officers near the bow, the woman and young man who accompanied him on the voyage.

The woman, Officer Leone, is an experienced harpoon gunner, so Shea put her and her fellow soldier to work manning the right gun under Tero.

"Hey," Shea offers, drawing Jo's attention.

"I really hate people not liking me." Jo sighs, looking behind her.

"That's crazy," Shea comforts, closing the distance and rubbing her hand up and down Jo's suited arms. "Who doesn't like you?"

"I don't like her; she's bossy for one thing," Caen pipes up.

Shea looks over at him with wide eyes, glaring at her quartermaster. She uncaps her waterskin at her side and quickly smacks him upside the head with a water whip.

"I was kidding," Caen gripes, rubbing the back of his head.

Shea summons the water back into the pouch and ignores Poseidon's wide grin at her blatant use of magic.

The only smile that matters is the one on Jo's face and the warm gaze from those beautiful blue eyes as they land on Shea in appreciation for making her feel better.

Shea's heart skips a beat.

James clears his throat and everyone looks back to the young helmsman.

"The ship is ready, Captain, we await orders. Do we sail?"

Shea takes a deep breath, looking at Jo, and then her eyes, of their own volition, find Beck near the starboard harpoon gun.

As if he can feel her gaze, he looks back to the steering deck.

She can just barely make out a smile.

Let the adventure begin.

"Release the sails, full speed ahead," Shea orders.

Caen salutes, but this time it's in all seriousness, and he steps to the helm's rail looking down over the quarterdeck.

"Mister Tero, release the sails! Batten down the cannons and prepare the chase gun."

"Aye, Mister Caen! Alright, ya old salts, I want those sails ready now! Lad, keep the look out," Tero shouts up to Aster, who calls back his assent.

Tero walks the line of the ship. Navy men and crew work together double-checking the bowline knots on the cannons, and Shea watches Beck being directed toward the bow cannon, the chase gun—looks like he's found his place among the gunners.

The sails release, catching the wind.

"Now let's ride the current all the way to Orena and Tenaro," Shea states, more to herself than anyone else, but she hears Poseidon speak nonetheless.

"Spoken like a true daughter of Poseidon."

She doesn't respond, but she doesn't have to, Caen growls in distaste for the both of them.

She crosses to the helm's rail, standing beside Caen, and Jo comes to join them.

Poseidon also ventures to the rail as the ship heads straight for the boundary.

Shea can feel all eyes on her rather than the magical border they're about to cross. She keeps her head high and her expression neutral, hiding every terrified thought she's having, and then, the ship's bow and figurehead cross the boundary.

It's strange, the boundary passing through their bodies as they enter the demon-filled waters beyond Nereid's borders.

Some cry out in shock like Jo, while others hiss in discomfort. It's as if the old magic inspects every part of them, filling their core.

It's almost the same as when Shea accesses her magic, but foreign and invasive.

She has to grab the railing, suddenly feeling lightheaded. Shea turns to check on Jo, but she seems to handle it better.

What catches her attention is Poseidon. His back is

straighter, his skin younger; she even thinks some of his hair has lost its gray. He looks powerful, and then Shea understands what they just crossed through.

A physical manifestation of Perses's power—and if he's that strong? The mere insinuation makes Shea's skin crawl as she thinks about her other brother, who's a god.

Shea's never felt so weak.

A moment passes as the last of the ship crosses through the border and then it all goes white.

Shea's forearm blocks her eyes out of habit; shouts of alarm can be heard all over the deck, and Shea knows it can't be sunlight.

The white light fades and in the center of the quarterdeck is a man with cropped dark red hair. He has freckles covering his face and chest, and his bloodred robes are open, exposing his muscled frame. His eyes are cold, a harsh teal, but Shea can see the resemblance.

There's a loud war cry from the bow, and Shea's eyes widen as she sees Beck with a sword—she guesses it belongs to one of his soldiers—charging toward Perses.

Shea's heart leaps in her chest, and before she knows it, she's ignoring Jo's objection and racing down the afterdeck steps. She stops short of Perses, who catches Beck's blade with his hand and breaks it.

Beck stumbles from the force, and Perses grabs him by the throat, lifting him off his feet.

There's something in her brother's eyes as he brings Beck closer—they wander across the other man's features until their faces are inches apart.

"Hello, little prince," Perses murmurs, and Shea feels a feral growl threatening to leave her throat as she thinks he might just place a soft kiss on his lips.

Meanwhile, Beck is gasping for breath, his hands scratching at Perses until her brother throws the younger man and he lands on his back in front of Shea.

Jo and Caen descend the steps, but stop behind her as

Shea reaches down to see if Beck's okay.

She briefly looks back to the helm and sees Poseidon is missing.

Beck coughs from the strain on his throat, but he whispers he's okay.

Jo kneels down beside Shea to check on him as well.

A silent moment passes between the two of them as Jo lays her hands on Beck's shoulders protectively.

Shea can feel Perses's gaze on her.

The rest of the crew and officers haven't moved. All of them are surrounding the mystical figure on the deck, just a couple feet away from where Shea stands and the double doors leading down below.

She looks up and meets his gaze. Pale white and green meeting vibrant teal, it feels like her body is on fire.

She stands, stepping protectively in front of Jo and Beck.

Caen is right beside her.

Perses examines her, and she watches him. She takes in his elven robes, noting that his feet are bare. She doesn't see the shell Beck mentioned, but she's sure he has it on him.

"And hello to you too, little sister."

"Perses, I presume?" Shea snarls.

He grins and it makes the skin on the back of her neck crawl.

"I've been waiting a long time for this, Shea. We look alike," he tells her, taking a step closer to his younger half sister.

Shea holds her ground, refusing to retreat.

"I'm nothing like you."

Perses's hand lifts and he flicks his finger toward himself, gesturing for her to come closer.

Shea has no intention of doing what he says, but the waterskin at her side bursts open and a giant hand made out of water solidifies and pushes her onward.

She stumbles, catching herself, but not until they're

standing a couple of feet apart.

Caen goes for his hammer, strapped on his back, but Jo shouts his name.

"Caen, no!"

Caen growls and takes another step, but this time the water-shaped hand transforms and creates a wall of ice around the two of them, blocking Caen from entering the ring.

Shea studies Perses's features, knowing that this display of magic would be a drain on her, but he shows no sign of effort or fatigue.

It puts her on edge.

"Now we can talk," Perses comments.

He tries to place a hand on Shea's arm, but she moves just out of reach.

He lets his hand fall back to his side.

"So talk. What do you want?"

"Nereid. Our people's freedom. Immortal power. And well, you."

"Me?" Shea questions, raising a brow.

"Yes. We're family. You and I are the only ones in the world who know what it's like to be children of Poseidon. Not only that, we both know the role humans have played in destroying our kind. We should be working together. I know you have him."

"Who?" she asks innocently.

"I can sense him. We may make him stronger but not nearly as much as he does for us. Blood is strength, Shea. Can't you feel the power curling in your veins just by standing so close to me?"

Shea doesn't respond verbally, but yes, she can.

She can feel the power vibrating over her skin, lifting the hairs on her arms. It's taking all of her focus to stay alert as the ocean roars in her ears.

"I know where he's leading you. Off to see big brother," Perses drawls, his eyes staying fixated on Shea, unnerving.

"Well then, if there's no point in denying it, the least I can say is we're going to stop you. Don't pretend taking over Nereid is an attempt to save the elves. They've erected their own barrier just to keep you out, so clearly they don't want your help either. Not to mention teaming up with the Empress of Slavery doesn't exactly help your cause," Shea spits, but her brother smiles at her with ease.

His body language is open and strong; he doesn't see her as a threat.

"She's a powerful ally and a more powerful enemy, though I don't believe I need to tell you that," Perses acknowledges, and Shea's brand burns on her chest.

She clutches the scarred skin with a gasp, but the pain dissipates as quickly as it appears.

"It's good politics to keep her close, and then once I have Arethusa, well. I'll re-evaluate."

"Why take over Nereid? Why help the elves at all? They banished you for something out of your control."

"Because their leadership lacks sight! I'm not just taking back Nereid for the elves; I will rule them, I will be the most powerful being on Nereid, and we will put man and the gods in their proper place. Below us," Perses growls.

He takes a step toward Shea, and she takes a step away, until they're stalking each other within the small circle of ice.

"Then you should just kill me. Because I won't allow that to happen. I want slavery to end, but I want equality. Not some reverse society crap. So if you're not going to do anything, get the bloody Underdeep off my ship," Shea commands, and stops pacing.

She walks the last few feet until she's right in Perses's face, staring him down.

What she doesn't expect is for his hand to close around her throat.

Shea gasps, his marble white fingers clutching her neck tightly, lifting her onto her toes.

"Little sister, I could never kill you. You, me, and even Triton are the next generation of gods. But in this pantheon, *I* will be king. So no, sister, I won't kill you, but I will teach you obedience. Something you desperately lack." Perses chuckles darkly, squeezing a little more until Shea's hands are scratching at his.

Her magic pulls from inside her and she can feel it trying to call to the ice wall around them, but it's like her magical grip keeps slipping. She can't close her fingers around the elusive power.

"I…" Shea tries but she can't catch her breath.

Perses cocks his head as if deciding whether he should let her speak, and then he loosens his grip just enough for her words to trickle through.

"I'm…going…to…stop," Shea rasps, "you."

"You can try." Perses grins.

Shea drops to the floor and she can distantly hear the ice collapsing around her, turning back to liquid and seeping through the wooden floor.

Hands are on her, more than two, touching her back, her hair, and her face as she tries to breathe.

She grips her throat and looks up, expecting to see Perses there, but he's not. She coughs, looking around wildly and finally notices Poseidon, who's standing over by the port quarterdeck rail, looking over the side.

"Off the port side, Captain! He's there," Aster shouts, pointing left from the crow's nest.

Shea pushes off the deck, waving Beck's and Jo's hands away, and stumbles toward her father, her hands gripping the rail tightly.

Down below, standing on the water's surface, is Perses.

A beautiful conch shell is in his hand, and he's looking straight at Poseidon and Shea as he places the shell to his lips.

He blows it and the sound is horrific. A terrifying screech like Caeruleus's sharp nails sliding down solid glass.

Everyone on deck covers their ears, but it's over

quickly.

And as if he was standing right next to her, Shea hears Perses's voice in her ear as he speaks from all the way down on the ocean surface.

She watches his lips move and hears him as clear as day.

"If you survive this, then you belong with me."

He's gone.

She blinks and it's as if he was never there.

The sea is quiet, only the wind howls as it passes over the ship.

"Get the cannons ready," Poseidon commands, and Shea turns to her father.

His lips are pressed in a thin line and his eyebrows draw together in concern.

"What's coming?" Shea rasps, clearing her throat.

"It's already here," Poseidon states.

It bursts through the water, screeching the same high-pitched shrill noise that Perses produced from the shell. Its eyes are a pale yellow and its body is larger than anything Shea has ever seen.

Water sizzles as it touches its red scales, and Shea's eyes bulge when she sees the large wings on the creature's back. Its mouth opens and water spews from its throat up into the air. Some of it splashes onto the bow of the ship, and screaming sounds from various crew members, steam rising from their seared flesh.

"We're dead," Beck announces from nearby.

"Not yet," Caen barks and starts shouting orders.

Naval officers and *Duchess* crew run to their stations. Men and women man the harpoon launchers, gunners adjust cannon aim, and Shea looks to her father.

"What is it?"

Poseidon takes a breath; he puts his hand out over the rail and when he pulls his hand back over, there's a trident made of water rippling in his powerful grip.

"A Megathirio."

Shea sighs, because of course. She translates for the rest of them.

"Water dragon."

CHAPTER 16: STRANGE BEDFELLOWS

Perses

Perses collapses back on the floor of the Lycon tent, breathing with some difficulty. His hands grip the soft carpet covering the hard ground miles away from the capital Acheron in Lycos.

It's been a month since they razed the Lycon countryside.

Ceto and her army, joined by his own dark magic creatures from the deep. Banished elves misshapen by their own temptations they found in the Underdeep, loyal to Perses because without him they would have remained the mindless creatures they had become. But he recruited them and, after stealing his brother's shell, amplified his magic enough to give them back pieces of their humanity.

Liquid drips underneath his nose and down onto his lip—he recognizes the copper taste and wipes away the blood.

He'll need to make the change soon. Without the immortality, his mortal body will fail from the excess magic.

All he needs is for Shea to return with Triton. If she

survives the Megathirio, that is.

Perses chuckles aloud and carefully stands from where he teleported to the floor.

A low moan alerts him that he's not alone, and before he turns to the bed behind him, he straightens out his clothing, wipes the residual blood away, and runs a hand through his hair.

The Lycon viper behind him would strike the moment she sensed weakness, and he can't have that, not yet.

"You've returned," Ceto's breathy voice finally speaks.

Perses turns toward her, shrugging off his outer robes until he's left in only red silk pants embroidered with gold dragon designs on the hem. He watches her eyes roam over his bare chest, and he notes with appreciation her nude form.

Her long black hair covers her breasts, and a white fur blanket lays over her lower limbs. She gestures for him to come closer but he does no such thing.

She doesn't make the orders.

She stares him down a moment longer, but he merely smiles.

Finally, she shoves the blankets aside.

She pushes out of bed and stalks toward him completely naked, only her hair offering her any modesty.

Torches are lit at various points of the extravagant tent and a war table sits behind Perses, leaving the couple in the center of the makeshift room.

She reaches out to touch Perses's chest, but he catches her wrist with ease. With his other hand, he reaches out and tucks the strands of her hair on the left side of her face behind her ear and cups her cheek.

"Did you see her?" Ceto asks, allowing the moment.

Perses grins, knowingly. "Yes."

"Was she beautiful?"

There's a dark lilt to her voice and Perses wants to laugh because he knows part of her wishes honesty and the other part hopes that he didn't find Shea more beautiful than her.

But of course, he did, because his sister is more beautiful than a mere human.

"Yes," he responds.

Ceto hums in acknowledgment.

"So they've gone then?"

"They won't be back for weeks."

Ceto chuckles. "Then we should march!"

Perses growls and pulls Ceto's dark form closer to him. His hand moves from around her wrist to instead wrap around her waist, until she's flush against him.

"No. We will stay on schedule. I need them to return. First, we will take back your precious Oceanus, and then once news reaches us that they're back in Arethusa, we take Thalassa."

"It's my army," Ceto states. "If I want them to march, they will."

"No," Perses murmurs, his lips inches from hers. "Not anymore. I'm running things now."

Perses kisses her deeply. She bites his lips and he tastes that bitter copper again. His hand moves from her face and instead grips her hair tightly, pulling until he hears her cry out in pain.

Once her mouth opens, he nips her tongue and she moans at the sharp bite. They pull away from each other, breathing heavily, blood smeared across both their lips, and they grin at one another.

"You may have the plan, Perses, but remember that I am the empress of Lycos and my army will listen to me. The deal still stands; you will have Arethusa and the Eastlands, and I will retain Oceanus and Lycos. We will rule together," Ceto declares.

"Of course, Your Majesty," Perses replies.

Ceto grabs his arms and he suppresses the flinch as her nails bite into his biceps, keeping his expression neutral.

"And Shea will be mine."

Perses inwardly laughs; he'd never let his sister fall into this woman's hands.

"You shall have her, Ceto," he tells her and smiles viciously when she laughs with joy.

"My empress, it's urgent I speak with Lord Perses!"

The tent flap opens and a Lycon high-ranking officer enters.

Ceto turns to face him with a thunderous expression plastered on her face.

He notices his lady's undress and quickly averts his eyes, kneeling before her.

"I apologize, my lady, but the creatures, I mean the Merrow, as Lord Perses calls them, have returned and the one called Coral Fang has asked to see him. They make the men nervous, my lady, they wish to know our orders, if we move out come daybreak?"

Perses examines the weak, quivering human as he awaits the lady's orders.

Ceto's dark expression turns sweet and sultry and she glances back to Perses with a smile.

"It appears our army needs us, my love," Ceto states.

"Yes, I believe so. I should speak with Coral Fang, he'll have updates."

Perses goes to leave, but before he reaches the soldier, Ceto stops him, gripping his forearm.

"Do I tell the generals we march to Oceanus?"

Perses considers the request and then nods.

"It'll give us time to make it over the mountain pass safely. There's many elven traps I'll need to break, old magic that will need to be dissolved. We leave come dawn."

The soldier looks up and places his forearm over his chest firmly. He starts to stand, but Ceto turns her gaze upon him.

"Did I say that you could leave, Captain?"

"No, Your Majesty, I just assumed..."

Ceto laughs. "You assumed, yes. I gave orders not to be

disturbed, and yet you entered my tent without permission."

"No, Your Majesty, I—" the soldier tries to explain, but Ceto cuts him off.

"No? You deny my claim? Are you saying I've lied?"

"No—no," he stutters, raising his hands up in surrender, "Coral Fang told me to fetch Lord Perses immediately."

"I am your empress! You obey me," Ceto shouts shrilly. She grabs the longsword near the bed and with quick precision removes the captain's head from his body before he can react.

Perses watches the officer's head roll until it stops at his feet, the poor man's cheek still twitching.

Ceto's chest rises and falls heavily, blood splattered on her face.

Perses calmly walks toward their bed and picks up the silk robe laid at the foot. He opens it up and places it on her as she puts her hands through properly. He even steps around and ties it for her as she pulls her hair out from underneath.

"Such strength," Perses compliments, and leaves a light kiss on her lips.

He chokes as her hand reaches out and grasps his cock through the silk of his pants, holding him by his genitals.

"After I inform the generals, I expect you to be naked in my bed when I return. I plan on having my way with you until daybreak. Am I understood?"

Perses clears his throat and vainly tries to speak clearly, "Perfectly, Your Majesty."

Ceto releases him and Perses takes a shallow breath, following her out of the tent.

She gracefully takes off toward the general's tent across camp, and Perses chuckles as he watches her human men stumble over themselves to bow as she walks by.

Perses smells him before he sees him. He looks over his shoulder to find Coral Fang's glowing milky eyes from the dark, where he's standing off to the side of the empress's tent.

"Coral Fang, you let her kill that poor boy," Perses notes

with a tsk of his tongue.

"Sorry, Master," Coral Fang admits with a razor grin.

Perses examines the Merrow quickly for injuries but finds none. The creature's body is disgusting, covered in scales and fish slime, with three rows of gills crossing the monster's neck. Long webbed fingers end in razor-sharp, coral-like nails, and knifelike fins extend off his ankles, thighs, elbows, back, and the top of his head. The Merrow are vicious humanoid creatures with no tail to make them mer-people, but not mortal enough to be considered elven anymore. With the help of Perses's magic, the Lycon blacksmith was able to create light armor for his Merrow army without restricting their fins or swim speed.

"Did you find an opening?"

"No, the boundary is closed to us until Master can accumulate enough power; there's no way into the Eastlands."

"I figured as much," Perses concedes, "but no matter, once I have immortality, my power will grow and then not even the great Ami will be able to keep me out. Speaking of, I have a new job for you, Coral Fang."

Coral Fang steps closer to his master, bowing. "Anything."

"I need you to see if the *Veiled Duchess* survived the Megathirio. It's on its way to Tenaro, but they'll find Triton is much closer than they realize."

"Orena," the monster spits.

Perses nods. "They're not far from the border."

He projects the coordinates into Coral Fang's mind, and he grunts in pain.

"If they survived, follow her."

"What do you want us to do? When we get to the island."

"Wait until they have Triton, I'll be able to sense it. I'll send you the order, and then burn it," Perses commands.

He turns to go back into the tent to ready himself for Ceto's return when a cold, slimy hand stops him. He looks back at the creature with disgust, and Coral Fang immediately drops his hand from his master's shoulder.

"The ship, my lord?"

"No, you fool. The *island*. Then return immediately to me for the Arethusian invasion. I need them to come home quickly, and that should give my darling brother and sister all the incentive they need to face me."

CHAPTER 17: TRIAL BY BOILING WATER

Jo

"Water dragon."

Jo can barely hear herself think as Shea's translation leaves her panicking.

Everyone is rushing to their stations.

The Megathirio, a water dragon, has risen out of the sea, but it hasn't blasted its boiling water across the deck yet. The monster is huge; it towers over the ship, steam rising from its blistering red scales.

Black horns twist off of its serpent-like skull. The boiling water blasts don't seem to be the only thing they have to worry about, as the talons on the creature's hands and the razor teeth don't look exactly harmless.

Jo eyes the wings with terror—how are they going to defeat this thing?

She notices Beck has already taken off toward the bow.

Jo calls after him as does Shea, but she can see him helping the injured crew out of the way so the rest of the abled crew can get to the harpoons and launch them.

"Aster!"

James shouts from behind them at the wheel.

They all look up to see Aster hanging from the crow's

nest—the force from the creature surfacing must have knocked him from the platform.

He has a rope tied around his waist, but with the Megathirio so close, the last thing he wants to do is go swinging toward the bow.

"Aster!" Shea shouts and she takes off to go after him, but Poseidon stops her.

"Let go of me!"

"Shea, if we're going to have any chance of living through this, I need you to listen to me!"

Jo looks up at Aster, watching his right hand fail as it lets go of the edge.

He's hanging on by only his left and the rope attached to his waist.

James runs down the steps of the helm, but Caen sees him and stops shouting at Mister Tero to start firing.

"James, you get back to steering this vessel away from that dragon or so help me gods it's not the monster you'll have to worry about!"

"But what about Aster," James growls.

"I'll get him," Jo says.

Shea stops listening to what her father's saying and turns to her with wide eyes.

"You're not bloody going up there!"

"Hey, if that's your kid up there, then he's mine too, so yeah I'm getting our boy," Jo orders and that shuts Shea up.

It must be enough for James too, because Jo turns to look at him and he's already back at steering.

The ship begins to turn, but it's not fast enough; the dragon's wings expand and one flap sends everyone falling to the ground.

"It can't fly, but it can create some strong gusts off the deck," Poseidon says. "The thing's too quick and has too much power to shoot at it unrestrained. The water's heat won't kill you; it's hot but you'll drown from the constant rush of it before you burn long enough to do any lasting damage."

"So what do we do?" Shea bellows and the dragon screeches again.

It brings a claw down, tearing through the front sail. Then it rears back its ugly head and Jo can see Tero tying ropes around sailors and connecting the ropes to the mast with Beck's help.

Searing water erupts from the creature's throat—Tero and Beck manage to avoid most of it by hiding behind the mast, but Jo loses sight of them, and many of the crew cry out in burning pain.

Aster screams from above; he's trying to pull himself up, but he can't.

Jo doesn't have a lot of time. She pulls the sword from her scabbard, the one she grabbed from Shea's room just in case, and realizes it's Shea's old sword. The one her father tried to kill her lover with. She stares down at the enchanted gold blade and part of her wants to throw it overboard but another part thinks its poetic.

"So what's the plan? He doesn't have much time," Jo demands.

She's looking at Shea, and Shea reluctantly looks to Poseidon.

"Well you heard her, what do you suggest?" Shea questions.

Poseidon smiles and gets to it. "Okay, Jo, you get to the kid and save him. Tell Beck to aim the harpoons off the port side and get the cannons ready. Shea and I are going to restrain it!"

"How?" Shea argues.

"We're going to imprison it in, well, for lack of a better term, a bubble of water. We hold it, suspended, and Beck and the gunners shoot."

"I can't do that, I don't have the power. It's too strong. I'll never hold it!"

"Shea," Jo yells, catching her attention.

Her captain turns to her, and she notices Shea's green eye catch on the blade Jo's holding.

"You can do this."

Jo doesn't wait for a response; she takes the sword and starts running to the rope ladder leading up to the crow's nest.

"Jo!"

Jo looks up in time to see a wave of boiling water rushing toward her.

A large mass hits her from the side and she lands between two cannons with a body on top of her—the sword clamors to the side.

Water rolls past but the little bit that hits her makes her cry out.

The figure on top of her groans as the water splashes across his back.

"Caen!"

Caen looks down at Jo and quickly helps her up.

The water dragon has ripped up the bow of the ship, the *Duchess*'s figurehead sinking into the fathoms.

Jo sees Beck in one of the harpoon chairs, and he takes a good shot at the creature, pelting it through the right wing, ripping through the thinner flesh.

The dragon screams in agony, and Beck jumps as a wave of boiling water blasts apart the harpoon launcher.

"Aster's still hanging on, you've got a clear moment!"

"Caen, tell Beck to get the gunners facing the port side and to aim the left harpoon off the rail. Poseidon and Shea are going to incapacitate the dragon, enough to get in a good shot."

The two of them look back to their captain and the god. Poseidon finishes saying something to Shea, and she nods with determination.

The next thing they can see is the father-daughter team walking down the center of the ship toward the Megathirio.

The dragon screeches when it sees them, and Jo hears Aster shout.

She looks and screams when she sees his last hand slip from the ledge.

Aster bellows as he falls, but he must have managed to grab his dagger at his right side because he quickly plunges the knife into the side of the mast. He's hanging from the dagger's handle now but it won't hold him long.

Jo and Caen take off.

The dragon screeches and it's louder closer to the bow.

Caen reaches Beck, and Jo reaches the ladder just in time for the dragon to open its mouth again.

This close she can see the water bubbling in its throat before it expels it at the deck.

Jo closes her eyes, preparing herself to withstand the full pain of the blasting heat, but it doesn't come. When she opens her eyes, she sees the water erupting from the dragon's mouth is being pushed back toward the Megathirio.

She turns and sees Shea and Poseidon with their hands outstretched, straining with obvious effort as they force the water coming from the dragon to encase the dragon's head. The more water it spits out, the more their casing expands down the creature's body.

Jo starts climbing.

She sheathes the sword and pulls herself up the rope ladder.

Aster is still struggling to hang on, but she realizes if she just gets high enough, Aster can let go of the dagger and swing to the ladder, and she just has to be ready to catch him so he doesn't swing past her and end up in the water prison with the Megathirio.

The dragon's tail breaks from the water bubble, as it panics from the magical encasing crawling over its body.

The sound of cannon fire echoes across the open ocean, but the cast-iron spheres practically bounce off the creature. The steel harpoons seem to be the only thing strong enough to pierce the monster's hide.

Its tail slams into the side of the ship, and the *Duchess* creaks from the impact.

Caen shouts for someone to get below and check the damage.

No use defeating this thing if the *Duchess* sinks.

"Aster," Jo calls out.

Aster looks over to the rope ladder and sees Jo a little farther down.

"I'm slipping," Aster croaks, beads of sweat dripping down his beautiful face.

"That's okay, I need you to let yourself fall. I'm going to catch you!"

Aster shakes his head. "If I swing too far over, I'll hit the thing!"

"I promise I'll catch you, Aster, just let go. I need you to trust me."

A strange gargling sound roars from behind them, and Jo gasps as she looks and sees the Megathirio almost completely encased.

Its wings and tail struggle, occasionally escaping the giant water prism.

It's incredible.

Jo turns her attention back to Aster though, who is staring at the magic casing in shock.

"Aster!"

He looks at her.

"Trust me, son."

His eyes widen.

He looks down at Shea, who's screaming at the energy it's taking to hold the Megathirio in place—and then, he lets go.

Aster falls quickly and as the rope tied around his waist pulls taut, he grunts in pain from the force as he swings toward Jo.

He's flying toward her, but she also notices he's coming in a little low. Okay, a lot low.

Jo scrambles down the ladder as fast as she can as he swings to the left side.

He's moving fast.

She reaches out and grunts as his body slams into her, and she uses his own momentum to propel them to the back side of the rope ladder.

Jo has Aster pressed against the rope, shielding him with her own body against any attack.

They're both breathing hard and the left side of Jo's body pulses from the hit, but she's got him.

"Thank you," Aster murmurs, and without really thinking Jo presses a quick kiss to the top of his head.

Jo hadn't even realized she'd closed her eyes until they shoot open at the sound of Shea shouting.

"I can't hold him, he's struggling too much!"

"Keep your focus on what I told you," Poseidon orders. "Now we've got to create an opening for them to shoot the harpoons through!"

"I'm barely holding him inside, I can't think about doing more," Shea screams, her arms quaking.

Her face is red, and Jo can see from here a tendon visibly popping from her throat.

"Careful!" Poseidon cries, as Shea briefly loses her hold—long enough for the dragon's mouth to shoot through the water prison.

It tries to spray the deck, but Poseidon manages to catch the water and push it back into the casing; the creature screeches from the feel of its own heat.

"Shea, concentrate, look at what you've done, the power you have! Beck has the shot, we just need to open the way."

Jo looks over and sees Beck in the harpoon contraption—he's got the gun primed, and he nods that he's ready.

"We can do this, I just need you to trust me!"

"I can't!" Shea bellows.

"Daughter," Poseidon commands, and Shea turns her head toward him with momentous effort, "trust me."

Shea takes a shallow breath; she turns back to the Megathirio.

She keeps her left hand outstretched but drops her right, and Poseidon does the same. Then they both bring their right hands up and begin to draw a slow circle in the air.

Jo watches the water bubble holding the dragon, but nothing seems to happen.

They've got him pinned by the pressure, keeping his chest open for Beck to take the killing shot, but they've got to create a window through the water first.

And then Jo sees it, a faint swirl in the water over the creature's chest getting bigger.

Shea is yelling at the effort, sobbing like she's in pain.

Jo looks down and her heart stops as she can see blood pouring from Shea's nose. Jo thinks she might collapse, but something else happens.

Gradually, Shea's eyes begin to glow. Her wounded eye slowly changes back to her normal shade of green and the scar knits back into smooth flesh. Her braided red hair flies free, turning brighter and richer than before. Her skin glows—not just tan but a true golden glow shining from her flesh.

"What's happening?" Aster cries.

Poseidon turns to his daughter and laughs but Shea doesn't seem to be aware of the changes. Her stature grows until she might even be the same height as Caen.

The window in the water opens and Shea's scream silences. She's quiet, her hands no longer shaking; instead of continuing the circular movement with her right hand, she uses a strange motion and water picks up one of the steel harpoons.

She pulls her right arm back and then pushes it forward like she's throwing an object.

The harpoon suspended in midair by water goes racing toward the Megathirio and plunges into the water dragon's chest.

The bubble of water encasing the dragon drops and the creature screeches in agony, gurgling on some boiling water it can't expel.

The crew watches in shock as the Megathirio collapses into the sea, black blood coating the ocean's surface, and the dead monster sinks below the rocky waves.

Jo makes sure Aster is holding on to the ladder and then descends as quickly as she can as Shea hits the deck.

At the same time, Beck races out of the harpoon launcher. Jo makes it to the bottom just as Beck manages to kneel down next to Shea.

As Jo runs closer, she notes that Shea's stature has already shrunken back down to her normal size. Her red hair covers her face and Beck pulls the captain into his arms as everyone gathers around to see if she's okay.

Jo kneels down in front of the two of them, her hand shaking as she reaches out to push Shea's hair away from her face, and when she does, she's not sure about what she finds.

She looks the same as she did before the battle; her hair has gone back to its regular color. Her scarred eye is still scarred, and with as much effort as Shea has left, her eyes flutter open just enough for Jo to see the beautiful green in her right and the haunting white of her left.

"Did we win?" Shea croaks.

No one can speak, no one's sure what to say.

"Yes," Poseidon answers for them all. "Rest. We have a long journey ahead."

Shea's eyes close without objecting, and she passes out in Beck's arms.

"You should take her below. We need to get the sails repaired, as much of the bow as we can, and get under way. Who knows what else will smell the blood and come swimming with its mouth watering?"

Caen, who had pushed his way through to Shea, opens his mouth to rip Poseidon a new one, but Jo stops him.

"He's right. We need to keep moving," Jo commands, and the rest of the crew agrees, pirate and officer alike.

Caen's mouth snaps shut before he responds, "Okay. We have extra sail down below, if we work hard enough, we can get the *Duchess* up and running, fast."

"How fast?" Beck asks, holding Shea close.

"As fast as we can. Alright, gents! I want a round off, who's alive and who's dead. Mister Tero?"

Everyone waits for Mister Tero's regular response, but it never comes.

"Tero?" Caen shouts.

There's no answer.

"Jim?"

Still no response.

"Didn't he go below?" one crew member asks.

"Well, let's find out!" Caen snarls.

The crew disperses, people go here and there, and Jo notices Aster kiss Shea on the head before running up to the afterdeck to check on James.

James is halfway down the steps before he catches Aster in his arms and kisses him deeply.

Jo's eyes tear.

Shea probably would have liked to see that.

"I can take her," Poseidon says, reaching for Shea, but Jo and Beck respond at the same time.

"No!"

Poseidon looks between the two of them with wide eyes, and Jo manages to compose herself first.

"I mean, that's okay. Beck's got her; we'll take her below."

Poseidon nods and heads off to wherever he needs to be.

Jo's eyes catch Beck's, and at first she thinks he might be angry with her, but then his eyes soften and his lips quirk into a soft smile.

"You were pretty brave out there, Your Majesty. I can

see why she likes you," Beck tells her as he stands and adjusts his grip on Shea's lax form.

Jo smiles, the tense pain in her stomach subsiding, and she takes in this strange boy. She can't see the attraction physically that Shea must see, but she sees the bravery and kindness this man exudes. Perhaps, maybe, she could learn to live with him being a part of their life.

"You too," Jo replies, and she walks beside him all the way back to the captain's quarters where they lay Shea down.

CHAPTER 18: THE COST OF POWER

Shea

It's been five days since they lost Tero.

Shea woke hours after the encounter—she didn't even remember killing the Megathirio, but all Caen had been able to offer was the old sea dog's sword.

These things happen. The deck crew saw him go down below. The last the lower crew saw of him, he was heading back up, and somewhere in the chaos of it all, Tero fell. Shea wishes they had a body to honor, but in a pirate's life sometimes they don't even get that.

Beck and Jo were there when she woke. They told her all about her amazing feat and the magic she displayed, but she couldn't piece any of it together.

Tero wasn't the only crewman who fell; they lost about six men overall and only two bodies were recovered.

As soon as Caen apprised her of the situation, she was pushing herself out of bed, much to Beck's and Jo's disapproval, but she had a ship to run, and now, a bos'n to replace.

She called James into her quarters and gave him the bittersweet news that he would be replacing Tero as bos'n of the *Veiled Duchess*. Then she called Aster in to join him.

Aster's right, he's too old to be her cabin boy. So, while

James trains with Caen to take over Tero's position, Aster will train with James to become the new helmsman.

Neither expressed much happiness at the promotions, although they were gracious. Every promotion is always bittersweet because more often than not it's a replacement.

After she excused them, she kept to herself, trying to remember. There were flashes of the fight, but it was almost like her brain was stopping her from seeing, as if it was protecting itself from whatever happened.

Jo stood at Shea's side later that night as the queen experienced her first pirate funeral. The bodies found were wrapped in cloth, the cloth was sewn up, and Shea did the honors of punching the needle through each dead man's nose.

Paetre had done the same. He hoped to see any sign of life before he condemned the bodies to the deep.

They laid the first man on the plank.

The torches burned in the dark, casting harrowing shadows over the crew's faces and the patched-up sails.

She thanked each man for his service, naming each one lost before she gave the signal for them to slide the bodies overboard. They hit the water with a resounding splash.

Shea produced Tero's sword from her jacket—she'd wrapped it in the same cloth as the corpses—and walked to the rail's edge, gripping the blade tight.

"Tero was a dear friend, a great bos'n. He served on this ship almost since Captain Phoebus. He was Paetre's confidant and someone we will never forget. Rest easy, old friend."

Shea dropped the sword overboard and watched it fall into the sea. She took a solemn breath as it sank below, gripping the rail tightly.

A hand touched her shoulder and she looked back to see Jo with tearful eyes. Shea smiled at her softly and placed her hand on top of Jo's.

"Right," Shea announced. "As you know, James will be

taking over for Tero. Aster will be our new helmsman. We've still got a week until we reach Orena; let's try to make the most of it. Mister Caen?"

Caen had stepped up and saluted Shea with the utmost respect. She glanced around everyone's sullen and withdrawn faces. They hadn't had a loss like this in a while.

"You have the deck," Shea ordered and retired with Jo to their quarters.

Poseidon stopped her on the way with the request to still start her training the next morning.

Without much reluctance, Shea agreed.

Four days passed since the funeral, and finally things have retained a kind of normalcy. They only have two more days before they arrive at Orena.

James has taken to his position swimmingly, though it is strange to see Aster at the helm at most hours. Everyone seems to be falling back into their place.

The rest of the repairs on the bow will need to be completed in Orena—with a great bit of luck, the hull of the ship hadn't been compromised from the hit it took from the Megathirio. They lost the figurehead during it all, something Phoebus will definitely comment on when they arrive.

Jo has continued working with Nol on his monster research, while Beck has found his own among the gunners. He's also taken to waking at the same time she does so that he can be on deck while Poseidon and her train in the morning. She can hear him cheer from the harpoon launchers as he does maintenance, when she gets something right. Furthermore, when the training is over, she finds he's brought up breakfast and the two of them share the meal at the bow over looking the ancient waters. They talk about everything and nothing at the same time. His friendship feels more like her anchor at sea, helping her keep her head when her overwhelming emotions try to take over. Beck has truly become one of her crew.

The only person who seems to be falling out of place

is...

"Shea!"

Shea shakes herself out of her thoughts as a blast of water slams into her chest and knocks her off her feet. She slams into the wooden floor of the quarterdeck, gasping, trying to catch her breath as the wind is knocked out of her. Her eyes flutter, and Poseidon comes into blurry focus, standing above her.

He reaches his hand out, which she takes gingerly.

Dawn has just begun to rise over the horizon. The deck is pretty much empty.

Aster is at the helm while James is supervising the end of the night shift, keeping the ship in top shape.

Beck even volunteered for an early morning shift in the crow's nest, and Shea can just barely see him up on the platform.

She groans as the wind catches the water soaking her clothes, causing her to shiver.

"Didn't I tell you to pay attention?"

"I'm sorry. I just have a lot on my mind," Shea tries, but Poseidon's not hearing it.

"We've been at this for four days and there's barely been any improvement. What you tapped into was a fight-or-flight instinct against the Megathirio. You cannot expect that to happen every time. You need to train, hone your skills. You were lucky," Poseidon growls, walking away from her.

Shea scoffs. She summons the water from the flask on her belt and blasts it at the back of her father's head.

He shouts in surprise.

"Lucky? I lost some of my best men that day! We've been training for four days and I still don't understand what I did or how I killed that thing."

Poseidon sighs, wiping the water out of his eyes. "You need to remember what I said—"

Shea chuckles, cutting him off. "I remember what you said! Choose an anchor, focus on that anchor, and use your magic to make it stronger, except I don't remember how I did it!"

Poseidon is quiet, the first time he has been in the four days they've been training.

The first morning he taught her new forms and hand positions for summoning and offense, and surprisingly most of them worked. But whatever boosted his power when they sailed through the boundary has really made him stronger. Every time Shea faces him in combat, she loses.

He always ends their lessons with a duel and when she loses, he pushes her overboard.

The first time he did it, Caen practically killed him, but Shea managed to use her powers to manipulate the water, so it put her back on the deck.

So far, it's been Shea overboard four and Poseidon overboard zero—today will make five.

"What did you think of? What was your anchor?" Poseidon demands, pacing in front of her.

"Jo. I guess. I mean, I saw Jo and Aster up on the ladder and I just lost it. I knew I needed to protect them, and then I saw Beck struggling at the bow and something in me snapped," Shea admits, trying to piece it together.

"Is that who you've been thinking of now? Beck, Jo, Aster?"

He takes a step closer to his daughter, examining her features.

"I suppose? I don't know. It's hard to concentrate. We're almost to Orena and when we get there, we have to gather all the supplies as quickly as we can. Get the repairs done, sail to Tenaro so we can find Triton so he can defeat Perses."

"That's the problem."

"What is?"

"You have to push all of that aside, and focus on what's important, what makes you strong."

"You want me to push all of my responsibilities aside

and focus on magic. I think that's going to be a problem," Shea drawls, rolling her eyes.

"You need to calm your mind, center yourself. The moment on the deck when everything was happening, the world around you was practically exploding, you focused because of what?"

"I don't know, that's what I'm trying to tell you," Shea stresses.

The wind passes through her water-soaked clothes again and she closes her eyes, reaching out with her magic to pull the water from the fabric. Surprisingly when she opens them again, she finds a ball of water in her hand and her clothes magically dry.

"You focused because you wanted to protect them," Poseidon tells her, smiling at her little trick.

Shea looks up at him with a raised brow and forces the excess water into her uncorked waterskin.

"You're a leader, Shea. A protector. Instead of focusing on somebody else, focus on that, focus on that quality in yourself. The need to protect. Think you're ready for our daily duel?"

Poseidon takes a step back into a fighting stance, summoning water from both sides of the ship, and the seawater encases his arms, extending them into tentacles.

Shea vocally gulps and pulls the water from her flask, stepping into the correct form.

"I'll give you to the count of three," Poseidon proposes.

Shea closes her eyes, searching for whatever power she supposedly holds inside. She thinks about Jo, Aster, Caen, and even Beck, though her mind starts to wander slightly at how much she's come to care for him. Inwardly, she yells at herself to focus.

"One."

Shea starts to panic; it's like she can see herself standing in a room in her mind. She's been here before, multiple times, but something new causes her to keep imagining the daydream instead of dissolving it into strategy.

A door is in the center of the darkness with power radiating off it.

She takes a step toward the door, and instinctively knows that behind it is everything she needs.

She reaches for the handle and screams fill her head. Aster's cries from the night Mariner cut his ears, Mariner's taunts during the duel, Paetre's gasping breaths as he died, Jo's sobs as she held Shea's dying body. All of it fills her head, and she can feel the water encasing her physical hands begin to falter.

"Two."

There's not enough time. She's going to lose, Perses is going to take it all. She's not strong enough. She's not.

The door rumbles and Shea takes a step back. From behind it, a voice is calling out to her, louder than all the screams and pain filling the darkness.

Light bursts from the door's cracks, and softer voices are slowly drowning out the cries.

Jo telling her how much she loves her, Aster telling her he's proud to be her son, Beck calling her brave, Caen reminding her he'll always be there for her, and then?

She hears Paetre, and a conversation from long ago.

A small child's voice filters from the door. *"Why did you choose me? I'm just a girl, an elf. I'm not anything."*

Paetre's voice rings through clear as the day he replied, *"You're something to me. You saved me, Shea, I was lost until I found you. And you were lost until you found me. Together, I know you're going to grow and do great things. You're a leader, Shea. Like me, but you have to believe. Even if you don't, fake it. Make them believe you're better, and someday, you just might be."*

Shea strides toward the door confidently; she places her hand on the knob.

"Three."

Shea opens the door.

It's like a blazing hot knife pierces her chest as the power from the door rips into her.

She chokes, her lungs burning in pain—she can feel it, everything. The magic filling her feet, legs, arms, torso. There's pressure behind her eyes. A strange sensation on the back of her neck.

She knows that right now there's a water blast racing toward her. She lifts her left hand and then opens her eyes.

Poseidon is stronger, for now, but with enough concentration, she freezes the blast in midair.

Her eyes meet Poseidon's gaze, and he's smiling at her with great triumph.

Using his distraction, she summons water from over the starboard side and then jumps out of the way, releasing the sly blast before Poseidon can recognize what she's done.

She forces a substantial column of water in his direction, throwing him over the port side of the ship.

Shea falls to her knees, shocked, landing in a puddle of water.

The buzzing feeling of power under her skin doesn't dissipate.

The morning crew is clapping at her accomplishment.

She can hear Beck whistling from above, and Aster crows from the afterdeck rail.

Poseidon reappears on deck, but what catches her attention is the reflection looking back at her in the puddle.

Her eyes are glowing, and the left is no longer pale. Her normal tunnel vision has expanded, and she realizes as she reaches a hand up and closes it over her right eye that she can see from her left.

The scar from her eyebrow to her upper cheek is still there, but she watches from the puddle as her magic heals her left eye until there are two glowing green irises staring back at her.

She doesn't even realize she's started to cry until Poseidon takes her in his arms.

"How?" Shea whispers.

"You weren't ready to heal," Poseidon replies.

And Shea allows him, just this once, to hold her. She doesn't even care that the deck crew is still watching.

A few moments pass and she manages to compose herself. Shea pulls away from Poseidon, standing shakily. Clearing her throat, Shea pushes a loose strand of her hair away from her face and glances over in time to see Poseidon make the same gesture. She laughs at the similarity.

"This doesn't mean you're done training," Poseidon reminds her, and Shea nods. "You've unlocked your magic, but you still have limits."

Shea's brow furrows. "You mean it could hurt me?"

"Every demigod has the ability to become a god; it's rare but it can happen if they survive the process. I saw a glimpse of your godly form when we faced the Megathirio. The change is permanent but dangerous. It's nearly impossible to survive. Now that you have access, you can do more, be more, but you're more at risk to experience the change," Poseidon explains solemnly.

"Are you saying I could become immortal?" Shea clarifies.

"Yes," Poseidon answers.

"Could Perses? Does he know about this?"

"Yes, I believe he does."

"If that happens. I don't know how we'd stop him," Shea murmurs.

Poseidon smiles. "It won't happen because we're going to stop him before he can accumulate enough power. Besides, even if it did, I doubt Perses would survive the change. The change is a gift, children who survive are usually those who earn it or, well, acquire it in other ways."

"What other ways?"

Poseidon opens his mouth to respond but is cut off when Beck interrupts them by hugging Shea. He picks her off the floor and spins her around.

Shea laughs, smacking him on the shoulder to put her down.

"Look at you." He laughs, examining her healed eye. "We've got to show Jo. She'll be thrilled."

Shea grins at him but she doesn't leave just yet. She waits for Poseidon to answer her question.

"You run along; the lesson is complete for today. You should tell your fiancée the good news," Poseidon remarks, gesturing to his own left eye before walking away to the bow.

"This is fantastic," Beck exclaims.

He pulls on her hand to walk with him to the medical bay.

Shea nods distractedly, staring back at her father, wondering what he meant by other ways to acquire immortality. But Beck's pulling becomes insistent and she thinks about Poseidon's advice. Perhaps she could push her responsibilities away for one day and focus on the wonders of magic.

CHAPTER 19: KINDRED

Shea

Jo's expression when she saw Shea's healed eye had been one of shock, for lack of a better word. She was standing in the medical bay with Nol looking over a shriveled monster hand from one of their previous encounters while the good doctor was extracting some kind of liquid from the creature's claws.

She'd kissed Shea so sweetly that the captain didn't notice that Beck had delivered her there and then left without a word.

The disappearance wasn't a surprise, but the longing she felt from his absence was something that caught her off guard.

Nol excused Jo for the day to enjoy this little miracle, and they spent the time together, talking and just being with one another.

Her magic was still thrumming through her body even after dinner passed, and as Shea got ready for bed with Jo, she found she couldn't sleep.

She assured Jo that she was fine, got dressed again, and decided to join whoever was on deck for the night, giving Caen the evening to relax. To her surprise she'd seen Poseidon and him talking at dinner; she tried to ask him about the moment of civility, but he dodged her question and headed off to rest.

Now, on her first round of the perimeter, she runs into an unexpected crew member.

"I don't remember assigning you to a night shift, Governor," Shea teases, sneaking up behind Beck.

Night has completely fallen, and the deck lamps are lit, shining brightly against the black. Everyone but James and the naval officer in the crow's nest are down below, either in bed or at the mess hall.

Beck is in the harpoon launcher fiddling with some part of the mechanics, an untouched bowl of stew on the ground, and colorful swear words spewing from his mouth. Parts and tools lie haphazardly around the machine, and Beck is still cursing by the time she sneaks up on him.

The starlight is bright over the water, the closer they get to Orena and Tenaro the bigger the sky feels, like they're sailing off the edge of the world straight into the night sky.

Beck practically dives off the machine in shock as Shea comes up behind him. He manages to hang on for the most part, but eventually he loses his grip and lands back-first on the ground.

"Bloody Underdeep, Hades's balls, what the Thanatos are you doing out here?" Beck groans, trying to sit up but failing miserably.

Shea laughs and helps him back to his feet.

"I could ask you the same question, are you breaking my equipment?" Shea nods to the stripped harpoon launcher.

"No! I mean no, I noticed that the firing gear was a bit sticky, thought I'd fix the launch time and make it a bit more efficient," Beck explains.

He's got black grime all over his face. The sleeves of his white dress shirt are rolled up to his biceps, he seems to have also lost his shoes, and his black capris are the only material below his waist. She spots his boots by the rail wall.

He notices her staring and looks down at his appearance. A soft blush fans across his cheeks.

"Oh, I—it's—just easier to work this way," Beck tells her.

Shea chuckles and holds up her hands in surrender. "No judgment here, I completely understand, you should see what I wear when I'm mapping," she jokes.

"Is that an offer?" Beck teases back, and Shea grins.

"Careful, Governor, you'll give a girl all sorts of crazy ideas."

The two dissolve into laughter, and as the laughter fades the other emotions are left, the unspoken want rigid in the air between them.

Beck clears his throat and begins collecting the tools from around the launcher.

"Great sparring matches the other night," Shea tells him, trying to keep the conversation going.

She doesn't want it to end and she inwardly hates herself for it.

"Yeah?" Beck says, glancing over to her.

"Yeah, you're a great fighter."

"Well, I learned a lot from my dad," he says.

He takes a rag off the launcher and starts cleaning his hands. He leans back against the railing, facing Shea.

Shea's eyes roam over his shoulders and she's taken back to the other night.

The crew had been antsy after a day out at sea. They'd had an encounter with some kelpies trying to rock the ship by barreling mercilessly into the hull.

Caen had been ready to give the order to fire upon them, but Poseidon had stopped them.

He'd walked out to the rail's edge and whistled down to the creatures below, still ramming their bodies into the ship. It was a mesmerizing tune, and to Shea's surprise from the afterdeck's rail, she watched as her crew became visibly drunk off the melody.

Various deck men swerved and tripped as the creatures calmed, and the song came to an end.

Even Caen had found himself tangled in the rope from the mast rigging. The kelpies had dove off into the briny blue after that, and Poseidon had continued on his way to the bow whistling a tune without an enchantment, but it still earned him nervous looks from the rest of the men and women.

Caen had suggested sparring matches to cool down everyone's nerves and bring the crew of the Duchess closer to the Arethusian Navy men and women.

Shea agreed with the tactic, so later that night, under the full moon on the quarterdeck, they lit the torches and spouted the rules. Swords were fine, but only swords: no killing and no cheap shots. The winner starts next round with a volunteered opponent.

The soldiers had looked at her waiting for more rules of engagement, but they soon realized there weren't anymore.

Shea watched a few matches; she'd given James the deck for the evening commanding the night crew till morning.

Jo even came up for a while and watched a couple of duels with her before retiring down below. Shea was about to turn in for the night as well.

Caen had entered the matches and had been the winner for four rounds; however, the pirates knew the brawls were over even if a few of the soldiers didn't.

But a loud voice volunteered to fight Caen for his fifth round, and it had Shea turning her attention back to the ring immediately.

Beck stepped into the ring, ignoring the objections of the two Oceanan soldiers he'd come on board with. Shea decided she wanted to see this, and her crew parted for her so she could watch from the inner ring of surrounding men and women.

Caen had laughed, but something in Beck's smirk had Shea intrigued. Caen waited a moment for him to make the first move. She could tell her quartermaster was impressed when he didn't, so

Caen took the first swing.

Beck quickly slid aside as the blade swung down. He ducked and parried each parting blow from Caen.

Shea grinned as she realized his strategy.

Beck was using Caen's height against him. Finally, as Caen swung down one last time, Beck somersaulted past and brought his sword up to rest against the back of Caen's neck, now behind him. He was achieving all of this with barely an offensive move.

Caen could have easily disarmed him in this position, and with the crew cheering and hollering, Shea wondered if he would do it to save his pride. But she could see the amusement on Caen's face, and he dropped his sword in a surrender allowing the younger man to win.

Beck dropped his sword as well, and the two clasped hands in a truce. Caen had taken Beck's hand and lifted it in the air.

"Anyone willing to take on the champ who beat me?" Caen teased and glanced around the circle of men and women. Most of the soldiers and pirates jeered and shouted, even held their hands up in surrender and shook their heads.

But Shea watched Beck's full grin and his confident style as he taunted the others while Caen laughed.

"I'll take a shot at it."

The circle went silent, and all eyes landed on Shea. But the eyes she waited for are a deep crushed cocoa brown, and they found her as soon as she spoke.

Beck's smile turned into a teasing grin, and Caen lowered the younger man's hand.

"We have a challenger," Caen announced.

The crew paused for either Beck to say something or Shea to move, but the captain waited for him to accept her challenge.

"It'd be an honor," Beck bowed mockingly.

The crew went wild, heckling each other, and so Shea took off her coat. She grabbed Caen's sword and stepped into the ring. They circled each other, their eyes hungrily absorbing each other's styles and moves.

Shea didn't need the first move. She attacked, but when

he tried to step away to dodge her blow as he did with Caen, her foot is waiting for him, and he tripped over her leg, falling to the ground.

The crew laughed, and they probably thought it was over, but Shea was just getting started.

She stepped away, laughing as Beck quickly righted himself and stood to position his feet.

"Nice," he stated, rolling his shoulders.

She returned his mocking bow from before with a teasing smirk. They stalked each other. Shea stepped forward with a swing, and he parried each blow with quick precision. She allowed him to counter, and they continued the flirtatious turn of the ring until they were back where they started.

Beck was getting antsy. He stepped forward too quickly and found themselves locked in a battle of strength, their faces pressed close, and their blades interlocked, leaving the two of them mere inches apart. Beck smiled as he pushed his sword against her strength, and his eyes roamed her features sending a shiver down her spine.

In an instant, her strategy was replaced with conversations that were had under the first warm light of each morning since the start of the voyage, and it overwhelmed her thoughts. She was too close, much too close to him, and she could barely think. She quickly disengaged and sideswiped his feet under him.

Beck fell back, and Shea moved to dance out of the way but arms wrapped around her waist as his discarded blade clattered onto the ground, and she fell with him.

Shea landed on top of Beck, and dropped her blade, to avoid impaling him or landing on it herself.

Beck huffed as her weight crashed into him. Her hair blocked their faces from the rest of the crew as it dropped down around his head like a halo.

She stared into his eyes, and she thought she could feel his hand moving up to brush her face, but a cough from behind her captured her attention. Shea sat up quickly, straddling Beck, and reached out for her sword that luckily fell nearby. She placed it at *his neck.*

The crew was silent as the two of them breathed heavily against each other.

"Mercy," Beck whispered with a smirk.

But it was Shea who felt like the loser of this round. She was still straddling him when Caen cleared his throat and said, "He surrenders, Captain."

She looked back, meeting Caen's gaze and chuckled awkwardly. She got off of Beck and extended her hand down to him to help him up.

He stared briefly at her hand before taking it, and when he finally grasped her forearm, she felt the shiver return and the need to pull him closer.

Except she didn't. Because she can't.

As soon as they were up, she dropped his hand and clapped him on the back.

The crew relaxed at the display of comradery, and Caen claimed her as Champion for the evening.

But even though she didn't look back at him, she knew Beck's eyes were on her as she walked away, retiring for the night. And he would be there waiting in the morning when she returned to the deck.

She flexed the hand that held his and suppressed the idea that it was tingling from his touch.

Shea breaks the memory from the night before, hoping she hasn't been lost in thought for too long and otherwise staring at Beck.

"Me too," she hums, running a hand through her hair.

She wraps her arms around herself and the two of them are quiet until Beck speaks again.

"What was he like?"

"Who?" Shea inquires.

"Paetre, your father. You know almost everything about mine; what was Paetre like?"

Shea raises a brow, but a small smile quirks her lips and she stumbles over to the rail, leaning beside Beck, their shoulders almost touching.

"He was incredible. Best pirate I've ever seen. Great fighter too, impossibly fast and skilled. He could take a man three times his size because their brawn was never a match for his wit. He was thirty-eight when he died. He seemed so old to me, but when he joined the *Duchess*'s crew, he was eighteen, worked his way to quartermaster at twenty-four, and became captain at twenty-five. I was eight when he found me, and he died when I was twenty-one. I really only had thirteen years with him, and I'd give anything for more time. He was the best father a girl could have, despite his mistakes and rough edges."

"I can understand wanting more time, I was sixteen when Lycons killed my mom. Now my dad, well he wasn't thirty-eight, and he would hate me admitting that, but it wasn't his time. There was so much more for him to do."

"I felt the same when Paetre died, even when the mutiny happened, I didn't even think it was a possibility. How could something so stupid take him away?"

"We hadn't had any attacks for a couple months you know, and my mom was this strong leader. She wanted to make sure the outlying villages on the front lines against Lycos were getting enough food. They caught her in a southern fishing village and tortured her to get to my father. When she died, Ceto sent us a message: the bravest among you has died, all that's left are the cowards. I wanted to kill her with every part of my being," Beck confides, his hands tightening on the rail behind them.

"I know the feeling," Shea humorlessly chuckles.

"That's right. You stole the Pearl of Lycos." Beck bumps his shoulder into her with admiration.

"Paetre's final score, it was the one job he'd chased for years. I never knew why, he didn't say, but I finished it for him. Took her down a peg. You know, with my eye healed, I thought maybe…"

Shea trails off, feeling a sense of worry wash over her,

and she places a hand over her brand.

"You thought what?"

"Nothing, it's stupid."

"Tell me, you can trust me," Beck consoles, turning so they face each other.

Shea looks up into his dark brown eyes and feels her nerves fade to calm. She feels safe, like she did with Paetre, like she does with Jo.

She sighs, breaking the eye contact, and brings her hands up to the strings of her blouse. She undoes the fastening and pulls the shirt down, so the top of her bandage shows.

Beck doesn't say a word, waiting for her to explain.

She pulls the bandage down just enough and hears him gasp when he sees it.

The brand is still there, all of her other scars and wounds have faded, but whoever charmed the scar was good. Even her wild magic hadn't been able to break the seal, leaving the ugly crescent moon with Scylla's tearful face and the snakes from her hair slithering around the half circle.

"How is it still there? What is it?"

"Ceto's personal seal. I offended her when I was young, embarrassed her. She caught me when I was around Aster's age and paid me back for my insult. Chained me to a table and let her court torturer carve her personal symbol over my heart so I'd always know who I belong to."

Shea lets the material fall back into place. She turns away, looking out over the dark ocean, the stars reflected in the watery surface.

"Someone really needs to kill that woman," Beck growls.

"If only." Shea sighs. "Anyway, the carver enchanted the brand. I've tried using my magic to get rid of it but no such luck."

"You could always ask Poseidon for help," Beck suggests, but Shea shakes her head.

"No, I'd prefer to keep this to myself. I'll find a way, someday."

"I get it."

"Really? Jo would call me crazy for not asking for help." Shea laughs.

"It's your pearl. You should get rid of it on your own terms," Beck explains and turns to look out at the ocean beside her, this time their bodies touching.

Shea stares at him fondly.

He understands her.

It's not until he catches her in the act that she realizes she's staring and quickly turns her attention back to the Old Sea.

They stand leaning against the rail together for a few minutes, when she sees a splash in the water.

Her eyes focus on the area and she catches a flash of luminescent color skim the ocean's surface before diving back down deeper. A soft, warm breeze fills the air, accompanied by more flashes of color.

She grins. They're over the Aiolos reef, her least and favorite part of the journey to Orena. They never know what they're going to get, such as the Aurai—wind spirits that they confronted when they passed over it last year—or something a little more friendly and even more beautiful.

It's the right time of year for them, she thinks, and a melodic chittering sound echoes across the water, like small bells chiming, confirming her suspicion.

"Beck?"

"Yeah?"

"You want to see something amazing?"

There's a pause and she keeps glancing down below, hoping they're still there and they won't miss them.

When she finally looks back up, Beck seems to have solved his internal dilemma and nods.

"Why not?"

Shea smiles widely, grabs his hand, and pulls him toward the ship's two pinnaces, the lifeboats.

"Get in," she tells him and gets to rigging the pinnace so they can lower and then pull themselves back up once they're done.

"Where are we going?"

"You'll see. Trust me?"

"With my life," he responds and jumps into the pinnace.

Shea grins and climbs in with the two ropes; she hands one to Beck and keeps the other.

"Pulley will do most of the work for us; go slow and I'll tell you when to stop."

Beck salutes her, and together they lower the pinnace to the ocean's surface. It's slow going, but they avoid any problems that way, and just when they're right above the ocean, so close that they could reach down and touch it, Shea orders him to tie off his rope and she does the same.

She gestures for him to come closer to the edge and she moves to the center of the small boat, pointing over, careful not to lean too far.

"What is it?" Beck whispers, but Shea holds a finger to her mouth to quiet him.

He listens to her.

She puckers her lips and starts to whistle the same tune Paetre used when he'd lower them down to the surface just like this, so she could see what really lived in the Old Sea.

"I don't see anything," Beck murmurs and then gasps.

Luminescent light appears all around them, blues, reds, greens, and yellows shining from underneath the dark ocean. It's bright and beautiful.

Shea keeps whistling the tune, and she moves Beck into the right position so he can see them.

The first, a female, chitters excitedly upon hearing Shea's tune. Her long tail shimmers just below the water with a vibrant red, her back fin the same; the lights from the other mermaids are so intense, it is easy to see her gorgeous features. She swims quickly by the pinnace and then jumps out of the water, giving Beck his first sight of a real mermaid. Her skin is a soft gray and her eyes glow a bright blue; she's more fish than woman, but her features are still distinctly humanoid despite her scales and the gills on the side of her neck.

Another pops through the water's surface and chitters at Shea before spraying her with water. Shea giggles at the playful nature.

Paetre had once equated them to dolphins in their intelligence and personality.

The one that sprays them is a bright yellow, her hair as vibrant as a sunflower's petals, and the luminescent vein running up her large tail is like sparkling gold. She also seems to have fins on her forearms as well as her back. The mermaid chitters for Shea to keep whistling the tune.

There's at least four now, swimming around them, one a bright green and the other a cerulean blue.

Beck is sitting beside her in stunned silence doing nothing more than gaping at the fantastical creatures in front of him.

"They're amazing," he finally whispers when his mouth has caught up with his brain.

"It was about this time of year that Paetre would take me to Orena to stay with friends, and if we got lucky, we'd see the merfolk as we passed over the Aiolos reef into the Old Sea."

"Are they dangerous," he asks.

She can see he's tempted to put his hand down to the water, but she places a hand on his arm to stop him.

"Not really, but I wouldn't give them the chance to pull you over."

Beck nods, grinning. "I've never seen anything like them. Thank you."

He turns, and she hadn't meant to put her face so close to his because when he faces her, they find themselves mere inches apart.

"Any time," she breathes, staring into his handsome eyes.

He swallows. Those warm brown irises study her, and he pushes a stray strand of hair back away from her face.

Shea inadvertently leans into the touch.

The mermaids are still chittering around them and Shea notices that the green merfolk is actually a merman, but suddenly that doesn't seem to matter anymore.

"They're beautiful," he repeats.

Shea can feel her entire body shaking with want, she licks her bottom lip and finds herself staring at his.

"They are," she whispers.

"But you know"—and if possible, he leans in even more, to the point there's barely a breath of space between them—"I've seen the most beautiful woman in Nereid, and I don't think they quite compare."

"Oh..."

"And you are without a doubt the most beautiful woman, Shea."

She closes the space between them. She feels as if she's been struck by lightning—it's a very similar feeling to when she kissed Jo for the first time.

She hears the merfolk chittering louder around them, and she deepens the kiss, listening to Beck moan, and she sighs as his arms wrap around her waist.

She wants to pin him down, to show him the extent of what she feels; she starts pushing him back and he goes willingly. She can vaguely hear the sound of rushing water, roaring in her ears, but nothing else matters. All that matters is that Beck and her are together.

"Shea?"

A shout breaks through her haze and Shea gasps as she hears Jo's voice call from the quarterdeck. She pulls back from Beck and looks around, her jaw dropping as she notices the water show around them, just like she created during her and Jo's first kiss. It's dancing along the surface, and the mermaids have been jumping through the hoops of water.

The water crashes back down, scaring the mermaids off and extinguishing their light.

"Shea?" Jo calls out again, more panicked.

Shea quickly runs a hand through her hair and Beck straightens as well, clearing his throat.

"Down here!" Shea answers, and Beck glares at her with alarmed eyes.

She sees her fiancée's head poke over the rail, and she smiles when she spots the two of them.

"What are you two doing down there?"

"We saw something in the water," Shea calls back. "We're coming up now."

"Okay, I just wanted to check on you. I'll meet you in the cabin, yeah?"

Shea nods and Jo leaves them alone.

Shea runs a hand over her face. "Oh gods."

"It's okay," Beck tries to comfort her, but Shea waves him off.

"No! No, it's not okay, because I love her. I'm marrying her, and I promised her nothing would happen and then I kiss you? Gods, I'm so stupid."

Shea hurries to her rope and begins to untie it, switching the lever on the pully, so it'll help her pull the pinnace back up.

"Shea, please." Beck reaches for her, but Shea shies away.

"Beck, stop. I can't do this."

"But you felt it, you feel this too," Beck states.

"I know, but there's no choice here, and if there was, I'm sorry but I choose her. She's who I want with every part of my being."

"Not every part," Beck snaps.

Shea glares at him. "You're right. You are...intoxicating. When I'm around you, I can't breathe without seeing you. But the same goes for Jo. Every emotion I feel for you, I feel for her. I love her and I want to be with her. And as much as I care for you, I won't lose her."

Beck looks as if Shea has just slapped him; he turns his back to her and goes for the other side of the pully, readying the rope.

"Beck."

"Let's just get back to the deck."

"I do care for you."

"Not enough it seems."

"Beck, please."

He sighs and turns around to look at her, his face riddled with pain.

"I can't explain it. And I don't want to hurt you."

"Too late."

"Beck. Do you believe that you can love two people at once? Not just liking two people and then choosing who you love more but to actually be in love with two people at the same time. To want to be with them both and see them happy, and taken care of, and to be there for them no matter what."

Beck is quiet and his eyebrows scrunch together like he wants to yell, but suddenly he sighs. His face relaxes with a melancholy touch.

"I don't know, but I do know that there's at least one person out there that I think I might be in love with. And I want to be with *her*. We should get you to your cabin."

Shea opens her mouth to say something else but thinks better of it and quickly shuts it.

They pull the pinnace back to the top, and as they haul themselves over the rail's edge, Shea comes face-to-face with Jo. There are tears in her eyes, but she hasn't shed them yet. She looks like she's in a lot of pain.

"Jo," Shea starts.

"Cabin. Now."

Shea nods. She doesn't look back at Beck, she can't. But as the woman she loves follows her to confront her betrayal and she leaves behind the man she loves alone at the pinnace, her heart breaks in two trying to mentally console each one.

CHAPTER 20: THE BOND THAT BINDS

Jo

They pass down the halls silently, not saying a word to each other. They barely speak to any of the passing crew and Jo keeps her eyes ahead. She can feel Shea following close behind her.

Her heart aches and she wants to cry, but the rage boiling from inside her is threatening to overflow before they reach the cabin.

Jo picks up the pace a bit and she can hear Shea jogging to keep up. Finally, they round the corner to the captain's quarters and Jo opens the door, gesturing for Shea to step through first.

She tries to catch Jo's eyes, but Jo stares stubbornly at the floor, trying to collect her thoughts so she doesn't do something she regrets.

Once Shea is inside, Jo walks in and closes the door behind her, locking it.

She's facing the door, one hand flat on the wood and her breath is coming faster than before. She bites her lip, trying to stop the burning sensation in her nose as her eyes water. She will not cry.

"Jo?" Shea murmurs.

Jo straightens, squaring her shoulders, and she puts the coldest mask she can muster over her features before turning to face Shea.

Jo's eyes roam over the elf, taking in her pained expression, the red curls framing her face, and as her vision slips lower, her eyes widen, noting that the top of her blouse is undone.

Jo's temper flares—she scoffs and rubs a hand over her mouth.

Shea looks down to see what has Jo reacting this way and also notices her unfastened blouse.

"It's not what it looks like," Shea states, tying her blouse back up.

"Really?" Jo chuckles darkly. "That's the best you can do?"

"What did you hear when we were in the pinnace?" Shea asks, warily.

"The two of you kissed," Jo seethes, stalking closer to Shea with a murderous expression.

It must catch Shea off guard because she stumbles back a step involuntarily.

Jo stops where she is and crosses her arms over her chest.

"How could you?"

"Jo, it was an accident. I—we were up on the deck talking about our parents and I saw the mermaids down below. I took him down to see them. I used to do that with Paetre. I was caught up in the moment, and when I looked at him, it just felt right. I wasn't thinking."

"So, what, you love him?" Jo snarls, trying to understand.

Her blood is rushing in her ears. Everything inside her is screaming to go back and kill Beck.

"I don't know…" Shea begins.

"Oh gods," Jo whispers, turning away.

Shea steps forward, reaching her hand out to place it

on Jo's shoulder, but Jo tries to shrug her off. Shea turns her so that they're facing each other and makes her look at Shea, holding Jo's face with her palms.

"Jo, please, I don't know how I feel about him. That's true. But I love you, and I would never do anything to risk what we have. You are everything to me, and this connection I have to him, I can't explain it and I'm so sorry. It just happened, but I need you to understand that if there was a choice, I choose you, I will always choose you."

Shea is crying and her hands are shaking. Jo takes a deep breath, trying to control her own emotions. Her hands reach up for Shea's and she carefully removes them from her face. She keeps them in hers, staring down at their joined hands.

"Aren't I enough?" Jo mutters.

"Oh. Jo, it's not about that, I swear. You are everything to me, love. Beck, I can't explain it. What I feel for him reminds me of what I feel for you. It's instinctive, when I'm around him I feel connected and safe. Just like when I'm with you. I never want to hurt you; I never would do anything to jeopardize what we have. So, I can stay away from him for the rest of the trip or send him home…when we reach Orena."

Even as Shea offers that last option, Jo can see the worry in her eyes at the thought of Beck sailing off alone. She's concerned for him.

Jo releases Shea's hands; she needs to take a step back.

She paces back and forth. She can feel that everything Shea is saying is the truth and there's one important fact that affects everything.

Jo loves Shea.

Shea is who she's meant to be with, and she will do whatever it takes to keep her.

"You are like no one I have ever met, you know," Jo tells her, pausing her pacing to look at the elf.

Shea is standing in front of her openly crying.

"From the first moment I saw you, it was like fate

snapped into place and all I could see was you. I knew that we could be something, something powerful, and when I woke up on this ship, I thought, well I guess we're meant to be enemies. And then I got to know you, and I fell harder than I did when I danced with you at my coronation ball. I sacrificed my family for you, I challenged my country to be with you, and I will not lose you now."

Jo walks back to Shea, whose breaths have been reduced to quiet hiccups.

"I'm sorry, I'm not usually like this," Shea mutters, wiping the tears from her cheeks.

"Well, we're not usually in situations like this," Jo laughs humorlessly.

"What do you wanna do?" Shea asks.

"I'm going to ask you some questions, and I want you to answer honestly, and depending on your answers, then I'll know," Jo tells her, nodding her head as she decides what to do.

"Okay," Shea agrees.

"Are you mine?"

Shea's eyes widen at the same question Jo asked her the first night they slept together.

"What?"

"Are you still mine?" Jo asks again, forcing Shea to look her in the eye.

"Yes," Shea answers, her eyes wide and pleading. "I'm yours."

Jo smiles, and takes a breath. "Do you still want to marry me?"

"Yes. Jo, I swear."

Jo nods.

"Do you love him?"

Shea breathes in through her teeth, her eyes scrunching closed.

Jo pulls her close until she's in her arms and waits for Shea to open her eyes again.

When she finally does, new tears fall.

"Yes, I think I do," Shea whispers.

And while the confession does hurt, it doesn't change Jo's decision.

"Okay."

"Okay?" Shea repeats.

"Okay," Jo answers. "I'm not saying that I completely understand, but I trust that you love me and want this. I was also warned about you and him."

"What? By who?" Shea demands, her eyebrows furrowing.

"Venus."

"How could she have known?"

"Goddess of love, dear," Jo reminds her, and Shea shakes her head.

"Our life has gotten so complicated."

Jo completely agrees.

"I'm sorry," Shea states.

"Darling, I know who you are. I know what you're giving up being with me, and I know that you are it for me. I just want you to be happy. And I'm going to do my best to make damn sure you are for the rest of your life."

Jo leans down and kisses her chastely on the lips.

"But from now on, this is mine, do you understand? Your kiss belongs to me unless I tell you otherwise."

As Jo pulls away, Shea pushes up onto her tiptoes and steals another kiss.

"Done," Shea promises her.

Jo smiles fondly. "I don't know how I'm going to deal with this just yet. But he doesn't need to leave. As much as I hate to admit it, I think he's a good man and someone we need on this journey. And maybe there's a way to sort this all out."

"Do you really think so?" Shea murmurs.

"I don't know, but I'm willing to try. Because this"—she holds up their joined hands—"is what I want. I'm not going anywhere. There are stranger things than this."

Jo takes Shea and leads her to the bed. She pushes her down onto the covers and climbs on top of her.

"One last question," Jo says.

"Yes?"

"Why was your blouse untied?"

Shea blinks a moment, her mouth opening and then closing. She sighs.

"I showed him my brand," Shea confesses. "That's it, I promise."

Jo nods and starts unlacing Shea's top.

"Then here is my vow. No one else will have you. Not unless I allow it. And the same goes for me. We're partners, and if there ever comes a time when we allow another into our bed, it will be on both our terms. Promise me that. Regardless, I forgive you, but I've seen marriages made out of secrets and lies, and I won't let that be us."

Shea pushes herself up until she's holding Jo on her lap and she lightly rubs Jo's cheek with her fingers.

"I promise. I promise," Shea whispers, pulling Jo closer till their lips are just about touching.

"I love you, Shea, and together we can solve anything."

Jo closes the distance and kisses her fiancée with all of her passion. She feels Shea's hands wrap around her waist and she bites the elf's bottom lip gently, pulling it and causing her to moan.

She pushes Shea back, enjoying the feeling of her body under her. Jo isn't stupid, she knows who Shea is and what she is. She will not persecute her for her nature because it's part of what Jo loves most.

She pushes the last of her thoughts away as her hand wanders lower; they have the rest of the night and she can decide what to do about Beck when tomorrow comes.

CHAPTER 21: THE MORE YOU KNOW

Beck

Another night is falling, and Beck tries to keep his eyes on his drink instead of watching Shea sleeping on her bed. Tomorrow they'll arrive in Orena, finally.

Earlier today, he practically had to carry her off the deck again after her sixth training session with Poseidon. They hadn't spoken since the night on the pinnace; he'd kept quietly to his work. He thought things would change since Jo had caught them, but nothing did. They were still together, and worst of all, they seemed even happier than before.

Beck had been crushed when he walked into the mess hall this morning after seeing the merfolk and seen them kiss over morning porridge.

He couldn't stop thinking about their kiss, there were no words to describe its perfection, but he kept his distance from Jo and Shea. He didn't want to cause any more trouble or heartache for himself.

He returned to the deck after breakfast to restore the harpoon launcher, when he saw Shea fall during training. He quickly ran to her aid without thinking and found her utterly exhausted because of her excess use of magic.

He didn't have another choice; he scooped her up into

his arms, much to her and Poseidon's complaint, and carried her all the way to the medical bay, trying not to focus on how adorable she was when she was tired. He found Jo and Nol working in the room and explained what happened. He didn't feel any hostility from Jo, who simply got to work following Nol's orders on what to get for the captain.

Beck laid Shea on the examination table, chuckling to himself, remembering how she'd magically knocked him out their first day together.

She smiled up at him goofily, probably from the exhaustion, and he couldn't remember seeing a face so beautiful.

Before the pinnace, they'd gotten close over the past week. They talked over shared meals, dueled each other when the days ran long, discussed both their pasts. In that moment, he wanted nothing more than to sail right past Tenaro and keep sailing the world, just with her, until they'd seen it all.

But it was fleeting, and then he stepped away so her fiancée could get closer to see her.

Jo fussed and checked her over for injuries while Nol did the rest. He left quickly because he couldn't watch Shea's love-filled expressions as she stared at her fiancée and laughed at her antics.

The rest of the day went by fairly quickly.

He's been spending time with James, the new bos'n.

He's working with Beck to get the harpoon launchers firing faster, and after Beck's discovery on how to fix the firing mechanism he shared the upgrade with the other gunners.

About midday from his work at the bow he watched Caen at the steering desk, talking to Aster and training him as the new helmsman.

In between tightening gears, and sharpening the harpoons, he saw Poseidon join Aster and Caen on the helm's deck and watched as Caen glared half-heartedly, alternating between the ancient sea god and the young elf speaking to each other.

James had glanced up at them too and smiled when the blond waved at him from his position behind the wheel before getting back to work.

Beck listened to James talk about Aster. He listened to him prattle on like a lovesick pup and laughed as the pirate blushed, asking for advice on how to talk to Aster about becoming more intimate. He laughed to hide his own heart from breaking, knowing that Shea and he would never be intimate in that way.

Beck had just finished sharpening the last of the harpoons, the sun had begun to wane on the deck, when Shea burst through the double deck doors with Caen, who he hadn't realized had left his post, following behind her. She stormed toward the afterdeck stairs, and Beck couldn't stop the small smile he had when he saw her look over at him, as if checking on him, before quickly turning her head back.

James had given him the go ahead to wipe down the harpoon, and then head in for supper when the shouting began.

They had both turned to see Shea arguing with Poseidon down the steps from the helm as she followed him below deck.

After that, James gave the rest of the deck crew their last orders for the day and sent them on their way so he could race for the afterdeck, to Aster.

Finished with work, he'd gone back to his room and wasn't surprised to find Poseidon missing. He cleaned himself up and headed to dinner where most of the crew had gathered.

Strom served up food with two navy men to help and the galley was packed with everyone perched in groups, now mixed as more days passed and the crew became one.

Once he had his food, he planned to head back to his room, but the worst happened. Jo caught sight of him and called him over to where she was sitting. He had quickly scanned the room for James, hoping to sit with his younger friend only to find him sitting on the other side of Jo at her table.

He couldn't do this; Shea was nowhere to be found, thank the gods, but still, it was Jo. And after the kiss, he couldn't imagine what she was thinking by inviting him over. But he really didn't have much of a choice.

He warily sat down at the table, digging into his food and ignoring her. If this was some kind of truce, he wasn't interested. He didn't want to be her friend.

Except, she started asking questions about his home, about Oceanus, and eventually he found himself laughing and falling into a rhythm with the queen. He couldn't figure out what game she was playing but every comment and question felt genuine, felt like she really wanted to get to know him.

Their conversation was later interrupted by Shea coming down the steps. He thought Poseidon would be with her, but no one else followed.

Caen had entered before her and had sat down next to James at their table listening to Jo and Beck's intimate conversation.

Beck couldn't help but notice the dark circles under Shea's eyes and before he knew what he was doing, he was excusing himself from the table, grabbing her dinner bowl from her hand, which she protested, and sat her down next to Jo.

He sat back down across from the two of them and he met Jo's eyes as they watched, concerned, as the redheaded captain ate her dinner in silence.

Shea quickly picked up on their staring. She glared and growled at both of them to knock it off otherwise she'd hang them headfirst off the bow.

They didn't stop staring.

But Jo got the conversation going again, asking Shea

about some couple named Phoebus and Dari and how they'd all be seeing them when they docked on Orena to collect their extra supplies.

The topic seemed to cheer Shea up. Soon he could see her eyes becoming heavy lidded, and as she tried to stand, she nearly fell over. Beck stood immediately, but Jo caught her easily and much to his relief.

He suggested she head to bed and Jo agreed, both of them going over Shea's head, who again protested.

Beck wished them a good night, but Jo asked for his help carrying Shea back to their quarters. He wanted to say no, but one glare from Caen told him no wasn't an option.

They'd carried her back to the captain's quarters together. Then laid her in bed and no sooner had her head hit the pillow, she was out.

He turned to leave again without a word, but Jo stopped him. She gestured to a bottle on the desk and the two chairs, and that's how he found himself sipping on a glass of rum watching his beautiful pirate elf toss and turn in her sleep, with the queen of Arethusa, and his enemy, sitting right beside him.

Now, he takes another sip of the rum, enjoying the warming sensation in the pit of his stomach, and glances at Jo momentarily, only to choke on his drink as he sees her staring.

He coughs. "Yes?"

"You don't have to look so afraid."

"Is that so?"

"I'm not mad, not anymore at least. To an extent, I understand."

"Do you? How modern."

"Don't do that," Jo scoffs.

"Do what?" Beck asks.

"Go on the defense. I'm really trying here, so if you could just, I don't know, drop the attitude that'd be great. You kissed my fiancée remember?"

"I know. Fine."

Jo doesn't respond and Beck goes back to watching Shea in her sleep while sipping on rum. Another few moments pass, and he can feel her gaze burning into the side of his face.

"What?" he asks.

"I know that look," she whispers.

He cocks his head, not quite understanding; she gestures to Shea's sleeping form with a nod of her head and he looks down at his lap.

"Sorry," he whispers back, but he's not really.

"No, you're not," Jo calls him on it, chuckling, "but I get it. She's hard not to like. And she likes you."

Beck nods. "She said that, yes." Shea's other words from the night of the pinnace come flooding back and he frowns. "But she loves you."

"Yes, she does," Jo agrees.

"So, what, you brought me here to rub it in?" Beck scowls.

"No," Jo tells him truthfully, "I asked you here to see if I could solve this dilemma we have on our hands."

"Dilemma? I love her, she says she loves me, but she also loves you. I kissed her, and you forgave her. End of discussion, I understand she's with you. I'm dealing with it."

Beck goes to stand, but Jo stops him.

"Please. Sit down."

Beck sighs, but he sits back down, grabbing his glass, which he set on the desk.

"Well, regardless of this"—Beck gestures to the three of them—"I am sorry about one thing. About everything I said on the steps."

Jo looks up at him, surprised. She reaches for the bottle on the desk and pours some more of the amber liquid into her glass; she offers him some more as well and he takes it, sure he's going to need it.

"Me too," Jo responds.

"I didn't mean what I said about your father," Beck murmurs, facing Jo completely. This, at least, he can be honest about, and it gives him a reprieve from discussing Shea.

Jo chuckles softly. "You weren't wrong. Your father loved you, and mine, Mariner...he didn't."

"Still. He was your father."

"I suppose."

They lapse into silence, drinking from their glasses.

"So, you do love her then?" Jo asks.

Beck chokes again, his head swimming, but he nods.

"I hate you," Beck tells her. "Or I hated you because ever since the steps I've gotten to know you and found out what a horribly good person you are. And even with what happened in the pinnace, with her"—Beck looks to the bed fondly—"in the back of my mind, I think you're better for her."

Jo snorts but doesn't respond. She allows him to continue.

"I hate that you're perfect for her. And now, with everything she said on the pinnace...I have no intention of coming between you two, and I'm sorry if I almost did. It seems you forgave her, and you should, because if you don't, then I will do everything I can to be with her. But I think you know how special she is, I mean how could you not? But, Jo, I can't." He runs a hand down his face, tears prickling at his eyes. "I like her, I—may even love her."

He hadn't realized that he looked down during his confession, and when he meets Jo's gaze, he freezes.

Her eyes are glittering with unshed tears, but what really catches him off guard is that she is smiling at him brightly.

"You're right. I do know how special she is, and I was really angry about the kiss. But I was also warned about it. You guys have had this connection since you met, and I don't question her loyalty because she has been honest about it from the start, and ashamed. She's also made it very clear that she's not going anywhere."

Beck scoffs and runs his tongue along his bottom teeth. "Well good for you."

"Beck."

He reluctantly meets Jo's gaze and she's still smiling at him.

"I love her with all my heart. I'm not blind. And I'm not stupid. I know how she feels about you, but I also know how she feels about me. I fell in love with her in an impossible situation and then we were separated for a year. We both changed quite a bit. Sure, we wrote letters every week, we always talked, but I hadn't laid eyes on her since the day she left. She's like a Lionbird. She is freedom. And someone that's not meant to be caged. And I wouldn't want her like that."

"So, what are you saying?" Beck demands, confused.

"I'm saying...that I think I can live with it. The looks, the feelings between you two. Beck. I trust you. And before you say you kissed my fiancée, I've gotten to know you quite a bit over the past few days too, and if they've taught me anything, it's that you're a good man. I just want her to be happy and she makes me happy; she's all I need to be happy, and I know that I do the same for her. I know that she loves me unconditionally and that is...rare."

Beck nods, putting his glass down on the desk as the room spins.

"But. You make her happy too. And I have a feeling, if we win this war, you'll always be in our lives. Not just as an allying state but hopefully as a friend."

"I don't understand. She chose you."

"And I am confident enough in our love to be able to give her a third choice, to not choose. I'm going to marry her, and she will be my wife, but if you truly love her and want her as much as you say you do, then maybe we could find a way for all of us to fit."

"This is insane." Beck laughs. He's never heard of anything like this.

"When has Shea ever been normal, it's naive of us to

think her love would be."

"So, you want to share her?"

"No. You're quite right in the fact that she did choose me, and I will remain her main partner, but I'm willing to see if there's a place in our life for you too. As a team, as…family. But until we figure that out, I'd like us to try being friends."

All this is surreal. Beck is beginning to wonder if this whole conversation is a hallucination from the rum.

"So, what do you say, Governor? Could you stand being friends, even family, with the queen and queen consort for the rest of your life?"

Jo drunkenly reaches out her hand across the desk, scattering maps onto the ground. Beck examines her flushed cheeks, the pink staining her high cheekbones, her burning blue eyes, and the light wisps of blond hair. He starts to see the passion and righteousness that he hated as positive characteristics now instead of flaws.

He can't believe she's won him over.

Beck looks over at Shea and back at the hand that just might begin something powerful that could last the ages.

"Yes," he replies, grasping her hand just as clumsily. "For a chance to be in her life, and even yours, blondie, I'll take it."

He winks at Jo and she bursts out laughing; they've had so much rum they can barely remember they're supposed to be quiet.

"You're almost pretty enough to be a girl, you know," Jo muses. "Unfortunately your equipment downstairs eliminates you from being my own mistress."

"Too bad," Beck jokingly sighs, and Jo cocks a brow. "We could have just eliminated the middleman and the two of us could have run off together."

The comment makes Jo laugh again and Beck finds himself drunkenly laughing as well.

"Hey!"

The two of them stop laughing like idiots and turn toward the bed to find an angry-looking redheaded pirate glaring at both of them.

"If you two are done deciding my love life for me, do you think you could pick your drunk asses up and find your way to the galley?" Shea growls.

"If she wasn't so cute, she'd be menacing," Jo drawls to Beck with a snicker.

"She's just tired from all the magic use today. Blondie, I don't think it'd be right to leave her," Beck suggests, gesturing toward the bed.

Jo grins as she understands his meaning. "You're completely right, Beck, we should definitely stay and make sure everything's alright."

"Oh no," Shea protests. "What happened to you two hating each other? I can't believe you drank all my rum."

Beck and Jo grin at each other and get up from the desk.

Shea watches the two of them warily and shakes her head as they both begin stalking toward the bed.

"I don't think so," Shea snaps.

But Jo has managed, with some difficulty, to make it to the left side of the bed Shea's on and scooches in, holding the pirate close as she begins to squirm.

Beck meanders to the right side and climbs on, lying across the foot so that all three of them are lying in Shea's bed.

He can feel Shea's obnoxious kicking feet and rolls over onto them, pinning them under the covers. Jo throws him down a pillow, and he pulls the outer quilt over him.

"You two are in so much trouble," Shea threatens.

But Jo is already fast asleep, and Beck is just about there; he's so out of it that he can't stop himself from saying, "It's because we love you, Shea."

And he passes out before he can see the tips of her ears tinge pink.

CHAPTER 22: BACK TO THE ISLAND

Jo

Jo wakes to find the bed empty of both Shea and Beck.

Morning light is shining through the cabin windows, highlighting the brilliant colors in the bedding.

Her head aches from the rum, but it's not enough to block out the previous evening's conversation she had with Beck.

What was she thinking? He makes her happy too. She'd forgiven Shea for the kiss. Everything Shea had said about Beck and her connection to him, Jo had heard her and accepted it.

She cringes at her drunken form displayed plainly behind her wincing eyes, but everything she told Beck last night was the truth.

He does make Shea happy.

Jo wants to spend the rest of her life with Shea, so she can deal with Beck. Because if there's one thing she doesn't have any doubt about, it's Shea's love for her. Shea chose her.

Jo knows in her heart that she is Shea's partner above anyone else. Besides, Beck is good for his word, and ultimately, he seems to respect Jo as Shea's partner.

A fist knocks at the door and an officer informs her

that they're docking at Orena.

Orena.

So many memories clash together over the name of the island where she spent her first true moment with Shea before it had collapsed into pain and fear.

Jo can't wait to see Dari and Phoebus again; she hasn't spoken to them since the last time she was here on this beautiful island. Jo hops out of bed and heads over to her clothes chest that they stored in Aster's old bunk to keep the floor clear. Shea had grumbled upon seeing all of Jo's luggage. Speaking of Shea's grumbling...

"You guys are in so much trouble."

Jo drops her naval uniform pants back into the chest as Shea's voice rattles her hungover brain. She supposes she and Beck had been a bit drunk the night before. The conversation slams back into her and her cheeks grow warm in embarrassment.

Shea heard everything they said.

Everything.

Last night, she was too intoxicated to even care, but now? She wanted to discuss the situation with him, possibly find a place for Beck in their life, and somehow last night was the result.

She doesn't have to choose.

What does that even mean?

Family.

There is now so much more to discuss, and on top of that, they practically decided everything for Shea, and their captain heard it all.

What the Underdeep is she going to do?

Jo finishes getting dressed, buttoning up her Arethusian military-style jacket, and rushes out of the small room, all the while trying to braid her hair back. She needs to see Shea. She needs to talk to her about what she heard.

She messily ties the long braid and pulls on her black boots; she barely glances into any of the mirrors before walking out the door. She steals away to the galley first, grabbing an apple from Strom partly because she's hungry and partly to avoid Shea's temper.

As she's heading out of the kitchen, she passes Poseidon on his way in, completely drenched in seawater and with a very familiar sour look on his face.

"Training?" Jo asks on her way by to the steps leading to the top deck.

Poseidon waves a hand over himself and pulls the seawater out of his clothes, drying the dark black pants and the unlaced white top, which fall better on his built frame. His shoulder-length copper hair with strands of silver and his gray beard remain soaked, dripping onto the collar of his shirt.

"She's in a merry mood this morning," Poseidon mutters with a harsh glint in his green eyes and continues on to the galley, where he's made friends with the *Duchess*'s cook.

"Have we docked yet?" Jo shouts to his retreating form.

"Just about," Poseidon replies and then he's gone.

Jo sighs and continues on. She climbs the steps to the top deck and opens the door to find Aster on the other side.

"Hello." Jo smiles around a bite of apple.

Aster chuckles and pats her on the arm as he limps past her, down the steps. "Morning. Whatever you did? I don't want to know."

Jo gulps, coughing slightly as the piece of apple goes down harder after his comment.

"What?" Jo queries after him.

"You'll see!" Aster responds with a twinge of pain to his voice.

Suddenly Jo has very little desire to walk onto the main deck. But she squares her shoulders and pushes on; Shea can't be that mad.

The sun is blazing on the main deck and its heat encases the crew with very little wind reprieve. Jo notes the crew preparing for docking procedure and she catches Beck at the bow furiously tying down the base of the harpoon launcher.

She waves at him until she catches his attention, and when his eyes land on her, he stiffens.

Caen shouts for him to get back to work, and she can see the redness staining his cheeks from here. He doesn't wave back.

Well that could be his own problem. It doesn't necessarily mean Shea ripped him a new one about last night.

Caen has also caught sight of Jo and gives the remaining orders to the bow crew to finish their work quickly. He storms over to her, and Jo's eyes widen at his twitching left eye and the hard curve of his brows.

"What did you do?" he asks, placing his hands on his hips.

"Me? What? I don't understand," Jo tries to explain.

"Right. She's in a great mood this morning. Whatever you did? Apologize," Caen states and then purposefully looks back to where Beck is at the bow, making Jo look over with him. "Both of you."

Caen pushes past her toward the afterdeck steps.

"Caen, I don't know what you're talking about," Jo says, following him.

She stops at the foot of the steps, a smile gracing her features as she stares out at the massive port of Orena.

Stunning fabrics span the market stands, intermingling with all kinds of people dressed in exotic styles and sheer clothing. The vines have grown, Jo notices. She can see a lot more greenery spanning the sand buildings that shimmer with the expensive gems scattered around.

Flowers Jo has never seen before sprout all over the new vines and trees, marking the city pathways.

Orena is full of life and cultures from across the globe; she feels welcome here.

She snaps out of her admiration and quickly takes the steps two at time to make it to the top of the helm.

James is steering the boat, with a strangely happy grin. He's easing the *Duchess* into port, and Caen walks to the rail ordering the deck crew to prepare the heaving lines of rope they'll need to connect the ship to the dock.

Everything seems okay so far, Jo thinks, and then her eyes finally land on her fiancée.

Standing at the map desk, Shea seems to be looking at a list of supplies along with the charting course they'll take from Orena to Tenaro, once everything's been collected.

She's radiant. Her long red hair is down, her captain's hat is missing, but she's plaited a front braid to frame her face. Her dark blue peasant blouse is tucked into her black pants, which are then tucked into her dark leather boots.

Jo can't help the smile that gathers on her features as she notices both her eyes the normal green, instead of the milky white her left used to be.

Finally, those green eyes land on the Arethusian queen. Jo's smile quickly fades. Those eyes have a burning fire behind them, and she's frowning upon finally noticing Jo.

Caen bellows the orders for the deck crew to throw the heaving lines, and Aster shouts that the below crew is ready to drop the anchor.

"Your Majesty," Shea mutters.

Jo gulps. This is definitely not good.

"Shea. Good morning, did you sleep well?" Jo asks, taking a step toward her.

She stops when she sees Shea's hand grip the desk tightly.

"Not exactly. I had a bit on my mind, as well as on top of me."

Jo thinks back to the night before and remembers climbing into bed. Perhaps she may have cuddled Shea with Beck lying at the foot of the bed, sort of pinning her legs down on accident.

Okay, so yes, she probably didn't have the best sleep.

"Do you want to talk about it?" Jo inquires, edging

closer to the table until she's on the other side, looking at Shea directly.

The ship lurches, making it to port, and Jo looks across the afterdeck until she sees Beck on the main, straining to keep the heaving lines straight as they progress toward the dock.

Shea sighs, and she loses some of the fire in her eyes. She looks...tired.

"No. Yes, I heard what you all said. No, I don't really know what to think. Yes, I've developed...emotions...regarding Beck. But I haven't had the time to really explore or even understand how I feel, and I don't need you and him figuring it out for me."

Jo winces at Shea's rant, but she agrees with every word.

"Jo."

Jo looks up, meeting those beautiful green eyes.

"I love you. He didn't change that. I'm not asking you to 'share' me with him. I am capable of being with you and only you."

"I know," Jo objects, and suddenly she can see the hurt in Shea's eyes. The doubt.

Jo recounts everything she said last night and then is reminded of how she called Shea a Lionbird, the epitome of freedom, and she can understand how she got the wrong idea. She doesn't think Jo believes she could ever settle down with one person.

"Shea, I know you're mine." Jo places her hand on top of Shea's. She lowers her voice when she sees Shea glance toward James at the helm.

"I know that you love me, and that you want to be with me. But do you remember what we said about our love being unfair? How one of us will have to give something up to be with the other?"

"I'm willing to do that," Shea remarks.

"Shea. You're giving up the *Duchess*, your freedom, to

become royalty. So, I thought if I could give you anything back, perhaps…" Jo trails off.

Shea's eyes widen in understanding. "You thought you could give me him."

Jo chuckles and her cheeks glow red. "Silly, isn't it?"

"Very," Shea states. Then she leans over the desk and kisses Jo on the cheek. "But sweet too."

Jo grins and catches Shea's chin before she can pull back, landing a kiss on her mouth.

The sound of a clearing throat has them pulling back to opposite sides of the desk once more.

Shea looks over in Caen's direction.

"Shall we drop anchor, Captain?"

"Yes, Caen."

Caen gives the order and leaves them on the afterdeck with James. They can hear the sound of the anchor falling and the gangway plank being dropped overboard and onto the deck, creating the walkway off the ship.

"Jo."

Jo turns back to Shea with a smile. She follows her as she walks over to the rail and places a hand on top of hers as they look over the main deck together.

Shea's eyes land on one particular crewmate, and Jo watches as Beck laughs with Aster on the main deck.

"I don't know what it is. This draw. But I do feel it. And I'm sorry," Shea's voice cracks slightly.

Jo's hand tightens on Shea's. "Do you love me?"

"Of course," Shea tells her, and she turns her head, looking up into Jo's eyes. "I choose you, always."

"Then that's all I need." Jo smiles. "I trust you. And I trust him, surprisingly."

Shea laughs and leans her head on Jo's shoulder.

"Besides, he'll make the perfect surrogate when this is all over for our kids."

Shea chokes, coughing, and pulls away from Jo with a weary expression.

"Kids?"

Jo laughs. "Well yes. We'll need heirs to the throne. I think it would be a smart alliance move to have Beck be the father."

Shea shakes her head. "I can't imagine you two…" She shivers. "And you're so stubborn now, I don't know how I'm going to deal with you pregnant."

Jo grins. "I can't imagine. But luckily, I won't be the one pregnant."

James begins a coughing fit behind them, and Jo laughs inwardly as he obviously heard her, but Shea doesn't react just yet.

"Right," Shea replies.

Jo can tell it hasn't sunk in, so she carefully removes her hand and starts backing away toward the stairs.

"Wait," Shea mutters. "What do you mean you won't be the one pregnant?"

Shea turns on Jo with a horrified expression, and Jo shoots her a cocky grin.

"Well, the ruling queen doesn't carry the heirs. There's too much risk, so the female consort does, or well, a surrogate mother if the consort is male."

"Jo."

"And don't worry. There's always a chance you could have a girl on the first try. And if not, we have more options for alliances with neighboring countries. Boys do run in his family though, from what I understand, but the more the merrier. Right, love?"

"Jo." Shea shakes her head, her eyes comically wide.

"And this way Beck will always be in our lives, he'd be family," Jo tells her, and the pieces are falling into place.

Jo can tell Shea is working the thought process out in her own mind and just how long of a game Jo's been playing since she realized she couldn't simply get rid of Beck. Now he's a political advantage and the perfect surrogate.

"You," Shea growls.

"Yes, dear," Jo replies and takes off down the steps away from her quickly angering fiancée.

"Jo!"

Jo laughs as she makes it to the gangplank, finding Beck standing at the top too. Jo hooks her arm through his, and he pulls to try to get away when he sees the raging ball of captain storming toward them, but Jo holds him steady.

"Oh, you don't have to be embarrassed, Beck, I calmed her down," Jo confides to him.

He looks at her with a concerned expression. "That's what you call calmed down?"

Shea notices Beck standing next to Jo and her ears turn pink. She can see her trying to find a calculated escape, but Caen finds her at the bottom of the helm stairs and begins pushing her toward the gangplank where Jo and Beck are.

James is no longer coughing but laughing when Aster joins him at the bottom of the steps as well.

Caen gives him command of the docked ship and James can barely raise his hand up to salute among all the giggles.

Aster volunteers to stay behind with James.

Shea glares at her son's boyfriend with menace.

Poseidon finally rejoins them on deck with a list from Strom, and Shea groans at the sight of him.

Jo nods a greeting to Caen and Poseidon, and she grins at the embarrassed looks Beck and Shea are throwing at each other.

Jo thinks, wickedly, she could definitely keep them both on their toes for the rest of her life.

"Everyone ready?" Caen asks.

The crew that needed to go ahead to the market have done so, and the rest will remain on the ship under James's command. That leaves Shea, Poseidon, Caen, Beck, and Jo to go to Dari and Phoebus's for supplies.

Everyone murmurs their acquiescence.

"Let's go," Jo commands, and she hooks her arm

through Shea's.

    Her other arm is still hooked through Beck's. She drags them both with her down the gangplank while Caen and Poseidon follow behind.

CHAPTER 23: THE FAMILY THICKER THAN BLOOD

Shea

And Shea thought overhearing the conversation between Jo and Beck last night had been embarrassing, but as the three of them along with Poseidon and Caen weave their way through the winding streets of the Orena port, Shea can't bring herself to even look Beck in the eye.

Becoming a mother to Aster had happened almost naturally, and sometimes he still feels more like a little brother than a son. But to actually give birth to Jo and Shea's child—correction Jo, Shea, and Beck's child?

Does he know?

Shea chances a glance in Beck's direction. He's standing with Jo in front of one of the Orenien vendors, examining the merchant's wares, pointing out things he likes to Jo as she does the same.

Shea can't help the smile that comes over her features, grinning at these two wonderful leaders who just so happen to see something amazing in her. She doesn't really understand why, but she's not stupid enough to question it—at least, not aloud.

Caen shouts from ahead for them to keep up, and Shea voices the same concerns closer to the two royals.

Jo shouts back that they're right behind them.

Beck picks up something from the vendor's table and exchanges Oceanan coin for it.

Here in the markets of Orena, anything with value can be traded for something else, there's too many kinds of people and nations prospering on the outskirts of the law.

Shea is trying to get a better look at what Beck has in his hands when a deep voice makes her jump.

"See something you like?"

Shea turns around quickly, her hands going to the waterskin on her belt, but she quickly meets a pair of similarly shaded green eyes smirking at her as Poseidon gestures toward Jo and Beck walking quickly to catch up.

"Just making sure they're okay," Shea explains.

She weaves past a group of prostitutes begging the two to join them inside for a good time.

Poseidon's eyes scan their scantily clad bodies and Shea rolls her eyes.

"You look like your mother when you make that expression," Poseidon tells her, chuckling to himself.

"You often stared at other women when you were with her?" Shea mutters, hoping she insults him.

Poseidon shrugs, pointing up ahead to Caen's fast fading figure when he sees Shea scanning the crowd for him.

They're almost at the crossroads for Phoebus and Dari's home.

Shea notes the abundance of greenery along the older buildings, surprised to see it so green this late in the year. Her thoughts come to a halt when Poseidon responds to her earlier snark.

"I did. Other men as well." Poseidon winks.

Shea looks back at Beck and Jo with slight distress, turning around before they can see.

"Attraction is attraction," he continues.

"Great, so not only did I inherit your insanely good looks, but also your promiscuity," Shea snarls, picking up her pace to leave him in the dust.

"You think I'm good-looking?"

They reach the crossroads and she can barely see Caen anymore. He must have gone on ahead. She knows the way to her old home like the back of her hand. She points down the correct street, waving her hand to get Jo's and Beck's attention, and they nod in acknowledgment.

She keeps going.

Poseidon catches up with her anyway.

"Just because I slept with other mortals doesn't mean I didn't love your mother, nor that I wasn't loyal to her. She knew who I was. She knew what I was, and she loved me anyway. As long as I came home to her at the end of the day, that was enough for her. Because she knew that she and I were the only two who had the kind of bond we did."

There are colorful crabs and coral-looking plants intermixed with the same vines and trees that the old elven structures have always been covered in, but something feels strange.

Shea can't help but be distracted from her conversation with her father because she feels something else. Something like magic flowing through the vibrant plants and new critters crawling through the old city, the elven ruins, almost like a new presence.

But the rest of what Poseidon has just said sinks in, and it makes her stop in the middle of the street. Poseidon pauses as well, staring around with confusion.

"Are we here?"

Shea runs a hand through her hair, a growl climbing up the back of her throat.

"What bond? You have a wife! Or is that all a lie, and does my fiancée and her queendom worship an imaginary figure?"

Poseidon sighs, his brows furrowing. "No, Amphitrite is real."

"So, then there's your bond! You married her; my mother, Ami, was just another mortal woman in your lineup. I get what you're trying to do," Shea lowers her voice as she sees Beck and Jo finally walk around the corner.

They're closing the distance between.

"But you and I are not the same. Our situations are nothing alike. I love Jo and I don't care about whatever ideas I might have about Beck. Jo is my bond. So, don't you dare try to justify how I'm feeling. You have no idea what's going on inside my head," Shea growls. "Got it?"

Poseidon opens his mouth to argue, if the fire in his eyes gives Shea any indication, but he closes it just as quickly, shakes his head, and gestures for her to lead the way.

Shea starts walking again, but her father speaks.

"I'm sorry."

Shea stops. "What?"

"I'm sorry."

"You said this already."

"Well, I'm saying it again," Poseidon snaps and Shea turns to look at him.

He crosses the small distance and stands in front of her, his eyes a lighter green than before and with a sadness that highlights the crow's feet, betraying his old age.

"I wasn't trying to explain away what you were feeling, I was trying to…comfort. I guess I'm not very good at it."

Shea hums but doesn't say anything in response.

"Shea. Even with Perses, and finding Triton, and everything else that has happened, the one thing I was excited about was meeting you. I didn't raise you, and I know I'm not your father in a way that truly matters but…I loved you, Shea. When I found out your mother had been pregnant and she had you, I was so happy."

Poseidon begins walking forward, and Shea walks with him.

Jo and Beck are now close behind them.

She thinks about scoffing and running away, but she finds herself rooted in place at her father's side, wanting to hear every word.

"When you were taken, I don't know if you remember, but there was a storm. One of the largest Nereid had ever seen. I wanted to bring you back more than anything. I searched everywhere, but by the time my scouts found you, you were with Paetre."

Flashes of lightning and heavy rain, the slavers a group of three horrifying men, dragging her to the slave markets of Lycos. The memories barrage her being and she has to look at the ground passing under her feet.

"Even then, I wanted to take you away but...your mother. She's a powerful elf, the highest priestess on the Erebos council. She had a vision. That one day Nereid would need you and they would need the woman who would be raised by a great man. And that great man wasn't me. It was your father, Paetre," Poseidon says, but his normally powerful voice holds an underlying tremor of emotion.

Shea doesn't know what to say, or even how to respond. How does she equate the image Poseidon is painting with the man she thought she knew and the man he's shown her to be?

"Why are you telling me this?" Shea finally asks.

"Because I love you. And it hurts knowing how much you hate me, but it hurts worse knowing that you might not realize that I love you as much as I love Triton, and Perses, and any of your other siblings. You are my children. Shea, you're my beautiful, intelligent, strong daughter and I don't like seeing you in pain. So that's why I said...what I said, but you're right—you're not like me."

Shea nods—she was waiting for the catch in all this, and there it is. She opens her mouth to tell him off, but he beats her to it.

"You're so much better. And I'm grateful for this

chance to get to know you and I'm thankful to your father for raising the woman you've become," Poseidon finishes.

He doesn't walk away though, he stays by her side, his head held high and his gaze straight ahead.

His words echo through her mind, and she studies him, truly studies him for the first time. His graying hair, and the small bits of copper still shining through, his greenish-blue eyes that change depending on his mood. His boisterous laugh when she gets something right in their training sessions, much like how proud she is when Aster surpasses her. And for the first time, she sees a man, not a god—not a celestial being but a father.

Her breathing quickens, and her heart feels like it might burst. She had a father, in Paetre, and father figures in Caen and Phoebus, but maybe there's room in her life for one more.

She glances down at Poseidon's right hand, hanging at his side as he walks beside her, and suddenly her left is filled with warmth and she realizes she's placed her hand in his.

Poseidon jolts, tripping on a step. He looks down at their intertwined hands. When he meets Shea's gaze, his eyes are a stormy blue and there's a smile on his face like the sun warming her on a cold day on the *Duchess*. He squeezes her hand and brings it up to his lips, landing a soft kiss on the back.

Shea smiles at him for the first time.

"Shea?"

She turns her head in surprise as Caen's masculine voice calls out to her from the courtyard in front of Phoebus and Dari's home.

She hadn't even realized they'd made it the rest of the way down the winding cobbled streets to the courtyard with the water fountain of Poseidon slaying the kraken. Shea's eyes wander over the stone carving of her father's face, and she finally realizes why the statue has always bothered her so much—the face is too cold.

Beck and Jo have stopped beside them, and Shea notices them staring at Poseidon and her.

Caen is also staring, although more like glaring down the two of them.

Phoebus is beside him, his expression unreadable and the grand door to their home is open.

Dari is sitting at the edge of the fountain with a beautiful smile, staring at something between Shea and Poseidon.

Shea looks down to see what it is and realizes she's still holding his hand. She quickly drops it and glances at Poseidon to see his reaction. The grand smile doesn't disappear when she breaks off his touch.

"Shea!" Dari announces, getting up from her seat where she seems to have been talking to Caen and Phoebus while they were waiting for them to arrive.

She looks beautiful. Her normally long white hair has been cut to her shoulders with bright silvery curls bouncing against the sunlight. Her dark black skin positively shines against the beautifully flowing purple dress fitted to her thin frame. She has a white shawl over her shoulder's concealing her missing left arm.

Phoebus has shaved his beard, although his hair has grown a bit longer, stopping just below his neck. He's standing next to Caen with his arms crossed, his short dwarf frame just as imposing as Caen's giant height.

Dari rushes forward, encasing Shea in a tight one-armed hug, which Shea returns with a laugh. They pull away just enough to look into each other's eyes and Dari lands a kiss on her forehead.

Shea can feel Poseidon's eyes on them, and Dari must too, because she turns to him with Shea still in her arm.

"Thank you," Dari says, and Poseidon cocks his head to the side.

"What for?" he asks.

Dari smiles softly at him. "For giving life to my daughter."

Poseidon's eyes widen and a smile of his own graces his features once again.

Dari turns back to Shea and she leans in closer to Shea's ear so only she can hear.

"She's still here."

Shea takes in a deep breath and nods.

"Okay."

"Don't worry. I don't think she'll say anything. We were going to give her passage to the mainland, but with everything that you said in your letter…"

"I understand." Shea smiles.

"We have much to discuss, Shea," Phoebus states and there's a strange look in his eyes that makes Shea believe him.

"It seems so," she responds.

"Jo." Dari grins, walking over to the blonde standing awkwardly off to the side with Beck.

Jo steps forward and hugs the older elf with a look of relief.

"Hello, Dari."

Dari pulls away after the hug and looks Beck up and down, making him blush. "And who is this?"

Shea opens her mouth to answer, but Jo beats her to it.

"May I introduce Governor Beck of Oceanus; he's accompanying us on our journey to find Triton on Tenaro," Jo explains.

"Please to meet you, ma'am," Beck tells her.

"You won't be going to Tenaro."

Shea, who had been watching the exchange, quickly turns her eyes to Phoebus.

"What are you talking about?"

"There's no need."

Shea walks the rest of the way until she's standing in front of him.

"Phoebus, we have to find Triton. I told you in the letter why."

Phoebus chuckles darkly and glares over at Poseidon.

"Aren't you supposed to be the All Father? The king of our gods? You're telling me the closer you got, you couldn't sense him?"

"My powers aren't what they used to be," Poseidon answers gruffly.

"I'll say," Phoebus spits.

"Okay enough," Shea growls. "Enough with the cryptic information. What are you talking about?"

"He's here."

"Or at least that's what the rumors say," Dari adds.

"After your last visit, when you dropped off—"

Dari coughs a warning and Phoebus doesn't finish his sentence.

Shea glares at him.

He continues stiffly, "After the last time you were here. Folks down at the markets say a man arrived from the west. He went inland. Many claim he's in the old temple, the old elven temple, and he hasn't returned. Merchants traveled inland to investigate, only one came back claiming something about the temple now being protected by creatures, monsters."

"How can you be sure it's him? He could be another powerful priest," Beck argues.

"Because we've both seen this kinda growth on Orena before," Caen snaps back.

"Years ago," Dari notes.

"Yes, when an immortal visited the island," Phoebus states.

"Who?" Poseidon whispers.

"It doesn't matter," Caen replies. "The point is Triton is here."

"You don't know that," Jo adds.

"Yes," Shea tells them, and they all turn to her. "We do. I could feel something ever since we arrived. Like a familiar presence or someone I'm connected to. I don't how to explain it, I just—I think they're right. Triton...I think my brother is here."

CHAPTER 24: CLOSE TO ME

Shea

"Let's take this inside," Dari commands, gesturing for everyone to follow her into her home.

After Shea's confirmation, the courtyard grew eerily quiet. Shea can't explain it, but the whole time she's been here, she's felt stronger. Her magic is snapping at the edges of her very being as if pushing at the inside of her flesh, snarling to break free, wanting to find the other magic on the island so similar to her own.

Phoebus and Caen both turn on their heel and march inside without looking back.

Poseidon follows a little behind, and Shea takes a step to join him but is stopped by a hand on her shoulder.

"Are you okay?"

Shea turns to find Jo and Beck staring at her with concern. Shea smiles at Jo's question and takes her hand, kissing the back.

"I'm okay. It's better if he's here, maybe we can convince him quickly and get home before they reach Oceanus. Maybe we can make it back in time."

Shea watches Beck's eyes widen.

"I hadn't thought about it. The fact that Oceanus

might be gone when we return."

He looks guilty and Shea grabs his hand too, without thinking.

"Hey, don't feel bad. A lot has happened and we've all just been focusing on finding Triton and hopefully figuring out how he can stop Perses from taking over Nereid."

Beck sighs and squeezes her hand in thanks.

Shea smiles softly but then realizes what she's doing and releases her grip. She looks over at Jo, but Jo doesn't look upset. Instead, she looks quite content.

Shea keeps Jo's hand in hers and starts walking toward the entrance of Phoebus and Dari's home.

The shop hasn't changed much, the marble counter is still there, though the herbs and supplies have changed around a bit on the shelves.

Caeruleus is sleeping on the bird tree, laid out over three branches on his back without a care.

Shea whistles and his greenish-blue ears perk up as he lazily opens his eyes to look at her.

"Dumb bird," Shea mutters affectionately as she gets close enough to scratch behind his ears.

He purrs in response, a large yawn exposing his sharp fangs, and rubs his face along her hand.

Jo gives him a tentative pet, which he takes.

He stretches and meows, taking off into the air above them and flying to the kitchen, probably to find some mice to eat.

"I'm glad he made it okay," Jo laughs and Shea nods.

Beck follows them the rest of the way into the giant dome with the beautiful oak tree in the center, spanning its massive branches and leaves over the room and acting as the roof of the building. Sun shines through the leaves, and Shea notices Dari has changed the floor to white rose petals instead of the usual enchantedly soft oak leaves. Magic invades every border of the walls and Jo chuckles at Beck's awed expression, probably reminding her of the first time she was here.

Dari walks past them with a tea kettle in hand, followed by a familiar woman from Shea's earlier travels this year carrying a tray of cookies and snacks.

Shea leads Jo and Beck to the dining area, which has a perfect view of the inner gardens. The monkeys are chattering softly across the grass and Shea can barely look at the glimmering pool as a pained sadness fills her.

"Where's Lena?" Jo asks.

Jo looks around the inner garden, blocked by a wall made of tree roots, an arched window with no glass making it possible to see through.

"She passed away, earlier this year," Dari tells her sadly, sitting down and pouring cups of tea for the rest of the group sitting at the giant mahogany table in wicker chairs similar to the grown furniture in the living space.

"Shea," Jo turns to her. "Why didn't you tell me?"

Shea sighs. "It never really came up. It's okay."

She pulls out a chair for Jo.

Shea tries to pay attention to the conversation happening around her, but she's focused on the woman who should be on the mainland by now.

Tall, and exceedingly beautiful, her skin is a shade darker than Dari's and her cheekbones would make any woman envious. Her amber eyes are similar to Caen's, though not as strikingly gold, and her dreadlocked hair is artistically done up in a gorgeous bun. She's wearing a similar dress to Dari's, and she's careful not to meet Shea's eyes.

The woman places the tray down quickly and goes to leave, but Shea can't stop herself.

"You're still here."

The lady stops, graceful as her upbringing implies, and she turns to Shea with a haughty expression.

"I would have left, but your parents insisted I stay for my safety."

She's been working on her accent, it sounds more

Orenien than Charisian, but it doesn't matter.

"Well, perhaps I could arrange safe transport down at the docks," Shea tells her.

Semele smirks.

"Shea," Phoebus barks, "Semele is our guest as long as she wishes, considering the circumstances."

Shea turns to Phoebus, examining his rigid posture.

This conversation should be fun.

Jo, Beck, Poseidon, and Caen all stay intelligently silent, but Dari is glaring holes in the side of her husband's head. At least someone is on her side, Shea thinks.

Semele bows mockingly in Shea's direction. Shea thinks she sees her change the color of her eyes to green, taunting her with a peek at her magic.

Shea's hands tighten on the top of her chair as she watches Semele leave the dining area.

They're finally all seated at the table, Phoebus at one end and Shea at the other.

"So, we're all seated," Shea announces, gesturing around the table. "What did you want to talk about?"

Phoebus glares at her callous attitude; he's been in a bad mood since she arrived and she's not fond of it.

"I'll leave the one subject for later, as it seems you don't wish to speak about it in mixed company." Phoebus points after Semele, and Shea rolls her eyes.

"Who is Semele?" Jo asks.

Shea turns to her with tired eyes.

"I promise I'll explain one day, but for now I want to stay focused. You said Triton is at the ruins, I'm not familiar with the route, is it possible to hire a guide?"

Dari finishes passing out cups of tea and Shea takes a sip as Caeruleus swoops down and steals a cookie off the table, flying back into the oak tree before Dari can finish chastising him.

Beck smiles up at the Lionbird and Shea chuckles at Caeruleus's antics.

Phoebus and Caen are not amused.

"You won't need a guide. I can get you there," Phoebus tells her, taking a cookie for himself.

Shea coughs on her drink of tea. "No. It's too dangerous."

Phoebus laughs darkly. "Remember who the first captain of the *Duchess* was, girl, I know what I can handle."

"She's just trying to protect you," Poseidon begins, but Phoebus snarls at him.

"I'll thank you kindly to keep your input to yourself. I helped raise that girl and if I need your opinion, I'll bloody ask."

"Phoebus," Shea growls.

Phoebus doesn't answer; instead he takes an angry bite of the cookie in his hand and ignores Shea's warning.

"I can take you and that's the end of that. The island isn't that big, and the temple is at the center, shouldn't take us longer than half a day to get there and half a day to get back. Especially if we ride."

"Great," Jo states. "When do we leave?"

"You're not going," Shea tells her.

Jo turns to her with an affronted expression. "Of course I am."

"No. I can't stop Phoebus, but I also need a guide I can trust. You, I can stop and you're not going. I need you to stay here. The fewer people going, the faster we can get there."

"Shea," Jo starts, but Shea covers her mouth with a hand and a pointed expression.

"No."

Jo glares but nods.

"Okay, so how many of us are going then?" Beck asks, standing from his seat.

"You're not going either," Shea chuckles.

"What? This is the whole reason I came!"

"No, you came to see the mission through; I'm going to do that, but you're also the governor of Oceanus. She's the queen, and you both need to make it back alive to lead your people through this crisis."

"This is ridiculous!" Beck growls.

"Hey, if I can't go, neither can you!" Jo argues and Beck groans, stomping off toward the entrance to the inner gardens.

"So, then who is going?" Caen asks, looking around the table at who is left.

"You," Shea tells him, and Caen grins in response, "me, Poseidon, and Phoebus. And we leave now."

"It's just about noon," Poseidon tells her. "Shouldn't we wait until morning, so we don't arrive in the dark?"

"Scared?" Caen mocks and Poseidon scoffs.

"I know the temple at the center of Orena, considering they worshipped me." Poseidon draws up to his full height. "This island was one of my first attempts to create a paradise for my people. It fell to slavers and traders." He glares at Caen and Phoebus, who both look offended. "But they protected the temple with magic, tests, and traps. Darkness is not a friend in a place like that."

"We don't have a choice. We don't have time; we need to leave now. But you knowing the temple is an advantage, and we'll use that considering we don't know what to expect," Shea commands. "Now was there anything else?"

"We can talk on the way," Phoebus responds. "I'll get my bag."

He pushes his seat away from the table and storms off in the direction of the bedrooms, down the white clay hall.

"I'll go get the horses ready, are there enough?" Caen asks Dari.

"We have five in the stables at the moment. Can I help?"

"No, I'm fine," Caen tells her and goes to leave, but Poseidon stops him.

"I'll come with you. Two sets of hands are better than one."

Caen nods and takes off toward the stables just outside the kitchen. Poseidon has to jog to catch up to him.

"Well, seems everyone's off on the grand adventure, I should get this cleaned up," Dari chuckles, and begins cleaning up the table, putting cups on the silver tray.

"I'll help you." Jo grins and starts gathering cups on the tray as well.

"Actually, Jo, can I see you a moment?"

Jo glances at Shea and then looks to Dari, who waves her on.

Shea leads her down the white clay hall, to the familiar bedroom that started it all.

They enter Shea's old chambers, and Shea takes a deep breath, feeling the tension fade from her shoulders as she takes in her familiar surroundings. They can see Beck from the balcony tossing stones into the pond and scaring away the obnoxious monkeys.

The floor is covered in the pink blossoms from the nearby tree and the bright sun is shining on the mythological mosaics spanning the walls and ceiling of the chamber leading out toward the open balcony.

Jo's hands wrap around Shea's middle, and Shea leans her head back against Jo's shoulder, her white-blond hair tickling the side of Shea's face.

"What is it?"

"What if he refuses to help?" she whispers.

Jo turns her around in her arms so they're looking at each other, and Shea wraps her arms around Jo's neck.

"What?"

Shea repeats, "What if he refuses?"

"He won't."

"But what if he does? All Poseidon has told me is, after something happened, he sent Triton to Tenaro to redeem himself for his actions. Since then he hasn't heard from him, and now, we find out he's not even on Tenaro; he came here. What if he knows about Perses already and doesn't want to get involved?"

"Then we'll find another way," Jo tells her.

Shea groans and breaks their embrace, stepping away.

"Who's Semele?"

Shea looks up, her hands on her hips, and she chuckles as she takes in Jo's guarded expression.

"It's not like that."

"Really? You won't tell me who she is, she makes you uncomfortable. What am I supposed to think?"

"It's not that. I saved her, you could say."

It's Jo's turn to laugh. "She must not have been very grateful."

"No." Shea smiles sadly. "She isn't. I got involved when I shouldn't have, I made a calculated mistake, and I almost paid for it. It cost her life. And so, I took her away, to teach someone a lesson. I don't know if what I did was right, I haven't really had the time to process."

Shea turns her back on Jo and stares out into the gardens, watching Beck sit down on the grass and pull his knees up to his chest. He takes something out of his jacket pocket and Shea cocks her head as he brings the long object up to his lips. A familiar tune fills the air and Shea realizes he's playing the flute.

"He said his mother taught him," Jo explains, her voice close.

Shea hadn't heard her move beside her.

"I recognize the tune," Shea murmurs. "It's elven."

"Oceanus has a lot of elven refugees from Lycos and the Eastlands, from what I understand; as long as they remain within the borders, they're safe."

"For the most part," Shea responds.

"Is she dangerous?" Jo asks.

Shea remembers they were talking about Semele.

"Yes."

"And Dari and Phoebus know?"

"Yes," Shea answers.

"Do I need to know?"

Shea thinks for a moment and turns to Jo with a tired smile; she takes Jo's hands in hers and looks her in the eye.

"When you do, I'll tell you. But for now, the story is a world away and we have bigger problems."

"Okay then," Jo states, "I trust you."

Shea reaches up and lands a soft kiss on Jo's lush lips. The queen pulls her fiancée closer and deepens the touch. Shea moans into the embrace.

"I should go," Shea whispers.

"I don't want you to," Jo says.

"I'll come back."

"But what if you don't? Shea, I don't want to lose you. I want to be with you, forever."

"We will be, Your Majesty," Shea promises.

She pulls away from Jo, and Jo reluctantly lets go.

A knock sounds at the door and Phoebus's gruff voice shouts that they're ready; it's time to go.

"Take care of him," Shea asks, pointing at Beck, who's still playing the flute in the garden.

"Anything for you." Jo nods.

Shea leaves her in the room.

She doesn't turn back. She starts heading toward the gardens to say goodbye to Beck but with everything that's happened what can she say. *I'll come back? It'll be okay?*

She doesn't want to leave without saying goodbye but everything between them, right now, hurts. She'll see him when she comes back. Hopefully. And if she doesn't come back? Well, maybe he'll forgive her someday in the underworld. She knows she's probably making a mistake but with a heavy heart Shea moves towards the kitchens instead.

Semele is sitting at a table towards the back of the room chopping vegetables from the garden for dinner that evening.

Dari brings in a tray and kisses Phoebus, hugging him tightly in the doorway to the stables.

"Come back to me."

Phoebus kisses her once again, then continues into the stables.

Shea hugs Dari and glares at Semele, who is watching the exchange with a wicked smile.

"If you say anything..." Shea begins and Semele laughs.

She closes her eyes, tapping into her abilities, and soon her body shimmers as one of her illusions settles over her frame. She looks just like him, the man who haunts both their nightmares from the adventure earlier in the year.

Her chameleon abilities have gotten stronger.

Shea can just barely see the ripple when Semele moves, giving away that the man sitting in front of her in Semele's place isn't real.

"You're stronger," Shea mutters.

"Dari's helped me learn to control my ability. I couldn't have done it without her," Semele says in that deep baritone voice of her husband.

"Semele," Dari barks, and the illusion ripples away, revealing her in the man's place.

"What? I didn't say anything." She laughs darkly.

"Thanks," Shea says to Dari.

"Shea," Dari sighs. "Be safe."

Shea nods and closes the door to the stable behind her.

Caen is already astride his large horse, and Phoebus has mounted his trusted pony, Kenna.

Shea wanders over to a new stallion she hasn't seen in the stable before, his coat a gorgeous dark brown.

Poseidon helps her up and she settles onto the horse, noticing the packs on each steed. Enough supplies to last them a couple days, should things go wrong. Hopefully things don't go wrong.

"Ready," Poseidon states as he mounts his horse.

"Right," Phoebus responds. "Everyone stay close. Follow my lead, we can slow down once we hit the roads at Starfish Cross."

Everyone voices their agreement and soon they're off. Phoebus shouts for Kenna to take off and they race through the streets toward the border of Port Town and the rest of the island.

The other parts of the island are separated into a starfish map of roads all leading to the center of Orena, the temple. Paetre used to quiz Shea on maps of places she'd been, but that was years ago. And the reason the rest of the island has never been mapped out is because not everyone believes the elves of old are gone, and most who have tried have disappeared.

The green vines and tropical plant life grow larger and thicker as the horses weave past the old elven structures. Finally, they break into the old city streets that remind Shea of the small flashes of memory she still has of Erebos, buildings half built of stone and trees.

They gallop away from everyone they love and toward the border, toward the temple, toward Triton.

CHAPTER 25: FOREVER ISN'T LONG ENOUGH

Jo

Jo isn't sulking. It's been about an hour since Shea left with the others, and she's still in Shea's room. Perhaps it's because she doesn't want to run into this new Semele and also because she can't help but wonder—what if Shea doesn't come back?

What if something happens and she's not there to help her? Her mind spins with scenarios and she feels as if she might start hyperventilating when a melody catches her attention. One her mother used to sing to her when she was a little girl. She stands from the bed in the corner of Shea's room and walks over to the balcony.

Beck is still in the gardens, but he seems more cheerful. He continues to play the flute he bought in the market, and the monkeys chatter along the grass as if singing along.

Jo makes up her mind, pushing her fears away, and heads out the door of Shea's childhood chambers and toward the music playing in the gardens. She makes it to the same doorway off the dining area and realizes she's never actually been on the garden's grounds. She'd watched from Shea's balcony, the night Shea asked her to stay on Orena; she'd slept on blankets the captain had laid out overlooking the inner gardens and had cried herself to sleep listening to Lena's trumpet trills.

A pang of sadness for the old elephant hits Jo in the chest, but she continues to venture into the beautiful garden.

Beck is sitting next to the sparkling pond, no longer with his legs pulled up against his chest but instead sitting cross-legged.

Jo realizes he's watching Caeruleus, who is swooping down from the trees surrounding the water and splashing Beck with his feathers playfully.

Every time he misses, he yowls in frustration and Beck plays a particularly loud note in retaliation before going back to the familiar melody.

He hasn't noticed Jo yet and she smiles as she hears the beginning of the song start to play.

"There were four cities / along the old trident road."

Jo sings the first two lyrics of the song, and Beck startles slightly, but he continues to play, smiling the best he can with the flute to his lips, encouraging her to sing the rest.

She clears her throat; she knows she doesn't have the best voice, if Beck's chuckles are anything to go by, but she thinks of her mom, imagining Triteia's voice.

He begins to play the beginning part of the song again and Jo sits down next to him and hums the first couple notes.

There were four cities,
Along the old Trident road.
It 'twas a pity,
Divided by code.

One day a great queen rose,
The ocean lord's gem.
They promised at the willow
And the el-vens did wept.

For the empire saw it,
And slayed the great queen.
It 'twas a pity,
United they would have been.

Now there are four cities,
Along the old Trident road.
It 'tis a pity,
Still divided by code.

Beck plays the last of the melody before dropping the flute onto his lap.

Caeruleus swoops down one last time and finally manages to swipe enough water at Beck, splashing him in the face.

"Caeruleus!"

Caeruleus yowls in delight and flies in through the open doorway out of the gardens and to the rest of the house.

"I think you pissed off the Lionbird." Jo laughs, and Beck wipes a hand down his face, trying to get rid of the excess water.

"Apparently," he remarks, looking over at Jo with a grin. "I didn't know anyone from Arethusa knew that song."

"It was one of my mother's favorites. The woman the song is about is my great-great-grandmother and the lord who fought against the empire for Oceanus's independence."

"A Lycon duke actually," Beck corrects but Jo doesn't mind. "But yes, he became the first governor of Oceanus. I'm a direct descendant of him. Governor Michaelan Orus of Oceanus, formerly Lycos."

"Our ancestors were lovers," Jo states and they gag at each other, laughing.

"The empire does enjoy taking things." Beck sobers, thinking of Lycos.

"Yes, it does. You know Shea and Ceto don't have a

great relationship," Jo begins to explain.

"I'm sure," Beck comments.

"We made the mistake of asking for her help once. No. I made the mistake. And it almost cost me Shea. Well," Jo laughs, "and my life. I would do anything to see Ceto fall and someone else take over Lycos."

"One of her first official acts was killing my mother."

Jo places a hand on Beck's shoulder, remembering the death of Governess Elizabetta of Oceanus.

Murdered, Jo's mind supplies.

"I'm sorry," Jo tells him.

"It was a long time ago."

Suddenly Beck laughs, startling Jo.

"What?"

"I just realized we're both orphans. Seems Shea has a pension for collecting people like us."

Jo thinks of Aster and she can't help the small laugh that escapes her as well. It would seem so.

"I couldn't say goodbye," Beck confides to Jo, standing from his place on the grass.

Jo stands as well, smoothing out her naval uniform.

"Am I the only one afraid that she might not come back? I mean, I know she can take care of herself, but the waiting, the not knowing?"

"It's almost worse than watching her die before your eyes," Jo finishes the thought for him.

"I'm sorry, I don't want to cause you more strife."

"I am afraid of losing her, if only because I haven't had the chance to become her wife. I thought at the end of this year, we'd be wed, and now I don't know if we'll survive the last of the month."

"We're going to beat him," Beck states, placing a hand on Jo's shoulder.

"Maybe." Jo nods and then a thought enters her head. "But I don't want to leave this world having not bound myself to the woman I want to be with forever. Having not proclaimed in front of the people I care about that I will honor and protect her until my last breath."

The idea is overtaking Jo's mind now. It is possible. Caen has the ability, being Shea's quartermaster by seafaring law, but…would she agree?

"Beck, would you excuse me?"

"Where are you going?"

"I have to ask someone a very important question."

Jo takes off at a run for the doorway leading into the house but is stopped when Beck calls after her.

"Jo!"

"Yes." Jo grins.

"Are you doing what I think you're going to do?"

"Perhaps. Want to help?"

Beck sighs. "No. But I will."

Jo waits at the doorway a moment for him to catch up and then she races off to find Dari.

They check the kitchens first but quickly back out the door as they find the strange woman, Semele, instead, who glares them out of the room.

They head off down the white clay halls and find a door ajar near the end, down a flight of stairs.

Jo steps out with Beck behind her and both their mouths drop as they realize they're standing in an orchard. Jo can just barely see the walls on the other side of the trees, and there's a vegetable garden growing to their left. They're in a room, but there's sunlight shining and a breeze whisking through the branches.

"I love magic." Jo smiles.

Dari is standing in the orchard with a basket, picking ripe apples and placing them in the wicker.

"Dari!" Jo calls.

The elven woman turns and waves at Jo with her right arm while holding a red apple.

"Joana, I see you found my orchard."

"This is incredible," Jo tells her as they meet each other

halfway.

Beck is still standing in the doorway with his mouth open.

"Thank you. What can I help you with? Are they back already, what's wrong?"

"No, not yet," Jo says, soothing Dari's concern.

"I need your help," Jo explains. "I want to propose to Shea. Regardless of what happens, I want to propose to her when she returns and then I want to marry her. Here on the island with you and Phoebus. I don't want to waste another second, and I don't know how much longer we'll have. So, I guess I'm asking for your blessing and your help?"

Dari is quiet; she doesn't respond, not yet.

Jo watches her face for any sign that she heard what Jo has just said, and then Jo notices her eyes glossing over, a bright smile tugging at the corners of Dari's mouth.

"You have it," Dari murmurs with deep emotion. "You have my blessing and my help. What do you need?"

"Do you think you could help me recreate that night?" Jo asks, her own eyes filling with unshed tears.

Dari laughs and hugs Jo tightly. "Who do you think helped Shea create it in the first place?"

They pull apart and Dari grabs Jo by the hand, tugging her toward the door.

"But first, you're going to need a dress, and I think I have just the thing."

CHAPTER 26:
I SEE YOU

Shea

They arrive just before nightfall. They'd reached the border fairly quickly, only having to stop once to cut down some of the foliage so that the horses could get through, but from there it had pretty much been a straight shot to Starfish Cross.

The old elven roads of Starfish Cross are paved with the same materials used to make the buildings in Port Town. The roads are filled with shimmering gems, and when you look ahead, the sun dancing off the precious stones blocks your sight from the path, obscuring your vision of what is to come.

They have to slow down the horses to avoid tripping over the jagged diamonds and other valuable stones.

But they march on, the deserts of Orena surrounding them on either side of the road for hours until they finally reach the edge of Orena's jungle at the heart of the island. The vines and tropical trees are too thick to lead the horses in, so from there they're forced to go by foot as the sun begins fading.

Phoebus and Caen tie up the horses.

Poseidon grabs two of the packs to carry with their

supplies.

Shea takes a branch from one of the jungle pathways and quickly gets to work transforming it into a torch.

There are stories, of course, of what lies within the Orena jungle but never anything truly confirmed. The only people who have returned from the temple in recorded history are insane or, not long after, dead.

They enter the jungle with Shea leading the group.

They walk for about an hour when Phoebus claims they're getting close. He started in the back but worked his way up, leaving Poseidon and Caen to talk among themselves.

Phoebus walks side by side with Shea, his sword drawn at the ready.

"Where is your sword, Shea?"

The condescension in his voice makes Shea's toes curl inside her boots. She keeps her eyes peeled on their surroundings.

The trees are huge, spanning at least fifty feet into the sky, and the plant life is so lush it's hard to see past anything but the path again. There's rustling around them but nothing has jumped out yet.

Phoebus keeps them on the path and gestures to continue moving forward. The light is waning until all that's left is the torch and diamond night sky. The moon looks huge in the openings of the treetops, as if Shea could reach out and touch it. It gives off just enough light to be of help.

"Your cousin blesses us tonight with the bright moon," Poseidon tells them all, and Shea realizes he's talking about Artemis.

Phoebus rolls his eyes.

"I don't need a sword," Shea finally answers Phoebus's earlier question, keeping her eyes on the path ahead.

Phoebus snorts. "You might be good, but everyone needs a weapon."

"I have a weapon," Shea responds evenly.

She uncorks the waterskin on her hip and summons a bit of water, slicing through a branch in their way on the path ahead before summoning it back to her flask.

"A real weapon. Suppose you get hurt, or you're unable to wield the water, then what will you do?"

There's quick movement up ahead, and Shea grabs her dagger from her boot and throws it with perfect precision, stabbing a snake straight through its head before it's able to strike Phoebus.

"How about that?"

Shea walks over and picks up the dagger, wiping the serpent's blood on her pants.

Phoebus grumbles and keeps moving.

The farther in they go, the darker it gets, and so Caen stops to light a torch of his own. They're getting closer, Shea can feel her magic drawing her in.

"So, who was the immortal you saw years before?"

"What?" Phoebus snaps and Shea actually jumps at his ferocity.

"The immortal you saw. That made you think this could be Triton?"

"Oh," Phoebus replies, "a woman. Can't remember who."

"Okay, what is wrong with you?"

Shea has had it with his attitude.

"What do you mean?"

"From the moment I got here, you have been a pain in my ass. Is it Semele? I told you I would have taken her to the mainland."

"What? No."

"Then what?"

Phoebus stops and glares at Shea, who glares right back, not standing down.

"Gods. You're just like your father!"

"You barely know my father," Shea retorts.

"Barely? I practically raised him! Your father is Paetre.

Not some absent god who decides to drop into your life and change you into something else," Phoebus shouts.

Shea chokes, understanding filtering into her brain.

Phoebus completely deflates, all the angry energy and the tough-guy act dissipating; he starts to look more like the man who helped raise her.

"Phoebus. Of course Paetre is my father, just like you're practically my grandfather, old man." Shea laughs, poking him.

"Watch it," he warns but Shea can tell he's kidding.

"When you sent the letter explaining you were coming, you called Poseidon…father. And my pride got in the way. It felt like he was claiming you. And then you needed to find your brother, and suddenly, you had family. Blood family. I worried Dari and I couldn't compete, not when your real father is a god. And then with Paetre gone, I just felt like I needed to compete for him."

"Phoebus, you're my family. You and Dari, and Caen and Paetre—Dad. I love you all with my very being, and at first I hated him." Shea looks back at Poseidon, who has somehow managed to get Caen to start conversing with him.

"But then, I can't hate him to make you feel better. But I will reinforce that he will never replace you guys, or Paetre, as my family. He's just an addition to who I am."

Phoebus reaches his hand out and Shea takes it without question. He squeezes.

"I really am glad to see you, my girl."

"I know," Shea responds, and as they break through a clearing, Shea gasps as the center of the jungle opens up.

A giant stone structure with incredible pillars down the sides stands before the four of them.

Caen and Poseidon find themselves beside Shea and Phoebus.

Stone steps lead up to two giant gold doors with carvings of mythological battle scenes. The architecture looks ancient, and none of the vines from the neighboring trees have touched the temple.

While the architecture dates it, the building is so clean it looks as if it was built yesterday.

There are torches leading up the walkway to the golden doors and the fire is blue.

"An immortal is within the temple," Poseidon states, gesturing to the blue fire. "The torches only light themselves when a god is within the temple."

"But is it Triton?" Shea asks.

"I think so," Poseidon replies and then growls, "It's like I can feel him, but the source of my magic is so far, I'm not strong enough to sense and confirm."

"But maybe I can," Shea murmurs. "Father, you said you're the source of mine and my siblings' magic. That you're stronger near us, but we're stronger near you. Can I sense and confirm it's him somehow?"

"Possibly," Poseidon answers.

She walks closer to him, handing her torch off to Phoebus, who takes it.

"What do I do?"

"Close your eyes, go back to the place where you unlocked your magic."

Shea closes her eyes and pictures herself in the room again, but this time the door to her magic is open, flowing within the room itself. It's no longer dark. A skylight highlights the door. Her magic dances around the room like the lights in the north sky she saw once, as a child on a northern voyage with Paetre.

"Okay, now imagine a link of some sort to that familiar feeling you had on the island when we arrived, when you thought you sensed him."

Shea focuses on the familiar energy around her, and back in the room another door appears, this one already open. It has water inside, heavy tumultuous water and also light bubbles like sea-foam, creatures swim within the deep, and when she touches her hand to the water, her father's face flashes before her eyes.

Poseidon laughs deeply. "That's me. My magic."

Shea chuckles, letting her hand reach inside the water, and she notices her own magic brightens in intensity as she connects with her father's magic.

"Alright, alright," Poseidon says, but Shea can hear the smile in his voice.

Shea pulls her hand out of the open door and looks around the room, searching for that feeling she's had in the back of her mind all day. On the other side of her magical door is a closed one.

Dark, murky blue magic swirls at the edges of the door frame. The door shakes from the power built up behind it. Shea can hear whispers around the edges, escaping from the small spaces in between.

"Thetis!"

"Perses, don't!"

"I'm sorry...I'm sorry...I'm sorry..."

She's never heard this voice before, she cautiously steps closer to the door, her hand going to the knob.

"I think I see it," Shea tells them.

Her hand clasps the handle, and as she touches it, a whole slew of emotions that aren't her own flood into her body. She gasps. Pain, fear, guilt, all of it runs her over like a carriage hitting her at full speed.

"Get out!"

Shea is physically flung backward by the force of the magic keeping her out. She opens her eyes to find herself on her back on the ground, staring up at Poseidon, Phoebus, and Caen all crowding around her.

"Shea?" Phoebus shouts, panicked, checking her over for any visible signs of injuries.

Caen throws out his hand and pulls her up off the ground.

"What the Underdeep happened?" Caen asks.

Shea brushes the dirt off her clothes, taking a moment

to catch her breath.

"Well, he knows we're here. But yeah, I think it's Triton," Shea says dryly, looking up at Poseidon with a raised brow.

"He's still got a lot of power in him, with me out and your and Perses's powers growing, it doesn't matter that the gates of Atlantis are closed."

"Because you're our power source and Atlantis and your trident are yours," Shea questions, "right?"

"We'll talk about it later. We found him, but first we have to get through the temple into the inner sanctum where the immortal garden is."

"Right," Caen announces with obvious sarcasm, "this should be fun."

Shea groans as she takes a step and leads the group down the path and up the stairs to the large golden doors.

The doors are massive, with incredible scenes of a battle fought long ago. It's not just Poseidon, Triton, and other sea deities on it though.

Shea has seen depictions of the air god Zeus before in other parts of Nereid and especially on other continents and islands. It looks as if the big six are on there, the original children of Kronos, the titan.

"What is this?"

Shea turns to Poseidon, and his face is a mixture of emotions. Pain, anger, and regret stand out among the many.

"The Titan War. The door should respond to our touch and open."

He doesn't say much more.

"Are your siblings alive? I mean, are they godly still or more like you?"

Poseidon chuckles darkly. "Most of us are still around. It's been a millennium since we were truly needed. So many of us integrated among the humans. Some have been able to become mortal while others simply fade or remain on the outskirts trapped in immortality. I haven't seen my other siblings in a very long time, nor most of my nieces and nephews. Those with varying skills didn't need to push day-to-day people around anymore. You mortals started doing a lot on your own, and many of us became obsolete."

"Great history lesson. Think we can get this door open now?" Caen gripes, pulling his hammer off his back.

Shea slams her elbow into his gut.

Poseidon is mumbling to himself and it seems to cover Caen's wheezing; he doesn't notice the interaction.

Poseidon places his palms on the temple doors, and they shake with effort, as if trying to open for the king of the sea. The eerie blue fire from the torches glows brighter, and it casts a frightening sheen on the scenes of the Titan War, like the carvings are watching them.

"Shea, I…" Poseidon begins, but Shea doesn't need him to finish.

She places her palms on the door beside him, and the door rumbles a little more before a loud screeching noise fills the clearing. The door presses back into the darkness of the temple and opens grandly for their small group.

Shea takes the torch from Phoebus and waves it forward into the darkness. Torches on either side of the entry hall spark with blue fire, brightening the room while casting a ghostly light, making the shadows flicker menacingly on the marble walls.

The entry hall is huge.

Shea can't see the end as it's still dark. They take one step inside and more torches light automatically for them.

"Okay. Everyone ready?"

"No," Phoebus groans, but he's the first one truly inside.

"Phoebus!" Shea whispers harshly.

He walks around the entryway, almost dancing along the floor.

"Well, I haven't been impaled by a magical spear, so I'd say we don't have to worry about booby traps just yet."

Shea sighs in relief.

"Alright, then."

They enter the temple, and as soon as all four of them clear the entryway, the doors close behind them.

Caen groans.

"We're dead."

CHAPTER 27: KEEP THE FAITH

Shea

"You said there was only one test," Caen shouts, leaning up against the wall and trying to catch his breath after the last disciple test they'd all just had to go through.

"Did I?"

"That makes two, Poseidon. We find another and I'm throwing you into the trap," Phoebus growls, storming toward the sea god with his sword in hand.

Shea steps in between them, patting herself down in case her hair wasn't the only part that got singed from the last test. Literally walking through fire. There was a pattern and timing of course, but Phoebus hadn't been fast enough, and Shea was the lucky girl behind him—providing a nice little burnt trim off the edges of her hair as a fire column had blasted out of the floor.

Before that, their first test had been solving a riddle. And surprise, surprise the answer had been water. Good thing they'd gotten it right too because Shea could feel about a lake of water behind the wall to their left that probably would have drowned them all had they gotten the answer wrong.

"*Are* there any more tests ahead?" Shea asks as she straightens and takes a glance at her surroundings.

They're in another stone chamber much like the one before, but it extends down a hall to another room. Torches are lit at certain intervals and it casts a blue glow on the stone, making it look like moving water. The hall narrows a bit, so they'll have to walk in single file, but the structure still looks brand new.

The magic is stronger in here, and she can sense her brother's magic trying to ward them off.

"It's been a while since I've been here," Poseidon points out.

Caen glares at him, tapping his hammer on the palm of his hand.

"Perhaps one more. Our culture does have a thing about threes."

"Air, water, and fire," Shea comments, thinking about her father and his two siblings, Zeus and Hades.

Well then, one could argue they had passed the test for water, and Hades was probably the fire they just walked through, leaving only air.

"I believe him," Shea remarks, taking a torch from the wall, her original having burned up in the previous chamber.

"Of course, you do," Phoebus growls, following behind her.

Caen and Poseidon take up the rear.

As they get closer to the next room, Shea spots a strange symbol over the arched frame; it looks like a lightning bolt. She steps into the new chamber and her eyes widen upon seeing what is inside. The torches light as she enters the room, and in the center is a large black hole.

There's a door on the other side of the chasm, but there doesn't seem to be a way across. Phoebus peeks around and places his hands on his hips, staring at their new test.

Finally, Poseidon and Caen shuffle in.

The door slams behind them, startling everyone in the

group. Caen latches his hammer to his back holster and tries pushing the door back open.

"No luck," Caen groans, putting all his weight up against the door, but still it doesn't budge.

"I guess we'll just have to find a way across," Poseidon states.

Shea takes a step toward the dark hole; she waves the torch over it, but it's like the darkness absorbs the pale light. She looks around the lit room and decides to give it a shot. She drops the torch into the hole.

It lights the way down for a few seconds and then disappears into the black. She doesn't hear a clatter from the floor either.

"It's too far to jump, even for me," Caen says, examining the chasm.

They're all at the edge, staring down into the darkness.

Phoebus puts his foot out, tapping the air like he's looking for something solid, but Poseidon has to reach out and grab him when he almost falls in.

"Phoebus, I could…"

"No," Phoebus responds, effectively cutting Caen off with a scowl.

Caen shuts his mouth and starts looking around the room at anything other than Phoebus's glare.

Shea has to slap a hand over her mouth, so Phoebus doesn't hear her giggle.

"No one is throwing me, not now, not again, and no one is getting thrown plain and simple, so. Mister almighty? How in Hades do we get across this thing?"

She nearly breaks when she sees Poseidon's lips squish together as he holds back his own chuckle.

Her father clears his throat and opens his mouth to answer when he stops. He's staring at something across the room and Shea turns and looks just in time to see a torch go out.

"Well?" Phoebus prompts.

Poseidon shushes him and Shea's eyes widen as another torch goes out and another.

Caen turns as well, seeing the slight panic on their faces, and he audibly swallows as the last of the torches goes out on the far side of the room, leaving it in darkness.

Phoebus on the other hand isn't paying any attention; his back is to the darkness and instead he's practically growling at Poseidon.

"Real mature! I can't believe you shushed me; you know, buddy, I've got a mind to cut you down to my size and deck you right in the—"

"Phoebus!" Shea shouts.

"What?"

Phoebus looks over at Shea with an arched brow, but he doesn't turn all the way. Instead he's staring at the wall with the door they came through.

"Ugh, guys?"

Caen, Poseidon, and Shea all turn slowly back the way they came in and are surprised to find two circles about the size of a ship's cabin window on either side of the locked exit.

Shea takes a step closer to the one on the right and as soon as her foot hits the floor, it begins.

Air shoots from the two new circular vents in the wall and it's enough to knock them all off their feet.

Phoebus goes flying backward, and Poseidon manages to grab him by the back of his shirt before he goes over the cliff and down into the chasm.

Shea is holding on tightly to a lip of stone on the floor, and Poseidon and Caen are doing the same.

The wind becomes harsher, she can feel her fingers slipping, she's losing her grip.

The last of the torches on this side of the room are going out.

"What happened to the other torches?" Phoebus calls out over the wind, finally noticing the darkness on the other side of the room.

Caen groans to Shea's right as he tries to hang on.

"We've got to get to the edge of the room and out of these wind tunnels."

Shea nods in agreement as Caen starts sliding to the right, and she looks over and sees Poseidon begin crawling to the left as he holds on to Phoebus.

Shea slowly inches her way to the right after Caen, her fingers trying to hold on to the small lip on the floor. But her foot slips and she's sliding backward toward the chasm. The wind is even stronger now, and it's got her over the edge, her hands scraping at the floor. She can feel the stone tearing at her palms.

Poseidon and Phoebus call after her, but they're not close enough to catch her.

Her boots can't find a grip, and the next thing she knows, half her body is over the cliff and she's about to fall into the chasm when a strong hand reaches out and grabs her hand.

Caen roars at the effort of trying to hold himself back from the edge against the wind while trying to keep Shea from going completely over.

She can feel his body slipping toward the chasm, and she's too far down now to grab the edge with her other hand. All that's keeping her from the darkness is Caen's strength.

"Caen," Shea shouts over the roar of the wind.

"I'm not letting you go; I'm going to pull you up!"

He tries to bring her up, at least enough to grab the ledge, but the air pushes against him with more force and she can feel it. She's dragging him down.

"Caen, it's okay."

"Somebody get over here and help me," Caen commands, but Poseidon and Phoebus are too far away, and it'd take them too long to crawl over.

"I'm not going to let you fall," Caen growls.

"There's nothing you can do," Shea tells him.

Tears are gathering at the corners of her eyes.

Is this how she dies? Not by Perses's hand or Ceto's? Not with her ship. She's pulling him down, she has to let go.

Shea uses her core strength and puts her feet on the chasm wall, it pulls Caen forward a little more, but she needs the footing to pull her hand out of his grip.

She won't let him die for her.

"Help us!" Caen yells again to Phoebus and Poseidon.

Shea opens her mouth to tell him he has to let go when a pain rips through her head. She cries out, clutching her hand to her forehead as she sees Triton's closed door in her mind shuddering. There's a pull toward the door and she feels it pinning her down.

"I have to go down," Shea whispers aloud.

The wind is too loud for Caen to hear, so instead she shouts out louder, "Caen let go!"

"No! I won't, not ever!"

"It's going to be okay, but I need you to let go. Trust me! I think Triton is down here!"

"What's she saying?" Shea hears Poseidon shout.

"She thinks Triton is in the chasm. It's too dangerous! I'm pulling you up," Caen tells her.

"Caen. Please, trust me."

Shea starts pulling her hand from his grip, but he holds on tighter.

"Shea, stop it!" Caen growls, but Shea keeps pulling. "Bloody Underdeep, Shea!"

Shea looks up at Caen and smiles fondly. "I can feel it, Caen."

"You girls and your bloody feelings," he mutters and lets go.

He lets go of the stone holding them up, and they both fall into the darkness together.

***

"Shea?"

Shea is back inside her mind, back in the room with all

the doors, and is it just her or are there more doors now?

Doors with symbols of shells, and tridents, and women with red hair. A flash of a woman with the most beautiful red hair fills her vision, the intricate details of her face blurred from Shea's mind.

"Shea?"

Something's shaking her; her head rolls to the side and as she opens her eyes, she sees Mariner's dead face staring at her. She gasps, choking—she can't catch her breath.

Pieces of his silver-blond hair are stuck to his wide-open eyes, the same as the day Jo stabbed him through, but this time those eyes don't stay open forever, this time they blink. His bloodied face grins at her with menace.

"You should have stayed dead," Mariner growls, blood sputtering from his mouth.

"Shea!"

Shea coughs, finally able to catch her breath as she sits up in Caen's arms, groaning from the force of impact where she landed on her back.

Her eyes wander over to where Mariner was lying next to her, but all she finds is empty grass.

Grass?

Now that the visions have passed, she takes a look around her.

Caen is checking her over for other injuries, but she quickly waves him off.

She attempts to stand but falls almost immediately backward.

Luckily Caen is there to catch her.

"Easy," he tells her.

Shea nods, laying her head against his chest for a moment just to catch her breath.

Wherever they are, it reminds her of the gardens in Arethusa. The ones infused with magic. Giant trees that appear to be made of coral tower over them, along with palm trees, but instead of coconuts they have pearls clutched near the top. The grass is glowing a soft, pale blue. Shea lifts her hand from its spot and a vague glowing impression is left behind. Above them is the dark chasm; they must have either fallen a long way and somehow survived or magic obstructed their view from up above. Shea sees the torch she dropped lying nearby.

Tan stone is scattered around the grass, as if this huge area used to be built inside but was overtaken by the exotic, glowing sea plants.

She looks around the strange chasm tunnel that goes up and then to the right inside the temple. She can see the night sky up above. This must be the sacred gardens Poseidon mentioned at the center of the temple. The light from the moon and stars are bright, but there are also random tall torches positioned at various points of the garden lit with the same blue fire from before.

Large marble columns lay in the distance and closer ones to their left, they must line the courtyard garden. The plant life is so thick she can't see the other side of this place.

A strange high-pitched noise fills the air, and Shea and Caen turn to the hole they came out of before Caen quickly starts pulling Shea away.

He drags her away from the drop site, and just in time too, as Poseidon lands on the grass back-first, and Phoebus lands on top of him.

There's an audible grunt from Poseidon as Phoebus slams into his stomach.

"Phoebus!" Shea shouts, forcing herself to her feet, albeit a bit wobblily.

She pulls him off of Poseidon and lays him softly on his back on the luminescent grass.

"Oh yeah, I'm fine," Poseidon wheezes, clutching his stomach.

"You're immortal," Shea snaps, and Poseidon waves her off.

Phoebus groans but he's awake.

"I think I broke something," he gasps, and Shea feels around his upper body until she looks down at his legs.

His right leg is twisted in an awkward position.

Shea reaches down, lightly feeling, and Phoebus barks a curse as her gentle fingers graze across his broken bone.

"Shit," Shea grumbles.

"Broken?" Caen asks.

Shea nods her head and goes to Poseidon, who luckily managed to hold on to the two supply bags he brought.

"We're going to need to make a splint," Shea orders.

Shea rummages through the supply bag and comes across some bandages; Caen grabs a sturdy stick nearby and brings it over.

"Can you set it?" Shea asks Caen.

Poseidon has managed to turn over; he's got his hand wrapped around his stomach but otherwise he looks okay.

Phoebus's face has gone a little pale from the pain.

"Only if I wanted to take his leg off," Caen chuckles. "We'll need Nol or Jo's delicate hands and expertise for this."

"Okay then, let's bind it. Can you carry him?"

"Please don't," Phoebus groans. "I'll get up."

He struggles against the two sets of hands before finally giving up.

"We need to go," Poseidon reminds them, looking around cautiously.

"In a minute," Shea tells him, and Poseidon looks like he might argue.

Shea turns her back on him before he can, helping Caen set up the splint, and soon he's got Phoebus in his arms.

Shea draws her water from the waterskin, scanning the perimeter, but she doesn't see any movement.

Caen gestures for Poseidon to take his hammer.

"I don't need it," Poseidon replies, but Caen doesn't take no for an answer.

"Take it, I don't see you carrying a water pouch, and Shea's proven she's magically stronger, so if I can't protect her right now because I've got him, then I need you to do it for me," Caen states, ignoring the glare Poseidon shoots his way.

"She didn't—" Poseidon starts but Phoebus cuts him off.

"She did," Phoebus gripes.

"Guys. Triton is somewhere in here, and I have a feeling he knows we're here too. And he's not happy about it, so I need the three of you working together so your son doesn't kill us," Shea commands, drawing up to her full height. "Understood?"

"Yes."

"Yes, Captain."

Phoebus nods.

"Good," Shea states.

She sees a trail with a torch leading into the heavier plant foliage. It looks worn down, as if someone has used it repeatedly and recently.

Shea finally notices a water source near their drop site. A pool of sparkling water, where she thinks she sees fish swimming.

"This way," Shea says and leads the party farther into the garden with Caen and Phoebus in the middle and Poseidon holding up the rear with Caen's hammer.

The trees reach high into the sky, obscuring their view of the pillars and the clearing where they landed. Torches are planted along the way, lighting the area for them to see. The path reminds Shea of the shell pathway in the Arethusian gardens, ground down until they're soft and smooth to walk barefoot upon. Strange chattering noises and beautiful birdcalls span the treetops. Shea looks down where she steps, and her footprint appears in the luminescence before fading away. Gorgeous plants of purple, orange, and white are scattered on both sides of the path; periodically Shea can see the marble columns through the plants, and she knows they're getting closer to the other side of the courtyard, and hopefully, closer to Triton.

Multiple paths break off from this one, going off into all sides of the gardens, but something tells her to stay on the straight path.

Shea thinks she can see the edge of this incredible garden and the pillars are so close, they've almost made it to the other side.

They break into a second clearing and this one has a stunning fountain in the center.

The fountain is a carving of a gorgeous man in a chariot drawn by dolphins, a crown sits upon his stone head, and he's holding the reins to the chariot in one hand and a conch shell in the other, lifted to the sky.

The conch shell is spurting out a column of water, falling into a glittering pool the statue stands within.

If they can get through this clearing, Shea thinks, they'll be on the other side of the courtyard finally.

A strange clicking sound stops her in her place. It catches her off guard and reminds her of someone's nails, impatiently tapping against a wooden surface.

"Do you hear that?" Shea mutters, and she looks back at her companions, who all nod.

Shea takes a step toward the clearing exit and something akin to hissing erupts from that direction.

"We're not alone," Poseidon states, tightening his grip on Caen's hammer.

Caen, Poseidon, and Shea all retreat together slowly until their backs are to one another.

Phoebus is struggling to get out of Caen's grip so he can help.

"What is it?" Phoebus asks.

As he does, something huge bursts from the clearing's perimeter.

A loud snapping sound rings in Shea's ears and she practically chokes on her tongue as an impossibly large crab comes barreling toward her.

The creature is big. A normal crab that seems to have

grown ten times its small size. Its shell is a dark blue, and some kind of moss is growing on its limbs and body.

It creeps toward the group, snapping its claws violently, its black eyes reminding Shea of a giant spider.

It hisses as it races forward, and Shea quickly moves into a correct stance and blasts the crab back using her magic.

She uses the water from her bag, but it's not enough force; the crab takes another few steps forward.

Shea throws out her left hand, summoning a wave of water from the fountain and slamming it into the side of the monster, throwing it off-kilter, and it almost topples over. Almost.

Another giant crab bursts through the other side of the clearing. It clicks something at the other crab, who clicks back and then starts running at the group.

Poseidon lets out a loud battle cry and slams Caen's hammer into the creature's face, sending it flying backward.

Caen laughs, caught off guard by Poseidon's strength.

"Let me down, you giant oaf, I'll break their shells in two," Phoebus shouts, trying to unholster his sword, but Caen holds him back.

Shea's crab is back at her again, charging toward her with more speed. She summons more water from the fountain to her side, bringing it up behind her. She pictures the water crystallizing and molding until she opens her eyes and finds icicles all around her. She pushes her hands forward and the icicles go slamming into the crab.

Most of them break on impact on the crab's shell, but she focuses a few at its legs, especially the joints, breaking off two in the process.

The creature screams in pain, collapsing in on itself.

"That's my girl," Phoebus praises.

Caen hollers in approval and Shea turns just in time to see Poseidon beating the other crab back. It's clearly wounded, and he seems to be going in for the killing blow when he's blasted backward off his feet by a column of water.

Shea whips her head around at Caen's shocked expression to find a man standing in the clearing with his hands outstretched. His face is solemn and covered in a short beard, his hair is a copper brown, and his eyes are so blue he looks blind. His face is familiar, as if she's known him all along, and there's an angle to his jaw that reminds her of the red-haired woman she saw in her vision when she landed.

Shea summons some water from the fountain to her side, getting into a fighting stance, but he simply turns on her, staring at her firmly.

He straightens himself up, his body lean but obviously muscular; it reminds Shea of a soldier.

His clothes are strange. His pants curve tightly to his frame with cord wrapped around the pant leg bottoms and he's barefoot. His shirt is short sleeved and there's a hood connected on the back. It seems to be made of some sort of leather. His ears are pointed, so maybe he's an elven priest who's somehow survived here all these years? Maybe he knows where Triton is.

The man allows his right hand to drop to his side and uses his left to snap his fingers.

Shea's bending falls away right in front of her. Her eyes widen in alarm and she tries to summon it back, but something is holding the water down; she can't pull it from the ground.

Poseidon sits up from where he landed from the blast, seeing the younger man standing before all four of them.

"Triton," Poseidon greets.

Shea's mouth drops open.

"Father. I'll thank you not to kill my crabs," Triton states, his hands going to his hips.

"They tried to kill us first." Shea scowls, not liking his superior attitude.

He doesn't respond, his eyes merely scan her frame. Once he's finished examining her, he rolls his eyes, much to

Shea's distaste, before turning back to Poseidon.

"I'm only going to ask you this once. What in Hades do you want?"

CHAPTER 28: BROTHER'S KEEPER

Shea

After their confrontation with Triton's pets, he leads them back to his makeshift camp up against the pillars and inner wall. A cloth canopy connected to three trees stretches over a cot, a firepit with cooking utensils and pots, a table with varying tools on it, and a rather modest living space.

The crabs follow behind them, and Triton shows Caen to his cot, allowing Phoebus to be placed down and cared for much to his complaint.

Shea stays close to Poseidon, watching Triton with fair interest but wariness. He obviously has a problem with their father, and apparently Shea.

Once Phoebus is settled, Triton picks up a clay bowl that has fish and vegetables inside. He brings it over to the firepit and lays the fish on a flat stone that he's heated over the fire.

Shea snorts as she realizes he's cooking dinner for himself.

"Triton," Poseidon begins, but Shea's immortal half brother quickly cuts him off.

"No."

"You said you'd listen," Shea snaps, taking a step toward him, but Poseidon holds her back.

"Oh, I'm sorry, go ahead, ask what you want," Triton sarcastically drawls, keeping all of his attention on the fish.

The giant crabs shuffle off into the garden, out of sight, and Shea notices Caen hasn't put his hammer away as he stays by Phoebus's side.

"Quit your mothering, I'm fine, Caen," Phoebus complains, slapping Caen's fussing hands away from his injured leg.

Triton pours some water into a pot over the fire and lets it simmer, periodically adding strange plant life to the concoction as it starts to boil.

Poseidon carefully walks over and takes a seat next to his son, watching him cook.

Shea sits on the opposite side of the pit, waiting for Poseidon to explain, but when he finally speaks, it's different from what Shea expects him to say.

"I need my net. You have it, don't you?"

Shea raises a brow, confused at the statement.

Triton understands perfectly though, and he chuckles coldly. "Right. Didn't have time to grab your trident before you shut the gates? I thought I sensed him. Perses is on the mainland then?"

"You knew Perses was back?" Shea growls, but Triton ignores her question.

She's just about to knock his cooking fish on the ground when he abruptly stands, scooping some of the boiling water out of the pot into a clay cup.

He takes the hot liquid over to Phoebus and Caen. He starts to hand it to Phoebus, but Caen grabs him by the wrist, stopping him. It spills some of the boiling water onto Triton's hand.

Triton winces but keeps his voice steady as he speaks, "It's a pain reliever. It'll also kick-start the healing process."

Triton takes a sip of the drink to show Caen it's okay,

and Caen takes it from him.

Phoebus sits there watching the whole exchange warily.

Caen smells it, takes a sip, gags a little at the taste, but it seems to be enough for him. He hands it to Phoebus to make him drink it.

"I just saw your face; I'm not drinking that!"

Caen grabs him by the neck, steadying him.

"I don't need it, you bloody pest!"

But Caen forces it down anyway, and Phoebus coughs from the heat of the liquid.

"There, I drank it. I don't feel any...any...different," Phoebus mumbles and promptly passes out on the cot.

"You're welcome," Triton mutters, but Caen ignores him, checking Phoebus's pulse just in case.

Triton returns to the pit and turns his fish to cook the other side.

"I didn't know for sure, but I could feel his magic. His door became visible again in my mind, and more powerful, so I assumed it was because he was alive and had my shell," Triton answers, and Shea realizes he's finally talking to her.

She notes that he also sees mental doors in connection to magic but pushes away the familiarity.

"Why didn't you come back then? You must have known we'd need you!"

"You don't need me," Triton tells her.

He takes the fish off the stone and takes it to the table with the variety of tools. One of the giant crabs enters the camp carrying leaves in its claw.

It hands the leaves to Triton, who takes them gently, brushing his hand along the claw in a soothing gesture. The crab chitters happily and creeps back into the garden.

Her brother picks up a rather large knife and begins to slice the fish into pieces. He lays each piece onto a leaf and Shea realizes then that they're plates. He takes two once he's done and gives one to Caen, then lays the other next to

Phoebus.

Caen, surprised by the gesture, actually thanks him, which the god doesn't respond to.

Triton goes back for the other leaves.

"And before you say it," Triton continues his earlier comment, "he doesn't either."

He hands the leaf to Poseidon, barely looking at him.

"He's here for something far more valuable than his immortal son, dear sister," Triton chuckles and hands Shea a leaf with her own slice of fish on it.

"You know who I am," Shea murmurs.

She notices that there isn't a slice left for Triton and yet he sits back down in front of the pit, stoking the fire.

"Easily, you look like…"

Poseidon cuts him off quickly, "Her mother. Triton knew Ami when she was elected to the elven council years ago, isn't that right?"

Triton raises a brow, but he doesn't object to Poseidon's interruption. "Sure."

Shea wants to ask him more about her mother, but unfortunately that has to wait. She picks a little at the fish before setting it down.

"Triton, you're not…"

"What you expected?"

"Yes," Shea agrees.

"Sorry to disappoint, but I'm still the same monster I always was, and if that helps you explain why I'm not going to get involved, that's fine with me."

"Perhaps we should start over," Poseidon attempts, but Triton laughs harshly in response.

"You're a thousand years too late."

"Look, the reason we came is because our father says we need you to defeat Perses. You're the only one who can take back control of your shell."

"The only one? Is that what you told them?" Triton asks.

"What do you mean?" Caen questions, standing.

He lumbers his large frame over, stopping behind Poseidon.

"Meaning, I'm a minor god. He's the king of the sea. He has total control of the shell just as I did because he made it for me many years ago, or well, he used to."

"Poseidon?" Shea says, trying to get him to look at her.

"I did, yes. But I can't take it from him now; I've been without a power source too long."

"Because you shut the gates and cut your power. Left your trident behind too, and I'm sure you were banking on your last resource. Who knew little brother could be so powerful for a mortal?" Triton spits.

"I was caught off guard, he used your shell to recruit the Merrow, and there aren't as many gods in Atlantis as there once were," Poseidon growls back.

"And whose fault is that?" Triton stands, anger coursing through his muscled frame. "I wondered why you opened your door. A year ago, on Tenaro, I summoned a tidal wave, just like that." Triton snaps his fingers. "I've never felt so powerful."

"Then you don't need my net."

"I don't have it." Triton smirks.

The clearing goes quiet. No one speaks, and Shea turns to see Poseidon's face clouding with anger, his eyes a shade so blue they look like they're glowing.

Shea stands slowly, and Poseidon does as well.

He lunges at Triton, practically picking him up off the ground by his shirt.

"What?"

"I lost it. Somewhere off Tenaro when I was fighting to escape," Triton tells him.

Poseidon is practically shaking with fury. He drops Triton to the ground, and he lands next to the firepit, knocking down the pot of boiling water. Poseidon kicks the pot, sending it flying to the other side of the camp with a shout.

He walks away with his hands on his hips.

"Hades, Triton! How could you be so careless?"

"I don't understand," Shea speaks, breaking up this argument between Triton and their father.

Caen is watching this whole exchange with his arms across his chest, studying Poseidon with a new ferocity.

"Why do you need this net? We found Triton, he can take control of the shell and defeat Perses," Shea recounts everything Poseidon has been telling her for the last week and a half.

"Oh, he didn't tell you. He didn't tell you anything." Triton shrugs, then stands and brushes the dirt off his clothes.

"I'm broken." Triton opens his arms wide like he's showing off why. "He banished me after I trained Perses and Perses tried to kill him. He banished me to Tenaro with his magical net as powerful as his trident. An anchor, which he needs, by the way, to restore his power, his last resource, to grant him enough strength to open the gates of Atlantis so he can return home. That's why he brought you all here."

"What is he talking about?"

"He closed the gates because he needed the power to banish Perses from the realm of the gods. But once he did that, he locked off his power supply from Perses and himself."

"Atlantis and the trident," Caen says, piecing this together much more quickly than Shea is.

"Right. I like you." Triton grins. "The net, like the trident, is his physical power as king, one touch and he'd be as powerful as he is when the gates are open, he'd have the ability to open the gates and return to Atlantis. Maybe he'd kill Perses for you. Maybe he wouldn't. Because in the end, he'd be back where he belongs. And he could lock off the Underdeep from the mortal world for good. That sum it up, Dad?"

Shea can feel her stomach turning.

"Tell me it isn't true," she commands, staring at her father's back. "Tell me this wasn't some wild goose chase to get you here. Tell me you didn't use me," Shea hisses, pulling her dagger from her lower back holster.

Poseidon stands with his back to the group, his hands on his hips much like Triton had done earlier.

"I would have killed him before I went back," Poseidon explains, but his voice turns into a background drawl as Shea's chest shudders.

"Could you have killed him before, on your own? Before Beck lost his father, before we lost Tero?" Shea rasps, her stomach churning.

"No," Poseidon objects, turning to face them all. "Well, maybe. Perhaps I could have summoned the shell, but it wouldn't have given me enough power to open the gates; it wasn't a guaranteed defeat. Venus and I searched for another way to open the gates but there wasn't one. I had hoped to get my net before we came to you, but it wasn't possible. I needed one of my children to get across the Old Sea alive. I wasn't sure you'd help me without…motivation. I assumed it'd still be with Triton. I needed more power to guarantee my return to Atlantis before Perses was defeated, otherwise I'm trapped here."

"So, everything you said about only a child of Poseidon could kill another child of Poseidon?"

Triton bursts out laughing, and Shea glares at him.

"Well okay, shame on you for believing that."

"So all of this was a waste of time?" Caen roars, taking his hammer off his back.

"Not exactly," Shea answers for Poseidon. "Because you definitely can't kill him now, you wouldn't even stand a chance against him."

Poseidon looks away, ashamed.

Shea can't stand it anymore; she throws her dagger, and Poseidon cries out as it enters his upper right shoulder. She's careful with her aim so that it doesn't hit anything important, but it hurts.

"Because without that net, and all the time wasted,

you're practically mortal now in strength. Right?" Shea snarls.

Poseidon lands on his knees, pulling the dagger out of his shoulder, and sighs, "Yes."

Shea curses and runs a hand through her hair.

Caen nearly throws his hammer.

"Underdeep," Caen growls. "We need to get back, now."

"We're not going anywhere," Shea commands, and Caen looks at her, confused.

"He can't defeat Perses, and I certainly am no match for him on my own. But we draw our power from our father like he draws his power from his trident or net, so the most powerful child of Poseidon is standing right next to us and he can still destroy Perses and take control of the shell," Shea explains and points at Triton.

Triton slow claps. "Well done. Perhaps you're not as slow as I thought."

"We don't stand a chance without you," Shea tells him.

"You're absolutely right. I am your only hope."

"So, will you help us?"

"No," Triton states.

He begins to turn away, and Shea makes a decision that she knows is wrong. She made a promise, but she doesn't see another way. So, she admits a secret that isn't hers to tell and she hopes she won't regret it.

"You have a son," Shea tells him with a wince.

Poseidon looks up in surprise, clutching his wounded shoulder.

Triton stops and looks back at Shea.

"What?"

"You have a son. Maybe you remember a woman by the name of Thetis. She had your son after you left her."

"The child survived," Triton breathes out, his face contorting with what looks like pain.

"You knew?" Caen asks.

"I saw her right before she was banished, and I felt the

babe growing inside. I'd never sired a demigod before, and it made me...feel. I tried to find her after she left Erebos, but she disappeared, and I never knew what happened to her. I found what I figured was humanity and then I found Perses."

"She was in Lycos and she had your son. Proteus," Shea tells him. "And he's in Arethusa right now; he's in danger as long as Perses is alive, and he's coming for Arethusa. To destroy everything, and I don't think he'll stop there. So, if you won't help us for Nereid, then do it for your boy."

"Didn't you hear? I'm broken. I can't save anyone, I'm not a hero. He banished me, and do you know why? Because I saw what I had become. And so I tried to train Perses to be better than when I found him alone and discarded in the Underdeep. I thought I could make up for everything, but I just created another me, a monster."

Triton sits on the table and runs a hand over his face. He looks exhausted.

"And when he attacked our father in Atlantis, I stopped him like a good son and soldier. He took my conch shell with him, but I ran my sword through his body and threw him into the deepest depths of the Underdeep. And then? I cried. And he banished me for it." Triton points to Poseidon.

"I fought. I fought every damn day, all the monsters of old on Tenaro, day after day. And I waited for you," Triton says, talking to Poseidon, who can barely meet Triton's eyes. "For three years I waited for you to come tell me that I was redeemed for all my wrongs, for Thetis and Perses. But you never came, and I realized that you couldn't absolve me because..."

Triton pauses, searching for the right phrase. "Because you're just like me. We thought we played by different rules, but we don't. We were immortal, but we weren't above it all. I hurt her," Triton says, before clarifying, "Thetis."

Shea is watching him, and she sees a single tear fall from his blue eyes and takes a step toward him. She can feel his door in her magic, straining to be opened, and it draws her closer to him.

She sees Poseidon in the corner of her eye go to stop her again from reaching him, but Caen grabs his injured shoulder and squeezes, making him yelp.

"I caused her unimaginable pain by making her love me. And she did. So much so that to make me stay and love her back she practiced forbidden magic"—his breath shudders—"my magic, a siren spell that lost her Erebos, her home. I didn't care because I'd done it before. Taken advantage of lovers not old enough to understand the consequences. I didn't care until it was too late. So. Tell me I'm not a monster."

"I can't," Shea tells him.

Triton chuckles coldly. "Perses isn't bad. He's just doing what we did first. I can't help you take him down. Besides I did it once before and it didn't stick, what makes you think I could take him down a second time?"

"I don't have a choice but to believe in you; look, it may not have been his intention to come for you here, but it was mine. I came here looking for *you*," Shea emphasizes, standing in front of him while he leans against the wooden table, "because I was told you could help me stop Perses. So, I'm asking, I'm—I'm begging you. Come back with us. As your sister, please."

"I don't know you. And I don't know that kid, there's nothing on Nereid that isn't protected that I care about so, I'm sorry, but you'll have to find another way. I can feel your magic, it's strong, but you should be careful."

"Why? I guess I'm going to need as much of my magic as I can develop if I'm doing this alone."

"Perhaps, but magic is what started all of this. I taught Perses everything he needed and more, but immortal magic wasn't meant for mortal bodies."

Shea raises a brow. "So?"

"So. He's dying."

"From magic?"

"Yes. That's why he needed Poseidon to make him immortal years ago; he's not fighting to take back Nereid from the humans. Everyone has a drive, a personal one, regardless of how righteous that being may be. Perses is fighting to live."

"But how would taking back Nereid do that for him?" Caen butts in, dragging Poseidon to his feet.

"I don't have all the answers; if I did, I wouldn't be here. Now if you'll excuse me, if you take that path there, it will lead you out of the temple. Pleasant travels."

Triton attempts to push past Shea, but Shea catches his upper arm and turns him back to look at her.

"I'm not leaving here until you say you'll help," Shea snarls.

"Then you'll be here a long time, princess, cause I'm not changing my mind."

"It's captain," Shea growls, her hand tightening on his bicep.

Triton smirks at her. "Whatever you say, now you best let go of me before I show you what a true child of Poseidon can do."

Shea is glaring up into Triton's eyes when his threat gives her an idea.

"I think I could take you." Shea smiles, and the change in her expression clearly catches Triton off guard.

"You really couldn't," he drawls.

"Wanna bet?"

"Excuse me?" Triton asks.

"I win, you come back with us. You fight with us for Nereid and you help me take down Perses before he hurts anyone else."

"And if I win?"

"You don't," Shea says quietly.

"And why would I agree to this?"

Shea grins at him with a challenge in her eyes. "What do you have to lose?"

"I won't be losing." Triton laughs. "So it'll be a shame when you go home empty-handed, after I've kicked your ass too."

"Um, Shea?" Caen interjects. "I don't think this is the best idea."

"You don't really get a say," Shea responds.

She lets go of Triton and he steps away, his hands up in a semi-surrender.

He points toward the path leading back to the second clearing with the fountain that she now realizes is of Triton.

"What are we waiting for?"

Shea follows him into the clearing but not before she sees Caen put Poseidon next to Phoebus. He tells him to watch the shorter man and then follows Shea and Triton to the clearing.

CHAPTER 29: MERCY

Shea

It's a bigger space than the camp, with coral trees all around them and the fountain pushed back from the center. Triton goes to the other side and Shea stays at the end of the path.

Caen steps away, his hammer still in hand.

"First one to ask for mercy loses," Triton says.

"Rules," Caen asks gruffly.

"Don't be the first to say *mercy*." Triton shrugs and that's enough for Shea.

She goes to grab her dagger at her lower back but finds it missing. She suddenly remembers throwing it at Poseidon, and then that she forgot to pick it up after.

She's only got her water magic, which he obliterated upon meeting her, and her fists. She hates it when Phoebus is right.

"Ready?" Triton inquires, positioning his feet into a familiar fighting stance.

It's the same one Poseidon taught her.

She allows her magic to spread out, feeling for the water to see if she can bend again, and she feels the connection.

Maybe Triton wants this to be a fair fight.

His mistake.

Shea summons a column of water to her from the fountain, bending it to her will, shaping it into a lasso-like form.

Triton grins, but he doesn't summon any of his own water.

Shea waits. And waits. She waits for him to make the first move until she can't wait any longer. She takes a step and with a cry she pushes the water toward him with immense force, hoping to knock him off his feet.

He doesn't move or flinch as the water barrels at him. He changes his footing and squares his shoulders; she can barely see him take a breath before he's taking control of her water and slinging it back at her with a graceful turn.

The water slams into her chest at full force and she's knocked off her feet, her back hitting the grass hard.

She hears him before she sees him.

He charges toward her, summoning water from the fountain and encasing his fists inside. He freezes the water around his hands and jumps into the air. His fist is coming for her face and she barely manages to roll out of the way.

The ice shatters on impact, but he summons more water and recreates the ice glove.

Shea uses her core and jumps to her feet; she pulls more water from the pool and goes on the defense as Triton attacks.

His fists are coming down hard and he's moving so fast she can barely keep up.

She doesn't block the attack fast enough, and his ice-encased fist slams into her jaw.

She stumbles backward, reeling from the hit. The ice shatters, but he steals her own water and re-encases it.

"Had enough?"

Shea spits blood onto the ground, wiping her chin and wincing at the pain.

"I could do this all night."

Triton grins at her and punches her in the stomach,

sending her tumbling back again.

He breaks the ice on his hands and tackles her around the middle, slamming her to the ground.

Her head bounces on the grass and it's not as soft as it could be—her vision blacks out a little.

He's on top of her, pinning her arms under his knees.

He's breathing heavily, but he still raises his hand and slams his fist into the other side of her face.

She cries out from the hit and she can see Caen running to pull him off her.

"No!" Shea shouts and Caen's steps falter.

Triton looks over at the giant warily, watching him.

"If you intervene, it's over. Stay out of this!"

"It's already over, just give in," Triton tells her.

"Never," Shea says, and she spits in his face.

It catches Triton off guard, and she manages to push him off of her.

She lands a solid kick to the side of his head.

He falls backward as Shea stands, and he shakes his head, clearing it. He examines her as she pulls up her fists, her feet dancing as she prepares for the next blow, and if she didn't know any better, she'd say he's impressed.

His hand reaches out before she can stop him, and another water column slams into her, knocking her farther away.

Her cheek is split, and she knows her jaw will be bruised tomorrow. Triton rises from the floor with the help of the water. She's no match for him with magic. There's got to be another way.

Then she remembers what he said about doors. That Poseidon's door being opened made him stronger.

Perhaps if she opens Triton's magic, she could tap into it somehow.

She closes her eyes, picturing the room of doors once again. She sees hers in the middle and looks around until she senses Triton's.

It's shaking as something pushes against it from the other side, murky blue and dark black shadows pour like water from the cracks, and she runs to it as quickly as her mind's projection can go.

She thinks she hears Triton call her name, but she tries to stay focused. She places her hand on the doorknob, and it's stuck. She tries to pull it open; she can feel Triton advancing on her. She forces her physical body to scramble back as she tries to unlock his magic.

"Come on," she whispers.

She forces herself to be calm, to breathe, and then, the door opens.

It hurts to pull in a breath—the power races through her, blending and mixing with her own magic. She can feel it ripping through her veins and she cries out, physically in pain.

She hears something fall on the ground and she opens her eyes to see Triton has fallen to his knees, clenching the grass with his fists.

She can feel everything, his pain, his anguish, his guilt. It tears her up in ways she didn't even think possible.

Images dance along her mind's eyes. Private moments: she sees Thetis, younger and naked, below her as she thrusts into her body. She can feel a kind of love etching at the surface of the vision. This isn't her memory.

She sees Perses also younger, with a bright face and sweet eyes. He's smiling as he spars with her, no, as he spars with Triton and beats him in combat for the first time.

She sees Perses's pained face as Triton runs his sword through his body.

She sees Atlantis, and she thinks her body is on fire. She's burning from the inside out.

"You're killing yourself," someone says, but she can't stop.

She sees the Atlantean throne room around her, and Poseidon looking as young as Triton with a trident in his hand and a crown upon his head.

She's choking on the water around her, the water instead of air.

She finds Perses's dying face again, the betrayal, as she yanks the sword from his body and he falls down into the pit in the center of the throne room, the depth's prison entrance so that they all can see the monsters below, watching them and guarding them.

Her eyes burn as his body falls and he takes Triton's shell with him, tumbling through a golden translucent barrier, and she realizes he's crying.

And just when she thinks she's going to die; when she can feel her body burning from all the power; when she realizes she's done exactly what Perses has done and is feeling everything her brother feels now; when the pain is more than she can manage, more than she can imagine...

She hears a beautiful voice whispering from the darkness she's succumbing to.

Beware the forest.
The darkening leaves,
The eyes that watch from the trees.

Shea recognizes the song; she feels it pulling her back from the edge of darkness. It's bright behind her eyes, like she's looking into the sun. The woman's voice is soft and gentle, and she thinks she can see her among the light.

Bright red hair, curly and long, materializes among the brightness, a tan face with pointed ears appear. A gorgeous smile, petite nose, and deep green eyes. The melody pours from her lips, and Shea knows her.

She knows her with every fiber of her being. The memory is associated with feelings of pain and love. She's sitting in a room covered in vines, in what looks like a wicker rocking chair.

She's wearing the most beautiful white robes and she's holding something in her arms, rocking it back and forth as she sings the song.

"Please come home."

A masculine voice speaks from Shea, and the woman looks up and smiles fondly. She keeps humming that melody, singing the ancient elven lullaby.

Beware the woodlands
The winding trails,
The never-ending roads,
Forgotten tales.
Forget the babbling brooks,
And weeping trees
A false calm giving you ease.

The memory starts to fade, and Shea is ripped from the comforting woman's voice with a loud cry of anguish.

Shea coughs as she comes back to herself, her fingers gripping the grass beneath her.

She's still alive. The door is open. She's connected Triton to her, but she's still alive.

How is this possible?

She's gasping for air, and Triton is stumbling to stand, he must have seen all of it too.

He manages to finally find his footing, and he grabs her by her foot, dragging her toward him.

Shea can see Caen running for them, and this time she won't object; she feels like all of her strength has been drained just from creating the connection.

Triton must see her eyes flicker toward him because he uses his own magic to manipulate water from the fountain. He sends the shot barreling into Caen, and it knocks him back.

It can't keep him down for long, she thinks, but despair sinks in as Triton uses the water to create a powerful ice restraint that keeps Caen locked to the grass.

He's struggling to move, to break it, but Shea knows he won't be able to.

"Triton," she croaks, but he shushes her.

His eyes are wild as he straddles and pins her beneath

him.

"I was playing nice before, sis. And then you go and do a thing like that. Invading my magic, my personal memories. I like my privacy. Why don't I return the favor?"

Shea is shaking her head; she only created a one-way link. If that was what it felt like creating one way, she can't go through it again.

But Triton doesn't seem to care.

He closes his eyes and his head jerks like he's rooting around for something in his mind until he grins in triumph.

"Got you."

Something breaks open in Shea's chest. It feels like two hands are inside her body, forcing an opening into her soul, and then like a bang, it slams open.

She cries out in pain and Triton gasps at the intensity of her own emotions.

Her own memories flash before her eyes: She sees herself taking the Pearl of Lycos. Meeting Jo. She sees herself saving Aster from Helios. Her first time with Jo. She sees Paetre and Caen. And Ceto carving into her chest, marking her forever as property.

She comes out of the trance briefly, and Triton's image changes; his appearance flickers, like he's not really there, and Ceto appears in his wake.

"Dark stuff, princess," Ceto whispers, and Shea shakes her head.

"What in Hades?"

"You forgot you said it yourself; you're dealing with the most powerful child of Poseidon," Triton's voice comes out of Ceto's mouth and it chills Shea to her bones.

She's had enough.

She headbutts Ceto, slamming her forehead straight into her nose, and the empress is flung back.

It's her in Triton's clothes, but the image flickers briefly as Triton's concentration breaks. He almost turns back into himself, but he manages to keep the illusion, and Ceto remains before her.

"How are you doing this?" Shea demands.

Ceto chuckles and it sounds just like her.

"I'm the father of sirens; not only can they enchant with their voices, but they can make you see what you desire most, or your worst fears," he spits in Ceto's voice.

Triton summons more water from the fountain, but this time he forms them into two ice swords. Shea tries to do the same, but she's too tired from opening Triton's door. She can't get the water to mold.

"You ready to say mercy yet?" Ceto growls.

"You picked the wrong image to get me to give up, because I will never give in to her," Shea snarls.

There's a holler from across the clearing. They both turn to watch Phoebus hobbling in from the path to the camp with Poseidon helping him. He's got his sword out of his holster and he brings his arm back as far as he can and throws it toward them. It lands a few feet behind Triton, stabbing into the grass.

Shea takes the opportunity while he's distracted and lunges toward him.

Triton turns, seeing her coming at him, and swipes his swords at her, but she slides under the blades and grasps Phoebus's sword out of the ground.

She takes up her proper fighting stance, the one Paetre showed her when he taught her swordplay, and grins at her brother.

"We gonna stand around talking all day or are we going to fight?"

She hears Caen call to Phoebus to break him out of the ice, and Phoebus orders Poseidon to take him over, which he reluctantly does.

So, while they're focused on Caen, Shea can focus on Triton.

Triton growls at her and storms forward.

She parries his blow and sidesteps, causing him to

stumble. He may be great with magic, but she trained with the best swordsman in Nereid, her father, Paetre.

She cracks one of his ice swords, and he has to roll back to avoid her swing, but she manages to slice his upper cheek.

He reaches a delicate hand up to his cheek, feeling the blood drip down Ceto's jaw.

He closes his eyes and Shea feels that strange sensation again. It's not entirely unpleasant; she just knows someone is there.

He laughs when he finds what he's looking for.

Triton stands slowly from the ground. The empress mirage fades away and the cut on his cheek knits back together.

He's a man once again—just, not himself.

Shea practically chokes. Her heart leaps to her throat as she sees Prince Mariner smiling at her.

He's still in Triton's clothes, which helps her remember he's not real, but then he speaks.

"So, it's not the empress you fear. I didn't go deep enough it seems. You fear a dead man, and you should because the one immortal thing in this universe is death. And now that you know we exist, then Hades must exist too. You're right in your assumption and it's only a matter of time before you see him again," Triton tells her in Mariner's voice.

"You're not real," Shea whispers.

"Oh yes, he is." Triton lunges.

Shea knows it's a distraction, but the duel from a year ago flashes in her mind. Mariner's words in her head, her fear, her anger. Everything he said about Jo and her, how they wouldn't make it, how they'd never truly be together. And then dying.

She's blocking him, blow for blow, but his grin, so similar to the one from their fight before, startles her and he slams his fist into her face.

She falls backward.

He kneels over her again.

Shea can hear Caen yelling at Phoebus to crack the ice harder, but it's too late.

Triton—Mariner, pins her to the ground.

It's so familiar; he runs his thumb over her left eye, and she shivers like she did before.

"Say it," Mariner commands.

"If I do? We lose," Shea whispers.

Mariner leans down until his mouth is right next to her ear.

"You've already lost," he whispers back.

A tear falls from Shea's left eye, and Mariner pulls back; he puts his knees on top of her arms and then wraps his hands around her throat.

He tightens them, and she chokes as the air stops filtering through. She stares up into Mariner's blue eyes, and she sees imaginary blood that isn't there, flashes of before.

Caen, Phoebus, and Poseidon vaguely shout in the distance. She thinks she can hear footsteps, but it's too late and he's right.

Say it, Mariner mouths, and he loosens his grip just enough.

"Mercy," Shea rasps.

CHAPTER 30: I FAILED YOU

Shea

The journey back to Port Town is strained. Everyone is lost in their own thoughts and Shea particularly can't get the encounter with her brother out of her head.

Triton let her go after the fight. Caen didn't even need to pull him off. He wasn't trying to kill her, he just wanted to make a point.

He reminded them all about the path again as Caen held Shea to his chest, tears visibly falling from her eyes.

Phoebus held her hand as she coughed and tried to catch her breath.

Poseidon watched from a distance, probably debating whether he would stay or return with them to Port Town. But before Triton could leave the clearing, Shea called out to him.

"Triton!"

He stopped, the Mariner illusion thankfully fading away, and he turned, looking back at Shea.

She pushed Caen and Phoebus away and tried to stand. She even made it a few steps before she fell, but surprisingly, Triton reached out and caught her.

"Thanks," she murmured, and he nodded.

Then he did something that caught her off guard; he smoothed her hair back from her face and helped her straighten up so she was looking into his eyes.

"You're a great fighter," Shea told him.

He smiled at her wistfully.

"I could really use your help against Perses."

He laughed and shook his head. "You don't give up."

"Not usually," she said.

"I already told you…"

"I know, but if you change your mind. We'll stay in Port Town a day, one day, and if you don't come…You don't come and we sail away."

"You're a glutton for punishment, you know that."

"Yeah. But I've also felt what's inside you, and I was wrong."

Triton raised his brow, looking so much like herself in that moment that she chuckled.

"You're not a monster, Triton. In fact, you're actually a lot like me. So, don't let him"—Shea pointed over to Poseidon—"win. Because staying here is what he would do, and I don't think you're like him anymore."

Triton stared into her eyes, searching for the lie, but he didn't find any, because she could feel him. She could feel his memories still, and his emotions, and she knew he could feel hers.

"Think about it."

And then they'd left.

Poseidon came with them, much to Caen's and Phoebus's objections. After all, he'd lied about Triton and why they needed to come here. But because of him, Shea had met Triton, and honestly, she was too tired to banish him.

They'd made it outside the temple and trudged to the edge of the jungle with Phoebus in Caen's arms. As they'd broken through the jungle's border, the sun rose over the horizon.

Everyone would probably be worried; they were supposed to be back by now. Shea could barely think let alone care. They ate some rations from the supplies and were happy to find the horses where they left them.

Caen hooked Phoebus's pony to his own horse, as he'd have to ride with one of them because of his leg.

Shea volunteered to take him, and soon they were back on the Starfish Cross.

Hours passed slowly as they rode along the desert and carefully avoided the gems in the path. Phoebus sat in front of her, cursing periodically because of his leg but also comforting her.

"It's gonna be okay, kid. Maybe he'll come."

"Maybe," she responded.

And then they'd lapsed into silence again.

Now, the sun is high in the sky as they finally reach Port Town's borders, and all Shea wants to do is take a bath and climb into bed with Jo.

The greenery has blossomed even more since they were gone.

Caen has to get down off his horse and cut through some of the plant life to make it back into Port Town.

By the time they break through, it takes them another half hour to make it to the stables at Phoebus and Dari's home, and it's early afternoon.

"Take him inside," Shea orders Caen, nodding to Phoebus.

Phoebus objects, but they all ignore his complaints.

"You got it, Cap. I can handle the horses when I get back," Caen tells her.

"No, it's okay. Let the father of horses do it," Shea responds and tosses her reins to Poseidon, who dismounts his horse next to her.

"Think you can handle it?" Shea asks, but it's not really a question.

"Shea," Poseidon begins, but Shea holds her hand up, preventing him from speaking.

"I'll get you to the mainland, and then you should probably disappear. I don't want to leave you here so Triton has to deal with you. I brought you here, after all, I'll take you back as was the deal."

Poseidon sighs. He starts getting the horses ready to be put in their stalls.

Shea walks in through the open door to the kitchens. She wishes she could wash up before they all see her; she looks a mess. Cut cheek, bruised jaw, split lips, hand marks bruised around her throat, and empty-handed after all. The wounds will heal quickly, and likely be gone by tomorrow, but the failure will still be there.

She's relieved when she doesn't find Semele in the kitchen. She can hear people in the dome, the main part of the house. She puts her hand on the wooden door and breathes, just for a moment, and pushes all of her fears as far down as they'll go. Because she lost, and now there's no way they can stop Perses. And she'll wait as long as she can for Triton, but he's connected to her, and right now she doesn't feel anything to indicate he's coming.

She can hear Dari cooing over Phoebus. He bravely recounts how he broke his leg and does not recall it being from falling down a hole.

Shea laughs to herself at his antics. She thinks she can hear Aster and it sounds like Beck is out there too. She nods to herself. She's not a coward.

It's time to face the music.

She steps into the main room and everyone looks at her. Her torn clothes, her bruised neck and face, her hair having fallen out of a braid during the fight. She looks like a wild child.

A single arm embraces her quickly and she freezes at Dari's touch before relaxing, remembering that it's alright. She's safe, for now.

"Look at you," Dari mutters, pulling back. Her white hair is in a low bun and a few loose tendrils fall around her face.

She's wearing a nice green dress and her eyes are roaming over Shea's face in a panic.

"I'm okay," Shea tells her, removing Dari's hand from her sore jaw.

Aster runs over to her and checks her for injuries as well.

"I should have been there," he tells her.

Shea looks up into his eyes, and she smiles because he's different.

He's grown somehow. He looks like a man. When did that happen?

"I'm okay, really," Shea tells everyone.

Beck walks closer as well and Dari steps away, going back to Phoebus.

She orders Caen to pick him up and take him to their bedroom, so she can get his leg set properly.

"You look worse for wear," Beck comments with a smirk.

Shea laughs and has to clear her throat as it's a little sore from Triton choking her.

"Where's Triton?" Beck asks.

Shea sighs. She looks him in the eye and shakes her head.

"I'm sorry. He's not coming. There's much to say, to explain, but I really just need a bath and sleep. I can explain more in a couple hours."

"Then it's over," Beck mutters, his eyes cast down.

"No," Shea says, "I left him with an offer; I told him we'd stay a day extra if he changed his mind, we can't lose hope, not yet."

But Shea doesn't admit she already has.

She whistles for Caeruleus, who flies down from the center tree with a yowl. He lands beside her, rubbing his body up against her leg, and she reaches down to scratch his head.

"Dari, can you get me some parchment and a quill?"

Dari does as she asks, and Shea quickly scribbles down her request for Thetis and Venus to mobilize the Arethusian army, joined with the Oceanan militia. She tells them to shut the gates and prepare for war. She writes at the end, *We're on our own.*

Once she finishes the letter, she hands it to Caeruleus, who takes it in his back claws.

"Arethusa, Caeruleus. And then wait for me there."

Caeruleus yowls again, what sounds like a groan, and flaps his wings, raising himself into the air. He rubs his face against Shea's briefly before flying out the top of the dome, toward their final front against Perses.

Shea turns to go to the bathroom with a sigh, eager to wash up, and runs unexpectedly into Dari once again.

"Where are you going?"

"The washroom," Shea tells her and goes to continue down the hall, but Dari stops her.

"Of course, but before you do, there's something you need to see."

Shea glares at her, confused, and then she realizes someone is missing from this little reunion.

"Where is Jo?"

"Shea…"

"Dari, where is she?" Shea asks, starting to panic.

She looks back at Aster and Beck, who both are trying to figure out how to answer, and that only increases Shea's fears.

"Is she okay?" Shea demands.

"Shea, everything is fine," Dari tries to calm her, but the past twelve hours are catching up with her.

Her mind is buzzing. She briefly feels a strange tug, like someone pulling on a cord in the back of her mind. She pushes the feeling away, her fear overriding her senses.

"Shea."

A voice breaks through the panic and she looks up and gasps.

Jo is standing in the entrance to the hallway looking absolutely radiant. Her hair is loose with a single braid framing her face, and petals are woven within the strands. She's wearing a familiar dress that's been slightly altered, the purple one Shea wore a year ago. There's a stunning white sash tied around her middle.

She runs toward Shea, and Shea opens her arms, catching her as she practically jumps into her arms.

Shea lets out a sobbing breath as she holds her close, smelling her clean skin and feeling her soft hair tickle her face.

"You're okay," Shea breathes.

"I'm okay," Jo repeats.

They pull away from each other and Jo looks her over. Shea can barely look her in the eyes.

"I tried," Shea tells her.

"I know," Jo says, and she takes her by the hand.

"Will you come with me?"

Shea sighs and smiles softly, nodding her head in assent.

Shea turns back to the room. Dari waves her on, while Aster fist-pumps the air, but what really worries her is the look of dejection on Beck's face as he watches them go.

She follows Jo down the white clay hall, past the many doors, before they arrive at Shea's old room.

Jo turns to face her before opening the door.

"Close your eyes," Jo tells her, and Shea has a sense of déjà vu.

"Why?"

"Trust me?" Jo asks.

Shea looks up into her eyes and she shrugs. "Always."

Shea closes her eyes. She hears the door open, and Jo gently leads her into the room.

Jo stops her just before the balcony and then lets go of her hands, leaving Shea feeling a little off-kilter.

"Okay," Jo tells her. "Open."

Shea opens her eyes and her breath catches. There are blankets on the floor, just like that night, and trays of food set in the center.

Pink petals are falling all around them and Jo is standing in front of the blankets in a *ta-da* kind of gesture. There are two goblets on the floor, and she leans over and picks up both that are already filled with a red liquid.

Shea's face has broken into a smile before she even realizes it, but a mental flash blocks her vision for a moment, and she stumbles back as she sees Mariner's face.

"Shea?"

Shea shakes her head, clearing it, and stands.

Jo rushes over with the goblets, checking to see if she's alright.

"Sorry, just reliving a lot of memories from last year recently," Shea chuckles, taking a glass from Jo.

"I'm alright really," Shea tells her.

She takes a sip from the glass, hoping it'll calm her nerves, and smiles.

"This is amazing," she states, walking over to the blankets.

Jo follows her over and they sit down together on the picnic. There are pillows there too.

"I thought you'd be back last night, so I was trying to recreate our moment under the stars, but things changed, didn't they?" Jo asks.

Shea takes another gulp of the wine and nods.

"They did."

"We lost," Jo murmurs.

"No. I lost," Shea admits.

"Shea, you did everything you could. You crossed an ocean of monsters to save Nereid. It's not over; we'll find another way. We still have Poseidon."

"He lied, Jo. About everything," Shea explains, putting the empty goblet down.

"What?"

"He lied. He came here to get his power back. I guess Triton had something that would give him his abilities once again. Triton could barely look at him, and so he had no interest in helping us. He didn't even have the object that could give Poseidon his power. We wasted valuable time. I can't defeat Perses on my own and Poseidon is practically mortal."

Jo absorbs as much as she can, but Shea can see the devastation on her face.

"I see," Jo comments, "okay."

"Okay, what?"

"Okay, we'll find another way. I refuse to give up. There must have been something you learned right? Something we can use?"

"I don't know," Shea states.

Jo grabs her hand, forcing her gaze up.

"Well then, why don't we play a game?"

"Jo," Shea groans.

"Come on, what do we have to lose?"

Shea's words from earlier echo in her mind, the same words she said to Triton.

"Nothing," she tells her, but in truth they still have everything to lose.

"Right. I'll make it easy, three questions this time. Everything's on the table, just like before."

Shea laughs, remembering that wonderful and horrible night from a year ago. When she'd asked Jo to stay and it hadn't turned out the way she hoped. She wonders what Jo is planning here.

"Why not. But I want more wine first," Shea demands, and Jo happily pours her a second glass.

Shea steals a grape off one of the trays and pops it into her mouth with a smile.

"Who's first?" Jo inquires.

"Whatever did you do without me while we were apart?" Shea asks.

Jo opens her mouth to answer, but Shea holds up her hand.

"Sexually," Shea finishes the question, and Jo smacks her on the arm.

"Really?"

"Yes." Shea grins, taking another sip of wine.

Maybe this will be fun.

"Well I, um. I didn't sleep with anyone, if that's what you're suggesting," Jo tells her.

"I'm not," Shea says with mock offense.

"Alright, then. Let's just say I used a gift that Thetis sent me as a birthday present for while you were away."

"And it is?" Shea inquires, very interested in what kind of gift was sent.

"None of your business. I answered, my turn."

"You know I'm remembering now; you were piss poor at this game," Shea jokes and she gets another slap to the arm for it.

"What was Triton like?"

Shea sobers at the question; she takes another sip of wine.

"I thought I'd find a monster, and in a lot of ways I did. But I found one that looked like me, and if things were different, I think he'd be here. He's powerful and smart, Jo, really smart. And even after the fight, I just wanted to get to know him more. Because maybe I could fix him, the way you fixed me."

Shea studies the rips in her pants and goes to pull off her boots when Jo catches her attention.

"Shea, I didn't fix you. No one can fix someone else. They do that all on their own, the only thing we can do is be there when they're ready. You gave him an option, maybe he'll take it."

Shea sighs, then brings Jo's hand up to her mouth and kisses the back.

"My turn. How are Rhea and Gaea? I didn't see them

before we left. And I remember reading one of your letters where you said you replaced them? I'm sure that went over well," Shea mutters, stealing another piece of fruit off the tray.

Jo chuckles but Shea can hear the frustration in her tone.

"It didn't. It was more of a promotion, but also, I needed my own ladies-in-waiting. They were my grandmother's and briefly my mother's attendants. They practically raised me, but I needed my own advisors. They're complicated. And I couldn't stand hearing them talk badly about the person I love most in this world," Jo justifies.

Shea realizes what she means, and she smiles.

"They love you, Jo. They want you to be happy, and the person you love"—she gestures to herself—"isn't going to be an easy road. People—that is if we survive Perses, some royals aren't going to agree with your choice. They're trying to protect you, they're your parents, Jo. They just want what's best even if they don't say it the right way."

Jo groans. "You're supposed to be on my side, not make me feel worse."

Shea laughs. "Well as queen consort, I'm also your advisor so…take my advice."

"But I also love Beroe and Eione; they've become my closest friends. I wish you could have met them before we left."

"I'll meet them when we get back," Shea tells her, and Jo nods in agreement.

"Okay. Did Triton know about Perses?"

"Yes. It's true what Poseidon said, he trained him. But not to be like he is. He found him in the Underdeep after the elves"—Shea stops—"after my mother banished him."

"Your mother?" Jo interjects.

"Yeah. Ami, I guess she's one of Erebos's leaders."

"So, I guess you could say you're an elven princess." Jo laughs.

Triton's words echo through her head from earlier.

"I'm not a princess," Shea snaps.

Jo stops laughing. She looks at her, concerned, as Shea brings her hand up to her head.

"I'm so sorry," Shea apologizes. "It just reminded me of something Triton said."

"It's okay, if this is too much, we can do this later," Jo tells her.

Shea almost wants to take her up on it, but there's something about all this, the picnic, the game, she has to see this through.

"No, I like being here with you," Shea says, scooting closer to Jo.

"Final question, right?" Shea asks, and Jo nods.

"Okay. What's this picnic all about?"

"Funny you should ask, because the answer is my next question," Jo answers, standing from the blankets.

She holds out her hand, prompting Shea to take it and they head closer to the balcony till they're standing near the edge.

The sun is shining on the sparkling pool and the animals are racing across the grounds.

Shea chuckles at the display. She closes her eyes and lets the wind wander through her hair.

There's an eerie sensation on the back of her neck, like she's being watched both from outside of her body and inside her mind.

She reaches out to the presence in her mind and sends a feeling of peace and warmth to them.

The connection stutters and then disappears.

Shea opens her eyes to confront the outside sensation and just about falls off the edge of the balcony.

Jo is down on one knee beside her, she's smiling up at Shea and in her right hand she has a ring.

The ring is beautiful. A white band made of what looks like pearl, as it shimmers in the sun.

Shea swallows, her breath caught in her chest. "Jo."

"Before you say anything, let me," Jo tells her, and Shea keeps her mouth shut because she's really not sure what to say.

"While I was hoping to do this under happier circumstances, I knew there was a possibility that might not be the case. I had this made after you left, and I've kept it with me everywhere I've been so that I'd always have a part of you close to me," Jo explains.

"I know what's happening out there, and I know this is probably crazy...but, Shea, I think everything happening is even more reason for us to do this. I don't want to leave this island not married to you. Because when we leave here, we can't possibly know what's going to happen.

"I want to marry you before we go back. Before we have to go to war. I want to have one last good thing in case this is it. And I want everyone to know how much I love you. I'm not selfish often, I've put my country before us times before. But I'm not doing that this time. This time I'm going to be selfish and I'm asking you to be selfish with me, just for one night."

Jo finishes her speech and gets up from one knee; she holds her hand out for Shea's left.

"So, what do you say? Will you marry me, will you marry me now?"

There are a million reasons to say no. A million reasons to tell Jo to get her head out of the clouds, to scream we have to go to war, and now? Now, Jo wants to stand in front of their friends and family and say *I love you* beyond all of the reasons they shouldn't?

Well, Shea was never one to listen to reason.

"Yes," she answers.

"Yes?" Jo asks, her eyes filling with tears.

"I should probably say no to get back at you, but Hades, yes. I want you; I want you for the rest of my probably very short life."

Jo laughs loudly.

Shea grins and hands Jo her left hand.

Jo slips the pearl band onto her finger and it's perfect. She takes Shea into her arms, holding her close, and Shea feels her own tears start to fall.

Cheers break out from down below, and Shea and Jo look out into the garden to see everyone standing there.

Dari is kissing Phoebus, Caen is clapping, and Aster hugs Beck, who is looking up at them with a soft smile.

Semele is even in the garden, and when Shea catches her eyes, she gives her a small nod before leaving them all alone.

"I guess we have a wedding to host," Phoebus announces.

"Which means those two need to be separated immediately," Dari shouts, leaving her limping husband in the garden and racing inside to find them.

"I'll tell the crew," Aster says before bouncing off into the house.

"I better brush up on my marriage vows, since I'm guessing you can't perform it," Caen sighs, talking to Beck, who ultimately laughs.

"Don't look at me."

"When?" Shea asks, turning back to Jo.

"Tonight?"

Shea smiles at her. "Gods help us. Tonight."

And Jo kisses Shea, deeply and passionately.

Because even if they die tomorrow, at least Shea knows she really is loved.

CHAPTER 31: THE WEDDING

Jo

Dari moves Jo to a separate room. She tells her she's welcome to look through any of Dari's dresses and see if she finds one she likes, but Jo decides that she wants to wear her naval uniform. It keeps a piece of Arethusa with her for the ceremony.

After that, Dari sends Aster up to keep her company and to help with anything she needs. What she doesn't expect is for Beck to be with him.

"Hello, boys." Jo smiles as she opens the door to the guest quarters to allow them in.

"You're not wearing a dress? Aren't girls supposed to wear a dress?" Aster asks.

"I don't think it's written anywhere," Beck tells him. "Besides, I think Jo looks very regal this way."

Aster shrugs and takes a look around the room.

"Thank you," Jo tells him, and Beck nods.

"How are you doing?" she asks.

"I'm happy for you both, truly," Beck states.

Jo decides to believe him.

"So, what can we help with?" Aster asks.

And suddenly Jo understands what Shea meant—he

has grown. He's just about the same height as Jo, at six feet, and most of his baby fat has left his cheeks.

"Well I'm trying to decide whether I should leave my hair down or put it up?"

"Up," both of them reply.

"Right," Jo snorts.

"I can help," Aster says.

He walks over to where Jo is standing near the door and brings her to the vanity in the room. He sits her down on the seat and they both look into the mirror.

"Venus taught me a little when I was younger. There wasn't much for kids to do in brothels. I helped her with Shea's hair for the ball last year."

Jo tries not to wince at the mention of V.

She smiles instead. "Well that was very beautiful, I think I'd like that."

Aster confidently grabs the brush off the vanity table and starts gently brushing out Jo's hair.

Beck strolls over and takes a seat beside her, watching the process.

She can see him playing with something around his neck. She turns a little to see what it is.

"What have you got?"

Beck, who seems to have been lost in thought, startles and looks up at Jo, blinking until her question filters through.

"Oh."

He holds up the necklace and there's two rings attached to it; one is silver and looks male by the size. The other is a smaller gold band with dolphins carved into the metal.

"My parents' rings," Beck states.

"They're beautiful," Jo notes, looking them both over.

"Thank you."

She can tell there's something else on his mind and she bets she knows what it is.

"It'll be okay."

Beck chuckles.

They're both two young leaders of large countries, responsible for many people, but in this moment, Jo sees a man with the world on his shoulders.

"How can you be so sure?"

"I'm not in the slightest." Jo laughs.

Beck grins at her.

"But I have to hope because I'm not allowed to give up. As a queen, that's not an option. So, I'm going to marry the woman I love and then go fight a war."

"You make it sound so easy," Beck croaks, clearing his throat.

"That's because I'm an excellent liar, and trust me, you'll be one too someday. It comes with royal practice, I've just been at this longer than you have," Jo confesses.

"What do you think?" Aster inquires, having finished Jo's hair.

Jo looks in the mirror.

"Aster, it's perfect!"

He plaited two loose braids and then laid them over her head, bringing them back around so he could cinch them at the top of her neck. Small blond tendrils frame her face.

She stands, brushing off her suit pants, and gives a little twirl for them to see.

"Well?" she murmurs.

"You look amazing," Aster tells her.

Jo reaches her hand out to him and he takes it with a smile.

"Beck?" Jo asks.

He looks up at her in acknowledgment.

"Could you step outside? I want to talk to Aster privately for a moment," Jo explains.

Beck nods and leaves the room without a word, but not before giving Jo a quick hug and whispering into her ear, "Don't trip."

She laughs at him and waits until he shuts the door to turn to the teen.

The elf is watching Jo curiously, probably wondering if he's in trouble. Like mother, like son.

Jo gestures for him to follow her to the long wicker bench at the end of the bed. She sits him down beside her and takes his hands into hers.

"I didn't do this properly," Jo tells him.

Aster cocks his head, confused.

"What do you mean?"

"Well, I asked Shea to marry me, but there's more to it than that. She becomes my family but then so does her son."

Aster's eyes widen in realization and he smiles at Jo with affection.

"Aster, you…are…brilliant. And becoming an amazing young man. I know Shea has been a mother figure to you, and to her you are her child, and she loves you. Which means I do too," Jo enforces, squeezing his hands.

"I want you to know that you can count on me, and that when Shea comes to live in Arethusa after this is all over, I want you to come too. You are Shea's son, and so I recognize you as mine, if that's alright with you. I want to ask your permission. Do you mind if I marry Shea?"

"You make us better, Jo; you make her happy. And I want her to be happy. We're a family now, and I'm happy to be a part of yours. I just," Aster stutters.

Jo squeezes his hand, letting him know it's okay to continue.

"I guess I didn't realize that, you guys getting married would be the end of Shea as captain of the *Duchess*. I always had it in my mind, that you'd marry and then we'd sail away, but we'd come home to Arethusa after each voyage. But we…she…can't do that, can she?"

Jo sighs and offers him a wistful smile.

"No. When she becomes queen consort, I'll need her in the capital. She'll have duties in Thalassa and responsibilities to uphold as my wife."

"Like having a baby?"

"James tell you about that?"

Aster blushes. "Yes."

"That's one duty. I'll need a successor, and unfortunately you're a man."

"You'd pick me?" Aster gasps, his eyes widening.

"If things were different, yes. But Arethusa can only be ruled by a woman. It's better that way," Jo states, thinking about Mariner.

Her expression darkens as she imagines her father's cruel smile. She'll never let a man rule Arethusa as long as she's alive.

"I wouldn't know the first thing about running a country anyway." Aster grins. "Besides, I have James, and well, it's hard to imagine settling down so soon."

"You truly love your life as a pirate."

"We're called pirates because we live by our own laws, but I like to think of myself as an adventurer," Aster explains. "There's so much world out there. I'd hate to never see the rest."

"You'll always be Shea's first son, any child we have will never take that away, and you'll be a brother to them. You have a place in the royal family in Arethusa."

"But what about James? And Caen? And Nol and Strom? And the others, the crew? Will they have a place in the court?"

"Perhaps," Jo starts, but Aster shakes his head.

"But you can't guarantee it, and even if you could, half of them wouldn't take it."

"Are you talking about James?" Jo asks knowingly.

Aster blushes then stands, breaking their touch. He puts his hands on his hips and chuckles.

"I wasn't meant for royalty. I'm a sailor, Shea raised me that way, and at my age…"

"She never would have settled down," Jo finishes his sentiment.

She walks over to him.

"You will always be welcome in Arethusa, and for your mother's sake, you better visit often," Jo orders.

Aster laughs. "That is if we survive the coming war."

Jo chuckles and hugs him close. "We'll make it, son. I promise."

Aster hugs her back, and Jo has to wipe a couple tears from her eyes.

"Okay, well enough about that. I also wanted to ask you something else."

"Okay." Aster smiles.

"Well, if you're not already spoken for, do you think maybe you could walk me down the aisle? If you don't want to or can't, it's no big deal, I can ask Beck…"

Aster cuts her off, "Jo."

"Yes?"

"Caen is walking Shea; I'd be happy to walk my new mom down the aisle."

Jo grins. "Good. I could get used to that new title; I think it almost beats queen."

Aster walks to the door.

"I'll go check and see if they're ready and I'll come back and get you."

"Sounds good."

**

A few hours pass, and Beck returns about an hour after Aster leaves to sit with Jo while they wait.

She asks if there's anything else she can do, but he tells her Dari has it covered. There are butterflies in her stomach, and she finally convinces Beck to play his flute while they wait.

He's cleaned up for the wedding; his hair has been pushed back and styled with what looks like water. He's wearing new black pants and a clean white shirt. It even looks as if he washed the outside of his brown boots. He looks nice.

Jo lays back on the guest bed and listens to him play an

old Nereidan tune; she hums the melody along to herself.

Her mind wanders through thoughts of Perses, and her queendom. About what life will be like if they defeat them, what Shea will look like in fabulous gowns and the consort tiara. Although Jo may order a new one to be made, as she remembers Shea in that mockery replica that Ceto made her wear to the diplomacy dinner.

Her fingers are tapping along the bed, as she thinks about little girls with red hair and even a boy or two with dazzling green eyes and brown hair. Her eyes widen as she realizes that her children could very much look like Beck if he agreed to be their surrogate father.

It's not uncommon in Arethusian culture to choose a man from court, and a man from a neighboring country would make her children twice as powerful.

But Jo also would have to pick someone Shea could trust; after all this, Jo can't imagine Shea wanting someone she didn't know to father their children.

But it would connect them in a way Jo herself could never be connected.

Formally they would be Jo and Shea's children, but truthfully, they would be Shea, Jo, and Beck's.

Could she live with that, could she live with that kind of tether for the rest of their years? The mannerisms, the traits, and appearances mixed between Shea and Beck. Girls with brown hair and wicked grins and boys with flaming hair and challenging brown eyes?

But then she sees the three of them, old, in her mind's eye. Their daughter crowned the next Arethusian queen, and she looks back and has three loving parents that would do anything for each other and for her.

Jo may never truly be connected to Shea like Beck would be as the other biological parent, but she would be Shea's wife and the partner that Beck can never have. It would be a three-way bond, and Jo realizes it would make them stronger.

"Do you want children?" Jo asks aloud.

Her eyes widen slightly as she just sort of blurts it out, and Beck's flute stops playing.

She draws herself up to her elbows and looks over at him; he's staring at her.

"Someday I suppose," he tells her warily.

Jo sits up entirely now so she can look Beck head-on.

"What about helping a couple who can't conceive on their own, offering your essence to help create their child?"

"I'm not sure where this is going."

Jo chuckles, standing from the bed. She walks over to Beck and kneels down next to the chair he's sitting in.

"You're aware that I'll need an heir. That Shea and I both will."

"Right."

"We're both women."

"Yes."

"So, we'll need an outside source," Jo slowly explains, waiting for Beck to understand.

"Are you asking me to have a child with you?"

"No," Jo says, and Beck takes in a sigh of relief.

"I'm asking you to have a child with Shea. With protocol and my own personal preference, I cannot carry a child. That would be Shea's responsibility as my wife."

Beck shakes his head. "Jo, this is— We don't even know what's going to happen when we go back."

"You're right. But I'm hoping for the best. And you and Shea have a bond. Just as she and I do."

"But I'm the governor of Oceanus, how could I be your surrogate? The children would be heirs to both state and queendom."

"If you'd like to name your first son heir to Oceanus, I'm okay with that. The first girl would be heir to Arethusa of course. But perhaps you'll marry and have children with your own partner. You'd be in their lives, but Shea and I would be the primary parents."

"This is a lot to process."

"It's a someday question, and you don't have to answer it now. But I trust you, Beck, and I trust her and I'm making our marriage bond today. But I think I could live with you two being connected like this, and I think the children would be something wonderful."

Beck sits there quietly a moment. He turns to Jo, examining the smile on her features. Perhaps looking for any lies, but he won't find any.

"If she asked, I would."

"I think that's the perfect answer," Jo remarks.

She stands and claps him on the shoulder.

He laughs at her antics, shaking his head in bewilderment at the conversation they just shared.

"I can't imagine myself as a father," he murmurs.

"I can't imagine myself as a mother," Jo laughs.

"Well then, maybe we'll learn together, how to be parents," Beck confides, and Jo nods in agreement.

She opens her mouth to add something else but a knock raps at the door.

She calls for whoever it is to enter, and Aster opens it with Dari beside him.

"We're ready," she announces.

Dari practically beams with happiness upon seeing Jo and walks up to her, placing her hand on her cheek.

"You're absolutely beautiful, my darling," Dari tells her, and Jo nuzzles into her hand a little.

"Thank you."

"Alright, well let's get you to the gardens, Caen has gone to get Shea. If I remember correctly, it's protocol for the queen to walk down the aisle first."

"Yes." Jo nods, smiling at Dari's knowledge but then remembering where it comes from.

Dari must notice her realization because she waves off Jo's sadness.

"There were happy times in Arethusa too. Your grandmother Doris's wedding was one of them. But she had a very special flower in her hair then."

Dari holds out her hand in front of Jo and closes her fist. She squints her eyes in concentration, her hand shaking slightly from the tightness. Her breathing turns deep and she sighs after, her eyes fluttering. When she opens her palm, an Arethusian rose, white with specks of blue on the petals, is lying in her palm.

It's smaller than usual but it's still there and Jo gasps in amazement.

"How?" Jo stutters.

Dari takes the stem and places it on the side of Jo's face, over her right ear.

"Our little secret," Dari whispers.

"My mother used Arethusian roses for her bouquet," Jo admits, touching the flower in her hair gently.

"A piece of her with you on this day, then."

"Thank you." Jo hugs Dari graciously.

"Are we having a wedding or what?" Beck asks, pushing Jo toward the door.

"You know how Shea is about people being late," Aster comments.

"Yes, we do." Dari laughs.

Dari takes the lead and they follow her down the halls, easily avoiding Shea's bedroom.

They enter the dome and Jo smiles at all the pink petals on the floor, the same as the ones in Shea's chambers.

White flower wreathes hang from the large oak tree, and the wicker furniture has been trussed up with Arethusian roses in the branch seams.

The dining area has been extended, and the backs of every chair has exotic flowers draped across. There's an incredible centerpiece with delicious food spanning the table for after the ceremony.

They exit through the door from the dining area leading into the gardens.

Jo grins when she sees the arch—it's circular, with luscious greenery weaved through the wicker. Beautiful pink petals strung on string fall under it, attached at the top as a backdrop.

Candles line the aisle, and Jo realizes it's just about sunset.

Dari has somehow even commanded the fireflies to come out early, and they dance above the chairs where various members of the crew and the Arethusian navy sit waiting.

Laughter and voices can be heard across the garden and there's stunning lanterns floating along the water in the glistening pool.

Beck leaves her side with a quick squeeze to her shoulder and walks down the aisle. He stands off to the side of the arch, and Jo spots Phoebus sitting with James in the front row with two open chairs, presumably for Dari and Aster, since Caen is performing the ceremony.

She grabs Aster's hand nervously.

Dari tells her she's going to go tell Caen and Shea that it's time.

Aster squeezes her hand and then wraps her arm around his in an escort position.

"Nervous?" he whispers.

The crew settles down as Beck begins to play a simple Arethusian tune.

Everyone takes their seats, waiting for the ceremony to start.

"Yes," she whispers back. "And no. Not to marry Shea, but what comes after we leave here. I thought marrying her before we left would make losing her a little less hard, but now? I'll just want more time."

"We'll get that time," Aster consoles.

Dari runs up behind them, slightly out of breath. She waves at Beck, signaling him and he waves back.

The familiar Arethusian wedding march begins. The

higher notes of the tune catch the rhythm of the wind, a swaying tone that allows the bride to glide down the aisle.

Jo always thought there was a bit of romance hidden behind the tune and most likely written by someone studying the feminine form. Detailing the curves of a woman's body in the notes of a song.

"Okay, dear. Your time is now," Dari whispers.

The crew and naval officers stand and turn their attention to Jo escorted by Aster.

Phoebus remains sitting, but she can see his face beside James, who she notices with pride, only has eyes for Aster.

Aster waits for her to take the first step.

She takes a breath and then walks in time to the music. She glides down the aisle, the fading sunlight warm on her cheeks. She hears the crew hollering and cheering but she tries to focus on not tripping and getting herself to the arch.

The fireflies are bobbing through the air, like they're dancing to the Arethusian wedding march.

Finally, they reach the end of the short aisle and Jo stands in front of it, her head tall and her back straight.

Aster gives her a hug and goes to stand beside James, but Jo stops him.

She gestures for him to stand beside her at the alter and he does so with a grin.

Jo looks down the aisle, but she's almost afraid to look up and see if Shea is there with Caen.

Her breath is short, but Aster lays a calming hand on her shoulder, and she hears many of the crew gasp in surprise.

Jo summons all of her courage and looks up.

She melts where she stands.

Caen has cleaned up, wearing what looks like a very cheap suit he probably picked up from the port market earlier in the day. And there's an Arethusian rose in his suit pocket and a blue sash tied at his waist in the traditional Arethusian knot.

Jo's breath catches as her eyes roam over Shea's form.

She's biting her split, rouged red lips, and her eyes haven't lifted off the floor yet to meet Jo's. In the fading light, her floor-length dress almost looks white, but there's a faded blue dye throughout the flowy material. It's light and airy but layered like an A-line ball gown. The neck is low on her chest, her breasts beautifully outlined by the material, the brand magically hidden, and there are wispy cap sleeves off to the side of each arm, faded with the same sparse blue. The tips of the Lionbird wings from her tattoo are visible on her freckled shoulders. Her red hair is down in sprawling curls, covering the top of what looks like a low back, along with the bruising on her jaw and black eye, beautifully displaying the bottom of her detailed tattoo, as she hugs Dari briefly.

Pearls have been placed among the red tendrils, shining under the sunset and the fireflies.

Caen offers her his arm and she takes it with her left before finally looking up.

Their eyes meet from across the aisle, and the smile that spreads across Shea's features leaves Jo completely breathless.

There's a dusting of pink across her freckled cheeks and Jo guesses the tips of her ears.

The melody in the air changes just a little, it's less traditional and there's a foreign tune intertwining with the original march. Jo wonders if Beck composed it just for Shea.

Jo tries to memorize every detail. She notes the bouquet of white Arethusian roses in Shea's right hand and the way she looks down every few seconds. She's mumbling something and when she's finally within hearing range, Jo almost laughs. Shea's counting her steps.

Finally, the moment arrives, Caen and Shea stop just before the arch and Caen extends Shea's left hand out to Jo, who takes it with a soft kiss to the back.

The sun has just about faded, and instead of the garden turning dark and muted, the lanterns bring a new light that rivals the sun.

The fireflies are dancing through the air over the ceremony and Caen takes his position in front of the arch, turning to face them so he can officiate.

Shea hands Aster her bouquet with a kiss to his cheek and then takes her position across from Jo, their hands interlocked.

"You're the most beautiful being I've ever seen," Shea whispers before Caen can begin and Jo laughs aloud this time.

"I couldn't be more beautiful than you are in this very moment," Jo responds.

Shea grins and they look to Caen to start.

"Well it's been a while since I've done this. So, let's see if I can remember how this goes. Is there any objection to this union this evening? Speak and challenge me to a duel or hold your tongue," Caen declares.

He places his hand on his sword's hilt and glares out into the audience.

Jo looks out as well, and spots Poseidon leaning up against a pillar, watching from afar. She wonders if he might object, but everyone stays silent, and when Jo turns back to face Shea, she sees her clenching her eyes shut.

"Are you okay?" Jo whispers.

"Did anyone object?" Shea asks.

"No, seems everyone agrees that you're perfect for me," Jo chuckles.

Shea opens her eyes and smiles, although her gaze seems to land on something behind her and her smile falters slightly before returning her gaze to meet Jo's eyes.

Jo can feel Beck's presence behind her, playing a soft melody, but she doesn't worry.

"Good. Now onto the vows. I'm going to ask you both some questions and then if you agree, just say I do, or I swear. Or even I ascent, though I suppose it might not sound as good..."

Dari clears her throat and Caen abruptly stops his rambling with a cough.

"Right, sorry. Anyway." He looks to Jo first.

"Do you, Joana, take Shea to be your wife, to be her constant friend, her partner in life, and her true love? To love her without reservation, honor and respect her, protect her from harm, comfort her in times of distress, and to grow with her in mind and spirit?"

Jo looks into Shea's beautiful green eyes and squeezes her hands. "I do."

Jo thinks she can hear Dari sniffling next to Phoebus, and Aster sighs from his position beside her.

But she can't tear her gaze away from Shea's gorgeous face and the glossy look to her eyes. They close briefly when Jo agrees to the vow and her head drops down with a little shake, a dazzling smile spreading across her face.

"And do you, Shea, take Joana to be your wife, to be her constant friend, her partner in life, and her true love? To love her without reservation, honor and respect her, protect her from harm, comfort her in times of distress, and to grow with her in mind and spirit?"

It feels like an eternity before Shea responds.

Jo knows it's only a few breaths, but her heart pounds nervously in her chest as she waits for Shea to either be hers or to realize she's making a mistake.

"I do," Shea answers.

Jo wants to pull her close and kiss her already, but the ceremony isn't over and so she settles for pulling her in for a quick hug before Caen separates them for the next part.

"Hold your horses, I'm not done yet. Triton," Caen mutters. "Now if there are any other vows you two would like to make to one another, take this moment to do so now."

"Other vows?" Shea asks, nervously.

"Personal promises, besides the normal jargon," Caen tells her.

Shea is practically biting through her lip.

Jo decides to go first.

"Shea," Jo says, catching her attention, and she smiles at her reassuringly. "I promise to always be there for you and to listen. Because I know you're a leader too. I promise that our union will be one of equals. I promise to stand by your side through everything and anything. And finally, I promise to always find you in this life, the after, and any life to come."

Nothing else matters but this moment, no one else exists but Shea standing before Jo. She gazes into Shea's beautiful green eyes. She could live within this moment forever.

Shea takes a deep breath.

"I promise to be your shield and to always have your back. I will most likely make you very angry on many occasions, but I promise to never let it fester or to sleep without making things right. I promise to be your family, I promise you my trust and my loyalty. And I promise to always love you. Because I do, Jo. I love you."

Jo just about kisses her right there, Caen be damned. But she keeps herself steady, her eyes glittering with unshed tears, and focuses on the woman staring back at her uncertainly.

"I love you too," Jo reassures her.

Shea chuckles and squeezes Jo's hands.

"Well then, the rings."

Jo turns to Caen, confused, but he extends his palm out to them and in it she sees Shea's ring that she proposed with and another band.

This one is simple, gold and elegant with dolphins wrapping around the ring riding on waves. It's absolutely beautiful, and oddly familiar. She wonders how Shea could have gotten something so perfect so quickly.

Shea takes the dolphin gold band and Jo takes the ring she had commissioned for Shea made of white pearl.

"Before the crew, family, friends, and the gods themselves, I bless this union. Exchange the rings."

Shea reaches for Jo's left hand and Jo gladly gives it. She carefully slips the ring onto her finger, and as the gold shimmers from the lanterns, Jo examines the intricate dolphins around the circumference. She realizes where she's seen this ring before. Around Beck's neck. This is his mother's ring.

Jo looks back at Beck.

He continues to play but catches her eye with a smile and a nod. That's enough of a blessing for her.

Jo reaches for Shea's left hand and easily slips her ring back onto her finger. They rejoin their hands, and both are bouncing in anticipation for what comes next.

"Now you are bound one to the other. With a tie not easy to break, may the bond always be strong, and may your union see calm seas ahead. I pronounce you partners before those you love; you may now kiss your wife," Caen declares, and the garden erupts in applause.

Jo steps closer and slides her hands around Shea's waist. She pulls her practically off her feet, and as Shea wraps her arms around Jo's neck, Jo kisses her wife.

Their hearts beat together as they pull each other closer and their lips meld.

Jo has kissed Shea before, but it's different now, it's a forever kind of kiss and it takes her breath away.

She uses all of her strength and picks Shea up, spinning her around, and Shea breaks the kiss laughing in surprise.

She puts her down at her wife's insistence, and suddenly they're swarmed by Dari, Aster, and the rest of the crew.

Congratulations fly, hugs are exchanged, and Shea is being dragged off inside for the reception, with Jo being pulled behind. She tries to slow the march and allow herself a moment to take in the garden one last time. This is the place where her life is now forever changed, and she doesn't wish to forget a single moment of it.

CHAPTER 32: THE LAST DANCE

Beck

The dome is full of laughter and music. A band that Dari had collected from the marketplace plays music of all kinds.

The crew and naval officers dance together, sustained by good food and drink. The floor is covered in stunning pink blossoms, and Beck smiles as Dari flitters around the room either replacing food on the dining table or replenishing people's drinks.

Aster and James catch Beck's eyes, as James timidly twirls Aster across the dance floor while the younger man laughs at him.

There's a general feeling of happiness and goodwill in the air.

Caen is with Phoebus singing an old ocean shanty, encouraged by their many glasses of wine, and lanterns float in the air above, casting a warm glow on the evening.

Beck knows how he must look, lurking in the shadows near the center tree with a goblet in hand, watching as Jo tries to stop Shea from wiping her finger across the wedding cake icing, which only ends in Shea drawing a line of blue down Jo's cheek.

They kiss and Beck barely flinches.

It hadn't been an easy decision giving Shea his mother's ring, but something about it had felt right when he had visited her in her chambers before the wedding.

He'd presented it down on one knee and when she accepted, he tried to pretend it was her accepting his own proposal.

He shakes the somber thoughts away.

Everything he told Jo was true: he knows they belong together, he knows this is what is meant to be. But fate can be cruel, so he takes a heady sip from his goblet, letting the alcohol warm his chest.

Surrogacy. He figures Jo meant it as a kindness, but all he can think is that it will always be a reminder of what he'll never have.

Shea and he would share children, but they would be Shea and Jo's first. Jo would get to be there for Shea. Jo would raise his child, and he would be nothing but a distant relative.

Not true.

The words echo through his mind and he sighs reluctantly because he knows his thoughts are wrong. Jo isn't like that and that's why she deserves her.

He's staring into his goblet at the swirling dark liquid, lost to the world, when a hand on his shoulder surprises him. He turns to find its owner and is shocked to see Poseidon standing next to him.

"What are you doing lurking in the shadows? You should be out there enjoying the party," Poseidon tells him, crossing his arms over his chest.

Beck raises a brow. "I could say the same about you. Father of the bride and all."

Poseidon wipes a hand over his mouth and shakes his head with a dark chuckle. "No…No, I've lost my place among them. But you've gained a special place in their hearts, you're a part of them."

"You're wrong. It's not the same. I'll always be on the

outside of what truly matters."

"And? Do you think you deserve more? In a love like yours, there's usually a winner and a loser. Although you didn't win, you certainly haven't lost like most. They love you."

"So, I just accept that I'll have her in some ways and not in the ones that are really important?"

"Isn't that enough? If you truly love her, if she's truly who you believe you belong with, isn't even a small piece of her enough?"

Beck stands quietly thinking about Shea, and his conversations with Jo. He thinks about his stolen glances and heated sparring matches with the red-haired elf, he thinks of how he makes her laugh and how her eyes sparkle when he talks about his adventures with his father.

He thinks about their heated kiss on the pinnace that night surrounded by mermaids.

Then he imagines brown-haired children with those same brilliant green eyes, and he sees Jo there. He sees the three of them in the throne room in Arethusa or the state's hall in Oceanus, smiling, childish laughter filling the air, and it feels…like family. Something he no longer has.

He opens his eyes, but instead of finding Poseidon beside him, he finds Shea standing in front of him.

The music has slowed to a softer tempo and he thinks he recognizes the melody.

She's gorgeous. Her dress flows enchantingly around her and the light catches on the pearls scattered through her lush red hair. Her hand is extended out to him and she casts him a shy smile, countering her confident personality.

"Care to dance?"

Beck looks around, making sure there's no one behind him. When he finds no one there, he returns Shea's soft grin with one of his own and takes her hand, following as she leads him onto the dance floor.

Crewmen, naval officers of varying genders, even Dari

and Caen, are slow dancing to the elegant melody.

Beck catches Jo's eyes from across the room.

A nervous tightening clenches his stomach in fear that she'll be unhappy, but Jo is smiling. She gestures for him to move along before turning back to Aster and taking his hand to dance.

Shea and Beck come to a spot, separated from the rest of the crowd, and face each other. Beck bows respectfully and Shea does her best with a graceless curtsy.

He steps closer and places her left hand on his shoulder and takes her right with his left. He quickly realizes that he's going to have to lead as she stumbles a few times through the traditional waltz and after the fourth smack to the shoulder because of his giggling, he takes control.

"Should I be worried I'm going to come out of this with broken toes?"

That earns him another smack to the shoulder.

"Jo never complains."

Beck laughs. "I highly doubt that. So, if you can't dance, why'd you ask?"

"I don't know," Shea deflects the question, trying to pull away. "We can stop if you like?"

Beck holds on to her, though, and uses his arm around her waist to pick her up off the floor. He casually spins her around before setting her back down, her joyous laughter filling his ears.

"I'm fine. In fact, this may be the best moment of my life," he whispers, letting his chin rest aside her head.

"Beck..."

"I know. Just for this moment, be here with me, okay?" Beck asks.

He looks into her eyes and Shea looks back wistfully before finally nodding.

He puts his chin back near her head and enjoys the feeling of her closeness, her warmth, her heart beating next to his.

"This is nice," she says.

Beck silently agrees.

"Am I crazy?"

Shea pushes away from him enough to meet his gaze.

"What do you mean?" she asks.

"Did I imagine it all? You, me, us? Do you even have feelings for me?"

"Beck. I just got married," Shea starts, and Beck sighs.

"Right, sorry."

He goes to pull away and leave her on the dance floor, but she stops him with unanticipated strength because he'd almost forgotten who she was for a moment under that dress.

"Please. Stay."

"Tell me I'm crazy, tell me everything I've felt, everything between us this past week, was nothing."

"It's not that simple."

"But it could be," Beck objects. "Because, Shea, when I look at you, I see possibility, I see a connection I've never felt with anyone else. You and I are connected somehow, and I just wish…"

Beck stops himself before he can say more.

"What?" she demands.

"I wish I had met you first. Because I care more deeply for you than I ever thought possible, and I can't help but wonder if you could have loved me the way you love her. If you had met me first? Could I be the one you're married to?"

He goes to leave again, and she almost seems to let him go but at the last second, she grabs his arm again and turns him to face her.

"Yes."

"Yes?" Beck breathes.

"Yes, I could have married you, loved you. I think in some ways I already do. But we didn't meet first; destiny brought her to me instead. And she's…she's my everything."

"I know," Beck sighs.

"But I also know that I don't want to let you go, because I do feel for you. So...I've been making a lot of promises today, and now I'd like to make a promise to you."

Beck looks around warily, waiting for Jo to appear, and Shea must see his expression because she laughs awkwardly.

"Don't worry, I have permission. It seems you've found a way into my *wife's* heart too."

"She's an amazing woman," Beck admits.

"Aye, she is." Shea smiles.

"So, a promise?" he prompts.

"Yes. There are conditions to my marriage to Jo, I recently found out, and one of them involves children," Shea begins, and a faint blush fans her cheeks and the tips of her ears.

Beck blushes too. "Jo mentioned."

"Seems she's already a step ahead," Shea mutters, but continues, "Jo and I are married, we're bonded, but she, somehow, understands my connection to you. Maybe it's a royal thing or maybe...She just knows me. And she's recognized that it doesn't affect my loyalty or promises to her. Beck, what I feel for you, there's no label—love, platonic or romantic, it's there and regardless of what may happen, I can't lose you. You're somehow a part of me, and I have permission to give you a piece of me too."

"You want me to be the father of your heirs?"

"I want us to be a family," Shea answers honestly. "Could that be enough?"

Shea is staring him down earnestly and the words run through Beck's veins.

Is it enough?

Next thing he knows, Jo is standing beside Shea. She takes Shea's hand and reaches out with her other for Beck's.

"I don't understand what we are," Beck murmurs, mostly to himself, but Jo speaks up anyway.

"We're a team. I think the three of us could do anything. But I need you to know that if you accept, if you're with us, I'm a part of this too."

"A family?" Beck repeats.

"Family." Shea smiles.

He looks at both of them and there's so many emotions tied to them, he can't possibly name them all. But one emotion stands out clearly. Want. He wants this. And it's more than most would get.

"So, what do you say?" Shea asks.

"Yes."

Beaming smiles appear on both of their beautiful faces, and Beck knows deep down he made the right decision.

"Of course, children won't be on the table for a while," Shea voices, and Jo kisses her wife's cheek.

"Yes of course," Jo teases.

"Considering we have no idea how we're going to defeat Perses or if we'll survive the encounter," Beck chimes in, and he's surprised when Jo leans over and places a kiss on his cheek too. For the first time he notices she's a couple inches taller than him.

"I choose that for tonight and for tonight only, I have faith. Complete faith that the three of us together will stop Perses. That we can take back Nereid and we will win. I have faith in us, and for one night let's pretend you do too," Jo tells them both.

Shea looks at Beck and Beck gazes back at her; their eyes meet and they both sigh. There's no point in trying to resist the queen, so they nod in agreement.

Jo grins. "Good! Now," she announces loudly so everyone can hear, "I believe this is my wedding and a night to celebrate! So, maestros, can I get an Oceanan jig if you please?"

The musicians readily accept her command and the room is entranced by a familiar tune. Jo holds out her hands to the both of them, which they take easily.

The crew begins to clap, and others take to the floor to dance.

The next thing Beck knows, he's spinning around the

room, with two beautiful women on his arms and the beginning of a new family in his life.

CHAPTER 33: FIRST NIGHT

Jo

"You'll make sure he gets to his room," Shea laughs as Aster and James take the weight of Beck on their shoulders.

Aster gives them both a thumbs-up as the last of the party retires for the night.

The dome is a mess, but a wonderful mess, as Jo examines the last pieces of her wedding to Shea. The musicians are drunkenly passed out on their instruments, various crewmates and officers lay scattered across the floor.

Caen stumbles with a sleeping Phoebus in his arms and Dari smacks him, whispering loudly for him to be careful as they retire for the night.

Jo could barely drink a drop; she wants to remember it all.

After their dance, Beck had gone back for another drink, which had turned into a few celebratory glasses, with the end result of him being carried out of the main living quarters by Aster and James.

Jo can see the hesitation on her wife's—*wife's*—face as Aster heads off with James alone, toward bedrooms and dark hallways. She places a hand on Shea's shoulder and the captain turns to her with a glowing smile.

"It's fine," Shea says as the three boys disappear down the hall and out of sight.

"I know," Jo agrees. "So where will we be retiring?"

Shea pretends to think about it before she grabs Jo's hand and leads her down the same hall the boys left through. Except instead of leading her toward the guest chamber Dari had prepared, Shea takes her back to a familiar door and opens the way into her old bedroom.

"My clothes are in here," Shea explains and Jo chuckles.

Lanterns have been lit in the corners of the room, casting shadows on the mural walls.

Jo loves this room; she loves every memory she's had in here and the memory they're about to make.

The bed has been pulled down as if Dari had expected they might return here. Jo sees Shea's clothes have been neatly folded on the vanity, and the mirror reflects all the light, making the room look brighter than it actually is. The stars burn overhead, and the moon shines.

Shea is standing just before the balcony, looking out at the garden, the light catching the pearls in her hair, shimmering. Her blue-and-white wedding gown still flows delicately over her fit frame and Jo can see the deep slit in the back vividly.

The blue faded throughout the dress enhances the blues and greens in Shea's tattoo. Her muscles flex under the ink, the massive wings reaching toward her shoulders highlighted by candlelight.

The dress falls just above her round bottom, covering the small of her back and the black talons of the Lionbird.

Jo's mouth waters with desire. She notices two glasses and a wine decanter have been placed on a short table close to the mouth of the balcony. She makes her way to it, pouring the red wine quickly before handing it off to Shea, who takes it easily.

Shea sips the lush liquid, leaving a stain on her bottom lip. She licks it away gracefully, and Jo melts.

She places her glass down, and while Shea looks out at the gardens, she undresses. She unbuttons her dress jacket, letting it fall silently to the ground. She smiles as it goes unnoticed. She works the pants down next, toeing off her boots silently.

Shea notes some things about the garden, and Jo hums either in agreement or acknowledgment, letting the captain ramble.

Finally, she slips her undergarments off and reaches for her braided hair, untangling the strands and letting it fall loose past her shoulders until she stands completely naked off to Shea's side.

"I was thinking, we both love it here. Maybe after we defeat Perses, we could make an escape home here. When palace life is…complicated. We could come here, just for a little while. We could be the pirate and the princess just for a moment again," Shea chuckles, taking another sip of wine.

Jo smiles at the idea, and wonders if that would be possible. She saunters forward until she's close to Shea's side before answering.

"It's something to think about," she whispers.

And when Shea turns to her with a smile, her eyes widen in surprise as she finally notices Jo's nude form.

Her forest-green eyes roam the length of Jo's body, and it sends shivers down the blonde's neck. Shea turns completely toward her. She sets her glass on the ground, and once her hands are free, she wraps her arms around Jo's waist.

"You could have told me, now I'm behind," Shea murmurs, her lips close to Jo's.

"Not at all, I wanted to have the pleasure of undressing you," Jo responds, their lips touching in a ghostly embrace before she pulls away grinning like a cat that got a canary.

Shea huffs as she tries to chase Jo's retreating mouth, and mock glares at her queen.

"Maybe I wanted the same pleasure," Shea drawls.

Jo smirks. "I'll make it up to you."

She pulls Shea's body back toward her and kisses her deeply. Her hands grip her hair, and the soft pearls elegantly scattered through her thick red locks caress Jo's palms. She opens her mouth, allowing Shea entrance, their tongues meeting, and smiles into the kiss as her pirate moans in delight.

Shea's rough hands guide their way to Jo's chest, massaging the two pale mounds, her thumb flicking over her right nipple.

It's everything Jo's been missing for the past year. She pulls back once more and takes Shea's hand, leading her to the bed. She pushes Shea toward the footboard, facing toward it, and steps up close behind her, easily parting the redhead's hair and exposing the dress's cinch at the top.

Pearls fall from Shea's curls to the ground, and Jo runs her hands down her body, tracing the inked lines creating the stunning Lionbird, causing the redhead to shiver in anticipation.

She kisses the marked skin on her upper back, leaving a trail of soft touches down her spine.

Shea arches into Jo's mouth, gasping at the feather-like feel of Jo's soft lips. She reaches back to touch, but Jo clicks her tongue and forcefully puts Shea's hands back on the wooden footboard.

Jo growls, "Stay."

Shea nods her head but otherwise doesn't speak, trembling as a soft breeze flows through the warm room.

The lanterns flicker, manipulating the shadows on the mural wall.

Jo's hands are reaching for the neck cinch when her eyes land on a short table next to the bed with a black bag laid on top and a decanter of oil. The bag is slightly open, so she tries to gauge what's inside. Her eyes widen in recognition.

She thinks back to the conversation she had with Dari

after the proposal, an awkward one at that, but she really wanted to get something special for their wedding night. Something that would bring Shea a lot of pleasure and something she would remember. She shakes her head in amusement, surprised Dari managed to retrieve one in town.

A chuckle escapes her as she wonders if she picked it up personally or sent someone like Caen to get it from the local cordwainer.

Shea turns at the sound, but Jo leans forward and kisses her neck, distracting her.

Her hands make quick work of the simple cinch and the beautiful gown flutters to the floor.

Shea's body glows in the lantern light, her muscled frame completely exposed. She's barefoot already and Jo briefly wonders if she'd been wearing shoes at all during the party and ceremony.

Jo reaches down and removes the gown, giving Shea an order to remain where she is while Jo sets the wedding dress aside. And she's pleased when she returns to see Shea has done as she commanded.

She steps up behind her, her longer legs placing her womanhood slightly over Shea's bum. She wraps her arms around the pirate and pulls her back until there's no space between them. She kisses Shea's neck, sucking marks into the strong flesh. She wonders if her marks will show up through the tattoo on her back.

Her hands pinch and caress Shea's breasts, her left hand slips low past Shea's chiseled stomach to her groin. She strokes the pirate's swelling clit surrounded by copper curls, softly rubbing in circles until Shea's chest is rising faster.

"What do you want, Shea?" Jo asks, brushing her left hand farther back, teasing Shea's entrance with her pointer finger.

The room feels warmer and Shea gasps at the feeling of Jo's hands on her body.

"I don't know," Shea murmurs, she seems to be having

trouble forming words.

"Do you want me to stop?" Jo teases, stopping her hands.

Shea jolts in her embrace, moaning an objection.

"No!"

"Then what do you want?" Jo repeats, mouthing a wet line along Shea's sharp jaw.

"Your mouth," Shea answers.

Jo smiles against her lover's face.

She kisses her sweetly on the cheek, and then promptly turns her around.

Their chests press together and Jo kisses Shea again, biting at her full lips, tasting the last remnants of the wine on her mouth.

She wraps her arms around her waist and guides her around the bed, until the edge is behind Shea's thighs. Jo breaks the kiss and pushes Shea back, enjoying the little yelp of alarm as she loses her balance and falls, landing on top of the bed.

She allows Shea to shuffle farther back onto the mattress, using her elbows, before climbing onto the large bed with her.

It's then that she notices Shea hasn't dropped the illusion exposing her Lycon brand.

"Did it heal?" Jo wonders, nodding to Shea's chest, and it takes a moment for Shea to catch her meaning.

"No," she answers, frowning at the spot where it's concealed over her heart.

"I want to see all of you, Shea, you don't have to hide from me."

Shea smiles. "I know. But it's not hard to keep the illusion up now, it barely takes any concentration."

Jo chuckles, kissing Shea's chest. She takes Shea's left nipple into her mouth and suckles the skin, pinching it lightly with her teeth. Not to hurt, but the masked pain causes Shea to gasp.

"I'd prefer if all of your concentration is on me," Jo insists, licking her nipple again.

The illusion fades and the enchanted mark appears. The mournful face of Scylla accompanied by tentacles and snakes.

She grabs a pillow from the top of the bed and places it under Shea's head. Then she reaches for the black bag on the table, moving it to the bed but keeping it off to the side.

Shea eyes it, seeing it for the first time. But Jo doesn't explain. Instead, she parts Shea's muscular thighs, her white-blond hair falling along the crease between her groin and upper leg. She lowers her face closer to Shea's sex, closes her eyes, and places a soft kiss on her folds.

She loves the way Shea smells, like saltwater and a scent belonging entirely to Shea alone. She licks a line from her entrance to her clit, enjoying the way Shea's thighs shake from the touch. She looks up through her eyelashes to see her wife's face, her eyes closed, biting her lip as Jo samples her again.

The captain's hands clench the fabric of the bed.

Jo lowers her mouth at last, thoroughly mouthing Shea's clit. She moans into the redhead's sex, letting the vibrations caress her.

Shea's breathing labors and the sound encourages Jo further.

She pushes her tongue against Shea's opening, fucking her deeply, and uses her right thumb to rub Shea's swollen clit firmly. Her left hand reaches up to massage Shea's breast. She's close, Jo can feel it, and that's when she removes her mouth.

Shea whines at the loss, reaching her hand toward Jo.

Jo catches it easily and straddles the elf with a taunting grin. She leans down, kissing Shea's full lips, tangling her hands in the red curls framing her face.

"What are you doing?" Shea murmurs in between kisses.

"Shh…it's okay. Close your eyes and leave your thighs open."

Jo kisses Shea one last time, before getting up from the bed. She opens the black bag but checks to make sure Shea's eyes are closed. She smiles at her lover. They're closed. She pulls out the object and examines the craftsmanship.

Jo whistles lowly, and she has to tell Shea to keep her eyes closed when she almost opens them at the noise.

It's a leather phallus, and well made, the cordwainer must have made a few before. She thinks it might even be softer than ones she has acquired before for previous lovers. The seams are well hidden and the cord that is exposed is soft to the touch, with a bit of a ridge to enhance the pleasure. The length looks to be about five inches with a three-and-a-half-inch girth. A little bit of wool sticks out from the seam but it's easy to push back inside. Jo reaches for the oil and generously lathers it onto the toy; she rubs the oil in between her fingers and gently climbs back onto the bed.

"Now?" Shea asks, asking if she can open her eyes.

"Not yet," Jo commands.

She kisses Shea's mouth, then her jaw, she trails down her neck lightly, sucking a mark onto her chest; she allows her tongue to wander down past her stomach. She lightly kisses Shea's sweat damp curls, and then lavishes her clit, alternating between sucking and nipping the small bud. Her lubricated fingers find their mark, and she thrusts her pointer finger inside, pressing against the upper wall, making Shea keen as she exhales.

She stretches her carefully, making sure she's completely prepared. At three fingers, Shea is at the edge. Her back is arched, and her hands are in Jo's hair, tugging, making Jo groan with want.

Her own sex is thrumming between her legs, she wants Shea so badly, but she's going to wait.

Shea's eyes are still closed as Jo grasps the leather phallus, lathering it with more oil off the bed, and positions the tip at her entrance. She kisses Shea's stomach, smiling as the muscle flutters under her touch, and then pushes the tip inside.

Shea's eyes fly open and her jaw drops in surprise. Jo meets her gaze with a satisfied grin.

"More?"

Shea rolls her hips and Jo brushes her clit with her thumb, making Shea yelp.

She nods harshly, as Jo pushes more of the phallus inside her wife, until it's halfway to the base.

"How did you?"

"Doesn't matter," Jo tells her, blanketing Shea's body with her own.

She captures Shea's mouth in a kiss, and it opens as Jo thrusts the last of the toy to the base inside.

Shea's breathing heavily and she whispers something that Jo doesn't quite hear.

"What was that?" Jo asks.

"Move, damnit," Shea groans.

Jo chuckles and pulls the phallus out before thrusting it back inside. She keeps up a steady pace, sucking and biting Shea's breasts as she penetrates her.

Shea moans for her to go harder and Jo relents to her command, sitting back so she can rub herself while she thrusts the toy inside Shea.

Shea watches Jo pleasure herself with heavy eyes and her own hands wander to her nipples, squeezing the areolas between two fingers.

"Jo…"

"I love you," Jo tells her, her own breathing speeding up as she rubs herself to near completion.

"I love you too, so much. I can't," Shea whines.

"Gods you're gorgeous," Jo mumbles, then she pulls her hand away from herself to keep from finishing just as Shea orgasms after a particularly hard thrust from Jo.

Shea's thighs fall completely to the bed, her breathing

releasing in staccato breaths. She looks to be on the brink of passing out, but Jo's not done with her yet. She gently pulls the phallus from her lover's entrance and places it off to the side.

"Come here, darling," Jo commands, pulling Shea up to her knees.

Shea stares at her through half-lidded eyes, her eyebrows furrowing in confusion.

Once they're both facing each other on their knees, Jo moves in closer until her right knee is between Shea's legs and Shea's left is between hers. They're so close to each other now, their chests are touching, and their knees are intertwined.

Jo wraps Shea's arms around her shoulders and she pulls Shea against her using her waist. Then she starts to grind her sex against Shea's thigh, pushing her own up against her clit.

Shea moans at the touch, her eyes screwing shut at the stimulation. "Jo," she swallows some air before continuing. "It's too much."

"Stay with me," Jo whispers, and she gets their hips working in a rhythm.

The position is intimate, and Shea's gorgeous green eyes stare widely into Jo's passionate blue.

She leans forward and captures Shea's mouth in a burning kiss, sweat dripping down their chests. They're starting to move faster now, and she purposely pushes her thigh harder against Shea's clit. Jo takes Shea's bottom lip into her mouth, dragging her teeth lightly across it, and that seems to do the trick.

Shea orgasms once again and Jo focuses on grinding herself harder against Shea's thigh until her own sex is pulsing and she feels herself coming hard against her wife's body.

They collapse together onto the bed, their legs still intertwined, Shea's head landing close to Jo's.

The pirate's eyes are closed, but Jo knows she hasn't

passed out, not yet. She gives herself a moment to come down from the high before reaching for the phallus to remove it from the bed.

But to do that she has to remove her legs from Shea's and the redhead quickly voices her objection.

"Don't move," Shea clumsily orders, and Jo laughs.

"Someone has to get you tucked in," Jo teases.

She manages to extract herself from Shea's legs and places the phallus on the bedside table.

"Where in the Underdeep did you get that?" Shea asks.

"It was a wedding gift." Jo winks, and Shea chuckles, slinging a hand over her eyes.

"I can only imagine," Shea murmurs.

Jo climbs back into bed, watching her beautiful wife lying there. She notices there are still some pearls left in her loose curls.

Shea realizes Jo hasn't laid down yet and removes her hand from her eyes, smirking as she catches her wife staring at her.

"We should sleep."

"We should," Jo agrees.

As she says it, Shea's legs part and Jo finds herself climbing in between them again. Jo mewls as her pirate kisses her deeply. Her eyes dart to the almost full oil decanter on the bedside table and decides it's full enough for a few more rounds. She lets her hands wander down.

Their wedding night continues in another wave of passion, distracting them both from the sinister change in the wind.

CHAPTER 34: WARM BY THE FIRELIGHT

Shea

"Time to come home, little sister," a wicked voice whispers from the dark. "We'll all be together soon. Enjoy the firelight."

A bloodcurdling scream breaks through the peaceful night.

"Wake up!"

Shea's eyes fly open as she gasps, her hand swinging out to catch whoever is standing next to where she's lying in bed.

"Perses," Shea cries out, still hearing his voice in her head.

The figure catches her fist, and her eyes adjust to the darkness. Triton is standing over her.

His clothes, brown pants with cords tied tightly around the calves and leather shirt with a hood, are obscured by a black cloak.

"I heard him too," Triton scowls.

Another scream billows through the air.

Shea snaps her head toward the bedroom door, which is now open.

Jo wakes to the sound of the second scream and yelps

when she sees Triton standing over their bed. She grabs the blankets and covers herself. Shea couldn't care less about modesty; she's already leaping from the bed, running for her clothes folded on the vanity.

"What's happening? What are you doing here?" Shea hisses as Triton stealthily moves to the door, looking out into the hall.

"After you left, I couldn't get you out of my head. I needed to close the connection, but your magic wouldn't let me. I needed to be closer, so I came to Port Town, and as I arrived, they did too."

"Shea?" Jo questions, pulling the sheet from the bed and using it to cover herself as she heads for her own clothes as well.

"Who did?" Shea asks, ignoring Jo for now.

"Merrow. Twisted fish folk that work for Perses. They're burning the city, killing everything in their path, and I'm pretty sure they're looking for you."

"Who is this?" Jo asks.

"Triton, meet my wife, Joana," Shea introduces them.

Triton nods to Jo in acknowledgment.

"I can see the resemblance," Jo murmurs, buttoning up her jacket as Shea finishes getting dressed.

"We don't have much time, I reinforced the elf's veiled magic on this home, but it won't hold much longer; they're going to break through."

"We need to get out of here," Shea orders.

Jo and Triton agree.

Shea starts for the door but then remembers why Triton came here.

"Well then, go ahead and close the connection so you can get back to the temple," Shea tells him.

Triton stares at her, his expression unreadable, and he shakes his head.

"I'll see you and your crew safely back to your ship, then I'll break the connection. It's the least I can do," he says.

Jo smiles at Shea subtly, and if Shea wasn't so worried about hearing Perses in her mind, she may have winked back. Instead she keeps her expression neutral and nods.

"I appreciate it. Thank you."

The sky overhead is black and orange. The city is burning outside and it's a harsh glare against the midnight blue.

Shea uncorks her waterskin now attached to her waist. She realizes Jo's sword is missing.

Triton doesn't seem to be carrying any weapons either, but she figures it'd be a mistake to underestimate him.

She leads them out into the hall, looking around for any trace of trouble.

They move quickly into the next room and run straight into Poseidon.

Jo catches Shea as she stumbles back, and Poseidon stops himself from falling by catching himself on the white clay wall.

"Oh. It's you," Shea growls.

Poseidon sighs. "I was coming to find you."

"Thanks for the concern," Shea scoffs. "Do you know what's happening?"

"Merrow. Dari, Caen, Phoebus, and some of the crew are in the storefront of the dome trying to keep the magic boundaries in place. They're surprisingly strong for elven magic," Poseidon states.

"I strengthened them, when I snuck through," Triton speaks.

Poseidon finally sees him as he steps around the corner.

"You're here." Poseidon smiles.

"Not for you," Triton responds.

Shea and Triton glare at Poseidon while Jo stands there looking uncomfortable.

"I know our family is a bit dysfunctional right now, but we should probably get going," Jo suggests, tucking a strand of hair behind her ear.

Poseidon clears his throat and unhooks something at his side.

Shea recognizes her old sword, the one Jo has been using, and he hands it to her wife.

"I know you don't trust me anymore," Poseidon says to Shea, and he's looking at both his children, "but you still need people to help. Let me do what I can. Because even though I've lost your faith, you're still my children and I want to protect you. Both of you."

Triton scoffs, turning away, but Shea takes a shaky breath.

She knows he's right, and even if he did lie, he's not completely worthless. He is still able to help more than most. Shea forces herself to put aside her anger and at least use him.

"We need to get to the storefront; have you seen Aster, Beck, and James?"

"I think they were in the kitchens," Poseidon reports.

"Okay, then let's go."

As she takes a step forward to lead the group again, the sound of glass breaking fills the air. Battle cries, men shouting, and people screaming echo down the halls. Clashing metal and banging is coming from the dome and Shea takes off in a run toward the sounds.

"They've broken through," Triton barks.

No shit, Shea thinks and startles when he responds.

"I was just saying," Triton snaps back in her mind.

She looks at him briefly as they run to the dome.

He gives her a humorless grin.

She shakes her head, turning back as they enter the dome.

It's chaos.

Shea has never seen the Merrow up close before.

Their bodies are humanoid, but their skin is covered in scales and fish slime with three rows of gills down the neck. Long webbed fingers end in razor-like nails and knifelike fins extending off their ankles, thighs, elbows, back, and the top of their heads. They're grotesque and misshapen.

They seem to be wearing some kind of armor, and all of them carry Lycon swords, black volcanic metal produced from the forges in Acheron.

Perses really is working with Lycos.

Shea can't believe Ceto is this insane—to be aiding him, an elf of all things, even for power.

The center tree is burning. Leaves are falling, creating small balls of fire cascading down from fiery branches, and the house lays mostly in ruins. They broke down the storefront with an explosion of some kind.

Shea doesn't see Dari, Phoebus, or Caen. She does, however, see Beck, James, and Aster fighting with albeit improvised weapons against two particularly nasty Merrow.

The first has orange fins and purple skin with brutal pure black eyes, while the other has overly large teeth spilling out of its mouth with white eyes and a gray ashen body, both covered in slime.

Aster seems to be wielding a large skillet, while James lunges with a pitchfork, and Beck swings a sickle he must have found near the hay bales in the stables.

They're holding their own.

Aster manages to slam his skillet into the orange-and-purple one's head while James skewers him with a pitchfork.

Beck dodges a nasty blow and slices the sickle into the gray one's middle, killing him but also losing his sickle in the creature's side.

Shea shouts to them and they turn, finding her quickly. They point toward the dining area and Shea turns to see Dari in a white nightgown, sword fighting a large Merrow. Phoebus is lying up against the wall, and Caen, in his vest, pants, and boots, is protecting him from two Merrow charging at them.

The one fighting Dari must hear Shea's shout because he turns toward her, and points.

He calls in elven for the other Merrow to attack her. Looks like he might be the one in charge.

Dari screams as she is unable to dodge a blow to her leg and the Merrow slashes her thigh.

Phoebus cries out and starts crawling toward her as quickly as he can with his broken leg.

"Poseidon, help Caen! Triton, Jo, go help Beck, Aster, and James. I'm going to go help my mom," Shea orders.

She takes off running into battle before anyone can object.

Jo and Triton head for the three boys.

Triton summons water from the air as he moves his hands in a precise gesture and water forms around both.

Jo draws her blade and they fight the oncoming Merrow together. There's not many left and if they can kill the last few, they can start making their way to the docks before more pile into the merchant's home.

Shea spots Caen swinging his hammer, crushing a Merrow's skull. His back is turned as another lunges at him with its blade.

Shea shouts for Caen to turn around but there's not enough time. She almost changes paths, narrowly avoiding a Merrow that storms her, swinging his blade across her chest. She uses the water from her pouch and wraps a lasso around the creature's throat, breaking its neck.

Poseidon has created a trident from the wedding wine. He rushes to Caen's aid and impales his trident through the Merrow attacking the other man, picking the creature up and throwing it across the room.

Caen side-eyes Poseidon with an angry glare, but he can't ignore his help and gruffly expresses his thanks.

Looks like they're a team for now.

Members of the Arethusian navy and Shea's crew battle the rest of the nightmarish creatures. A few of their allies are dead on the floor.

Shea finds the two Oceanan soldiers who accompanied

Beck at the beginning of this voyage on the ground.

The male officer has been decapitated and the woman holds his detached head in her lap, her eyes wide and unseeing, blood soaking her clothes.

Shea takes down another Merrow that tries to sever her arm as she bends the water offensively. She forces the liquid down his throat and changes it into icicles, ripping his throat out from the inside.

Semele has found her way to one of the dead Merrow's swords. She's fighting off another, keeping him off Dari's back, while Dari summons burning vines from the center tree to wrap around the Merrow attacking her.

Shea's almost to her, only a few steps away.

Dari's leg is bleeding badly, and just as Shea's about to make it to the two older women defending the dining area, she spots Phoebus.

He's still crawling toward Dari, his broken leg splinted around his leather pants and his peasant shirt ripped, but now a Merrow has noticed him.

The creature smiles at the slow-moving dwarf.

Phoebus winces in pain as his broken leg slides across the ground.

It advances from behind him and Shea makes a choice.

Semele and Dari seem to have things in hand, so she veers off course and runs toward Phoebus.

The abomination growls, alerting him to its presence in time for him to see the Lycon sword coming down on him.

Shea shoots out her hand with a guttural cry, the water changes form midair, solidifying into a solid ice spear that hits the Merrow in the chest, throwing him off his feet to fly backward.

A feminine scream catches Shea off guard, and her steps falter. Shea turns to find Jo, searching for her desperately, and her eyes land on the queen near the broken storefront helping Beck kill an incoming Merrow.

Jo turns around as well, relief visible when her eyes

land on Shea, but then they widen in horror as she stares beyond her.

"No!" Phoebus cries, his hand flung out.

Shea turns to where he's pointing and finds Dari with a Merrow standing behind her. His sword is thrust through her chest, lifting her off the ground.

Semele is the one who must have screamed as she tries to fight harder against the Merrow she's battling to get to Dari.

Nausea grips Shea's stomach. There's a roaring in her ears, a gushing noise like river rapids. She can feel her veins thrumming with power.

The Merrow behind Dari pulls his sword from her chest, dropping her to the ground like a discarded object.

Shea's vision tunnels; her hands are moving of their own accord, and there's a sensation like an invisible rope in her hands that she's pulling on.

A thunderous sound echoes throughout the dome as Shea screams. A wall of water rushes from the garden, breaking down a part of the dome. Water tentacles shoot from the turbulent column and grab at the remaining Merrow in the dome.

All of them.

They're sucked inside the liquid wall. Shea thinks she can hear someone shouting her name, but she ignores it. She's going to kill them; she's going to kill them all.

Once they're inside, she clenches her fists slowly. Ice inches its way up the water, freezing everything inside the churning wave, even the Merrow, until frost obscures the view.

She pulls her clenched hands together, feeling the raw power humming inside. She thinks she can hear a man's voice in her head whisper…

"Beautiful."

But she's not beautiful, she's dangerous.

She pulls her hands apart, and the wall of ice shatters,

the creatures inside bursting into a million pieces of ice and flesh.

It falls to the ground with a loud crash.

Shea lands on her knees, the ground around her pulsating with power. She has to keep going, she has to destroy every last one of them.

A man's face appears in her vision. A familiar one, with light blue eyes and copper-brown hair. He's saying something to her, but she can't hear it. All she can hear is the sound of the ocean.

She watches his mouth because he seems to be repeating the same phrase over and over again. She focuses on the movements of his mouth until his voice filters in.

"Epistrépste se mas tin mikrí adelfí. Eímaste to máti kai i kataigída den boreí na akolouthísei."

He repeats this phrase until her brain finally translates the elvish: Come back to us, little sister. We are the eye, and the storm can't follow.

"Triton," Shea whispers, her voice hoarse from screaming.

He nods, and even grants her a smile.

"Are we safe?"

"For now," he comforts.

"Dari," Shea breathes.

She looks past Triton and sees Phoebus sitting on the ground with Dari in his arms, rocking her in his embrace.

"No," Shea grunts.

She stands as quickly as she can, waving off Caen, who has come closer to help.

Semele has her head bowed and seems to be murmuring something to herself, a prayer perhaps.

Beck and Jo are standing behind Phoebus, watching him with Dari while James holds Aster, who's buried his head against his shoulder.

Shea runs as best she can, and as Phoebus looks up and sees her, a single tear escapes his eye. He gestures for her to come closer.

She kneels down and sees that Dari is still breathing. Her heart leaps.

"She's alive," Shea exclaims.

"Not for much longer, my little one," Dari murmurs.

Shea places a hand over the wound in Dari's chest, but Dari pushes her hand away.

"No, it'll only delay the inevitable."

"We can get you to Nol," Shea argues, but Dari raises her hand weakly and presses a finger to her mouth.

"It's okay. I'm ready, but you all need to get out of here, more will be coming."

"We're not leaving you here alone," Shea commands.

"She won't be alone," Phoebus states.

He pushes some of Dari's white hair away from her face and Dari smiles at him.

"What?" Shea croaks.

"I can't leave my wife, and my leg will only slow you down. Dari's right, you need to go."

"If you stay, you'll die, Phoebus," Caen emphasizes.

"And we'll die together."

"I can't leave you both behind, you're my family," Shea pleads, tears starting to fall.

"And we always will be," Dari says. "But you have other family who can be helped now, and you need to get them out of here."

"No," Shea stubbornly refuses. She turns to Triton and Poseidon standing behind her. "All of our power, there must be something we can do!"

Poseidon looks away.

Triton glares at their father, disgusted with his cowardice. He looks Shea dead-on.

"Death is not our dominion. There's nothing we can do."

"I'm sorry, Shea," Poseidon tells her.

"That's not good enough!" Shea roars back.

"Shea!" Phoebus barks.

She turns to face the man she considers a grandfather, tears brimming in her eyes.

He gazes at her with fire, and a set expression.

"Who are you?"

"Phoebus..."

"Who are you? Who did we make you, who did Paetre make you?"

"Captain," Shea grits. "Captain of the *Veiled Duchess*."

"And a leader. Their leader, and being a leader comes with sacrifices. You have to get your people to safety. You have to make sure our deaths are not in vain. You have to kill Perses. But in order to do that, you have to live. Leave us and get to the ship."

"But you're my people," Shea whispers.

Phoebus laughs and Dari smiles, a choking sound escaping her throat.

"And we always will be," she gasps. "We love you, little elf, and we will always be with you just as Paetre is."

"We love you, Shea," Phoebus adds.

Shea bites her lip to keep from sobbing. She hugs them both the best she can and kisses Dari's forehead and Phoebus's cheek.

"If we're going to leave, we best do it now before more of them come," Caen advises, gritting his teeth.

Shea stands shakily and Jo races toward her, catching her as she falters.

"I've got you," Jo tells her.

Beck is at her other side, helping as well.

"Jo," Dari rasps.

Jo turns, kneeling down beside Dari and Phoebus.

"Take care of our girl."

"Always. Thank you...for everything."

Jo squeezes Dari's hand and stands.

She recruits Beck to go and scout the caved-in storefront. James offers to follow as well.

Aster kneels down, hugging Dari as tightly as he can without hurting her, and she kisses him on the head as Phoebus ruffles his hair.

"You're the man now. Caen's an old softie, so you got to be the one in charge of them," Phoebus orders.

Shea laughs while Caen looks mock affronted.

Aster sniffs, nodding. He stands next to Shea and takes her hand.

She knows he won't leave her side.

"Caen. It's been a lifetime," Dari chuckles.

"I never thought I'd be the last one left," Caen jokes, wiping his thumb across his nose quickly.

"Well you are," Phoebus drawls. "So don't let us see you anytime soon. You get old. Well, older than you are."

Caen laughs but it's hollow.

Phoebus reaches up his hand.

Caen leans down, taking it, and squeezes gently. Then he stands and salutes with his hand over his heart.

"It's been a pleasure, Captain," Caen states, "and a privilege, my lady. Tell Paetre…" Caen looks away. "Tell him I… never stopped loving him, missing him."

"Will do, brother," Phoebus sighs.

Shea is surprised by the way Caen phrases his message to Paetre. She almost wants to stop him, clarify what he means, but there's no time.

It's time to go.

The last of the crew that came to the wedding, who survived, are all at the broken storefront with Jo, Beck, and James.

Aster keeps his hand in Shea's.

Caen walks away without looking back, and Poseidon follows.

Just as Shea turns to go as well, she notices that her immortal brother is still with Dari and Phoebus.

"They're going to come," he tells them.

"We know," Phoebus growls with his head held high.

"Merrow are cruel folk. And while I think your wife will pass before they arrive, I would rather you not suffer a worse fate," Triton explains.

"I'm not leaving her," Phoebus yells.

"I know."

Triton reaches under his cloak and Shea realizes he has a travel bag. He reaches into the pack and pulls out a black plant with blue veins riddled through it. He kneels down in front of Phoebus and Dari and shows it to them.

"This is Azulshade, it grows only in the depths of the Underdeep and the shallows of Tenaro. I managed to collect some during my time there. If you turn it into a salve, it has incredible healing properties. I would have used it on your wife, but by the time I could have made the right poultice for her, it…Well. But if you were to eat it, it would stop your heart inside of thirty seconds."

He offers it to them.

"Take it when we leave. It's a peaceful way to go, you won't feel much, perhaps a little discomfort and then it'll all be over."

Phoebus shakes his head. "I couldn't—"

But Dari reaches out and takes it weakly.

"Thank you," she tells him before looking up at Phoebus. "Just as you don't want me to be alone, I do not wish you to suffer, my love. We'll take it together."

Phoebus leans down and kisses his wife soundly on the lips.

"Thank you," Phoebus sighs, catching Triton's eyes.

"You shouldn't thank me. I should be thanking you for caring for my sister. I'm sorry."

"This isn't your fault," Phoebus scoffs.

"It might as well be. I tried to kill Perses before, and if I succeeded this wouldn't be happening."

"So, try again."

Triton looks at Dari with surprise.

"I failed," Triton explains. "Who's to say I'd succeed

this time?"

"Who's to say you won't," Dari demands. "Shea told me about meeting you. She believes in you, that you're better than you were. Now I've always had faith in the gods, but my daughter not so much. Do you want to be better?"

"I've caused so much pain," Triton states, but Dari scowls.

"I didn't ask you if you felt guilty. I asked you if you wanted to be better."

Triton is quiet.

Shea tells Aster to go ahead.

Caen is conducting groups of four out of the dome to head for the docks.

Beck and Jo are staring at her from the door.

She knows it's time to go, but she has to hear this through.

"Yes," he finally admits.

"Then stop him. Save Nereid. Help your sister. You're a part of this world whether you want to be or not. Stop hiding and do better. You can start with protecting my daughter and making sure we don't die here for nothing."

"You heard her," Shea interrupts.

Triton turns toward her, not realizing she was so close.

Shea holds out her hand for Triton to take.

"You with us?"

Triton is staring at her curiously. He clicks his tongue and shakes his head in exasperation.

"I can see where she gets her stubbornness from," Triton murmurs to Dari.

Dari reaches her right hand out and Triton kisses the back.

Shea still has her hand out as he leaves them on the floor and faces her.

He takes it.

"I'm with *you*. It's time I fix my mistakes."

Shea takes one last look at Phoebus and Dari, at the dome where she partially grew up, and she places a hand over her heart as a sign of respect. Turning her back on them is as hard as when she watched Paetre die. Her steps fumble, but Triton keeps hold of her hand and helps her to the door.

James and Aster have gone on ahead, leaving Caen, Jo, and Beck, as well as an unexpected face.

"Semele."

Semele gives her a ghost of a smile.

"You're welcome to come with us," Shea offers, but Semele is already shaking her head.

"I'm not willing to enter another war, Shea. I've seen enough violence in my life, you know that."

Shea does.

"Where will you go?"

"I hear Helios is nice this time of year, and from there, perhaps even farther south. All I know is I can't go back. I never thanked you."

"You'd require a thankful bone in your body," Caen drawls, glaring at Semele.

The lady smirks.

There's a loud crash from down one of the streets, screams can be heard in the distance, and inhumanly growls echo off the wind.

They're coming.

"I never expected you would," Shea chuckles.

Beck is peering farther down the cobbled stone streets and he waves for them to hurry.

"Hate to interrupt," Jo remarks, "but we need to go."

"Goodbye, Shea," Semele imparts.

"I don't think it's safe for a woman to walk these streets alone right now," Jo argues, but Shea holds her back from reaching out to Semele.

Caen sends Shea a knowing glance as Semele laughs.

"I won't be a woman then," Semele responds.

Her body ripples and molds, her frame changing

shape, sharp edges protruding from her once slim frame until one of the disgusting Merrows stands in front of them.

Semele waves with her clawed fingers, and stealthily scurries away.

"But she's—" Jo stutters. "She was human. No human has magic."

"No human Nereidan," Caen tells her, drawing his hammer. "But she wasn't Nereidan."

"Time to go," Shea announces.

Beck sighs in relief as they finally begin to follow behind him.

They keep to the shadows and away from the firelight.

Caen knows the alleys of Orena like the back of his hand. And they make it to the docks in an hour or so.

The remaining crew on the *Duchess* would have known to sail the ship to the old docks, past the newer built and busy marketplace, along the shallows where the old town docks sit rotting without lanterns.

The shadows would hopefully have obscured them, but the city is ablaze. Everything is on fire and the shadows have receded in sight of the flame.

The new port is burning, falling and being swallowed up by the sea.

They make their way to the crumbling old port with few encounters.

A particularly nasty duel ends with Caen earning a head wound and Beck on the ground, but when Shea runs to him, he's up just as quickly.

She tries to see where he's been hurt but he assures her he was merely knocked down.

Between Shea and Triton, they're able to support Caen and make it the rest of the way.

They watch their step along the rotting wooden planks, and in the distance, Shea can make out her familiar bloodred sails.

They're met halfway by Aster and Billius, a *Duchess*

gunner.

They aid a stumbling Caen, and soon after they're all on the main deck of the *Duchess*.

The ship is silent. No evening lamps burn, as the island gives off enough light for everyone to see each other's faces.

The screaming is dying out, and the fire blazes like Hades's fire.

Orena is gone.

Dari and Phoebus are *gone*.

Shea looks around at her crew; at least half her men are dead. This was more than a loss; this was a vision of things to come. What just a few Merrow could do and how Perses could orchestrate it from miles away.

"What are your orders, Captain?" James asks.

She chuckles painfully to herself, because with Caen injured and being taken down below, James is next in line.

All the people she's lost, and gods, she could still lose more.

She's losing her mind, and a strong hand steadies her. She looks back to see Triton with a solemn expression. She has to be strong. She's the captain.

"Weigh anchor, set sail, and get us the bloody Underdeep out of here," Shea orders.

James nods, squaring his shoulders under his new responsibility as quartermaster and bos'n. He takes a deep breath.

"You heard the captain," he growls, his blue eyes piercing every member of the crew on deck.

The surviving men straighten at James's voice—it seems to snap them all out of their stupor and they start moving.

"Get those sails up. I want that anchor out of the water now! Aster!"

James finds Aster, who freezes at his boyfriend's hard voice.

Shea can see James's eyes soften, but he remains strong and firm.

"To the helm."

Aster takes the helm stairs two at a time, and before long, Shea can feel the wind on her face.

She wanders over to the rail, placing both hands on the wood, and watches the burning city's reflection on the midnight water. The stars shine dimmer in comparison. She's always hated the orange of fire.

There's a presence at her side and she finds her wife's hand gripping her left. Another person appears to her right, and Beck's shaking hand covers the other.

They watch the fall of Orena together and Shea can't help but wonder if the fire has reached Dari and Phoebus yet.

CHAPTER 35: LAST NIGHT

Phoebus

"They're gone?" Dari whispers.

"Yes," Phoebus confirms, still staring at the caved-in storefront where their surrogate daughter disappeared.

"I can't feel my legs," Dari chuckles.

Phoebus's eyes close, the pain of those words seeping through his mind. He sniffs, stopping the tears from coming. It won't be long then. He opens his eyes and huffs as he sees Dari's smiling face.

She won't need the plant; she's got minutes left.

"Do you remember when you brought home Lena?" Dari croaks.

She grunts as Phoebus readjusts her in his arms, but the wrinkle of discomfort disappears from her forehead as he supports her neck better.

"You mean when you almost killed me?" he jokes.

Dari laughs, but it turns into a bloody cough, a trickle of red escaping her mouth.

"Well what was I going to do with an animal that large, I was terrified she'd crush Shea. Our little elf was so small for a sixteen-year-old."

"But brave. Fiery. Strong like you." Phoebus smiles wistfully, remembering the wee elf they once cared for.

"I hate leaving her," Dari sobs.

Phoebus holds her close now, rocking her injured body against his.

"Shh…my love, she'll be okay. I know it."

He keeps rocking his wife until her sobs begin to dissipate.

"We'll all be together someday. You were the best mother she could have had. Gods, you were the best wife a man could have. I love you; I may have saved you from Arethusa so long ago, but Dari, you were the one who truly saved me," Phoebus says, expecting an argument from his wife, the way they always banter.

But no response comes.

"Eh? Dari?"

Phoebus pulls her away from his chest and his eyes meet her wide unseeing ones.

"Ohhh…"

Phoebus cries, and the tears fall freely. He kisses her dead lips and pushes her hair back.

"Oh, my darling."

An explosion rocks the remaining structure of the dome and there's visible fire surrounding the splintered wood of the doorway. Loud growls and battle cries can be heard from outside.

Phoebus opens Dari's lax right hand and plucks the Azulshade from her palm.

He looks around their home, their memories of fifteen plus years, and he kisses his wife one last time.

"I'm coming, love. It's going to be okay. You're okay now."

Phoebus eats the Azulshade. He chews it quickly and swallows the best he can. He's tempted to count the seconds but instead he pulls his wife closer, kissing her forehead.

A dull pain starts in his left arm, it's growing sharper,

and he chokes. He can't take in any air. He suppresses the panic that threatens to overtake him.

A loud bang echoes throughout the dome, and Phoebus looks up in time to see a group of ugly Merrow storming their home.

His lips twist into a harsh semblance of a smile and he uses his last breath, "Too late."

Hades takes him.

The last living thought that graces his mind is of his wife and how he can't wait to see her again in the underworld.

CHAPTER 36: LAST RITES

Shea

The ship is quiet even hours after Orena has faded from the horizon. Dawn rises but most can't decide whether the orange light is sun or fire.

By the time Nol has patched up Caen's head and he's walking around, James has the list of the dead.

All but five Arethusian naval officers have been killed, something Jo has a hard time processing.

When the *Duchess*'s crew arrived in Arethusa, they had fifty men. After the Megathirio, it had dropped to forty-three. Now Shea has twenty-six of her original crew left. They're down sailors, but the voyage isn't impossible to make. As long as they don't encounter any major monsters like the water dragon on the way home, they should be able to sail the *Duchess* without struggle.

By midmorning, the once bright sunny sky has faded into a gray and murky one.

Shea can feel a storm brewing as she studies the charts on the navigation table up on the afterdeck. Caen returns to his duties as quartermaster with Nol's permission, leaving James to go back to his responsibilities as bos'n.

There's no time to mourn.

Jo refuses to retire after hearing the number of soldiers she's lost and runs to Nol to help with any injured.

They'll need every hand available.

The winds stay strong, leaving little for the crew to do besides maintenance and smaller tasks. It allows time for the losses to be felt, and by afternoon, the ship is more like a funeral hall than a sturdy crew.

Shea needs to cut down the time of the voyage somehow, she needs to get them all to Arethusa faster. Because if what happened to Orena was merely what a platoon of Merrow could do, what would happen when they had a whole army at their backs?

"Damnit!" Shea growls, slamming her fist onto the map and causing both Caen and Aster to jump.

"We're making good time," Caen begins, but Shea holds up her hand for him to stop.

"There's got to be some way. Some way we can make the *Duchess* move faster," Shea murmurs, pacing back and forth.

"We don't have the manpower. We barely have enough to sail the ship as it is," Caen reminds her.

"Hades! If we don't get there in time, then it's all pointless anyway," Shea snarls.

Her temper gets the better of her, and before she knows it, she's pulled a lasso of water up over the edge of the ship and she slashes it down on the opposite rail, cutting the wood deeply.

"Careful!" Caen remarks. "Don't take it out on the *Duchess*."

Shea runs her hands through her hair, trying to come up with a solution.

"What about Beck?"

"What?" Shea turns sharply to look at Aster behind the wheel.

"Well, remember how he met Perses? Before all this? He said one minute he was out in the ocean and the next they were all on the shore of Arethusa."

"Aster," Shea breathes.

She runs over to him, cups his face between both her palms, and kisses his forehead. "You're a genius!"

Shea runs to the rail and shouts for Beck, who races to the bottom of the stairs.

"What do you need?" he asks.

"Find Poseidon and Triton, tell them it's urgent and to meet me on the afterdeck."

Beck nods and takes off.

A few minutes later, he returns with Triton and Poseidon following behind him.

It's then that she truly sees the differences between the two. When she'd met her father, his shoulder-length hair had been gray and his copper beard graying, but his face had looked as young as a thirty-year-old man. His whole presence exuded a sort of youthful aura and his stature was strong and powerful.

Not so anymore.

His hair and beard are completely white, and he looks to be about the same age as Caen. His power isn't as tangible as it was before.

She can still feel it within her mind's room of magical doors. She touches his open doorway and a wave of power washes over her, but as a sort of strength seems to rejuvenate herself, when she looks back at her father, he looks tired.

Triton on the other hand is practically generating energy where he stands. She can feel the ocean's power radiating off of him, and he looks the same age as she is.

"What's happening to you?" Shea demands, confronting Poseidon, who's leaning up against the helm's rail and facing the main deck.

"I'm fine," Poseidon states.

"Bullshit, and why do you feel so…" Shea stares at Triton, trying to find the right word.

"Powerful?" Triton supplies.

"Yes."

"Easy. For one, he's here." Triton points to Poseidon, who rolls his eyes. "And two, my shell is here. It's not locked in Atlantis. I draw my power from both, mostly from our father, but my shell gives me an incredible boost. As long as it's in the mortal world, my abilities will only grow."

"Are you dying?" Shea inquires, semi-worriedly, at Poseidon.

"No!"

"No."

Triton and Poseidon answer at the same time, although Poseidon is much more forceful.

Shea raises her eyebrow.

"I'm not," Poseidon answers. "The original gods, my siblings who were born of the titans, we were given dominion over pieces of Earth and humanity. Along with those dominions, we were given objects that grounded and connected us to our power. Should those objects ever be removed, it would leave us with our base abilities. My brother Zeus was given a lightning bolt to rule the skies, I was given a trident to master the seas, and Hades was given a bident to control the dead. Each of these objects made us more than our immortal selves. They made us invulnerable. Take them away and we'd still have our immortality from our parents, the titans, but we would be vulnerable to mortal death."

"So, you're becoming vulnerable?" Caen inquires.

Poseidon sighs. "Yes. I told you that the gods faded or left their posts, and some of them did, yes, but they faded either because they lost their objects or because their godly parents were destroyed."

"I don't understand," Aster chimes in, as he's been listening to the whole thing.

"To make sure another Titan War didn't happen, the original gods tied their children, the minor gods, to themselves instead of objects. Destroy a parent and the child would lose their invulnerability. It definitely inspired loyalty," Triton muses.

"So, if our father dies?" Shea asks.

"Then I start the same process, I begin to lose my invulnerability. Not to mention the call would begin to replace him. But yes. Our powers would be greatly reduced. You'd most likely lose your healing abilities, and your bending would be more like it once was."

"What call?" Shea asks warily.

"You shouldn't worry about it, I don't plan on dying anytime soon," Poseidon gripes, glaring at his son.

"But didn't you say Perses tried to kill you in the Underdeep?" Caen mentions.

"Yes, with celestial steel," Poseidon explains. "The only metal that can kill an immortal and invulnerable god. Created by Hephaestus himself in the underwater volcanoes of the Underdeep. There was an old legend that claimed if a god was ever stabbed in the mortal realm by a mortal man with a celestial steel blade, their immortality would be transferred to them."

"A myth. But he stole my sword while I was sleeping. Maybe he thought it was real," Triton states.

"Did you get it back?" Aster asks from the helm, enthralled by the story.

"Yes," Triton murmurs. "After I stabbed Perses through, I withdrew the blade. I couldn't bear to wield it again, so I threw it down to the depths with our brother's body."

"I still don't understand why he's doing this, if he's dying, I mean?" Shea murmurs. "What does he have to gain from taking over Nereid?"

"That, dear sister, is an excellent question, and one that makes me curious as well."

"I'm sure you didn't call us up here for a theology lesson, how can we help?" Poseidon inquires.

"Actually, I'm going to need Beck for that, considering I wasn't there."

"I thought that's why you wanted them," Beck's voice speaks up from behind Poseidon and Triton, who step aside to let him through.

"How long were you there?" Shea demands.

"Um, the whole time. I wanted to know what was happening." Beck shrugs.

Shea pinches the bridge of her nose.

Caen chuckles beside her.

"This is about how he transported us to Arethusa, right?"

Shea nods.

"Who?" Triton asks.

"Perses," Beck responds. "When he attacked my father's ship weeks ago. We were all in longboats, he spoke to me, gave me a message to give to Jo, and then he blew the shell and we were transported to the shores of Arethusa."

Triton and Poseidon catch each other's eyes, alarmed.

"What?" Shea asks.

Triton ignores her in favor of asking Beck another question.

"What did it feel like? And the sound, what sound did the shell make? You actually saw him blow it?"

"Yes, it was shrill. Painful. When we moved, it was sudden, almost instantaneous, and it felt like my stomach tried to eat itself."

"Did your vision go dark?"

"For maybe a moment."

"It's not possible," Triton tells Poseidon.

"But it sounds like it. Either he's getting help from my brother or he somehow accessed it using the shell."

"Somebody please explain what is going on!" Shea shouts, and everyone turns to her.

"There's no need," Triton remarks.

"No, there is," Shea argues. "I need you to do whatever Perses did."

"I can't."

"What did he do?" Caen growls.

"Shadow magic."

"Shadow magic?" Shea repeats.

"Yes. It's a traveling magic. A god or someone claimed by Hades, a demigod or elf, can use that magic to move within the shadows. It's like a world of mirrors. You enter into the shadows and you can choose which one you leave through. It's easy to transport yourself, harder to transport others but not impossible."

"You've done it?" Shea interrogates.

"Yes." Triton nods.

"So, you can do it now?"

"No."

"Why not?" Caen almost whines the question.

"I don't have my shell. I'd need it in order to do it; it's not technically in my dominion so I'd need it to boost my power to access that kind of magic."

"Okay, so you do it." Shea points to Poseidon.

Poseidon actually has the audacity to look sheepish.

Caen scowls. "Let me guess, you'd need your trident?"

"Yes," Poseidon sighs.

Beck groans. "We're doomed."

"What can we do?" Shea exclaims.

She looks between her brother and their father, waiting for a response.

"We can use what abilities we do have," Triton murmurs, leaving them all on the afterdeck and heading for the bow.

They look between each other and then take off, racing after him.

Shea has to stop and order Aster back to the helm.

Beck, Caen, Poseidon, and Shea all make it to the bow where Triton is looking out over the starboard gunwale toward the water.

"What's happening?" Beck asks.

Shea doesn't answer; instead she watches Triton step

back from the rail. He takes a deep breath and centers his stance, placing one foot in front of the other. He raises his hands out toward the front of the ship and then flings them both back across from his right side.

The ship lurches ever so slightly.

He does it again, and again, and again, until Poseidon and Shea realize how he's bending the water. Like he's pulling the ship along on an invisible rope.

Poseidon meets Shea's eyes. He nods and heads for the port side of the ship.

She heads to the right with Triton.

They match his stance, Poseidon doing everything on the opposite side and Shea following Triton.

"You got it?" Triton huffs, teasingly.

"No problem," Shea snarks with a cocky smile.

On the count of three, they extend their hands.

She feels the water with her mind. Imagines she's touching the cool ocean, and she can feel the invisible cord within her grasp. Once she has a tight grip, she pulls it back.

The ship lurches forward. Caen and Beck fall backward, unprepared by the wind and speed. Shouts from the crew can be heard all over, and Caen suddenly realizes tying everything down would probably be a good idea.

Poseidon, Triton, and Shea keep going as the crew scrambles around them, tying down loose cannons and crew members.

She vaguely hears Jo in the background, shouting and asking about what's going on, but she has to focus on the task at hand.

They keep going and the ship is moving so fast that small waves of water grace the deck, splashing and soaking various crew members until Caen orders most of them below.

They bend the water for hours. They keep it up until it's time to light the torches and the stars have appeared.

It took them seven days to get to Orena from Arethusa even with the Megathirio.

Shea's tempted to keep going but Triton nudges her and gestures over to Poseidon, who looks about to drop. Not to mention she can hear half her remaining crew puking over the sides of the rails.

Shea drops her arms, and as soon as she does Poseidon does too, almost collapsing where he stands.

He manages to catch himself on the rail and Shea almost runs over to help before she remembers she's still mad at him.

James is lighting the deck lanterns, now that they've slowed to a natural speed.

Triton reaches over for her and she doesn't realize how tired she is until she finds herself gratefully leaning into him.

She looks up to say thank you but flinches back when he reaches down and wipes a finger under her nose.

"You need to be careful," he says.

He shows her his finger and her eyes widen when she sees the blood smeared across it.

She reaches up, wiping her nose, and comes away with a little more blood, but the flow seems to have stopped already.

"Magic isn't built for mortal bodies," Shea repeats, remembering what Triton said.

"It's why human Nereidans can't practice it anymore, and why it's even dying out among the elven race. The older you get, the more powerful, it's only natural," Triton explains. "But the more powerful you get, the more your soul burns through your body, exhausting it. You'll need to be careful as you get older. I thought it might be different with you because of—"

He cuts himself off and clears his throat to stop himself from finishing his sentence.

"Different because of what?" Shea asks.

"Never mind." He smiles.

Jo arrives on deck and grins when she sees Shea. She jogs over to her wife, kissing her hello.

"Somehow Strom had the steady hands needed to make supper. He says we can all go to the galley now."

"I need to check the charts," Shea says, but Beck is already at Jo's side.

He leans against her a bit, his eyes slightly lidded in exhaustion, and interrupts.

"Caen wanted me to let you know, we'll be in Arethusa in two days."

"We did it." Shea laughs, and Triton claps her on the back.

She looks up at Poseidon and is surprised to see Caen there with him.

He helps Poseidon up from where he sat down against the gunwale and they clasp each other's forearms in what looks like a truce.

Shea wonders what that's all about and why Caen has suddenly decided to forgive him.

"So, dinner?" Jo asks.

"You know," Shea sighs, "I don't really feel like going to the galley."

"Me either," Beck admits tiredly, holding his arms against his chest.

"Well, why don't we eat on the deck?" Triton asks.

Shea stares at him, then looks up at the stars, at their comforting light.

Dari always preferred starlight too.

"Let's do it. Triton, Beck"—Triton stands at attention, while Beck tries to hide his exhaustion behind a smile—"round up anyone who'd like to eat on the deck tonight, start bringing up the meals."

Triton gestures for Beck to show him where and Beck realizes that he's going to have to take the lead. He heaves a breath and tells Triton to follow him.

Shea almost calls after him, but Jo grabs her hand, distracting her.

"What shall we do?" her wife asks.

"You and I"—Shea smiles, leaning in and kissing Jo with a gentle touch—"are going to take a little trip to the ship's rum caskets."

About an hour later, almost the entire crew is on deck. Chairs and barrels have been brought up from below and everyone is sitting around with steaming bowls of stew and mugs of rum.

Strom, with the help of Aster, even brought up a small table and the pot so he could refill anyone's empty stomachs. With the lack of mouths to feed, rationing is no longer a requirement.

Poseidon sits near Caen, who seems to be talking with him quietly.

Other members of the crew are talking among one another and sharing stories of those they lost.

Beck sits down gingerly on one side of Shea, careful not to let his back touch the barrel he's leaning up against.

Shea tries to ask, but he waves her off and she doesn't have the energy to push.

Jo sits on her other side, sipping on the warm broth of the stew.

Triton is talking animatedly with James and Aster about something she can't hear.

She simply takes in the feeling of life all around her. Her eyes water as she thinks of Dari and Phoebus, as well as the crew she lost on Orena.

Beck watches her intently, and he reaches into his jacket pocket, searching for something, his body rigid and tense.

Shea reaches out to touch him, but Jo places a hand on her leg.

She must have noticed Shea's change in mood as well.

Shea looks over at her and kisses her softly in gratitude for the comfort.

A note fills the air, and then another, and Shea turns to see Beck has pulled out his flute.

He seems to have a little trouble holding up his arms, but then he adjusts his position so his elbows can rest on his knees and it seems to help.

Was he injured? Shea wonders and is about to ask, but then he plays a couple bars of a familiar tune.

She smiles as the music relaxes her and she closes her eyes a moment, allowing herself to really focus on the melody from the flute.

Footsteps alert her to someone in front of her, and she looks up, surprised to find Triton.

James and Aster sit down near Jo and Beck until they've created their own small circle, their own group.

Triton sits as well, bringing his knees up to his chest like Beck.

"Tell me about them."

Shea doesn't need to ask who he's talking about.

She shakes her head, scrunching her eyes tightly closed to stop the tears.

"I can't," Shea mutters.

There's a moment of awkward silence and even Beck stops playing.

Shea almost gets up to go to bed, when Triton speaks again.

"You look just like your mother. Ami."

Shea's eyes fly open, and she stares at Triton in shock.

"You knew her?"

"Ami?"

"Yes," Shea breathes.

Triton glances back in Poseidon's direction, and she looks over as well, noticing that his face has darkened at the mention of her mother's name.

"I did, I knew her very well."

"Triton," Poseidon warns.

"We're just sharing memories, Father. She was a kind mortal elf, right?"

Triton's eyes flash challengingly back at Poseidon,

who's still sitting next to Caen. It seems as if their father might argue, but Poseidon sighs and gestures for him to go ahead.

"You liked her?" Shea inquires, a little surprised considering that means their father cheated on Triton's mother, Queen Amphitrite, with her.

"Oh yes," Triton smiles. "It's different for the gods, the concept of infidelity. Well, except for our aunt Hera, but then our uncle Zeus never knew when to keep it in his pants. But no, my mother didn't care about the relationship."

Poseidon chuckles in the background.

"Your mother is Amphitrite," Jo whispers.

Triton looks over to her and places a gentle hand on hers.

"She really loved Arethusa. She truly felt honored to be your patron."

"Loved?" Jo asks.

Triton nods. "My mother gave up her relic willingly to live among the mortals like my cousin Aphrodite."

"Cousin?" Shea repeats, trying not to think about the familial implications of being a demigod and sleeping with a god.

"Incest is also different for us. Our family connections are soulful, not by blood. It prevents abnormalities that way."

"Gross," Beck comments.

James and Aster agree, if their facial expressions are anything to go on. They all look at Shea tragically, remembering her past relations with V.

"Okay, so back to my mother." Shea chuckles, rolling her eyes at their judgmental looks.

Triton grins. "Ami. Ami is...stubborn, incredibly smart, I never met a being who could outwit her. She could be quite traditional, never a break in protocol. She had such a connection to the water, like you do," Triton murmurs, lost in reverie.

Shea tries to imagine her in her mind, but she can't see

her; nothing about Ami comes to her.

"I wish I knew what she looked like," Shea laments.

"You do."

"No. I don't remember my mother. Paetre seemed to think it had something to do with the blow I took to the head from one of the slavers who took me from the Eastlands."

"You never told me that," Jo says.

"I had Dari. She was my mother for all intents and purposes."

"She was," Triton agrees. "But you have seen your mother."

Shea shakes her head, raising a brow.

"When you opened my door," Triton reminds her.

"I saw a lot of things when I opened your door," Shea quips, thinking of the intimate moment between him and Thetis.

Triton blushes, the tips of his pointed ears a light dusted pink, and everyone laughs at his show of modesty.

"The last memory, smartass."

Shea tries to think back to their duel in the temple, the flashes of Perses, Thetis, and…her mind settles on the image of a woman. A red-haired woman singing to a babe in a wicker rocking chair.

"That's…that was my mother?" Shea murmurs.

"Yes."

"But you…" Shea thinks back to the memory; she can vaguely recall Triton saying something to her. "You said…"

"I used to visit when you were born. You were one of my father's children I knew about, and I liked Ami, so I would visit you both sometimes. She'd sit in that rocking chair and sing to you for hours. She loved music," Triton says wistfully.

She can hear the vague whisper of a tune from the back of her mind. She begins to hum a bit of the melody, and as she does, her eyes widen.

"I know that song!"

Beck takes his flute back out of his jacket with a wince.

"I think I do too."

Shea wants to ask him if he's okay, but Triton interrupts.

"It's an old elven lullaby. It was a warning to keep children from wandering into the woods and to warn them about the fae, elves who practice dark magic," Triton explains.

"No." Shea shakes her head. "I mean yes, I know the meaning, but I know that song. I…"

She closes her eyes, searching her memories until a soft, wispy voice enters her head and suddenly she can see her much younger self and Dari sitting on her bed, singing her a lullaby.

The first nights when she came to visit and was no longer on the ship, and Paetre was far away, were always the hardest. The only way Dari could get her to fall asleep was if she sang to her.

Shea smiles with tears in her eyes. "Dari used to sing that to me too."

"Maybe you'll sing it to our kids one day," Jo tells her with a watery smile.

Aster leans his head against James's shoulder and chuckles. "Oh, she has. She must not remember, but she sang that song to me on one of my first nights on the ship when I couldn't sleep."

Shea laughs as the memory surfaces. She thinks about the old lullaby and hums a bit of the tune. She's sure the rum is probably encouraging her as she begins to sing a bit of the beginning.

Beware the forest.
The darkening leaves,
The eyes that watch from the trees.

Shea trails off, and the crew around them hollers and cheers at the sound of her voice. She startles, forgetting that most of the crew is there.

Caen whistles in encouragement, and Poseidon laughs

at his antics.

Shea blushes deeply, but everyone is clapping for her to continue the song.

"You never told me you could sing," Jo exclaims.

Shea's ears are a bright red.

She groans, wiping a hand down her face. "I don't advertise it."

Beck, the traitor, seems to have picked up enough of the melody and begins to play it on the pan flute.

Triton taps a soft beat in time to the song and she's mildly impressed until she remembers he's the father of sirens—of course he'd have perfect rhythm.

"Give it a go." Triton grins.

Somehow, she suspects he knew this was going to happen.

Shea grabs her mug of rum and downs a bit of it before clearing her throat and catching the tune to begin the next verse of the song.

Beware the woodlands,
The winding trails,
The never-ending roads,
Forgotten tales.
Forget the babbling brooks,
And weeping trees
a false calm giving you ease.

Shea scans the crew, and she can't help but smile as they're sucked into the story.

She remembers staring at Dari in a similar way as she sang about the dangers of the wood. She'd imagine that it was fae who took her away from the Eastlands, and Paetre saved her from them.

She continues to sing along as the melody builds.

Beware the magic,
The howling winds
Full of whispers and mischievous grins.
Into the woods,

Beyond the edge,
Their fae rings hide beneath the forest bed.

She catches Aster's eyes and remembers those nights where she'd threatened to hang him over the bow if he told anyone about her voice.

She'd lay in bed next to him and sing old shanty songs and lullabies she'd learned from free and enslaved elves alike over the years, just to get him to laugh or smile.

Her favorite part of the song comes next, but this time she has backup.

Triton sings along with her, and she loves how their voices sound together.

Jo claps, loving every minute of this, and it causes Shea to laugh a little, fumbling her voice.

Beware the horn
The hunt's begun,
The horses' ride,
The sound like drums.
They seek dangerous game
They love the chase.
They'll hunt you down
To your disgrace.

Others who know the song begin to chime in for the last verse and Shea realizes that this…this is Phoebus and Dari's memorial.

This song is for them, and the crew they lost, taken by fae, by Merrow, too soon.

But someday they'll be together again.

Shea's going to bring her people out of the forest and back into the sun. And Perses is going to have to kill her if he wants to stop her.

So, beware the forest,
sweet little one,
Beware the forest,
And if you must, run.
Break away from the branches

And back to the sun.
Back into the light
Past the woodland's sight.
And never look back
From whence you've come.
Beware the forest, dear little one.

The crew cheers and bellows as they all finish the song.

Some start to cry, but there's a smile on every face.

Shea reaches her hand down to Jo and to Beck. She squeezes their hands in hers. Her eyes dance from person to person.

She smiles fondly as James kisses Aster sweetly.

And she even notes how close Caen and Poseidon are sitting as they watch her fondly.

She breaks her handhold with Beck and Jo. She reaches down, grabbing her mug, and lifts it to the sky.

This one's for you guys. Phoebus, Dari, Tero, Paetre. I'm not giving up hope. I'm going to make you all proud, Shea thinks as she stares up into the beautiful and distant starlight.

She lowers the glass, takes a sip, and her eyes harden as she looks back up at the stars.

And I'm going to kill Perses, gods help me, I promise you.

And she decides to take the shooting star that passes over ahead as encouragement.

CHAPTER 37: DON'T TELL

Jo

Jo laughs as another crew member takes Nol's hangover remedy gently from her fingers. They're lucky it has a nausea-reducing effect, as Jo has to grab onto one of the hanging cots to catch her balance as the Duchess hits a hard wave.

Last night had ended in too much drink for everyone, and by the time the sky was beginning to lighten, soldiers and crew had to drag their fellows to their beds to sleep off the rum until the morn.

Shea's voice was mesmerizing.

Jo smiles as she recalls last night, and the way her wife's voice had enchanted the old song like she was reciting a spell or incantation. It had been a somber night for all.

Jo could still barely ponder the fact that so many of her soldiers had been lost on Orena, all because she had to have her wedding.

She shakes her head; she doesn't want to feel guilty for marrying the woman she loves.

She steps around the hammocks and heads for the doors, leaving the crew's quarters.

She has a couple of vials left so she heads up to the top

deck to get a better look at who's not up yet.

When she arrives, a few more men gratefully take a vial from her.

Her eyes wander onto Shea's strong form as she bends the water beneath the ship at the bow, moving the *Duchess* quicker than before.

Triton and Poseidon are there with her too, and a small part of Jo hopes that Shea can keep this family even if they are immortal.

She hands off the last remedy in her pack to an Arethusian soldier she recognizes. Lana, or Leila? Either way, Jo smiles at the soldier and exchanges gratitude for her service, and the soldier thanks Jo for the delivery of the concoction.

When Jo woke this morning, she'd found a note on the pillow next to her head from Shea, asking that she report to Nol immediately.

She'd gotten dressed as fast as she could, and as she was pulling on her boots, the ship lurched forward.

Poseidon, Triton, and Shea were at it again, which meant more anti-nausea elixirs.

When she'd arrived, Nol had greeted her with a dazzling smile. The anti-nausea vials looked different today, a brown mixture instead of the light gold from the day before. He explained that a hangover concoction would be more beneficial.

Jo had chuckled as she realized his smile was because he wouldn't have to deliver them all.

Thoughts of the drunken crew filtered back into her mind from last night's memorial—at least it had felt like a memorial—and Jo headed off with the vials to hand out to those too sick to move from the public quarters.

As she'd stepped out of the medical office, she'd looked down the hall at the sound of a door closing, happily surprised to find Caen leaving Poseidon and Beck's room.

She tried not to feel discouraged when he spotted her, barely nodded in acknowledgment, and hurriedly rushed past her. He must be needed back up top, she tried to reason to herself, and had headed off to hand out the elixirs without worry.

That had been an hour ago.

Beck had offered Triton the bedroom to share with Poseidon after the song, and that had gone about as well as one could imagine. Triton had politely declined and had headed off toward the crew's quarters to find an empty cot to sleep.

Jo doesn't see Beck on the top deck surprisingly, he's usually one of the first ones up, helping James and keeping the harpoon launchers in top shape.

She didn't think he drank that much, since she'd seen him drunk before; his words hadn't been slurred when he left the deck last night, although he was a bit pale and sweaty.

He'd excused himself, murmuring his exhaustion, and they'd let him go.

Jo is coming down the stairs below deck when she sees Beck walking, no, limping down the hall from the storage bay toward his room and the medical quarters. She's tempted to say something but stops when he catches himself weakly against the ship's wall. He leans heavily against the wood, wiping his forehead across his arm, and then stands with a breathy groan before continuing.

His coat is still on, which Jo finds surprising; he usually only wears a peasant shirt while working around the *Duchess*. Come to think of it, he'd been wearing that jacket since they boarded a day ago.

Jo follows him.

She stalks him down the halls, and watches as he avoids touching or bumping into any crew members. Finally, they reach the medical quarters, and he stops himself in front of the closed door. He takes a breath and forces his shoulders back so he's standing straight with a pained grunt. He bites his lip hard, and Jo thinks she sees a bit of blood escape as he splits his lip in the process to hold back any sound.

Once his back is straight, he wipes a quick hand across

his brow and opens the door with a huge smile.

She hears Nol greet him and the door closes behind them. Jo waits a few moments, deciding whether she should walk in or not, and when she finally comes to the decision to enter the quarters, the door opens. She hides behind the corner again.

Beck edges out the door with a hand behind his back, and as she looks closer, she sees it's gauze.

"I'll get it to him right away," Beck tells Nol, holding up a vial with the hand not behind his back.

"Very good, thank you, Beck," Nol responds and shuts the door softly on him.

Once the door is closed and Beck thinks he's alone. He stumbles, bending over, his mouth open in a silent cry. He breathes heavily and then stands the best he can and limps his way to his room at the end of the hall, which is empty because Poseidon is upstairs moving the ship with Shea and Triton.

He closes the door behind him, leaving Jo alone in the hallway.

There's no way she's not intervening. She rushes to the medical bay, handing off the pack to Nol and telling him she'll be back. Then she rushes out of the room, down to Beck's door.

She thinks about knocking but figures he'll either hide or not answer so she decides to walk in.

She opens the door quickly and nearly cries out at what she sees.

Beck is standing in the middle of the room. The bed on the right is completely made, while the bed on the left looks like whoever slept in it wrestled around with another occupant.

She tries not to focus on that now. She stares at Beck, who is glaring back at her with wide eyes, the gauze he stole from Nol in his mouth, and his jacket and shirt are off.

His bare back is completely exposed to her, and starting from his left shoulder all the way down to his left hip is a large gash from what Jo presumes is a sword. His jacket and what's left of his bloody torn shirt are sitting on the made bed.

"Jo?" Beck tries to speak around the gauze roll in his mouth.

Jo slams the door shut and rushes to his aid, scanning his back and trying to gauge how bad it is.

"When?" Jo screeches. "How?"

"It's nothing," Beck tells her once he's taken the gauze out of his mouth.

He tries to push her away, but the effort obviously hurts, and he almost falls to the ground.

"Don't do that again," Jo orders.

It seems like he might object, but he finally sighs and nods.

"Lie down on the bed on your front, I need to examine the wound. Gods, Beck, you may have needed stitches! You could have bled out." Jo winces as Caen's voice from a year ago echoes through her head.

She remembers Shea's broken body after the duel with her father. *She'll bleed out.*

Jo helps Beck onto the bed, removing his bloody jacket and shirt and tossing it to the ground; she'll need to get him a new top.

"Stay, I'll be right back," Jo orders, but Beck jumps up.

He cries out from the sudden movement, but he grabs her hand anyway.

"Please," he begs, his brown eyes wide and in pain. "Don't tell Shea, or Nol because he'll tell her. Please don't tell her."

"Okay," Jo soothes, if only to get him to lie back down. "Okay, I won't. But I have to clean it; I need to grab a needle and thread just in case, and then proper bandages, not just gauze. I won't say a word but only if you let me treat this properly; it might already be infected."

Beck sighs, and finally nods, allowing her to leave.

Jo races down the hall, storming into Nol's office. She tells him she needs to grab a few things and she can't answer any questions.

Nol completely trusts her and allows her to do as she wishes.

She grabs a bowl of clean water from the medical jug, a sponge, a bit of salve concocted by Nol to help the healing process, some proper bandages, and a needle and thread just in case.

She kisses Nol's cheek as a thank-you and he laughs, telling her to go.

She hurries as best she can without spilling the water, especially with the ship moving so quickly, and opens the door gently, closing it with her foot behind her. She's relieved to find Beck lying where she left him.

She sets her supplies down on the floor next to the low bed, and before kneeling on the ground, grabs one of the fallen pillows on the floor next to the other cot to place under her shins while she works on Beck.

Once that's done, she takes a good look at the wound. He's extremely lucky it's not infected, and that is partially because he doesn't need stiches.

It may have bled a lot, but it's not as deep as it looks. It'll leave a nasty scar though.

She grabs the sponge and dips it into the clean water to start the cleaning process. She doesn't say a word as she places the first dab at the top of his shoulder and decides to work her way down.

Beck doesn't seem eager to speak either.

There are a few hisses, and a couple curses, and once she's made it to the bottom of his shoulder blade, she decides it's time to find out why in Hades he didn't tell anyone.

"That last encounter, with the Merrow. When Shea found you on the ground. That's when it happened?"

Jo remembers it vaguely; she had gone to help Caen,

who was bleeding quite a bit from a forehead cut, while Shea went to check on Beck. The next she'd seen of him he seemed fine.

"I had my back turned and it came out of nowhere, crawling up out of the water onto the old dock. Sliced my back, I barely made a sound. I was too busy turning with the sickle I'd retrieved to take its head off. I hit the ground after, and when Shea came to me, she was so tired and grief-stricken, I didn't want to add to her pain," Beck states, his head on his arms and turned in Jo's directions, so their eyes meet.

"You should have told someone," Jo scolds.

"I couldn't, there was so much pain. From everyone. I didn't want to add to it. The bleeding stopped, so I figured if I could clean it myself…"

"Why didn't Poseidon say something. He must have seen you undress for bed last night?"

Beck buries his face in his arms.

"I didn't…" he mumbles, and Jo isn't able to hear the rest.

"Beck," Jo warns.

"I didn't sleep here last night." Beck sighs, turning to look at her.

"Then where did you sleep?" Jo glares.

He blushes. "The storage room."

"What?" Jo growls, accidentally pressing a bit hard about mid-back and Beck arches away from the touch.

Jo doesn't apologize but she does alleviate the pressure.

"It was no big deal, there's a cot down there I found a few days back on some barrels. I just slept there on my front. It was fine until the ship lurched and I fell off and landed…on my back." Beck winces thinking about it.

"Well serves you right, perhaps it'll teach you to have more sense. No, you listen to me," Jo growls, grabbing the back of Beck's hair and forcing him to look at her after he turns away, rolling his eyes.

"You being in pain does not alleviate our pain. Do you know how I felt finding you like this? Huh? Worry, stress, pain that someone I care about, someone I just admitted to being like family, is hurt. You think you don't matter, well you're wrong. You matter to us; you matter to me."

Jo releases his hair once she's done with her tirade, and he rests it back on his arms, blinking as he absorbs everything she said.

"Gods, it's like having another Shea around. You think martyrdom is cute? It's not. My children are going to have no sense of self-preservation," Jo mutters to herself as she finally comes to his hip, cleaning the last bit of the gash.

They remain in silence as she finishes cleaning the wound—the once clean water is dark red when she places the sponge inside the bowl. She picks up the jar of salve, and takes a good amount out, starting at the top of his shoulder again.

"I'm sorry," Beck finally says, breaking the silence.

Jo hums in acknowledgment but doesn't answer.

"I should have told someone. I—I didn't know you cared that much."

Jo's hand freezes; she stops mid-back and places the jar down. She shuffles over so that her face is in front of Beck's and looks him in the eyes.

"You are my friend. And one day, you will be the father of my children. Of course I care for you. You also mean a great deal to Shea, which makes you one of my own, and I protect my own, just like I would protect Aster, James, Caen, Nol... You're a part of this family, and I don't take kindly to those hurting my family, especially when it's one of them doing it to themselves," Jo states.

She grips his chin in between her fingers. "If you ever do this again, I will thrash you myself. Is that understood?"

His eyes widen, and she knows the moment he realizes she's serious.

He wets his bottom lip and swallows. "Yes, ma'am."

Jo nods with finality. "Good."

She finishes putting the salve on his back and then tells him to sit up so she can place the bandages and wrap the gauze.

He does as he's told immediately, and Jo smirks at the compliance.

"Are you going to tell Shea?" he asks as she starts wrapping the gauze after placing the bandages correctly.

She starts with wrapping it around his left shoulder and peck and then begins to wrap it around his middle. She doesn't answer, not yet. Instead as she's wrapping the gauze her mind starts to spin.

Had this been worse, he could have died.

Shea could have lost another person in her life; someone she even possibly loves as much as she loves Jo.

And it's not like Jo doesn't care for him. Beck is her friend, someone who knows what it's like to have to lead a country, to lose things most people never will, and he knows what it's like to love Shea, the fear, the excitement.

He is the closest thing she has to a confidant and ally. All this time Jo has looked at the future in the most positive light, but what if they all die upon arriving in Arethusa tomorrow? What if Beck is the first person Perses kills?

How will Jo react? How will Shea? She doesn't want to leave this world with any what-ifs, and she certainly doesn't want Beck and Shea to.

But is she really willing to do this, to allow what she's thinking to happen? She'd have to talk to Nol about precautions, but if this voyage is the very last time they may all be together and relatively safe? Then at least they'd leave this world knowing if all of their decisions were the right ones.

"No," Jo tells him, making her decision, and Beck seems to deflate with relief. "You're going to tell her tonight."

"What?" Beck inquires, staring at her in horror.

"Yes, you'll come to our quarters, tonight after supper.

And I will track you down if you do not appear. Understood?"

"Jo..." Beck groans, wiping a hand down his face, and then gasping when Jo ties the bandage off harshly.

"Am I clear?"

"Perfectly," Beck croaks.

"Now," Jo stands with the bloody water bowl and jar of salve. "How do you feel?"

Beck rolls his shoulders a little, wincing slightly, but his coloring is much better already.

"Better," he states, smiling softly up at her.

"Excellent. I have work to do, and you will not be working today." She holds up her hand when he tries to object. "If you work, the wound will open and bleed. Stay put. You can go to the galley for dinner and then I'll see you at Shea's quarters after. Right?"

Beck nods sullenly.

Jo makes her way to the door, stopping when she opens it. "Oh and, Beck?"

Beck looks up at her, and for a moment, she almost laughs. He looks so young suddenly.

They all are, really—young. She pictures that young face, bloodied, with wide eyes unseeing, and it hardens her resolve.

"Don't be late."

***

Jo is just finishing a chapter of an old manuscript she found in one of the piles of Shea's treasure hoards in the corner of the chambers, when Shea stumbles in looking exhausted.

Jo has a steaming bowl of stew waiting for her at the desk where she's sitting, reading an old tale from long ago. A tragic love story, meddling gods, and a world that forgets them all. The irony of their situation is almost poetic.

She places the illuminated pages aside and gets up to greet her partner, offering her the chair on the other side of the desk.

"I'm starving, thanks, love," Shea mutters, digging into

the food.

Jo kisses the top of her head and returns to the other side of the table to sit. They talk about their day, Jo not mentioning Beck and his injury at all—she'll leave that to him. She looks toward the windows as Shea finishes, and if Beck does as he's told, he'll be coming soon if the moonlight is anything to go by.

"Strom never fails to impress." Shea chuckles, a bit of energy returning to her now that she's eaten.

"Would you like some wine?" Jo asks, standing up to get a glass.

Shea nods, staring fixedly at Jo with a creased brow.

Jo walks back over with the glasses and catches her curious expression. "What?"

"Something's up," Shea states, looking around the room.

She stands from where she's sitting and advances toward Jo. She stops in front of her with her hands on her hips.

"What's going on?" Shea inquires.

"Nothing," Jo responds quickly, moving past her to place the filled wineglasses down.

Shea steps up behind her, and Jo turns, looking down into those fiery green eyes.

"I can't put my finger on it, but something is bothering you. Are you okay? Are you hurt?"

"I'm fine," Jo laughs, waving off Shea's concern.

Jo sits down, amused, watching as Shea starts to pace.

"You're fine? Hmm, so is someone else not fine? Is it Aster?" Shea stops moving, turning to her worriedly.

Jo straightens in her seat and looks at Shea seriously. "No. He's fine. Don't worry, everything will be explained soon."

"Right…Now I'm worrying," Shea gripes and goes back to pacing.

A knock sounds at the door.

Shea looks over at Jo and takes a step to go and open

it, but Jo gets up and runs to the door before her wife can get there.

She opens the door, and finds a nervous Beck, practically wringing his hands. She gestures for him to come in and when Shea spots him, her face pales.

She looks him over, vivid concern on her features.

Jo steps away, watching as Shea moves quickly toward him. She takes his face between her palms, searching his eyes.

"What's wrong? What happened?" Shea panics, her hand falling to his shoulder, and he winces at the touch.

Shea's eyes dart to his left shoulder and then to his face, her eyes narrowing.

Jo is watching the exchange, more amused than anything else. She realizes she's not jealous in the slightest.

"I knew it," Shea whispers, "take it off."

"Shea," Beck sighs.

"Now," Shea orders, and Beck looks back at Jo as if for permission.

Shea follows his gaze and when her eyes land on Jo, she startles. She must have forgotten she was in the room with them. Shea steps back suddenly, like Beck's touch has burned her, and her ears and cheeks color. She looks ashamed.

Jo will have none of that.

She crosses the room to her wife, wrapping her arms around her middle and kissing the side of her face. She whispers into her pointed ear, "It's alright. Truly."

And then she looks up at Beck.

"Do as she says," Jo tells him.

Beck looks up at the ceiling, like he's hoping for divine intervention, but no help comes, and so he gently removes his jacket. He's wearing the same bloody peasant shirt, and Jo curses, remembering that she forgot to find him a new top.

She files that away for later. Jo removes herself from Shea but remains at her side, holding her hand.

Beck carefully takes off his shirt, exposing the white bandages underneath. Jo turns to watch Shea's expression now as she sees the bandages, and she notices Shea's eyes are wet.

It confirms for Jo that she's making the right decision. She feels even more confident, all that will be left is convincing them it's alright.

Shea steps forward hesitantly to where Beck is standing awkwardly, and Jo pushes her toward him.

Beck catches her with a grunt and Shea straightens abruptly, turning back to glare at Jo, who shrugs with a soft smile.

Shea goes back to examining him, and she pushes at his right shoulder for him to turn around. Her coarse but small hands caress his injured back and there's a little blood from where the bandage is protecting the wound.

Jo will need to change those soon.

"The Merrow, when you were on the ground?" Shea asks.

Beck nods. "I'm sorry."

"I can't believe Nol didn't tell me," Shea growls.

"Nol doesn't know," Jo tells her.

Shea looks back at Jo, confused.

"You dressed the wound? Why didn't you tell me?" Shea asks, her voice taking on a sharp edge.

"She didn't know until this morning," Beck objects.

Shea turns her attention back to him.

"Wait, I'm sorry, you've been walking around with a major gash in your back for almost two days and you just this morning got it dressed?"

"Yes," Beck responds nervously.

"What the bloody Underdeep were you thinking? It could have gotten infected; you might have needed stitches! How did Poseidon not notice, you two share a room." Shea shouts, berating Beck for his stupidity.

The governor looks to Jo for help, but she doesn't

intervene—he's earned this.

"Well?" Shea growls.

"I may have slept on a cot in the storage bay to avoid any questions," Beck explains, and Shea smacks him on the head in response.

"Ow!"

"Do you know how hard an infection would have been to get rid of? To know you didn't die by some creature but something that could have been easily fixed, or you could have bled out and we would have found your body days later being chewed on by the rats," Shea's voice is thick with emotion, and Jo can't see it, but she thinks she might be crying.

"I can't do that. I can't lose anyone else right now. I can't fucking lose you!"

"I'm sorry," Beck says, tears falling as well. "I was trying to save you the pain."

"Well that certainly backfired!"

Jo can see Shea's shoulders shaking—the stress of Orena, her losses finally catching up to her—and she takes a step toward them.

Beck puts his hands on Shea's shoulders, trying to comfort her.

"You should kiss her."

There's a choking noise, and Shea turns to face Jo.

Beck looks up as well, and the queen stares back at them, amused by their shocked faces.

"What?" Beck whispers.

"I said, you should kiss her. You're sorry, aren't you?"

"Jo," Shea exclaims.

But Jo cuts her off, "Aren't you?"

"Yes," Beck tells her.

"You love her, as I do?"

"Yes."

"You love him as you love me?" Jo directs her question at Shea, who has stepped away from Beck.

"Jo, what is this?"

Jo chuckles softly to herself. She looks down at her hands, joined together, and then meets Shea's questioning gaze with complete honesty.

"I am not confident we're going to survive what's next."

Shea and Beck both open their mouths to object, but again Jo stops them.

"Please let me finish. I love you, Shea. I am secure, and safe, and…marvelously happy with our relationship. And I know you are too; I don't have any doubts or questions. I know you love me…and I know you love him. But if we're not going to survive? If we're going to die in Arethusa, come the next few days? Then our plans for the future are forfeit. And I don't want any of us going to the underworld with questions or regrets. So, I'm asking the two of you to forget with me tonight. To answer a question and not worry about the consequences. Because I'll be happy to deal with it if we survive."

Shea and Beck are gaping at Jo in surprise; neither look sure of how to respond.

"And I'm not saying we have to, and if you don't want to…"

Beck remains quiet, and she can tell he's refusing to voice his say. He's waiting for Shea's response instead.

"Jo. I am…I don't know what I am, but the faith you have in me is…extraordinary. I—" Shea shuts her mouth, shaking her head.

Jo encourages her to say it, walking the rest of the way to her, taking her wife's hands in her own.

"It's okay. You want it?"

A tear falls, and Shea's voice cracks, "Gods help me I do, I'm sorry."

"Shea," Jo soothes, "I'm asking. I'm telling you it's okay. And I don't want you to be sorry. I'm okay with this. I care about Beck," Jo tells her, looking to him.

He smiles at her.

"I'm okay with this," Jo states, casting her gaze between them both.

"The question is, do you want to do this?"

Shea takes an unsteady breath and looks up at Beck as he waits for her response.

"Yes."

Jo smiles.

"Beck?"

"Don't really want to sound too eager here," Beck mumbles. "I want to, of course I do," he says, but takes a step back away from Jo and Shea.

"But...we can't take the risk."

"What do you mean?" Jo asks.

Shea is looking at him, confused as well.

His resigned expression changes into wide eyes and he looks between them both.

"We can't risk Shea ending up with a child. Not now," Beck explains, like it's obvious.

Jo giggles as realization filters in and Shea smirks.

"What?" Beck asks, affronted.

"There are ways around that." Jo laughs.

"Nol has made me morning-after elixirs before—before Jo and all this. I'd just drink it tomorrow, and it would prevent the conception of a child."

Beck gasps. "I've never heard of such a thing."

"Yes well, men don't traditionally have to deal with these situations," Jo murmurs, teasingly.

"So then are we doing this?" Beck stutters. "Um, this may sound like a stupid question but how are we doing this?"

"Are you a...virgin?" Shea asks, taking his hand in hers.

"Well, no, I mean I have experience with girls," Beck starts to explain, but Jo can see right through him.

"But not enough to know about contraceptives, otherwise there'd already be little Becks running around. Are there little Becks running around?" Jo inquires.

"No!" Beck yells, before quieting his voice. "No. I've...been with women...just, not all the way."

Jo giggles at Beck's blush, which travels down his neck almost to his chest.

"Oh dear," Jo whispers.

Shea squeezes Beck's hand. "That's okay. I don't mind taking the lead. Although, would you be comfortable with Jo in the room?"

Beck looks slightly surprised at the question, and nods very quickly. "Whatever Jo wants. I'll do whatever she wants."

Jo smiles at his honesty, and it makes her even more trustful. She looks at his nervous form, the way his hands are slightly shaking, and she knows that participation from her would probably be a bit much. So, she suggests the next best thing since she doesn't feel too comfortable leaving them alone in the room.

"I'll watch," Jo announces, "from here." She loosens her clothes, unbuttoning her pants, and unlacing her shirt a bit. She sits down at the chair at the desk, getting comfortable.

"I'll join you to sleep. Is that okay?" Jo asks.

Shea smiles, nodding, and Jo is surprised to see Beck staring at her untied blouse, feeling his eyes roam over her frame. She takes it as the compliment it is.

They're standing in the middle of the room, and she realizes they're waiting for her command. She grins.

"You may begin."

Shea looks at Beck, and then back at Jo, and quickly walks over to Jo. She bends down and kisses Jo deeply and passionately, allowing her entrance to her mouth.

Jo feels Shea bite on her bottom lip, and as they pull away, they're breathing heavily in each other's faces.

Shea is staring into her eyes, and Jo knows what she wants, she always knows what Shea wants.

"Go ahead," Jo whispers, giving her the okay.

Shea nods and turns back to Beck, who is watching her with admiration. Shea's hands fly to her shirt and she starts unlacing the top. Once that's done, her hands go to her hair, which is braided back, and she removes the leather tie. She shakes her hands through her lush red hair, letting it fall down past her shoulders.

She kicks off her boots, and all the while Beck stands there watching, completely mesmerized, and Jo concentrates on Shea as well. She lets her hands wander over her own body and she feels her breast a bit as she watches Shea undress.

Beck bites his lip as Shea slides her brown pants down her muscled legs until they fall like a puddle around her feet.

She's left in only her peasant blouse.

His arousal is evident through his pants, and Shea closes the distance between them.

She takes his hand gently and lays it on her body, allowing him to feel her form through the blouse.

Beck slides his hand down her curves until he reaches the shirt's hem. He looks at her with a questioning glint, and Shea nods, giving him permission.

Beck lifts the shirt up over her head, until her nude form is before him. Her hair is long enough that it covers the tops of her breasts but that's the only modesty she has left.

Beck is staring at her nervously, but from the way Shea is holding herself, Jo knows there's a cocky grin on her face.

She's not embarrassed at all. And she shouldn't be, Jo muses, running her hand into the inside of her pants, it's a beautiful body.

Shea's hands reach out to Beck's waist, and she looks up at him, her head tilted and her hair falling to her back, exposing her tattooed shoulders.

Beck smiles and lets out a shaky breath.

Shea's body obscures the view, but Jo can hear the leather cords tying his pants being unlaced.

Beck runs both hands over Shea's bare shoulders, and she smiles fondly as his fingers trace the tips of the Lionbird's wings. He quickly kicks off his shoes as Shea finishes with the lacing, and Shea takes a step back so he can slide out of his pants.

He glances in Jo's direction, hesitating as he sees her staring, but then he looks back at Shea, and it must help him make up his mind because he slides his pants and undergarments off.

Jo can appreciate his body, but it doesn't hold the same attraction for her as Shea.

Shea, on the other hand, gasps at the reveal and Jo guesses she must like what she sees.

His muscles are lean, his legs are long and defined, and there's a hint of abs gracing his strong stomach under those bandages. His length is decent, Jo supposes, for women attracted to such things. It's hard and perhaps a little larger than the phallus they had used on their wedding night, hidden within dark brown curls.

Shea steps toward him and carefully wraps her arms around his neck while he wraps his arms around her waist, pulling her close.

He leans down slowly, stopping just before their lips touch.

They're both breathing heavily, but they don't seal the kiss, they remain close, touching.

"Something wrong?" Jo murmurs, a moan catching her throat as a spark of orgasm threatens to overtake her from her own ministrations.

"Can we?" Beck croaks.

Jo stops her hand; she stares at the two of them locked in a naked embrace, and suddenly she feels as if she's the most powerful person in the room.

"Are you asking my permission?" Jo inquires.

"Yes," Shea whispers, her voice barely audible.

Jo hums, as the answer sends a chill down her spine. She likes that, she likes this newfound power very much.

She leans back in the chair, resuming her hand movements upon her womanhood.

"Yes. Kiss her," Jo orders.

And he does. He captures her lips in a powerful display.

From Jo's position, she can see everything, the way Shea's breasts push against his bandaged chest, and his hard length rubbing against her firm lower stomach.

Beck reaches a hand down, massaging Shea's bosom, feeling his way across her nipples. Shea moans into the kiss as he scratches his thumb across the sensitive bud.

"She would prefer your mouth," Jo tells him breathily.

They break the kiss, their breaths mixing together as they stare into each other's eyes.

"Take her to the bed," Jo demands.

Beck offers Shea his hand and she smiles at him, dazzling both Jo and Beck with it.

She takes his hand and they walk slowly, sensually to the large bed. He lays Shea across it on her back and climbs on top. She opens her legs for him to lay in between and he gratefully takes the chance, positioning his knees there.

He lays down on top of her, his forearms supporting his weight, and Jo can tell it hurts, but he doesn't let himself down. He protects Shea even from himself. Beck captures Shea's lips once again, their mouths moving in a symbiotic dance, and there's no space between them, as he grinds his hard length against her hip.

Jo moves her hand a little faster, bringing the other up to her own chest, stimulating her nipple as Beck kisses his way down Shea's throat.

He moves lower and lower until his face is above her rising chest. He waits again.

"Take her nipple into your mouth, Beck. Pleasure her," Jo groans, arching up into her own hand.

Beck does as he's told. His tongue reaches out and he swirls the tip around Shea's nipple.

Her back arches as she moans at the sensation.

He steadies himself onto his left forearm, and his right hand cups her breast as he focuses all of his attention on her areola.

Shea's hands almost touch his back, but she remembers herself and his wound at the last moment and grips the blanket on the bed instead. She is writhing beneath his touch and Jo can see a wet trail along Shea's inner thigh from Beck's heavy manhood.

"You need to prepare her," Jo moans.

Beck looks up at her comment and he bites his lip. Shea catches his eyes and she smiles at him sweetly.

"It's okay. Three fingers should be enough," she explains.

Jo finds the comment strange until she remembers that Beck has never done this before.

Beck returns his mouth to Shea's breast, keeping up his attentions as his hand moves from her chest to sidle down to her opening. His body blocks Jo's view but she can see the moment his first finger penetrates Shea, her eyes open and a small whine escapes her lips as he thrusts the digit inside.

Beck pulls his mouth and his hand back, sitting up on his haunches, worriedly.

"Are you okay? Did I hurt you?"

His brown eyes are ridiculously wide. He looks like a puppy after his mistress tells him no.

Jo laughs at his innocent expression.

But Shea takes a much kinder route, biting her lip to keep in her amusement. She pushes herself up onto her forearms, shaking her head.

"No, I'm okay. It felt good actually," Shea explains lightly.

"Oh," Beck sighs in relief. "Should I do it again?"

"I think she'd like that very much," Jo comments.

Beck blushes as he's reminded of her presence once again.

Shea reaches for him, her hand falling below his waist, and Jo sees her arm start moving in a pulling gesture.

Beck's mouth opens in delight, and he gasps at the feeling of Shea's hand on his length.

Shea keeps up the pace until Beck is up and pushing her back against the bed.

He moves back into his former position, his mouth on her breast and his hand falls down to her opening. He enters her again.

Shea bites her lip to keep the sound in, so she doesn't scare him away.

Jo watches Shea's face and imagines herself in Beck's position, sliding her fingers inside of her gorgeous wife, making her fall apart. She opens her eyes as she comes by her own hand and she hadn't even realized she'd closed them, lost in the fantasy. At least a minute or so must have passed because as Jo comes down from her high, her head snaps to the couple on the bed as Shea cries out in ecstasy. She smiles as she sees the two of them joined.

Beck's body is shaking in effort as he holds himself still, his thick length pulsing within Shea's magnificent body. They're kissing each other in an intimate moment and finally Shea breaks the kiss to tell him to move.

Jo starts moving her hand again. She watches Beck pull his hips back gently and thrust himself inside Shea.

They keep up the slow, steady rhythm, kissing each other as Shea's hands curl into Beck's thick hair and Beck mouths his way down Shea's long neck.

The whole room feels heavy, all Jo can hear is their breathing and her own.

His hips start to move a bit faster as Shea wraps her legs around his waist, and she whispers for him to move faster and harder.

At Shea's directions, Jo follows her orders, moving her own hand in time with Beck's thrusts.

She's going to come, and she practically climaxes again when Shea lets out a pleasure-filled cry as Beck thrusts quickly into her body over and over as they spill over the edge and come one after the other.

Jo gasps as her orgasm rips through her core, and she collapses back against the chair. Her breath is heavy, and she knows she has a lazy smile spread across her lips. She startles as a hand wraps under her knees and another under her back. She opens her eyes to see Beck, and she quickly but carefully wraps her arms around his shoulders as he moves her to the bed on the left side of Shea.

They're both still naked.

Beck climbs into bed on the other side, leaving Shea in between the two of them.

"I guess that answers that question," Jo murmurs, as they're all lying together looking up at the ceiling.

"Hmm?" Shea looks over at her, their hands intertwining.

"You guys were amazing together," Jo chuckles, and they all laugh quietly.

"Do you still think we'll win?" Beck asks, not really directing the question at anyone specific.

No one answers. But Shea takes his hand as well, and they all continue to stare up at the ceiling.

Jo watches the moonlight waver on the wood from the reflection of the ocean. She studies the light, focusing on how calm and beautiful it is, and smiles to herself. She may not know if they'll win against Perses, but with all the beauty that's been given to her in this lifetime, she knows she can never lose.

Beck's breathing evens out first, and then Shea's follows soon after.

Jo listens to the sounds of their sleep, and she lets it comfort her as she tries not to think about what awaits them in Arethusa tomorrow.

CHAPTER 38: ONE LAST HOPE

Shea

"Captain!"

Shea bolts up in bed at the sound of banging at her door. Her heart is beating quickly, and as she sits up, she sees two faces in her periphery.

The banging continues as Shea looks over at the panicked faces of Jo and Beck, all three of them inwardly praying to the gods that whoever is at the door doesn't walk in. Because Shea's pretty sure she didn't lock it.

Not that she was expecting what happened last night to happen.

"Captain!"

"Yes?" Shea calls out with strangled fear.

She pushes back the covers, revealing her naked form. Leaving Beck and Jo in bed, she rushes to the door. She grabs her jacket off the back of one of the desk chairs and wraps it around her as she leans her entire body up against the door to keep it from opening.

"Yes? What is it?"

"Captain, you're needed upstairs immediately."

Shea pins the voice down as James, and relaxes up against the door because unlike Aster, James won't come in without an invitation.

"Very good, I'll be up soon," Shea answers, but as she lets go of the door, it starts to open.

Shea rams her body up against it, shutting it on her young bos'n.

"James!"

"I'm sorry, Captain. I just felt perhaps a face-to-face would be better. We need you now. It's extremely urgent."

Shea looks up at the ceiling and then looks over to the bed. Jo is as white as a sheet; she leaps from the bed and starts dressing as quickly as she can.

Beck seems pinned with fear, and with every movement he winces, his back probably bothering him from last night's activities.

She tries to angle herself to see if James would see the bed from cracking the door open a little.

She shakes her head. These things were so much easier when she wasn't married. She decides to stick with her original plan of keeping the door closed.

James knocks again when he doesn't hear an answer.

"Shea?"

"Sorry, yes. Okay, I'll dress quickly and be up. Is something wrong?"

There's silence from the other side of the door, and at that Shea's tempted to open up, to Hades with the consequences, but James luckily responds.

"Yes, Captain. Also, I would suggest having Jo find Beck, I don't think it would be prudent for him to be on the main deck right now."

At that, Beck is leaping from the bed.

Shea tries not to focus on his still, gorgeous, nude form, and she has to stop him from opening the door with her hands outstretched, pushing him back by his pecks.

"Why?" Shea inquires, her voice straining from the effort of holding Beck back.

She almost falls when he quickly walks away, scrambling for his clothes.

"You're going to have to see this for yourself, Captain," James tells her, and she hears his footsteps walk away.

"Beck," Shea tries, but he's already got his pants on.

He looks at his mangled shirt and leaves it on the ground, storming toward the door with a worried expression.

Jo is almost dressed. She's pulling her boots over her naval uniform pants, hopping, trying to get them on faster, as Beck gently but firmly moves Shea aside and runs out the door, heading for the main deck.

"Jo," Shea says, but Jo's already moving.

She kisses Shea's cheek quickly.

"I got him! You get to Nol for the elixir."

Shea gasps as she almost forgot. She nods, but Jo doesn't see it as she's barreling out the door after Beck.

Shea finds some clean pants, well mostly clean, discarded on the floor. As she's pulling a black peasant blouse over her head, she notices a strange fog sitting on the water outside her cabin windows. At this time of year, it's extremely odd, and anything odd usually means there's a problem.

She slides into her boots, attaches her waterskin to her side, and breaks into a run for Nol's quarters. She passes some crew who are moving quickly; they seem to have orders of some kind. Shea races to get to Nol, so she can take the elixir, and get up top to find out what's going on. She turns the last corner, finally making it to the right hall. She's just about at Nol's door when she looks toward the end of the hall, where Poseidon and Beck's room is, Caen's regular quarters, and sees the door open.

She expects to see Poseidon, but to her surprise she sees Caen—and in a state of mild undress. His vest his draped over his forearm, leaving him bare-chested in only boots and his leather pants. His back is facing her, and he seems to be talking to someone inside the room.

She takes a step forward to find out who he's talking to when her father appears at the door in a similar state.

His hair is a mess, and his chest is also bare.

Her eyes widen as her father sidles up to Caen, positioning himself in his arms, and Caen actually chuckles, smiling.

Shea feels her heart beating faster, shaking her head. This doesn't make sense.

Then Caen leans down, his hands moving to Poseidon's white hair, entangling in the curly strands, and he kisses him deeply. Poseidon returns the kiss with a grin.

Shea stumbles back, her entire world turning upside down. She doesn't understand. All thoughts of Nol and why she's here fly from her head.

They break the kiss, and Poseidon's eyes wander over Caen's face with amusement before flickering down the hall, catching Shea in his gaze.

His eyes widen dramatically; they look the same shade as Shea's, she notes hysterically, as he opens his mouth, saying something.

Caen stiffens, and he turns down the hall to find what Poseidon's staring at.

Shea, seemingly frozen, hasn't moved since Poseidon spotted her and she meets Caen's eyes as he turns.

His face goes from relaxed to horrified, and he steps immediately out of Poseidon's embrace, moving toward her, but Shea takes a step back.

Her eyes are burning, and she's not crying—she feels angry. Confused. And she doesn't want to know why just yet.

Caen starts walking toward her and Shea turns and runs away like a coward.

She can hear him calling her name, but she doesn't listen. She keeps running until she makes it to the stairs leading up to the main deck, taking the steps two at a time.

She breaks through the double doors and coughs as she inhales a large amount of smoke, not mist. There's smoke everywhere, and she finds most of the crew staring off the starboard side of the ship.

Triton is hanging off the mast rope ladder in a way Shea has done so many times before. He's got his head bowed and he seems to be whispering something to himself.

Beck is on his knees, both his hands in his hair, openly crying at the view before them.

Jo has a hand on his shoulder, comforting him, but she looks almost as upset as he is.

Shea turns and looks, really looks, at what they're all staring at and her mouth dries.

Oceanus is gone.

They're sailing past the wreckage of it all. The once colorful markets, and varying stone buildings of the capital, lie in ruins. The capital coliseum is missing an entire wall. The docks of Metis are burnt to a crisp, what's visible is black and gnarled with burning embers, the rest is in the shallows of the ocean. But the worst part of all is the silence. There's no screams, no cries, no pleading.

Oceanus has been conquered.

Perses actually did it; he helped Ceto wipe Oceanus from existence, and Shea knows that if they don't stop them, they'll do the same to Arethusa.

She feels a hand on her shoulder and turns sharply to find Caen staring at her with a woeful expression. She wants to lean into his hand, the comfort she's sought so many times, but the kiss between him and Poseidon flashes before her eyes, and she pulls away.

He's visibly hurt by the action, but Shea doesn't have time to deal with his feelings.

Suddenly the reality of the situation seeps in and she wonders how long her ship has been sitting here, mourning the city, yes, but also perfectly in the open. For all they know the Lycon army, the Merrow, Ceto, and Perses could still be there, now watching them from afar and getting ready to strike.

"James!" Shea shouts, and her bos'n comes running from the bow.

She sees Aster at the rail, and he turns at her voice. No one's driving her bloody ship. She lets her frustrations fuel her. She has to be the leader right now, which means she needs to be as cold as her enemy is.

"Are we waiting to be blown from the water?" Shea growls.

James, who has come to attention before her, seems shocked by her aggression, and that won't do. She's gotten soft, and if she's going to win a war? If she's going to save her people, she needs to be the reason the *Veiled Duchess* was the most feared ship in all of Nereid.

"No, Captain," Caen answers for him, switching into quartermaster mode, and that Shea can deal with.

The crew has turned, watching the exchange.

Beck is still staring out at his lost home, but Jo has turned to face her, her features also looking surprised at Shea's sudden harsh tone.

No more dallying, they need to get to Arethusa immediately. She watches Triton jump down from the mast rope and begin walking her way. She feels comforted by his presence and it reinforces her decision.

"Then let's get this ship moving," Shea bellows. "I want my gunners at the ready. Jo get Beck down below. If he can't work, I need him out of the way."

Jo frowns at Shea's coldness but nods, helping him up.

Beck looks like he's in a state of shock and Shea understands, truly, but if she really wants to help him, she'll get them to Thalassa.

"Aster, who gave you permission to leave your post?" Shea snarls, storming onto the deck as the gunners and deck crew start scrambling at their captain's wicked tone.

They haven't seen her like this, well, in a long time.

Aster visibly flinches, but as his eyes scan her features, he seems to understand and he straightens his back, his jaw clenching.

"No one, ma'am," he responds, not meeting Shea's eyes.

"Then get back to it," Shea grounds out, stepping up close to him, "now."

Aster gives a short nod, and starts running toward the helm.

James is barking orders at the deck crew to get this ship moving, and Shea can feel Caen at her back like a shadow.

"If you'd like to retire down below," Caen murmurs.

He grasps her arm, stopping her from continuing toward the bow and Triton, who seems to be waiting for her.

They're standing in the middle of the deck, and Shea can feel curious eyes watching them from their jobs. They're a distraction.

She refuses to look at him, and she removes her arm from his grip.

"I can take over up here, so you can check on him," Caen finishes.

Shea scoffs, turning to face him with a sharp stare. "I've been *retired* long enough. Obviously, my crew needs me. I'm not leaving this deck until we arrive in Arethusa in, if my calculations are correct judging from where we are"—Shea gestures—"around six hours."

Caen opens his mouth to respond, but as he does, the deck doors open behind him.

Poseidon steps out, fully dressed.

Shea's eyes narrow on her father and she looks back at Caen. She juts her chin in Poseidon's direction, and Caen turns to see where she points, sighing deeply when his eyes land on the sea god.

"But if you'd like to *retire*, Quartermaster, I've got things covered up here," Shea drawls, her words dripping with venom.

She turns to leave him but stops, her magic jolting in

her chest, causing her anger to fester. She glares back at him.

"You know you really had me fooled with the whole disapproval, hate thing. So, tell me, when did you decide fucking my father, who lied to all of us—who, if it wasn't for his lust of power, Perses would be dead by now, and Dari and Phoebus would still be alive—was a brilliant idea?" Shea practically spits the word *fucking* and Caen winces, giving her the smallest amount of satisfaction. "Because I certainly don't understand why. Nor do I really want to at the moment. Were you truly that desperate?"

At the mention of Dari and Phoebus, Caen's eyes remain glued to the ground. He doesn't look back up at her, not once.

Shea wants to walk away, but she can't just yet. Everything she's been feeling the past couple days is bubbling out. Her magic is buzzing from her hands up her arms, egging her on, urging her to destroy.

"I don't care if you fuck men." Shea laughs coldly. "My son certainly does. I do! In fact, probably half the world does. But why, in Hades, did it have to be him?"

Shea shakes her head, all of her thoughts burning through her mind like wildfire. She's barely listening to what she's saying anymore and if she had been, she never would have said what she says next.

"You know I heard what you said to Phoebus," Shea growls. "And at the time, I didn't really understand what you meant—the message for Paetre. And perhaps I always knew. The looks when you knew he wasn't looking, how you cared for me after he was gone."

Caen looks down at her now, his expression unreadable, but he turns to face her completely.

"Shea," he objects, not liking where this is going.

"Perhaps that's why you stayed all along," Shea hisses. "Was it a promise? Or did I just remind you of him? So maybe that's why, huh? You never got to have the real thing, but hey, Shea's birth father, that's close enough, right?"

Shea screams the last sentence loud enough that she knows most of the crew probably heard. And by the time it's out of her mouth, regret is already swimming up her throat and closing off her air. She chokes on her wickedness, her magic disappearing, leaving her to drown.

Caen's gaping at her. His eyes wander over her form, and he cocks his head, a humorless smile replacing his shocked expression.

"You're right about one thing," Caen tells her, his voice devoid of any emotion. "You're just like him. Paetre. Never knew when to hold his tongue either. Got him into a lot of trouble. So, I'm only going to say this once."

Caen marches up until he's towering over her.

Shea holds her ground, but her heart is beating like a hummingbird. She thinks he might hit her, but he just leans down, so his face is right in hers.

"My reasons are my own. And I don't need you to understand. My personal relationships are my own, including those with *both* your fathers. You're my kid, and if anyone else would have spoken to me like this, they'd be run through right about now. I do love you because of Paetre."

Shea can't take in any air, her lips thin at his last statement.

Caen's eyes search hers, and he nods like he knows his comment did some damage.

"Because it was *Paetre*," Caen emphasizes, "who brought you into my life. You're angry, you're upset, and you've lost more than most. I'm not going anywhere, but— Do. Not. Test. Me. If I have to treat you like Paetre, I will, and I hit his pretty jaw more often than not without any reservations when he pushed me too far. So, I'm going to do my job and if you need anything, let me know."

He walks away from her after that.

Shea stumbles over to the rail, looking out over the water as Oceanus starts to fade away.

Triton steps up beside her and simply places his hand

over hers.

    She doesn't speak or acknowledge it. She just stands beside him for a moment. If she's not careful, she's going to lose more people to herself than to Perses. They've got six hours until they reach Arethusa. Shea finally looks over at Triton and gestures for him to follow her to the afterdeck. It's time to start planning how exactly they're going to win this war.

CHAPTER 39: DARKEST EDGE

Shea

They arrive in Arethusa about noon. The sun shines brightly overhead, and the smoke they had experienced sailing past the destroyed city of Metis is gone. If they didn't know any better, it would seem like a pristine day.

There's nowhere to dock; the royal fleet has been brought to the Arethusian port, and there are a few ships marked by the Oceanan flag scattered among the navy.

Shea makes the decision to lower their anchor farther out from the docks and take the two longboats to shore. She chooses the crew that will remain behind in case of an evacuation, and she takes a bit of pleasure when Caen practically storms off at the order that he will be one of the crew remaining behind. She knows she should probably apologize before she leaves, for all they know she could be dead come the invasion's arrival, but for now she focuses on who will be going ashore.

Triton and Shea have been discussing battle plans for the last two hours up on the afterdeck, and they've hopefully constructed some ideas that just might work. Once she's chosen the select few, she counts off to herself as a reminder.

Beck.

He'd come back up not long after they had traveled farther out to sea, making their way around Nereid to Arethusa.

She'd watched him briefly report to James for work and then seen him climbing the mast for maintenance before pulling her attention back to the plans. She'd seen that expression in a mirror before—vengeance, anger—and Shea hopes that'll keep him alive since she knows she can't force him to stay behind on the *Duchess*.

Jo.

About an hour out from her queendom, Jo returned to the main deck.

Caen shouted her name, and when Shea looked up from her discussion with Triton on evacuation details for the civilians, their eyes had met. She wondered if Jo was still upset with how she had acted earlier, but her worries melted away as her wife smiled at her encouragingly. Shea frowned when Caen took Jo aside for some reason or another, but she didn't have time to investigate.

Poseidon.

He'd attempted to walk up the afterdeck stairs three times on the last stretch of their journey before finally making his decision and coming up. At first, he'd stood by his children, silently observing as they discussed the weaknesses of Arethusa's perimeters but when they'd come to a particular problem, he'd offered a simple solution, breaking his silence.

Shea wanted to ignore him, but his advice was sound, and Triton looked up at her, whispering in her mind, *"He's won many wars."*

Shea had gestured for him to join them and they discussed strategies until Arethusa's capital, Thalassa, had appeared on the horizon.

The glimmering castle on the cliffs shone like a diamond among darkness. As if it were the last safehold in all of Nereid.

As she looks around her surviving crew, Shea realizes

she won't risk any more of her men, she can't because she'll need all that's left to sail the *Duchess* away if this goes south.

The remaining Arethusian soldiers will accompany them to shore.

Aster confronts her as they're boarding the longboats.

"You're not taking Caen?"

Shea sighs, nodding for Jo to get in ahead of her. Beck is already on the first longboat with Triton and Poseidon and a few Arethusian soldiers.

Two of her crewmen are lowering them down to the ocean's surface while the last of the naval officers board the second longboat with Jo.

Shea's eyes flicker to Caen, who's standing on the afterdeck looking out at Thalassa.

"No," she states, turning to board the longboat, but Aster grips her arm tightly, stopping her.

"Don't do this."

"Why are you asking about him? Hmm? Don't you wanna go?" Shea laughs, but the sound is hollow.

"Yes. To protect you, always, but I know I'm no match for them. And I'm not going to get in your way," Aster murmurs.

"You're doing a fine job of that now," Shea comments, gesturing to his hand on her arm.

"Because right now I can protect you, and you're making a mistake."

"I don't feel like I can trust him right now."

"Why?" Aster objects.

"It doesn't matter." Shea yanks her arm out of his grip, but he steps in front of her, blocking her path to the small boat.

"Because he slept with Poseidon?"

Shea's eyes widen and she shushes him.

Aster scoffs.

"A bit late for that since you practically announced it on deck. Why does it matter to you? What are you really blaming him for?"

"I don't blame him," Shea growls.

"Then what is it?" Aster hisses, getting up in Shea's face. "Because leaving him behind is a mistake, he's had your back, he's always had your back."

"Can you just leave it alone?"

"No," he argues.

Shea's looking into those anger-fueled eyes and she feels like she's using her mirror magic, staring at an image of Paetre and her.

"You're pushing him away—why?"

"Because," Shea spits, "because I already lost Phoebus and Dari, and I can't lose him too. And when I saw him with… Poseidon…All I could think about was how because of Poseidon and because I wasn't good enough, Phoebus and Dari died. And I panicked because…I can't lose Caen to him too. I won't. I'd rather die."

"You truly believe that," Aster breathes, searching his surrogate mother's eyes.

"Yes."

"Then I know I can't change your mind."

Shea nods, taking a deep breath. She starts to move around Aster, but he stops her again by grabbing her hand.

"But if you…die," Aster falters on the last word before continuing, "you lose him anyway. So, why don't you do the smart thing, because my mother is not an idiot. She listens to strategy and she knows how to win. But she also can't do that without Caen. So. Are you going to *stop* being an idiot?"

Shea's mouth hangs wide open as she stares at her child—no.

He's not a child anymore.

She tries to recover, but she finds herself jittery and unable to look him in his eyes. She glances over at Caen, standing at the helm, and clears her throat. When she finally gathers the courage to look up at Aster, she sees she's not leaving unless it's with Caen.

He's really not a child anymore.

Shea huffs, a somber chuckle escaping her lips. He's only sixteen, just barely, but pirates are never children long anyway.

She likes to think he got longer than most.

She sighs, flashing her son a soft smile, before turning her body in Caen's direction. She steels her features.

"Mister Caen!"

Caen snaps his head toward her. He seems to straighten up and his arms flex as he grips the banister tighter, awaiting what she has to say.

"Do you think this ship will be able to run without you?" Shea shouts.

There's a moment of silence, and for a second, Shea thinks he might not respond. But his hardened mouth turns into a teasing grin and Shea can already feel her anxiety falling.

"No," he responds. "But I'm willing to let it try, Captain."

Shea nods. "Quickly then, give James your orders. We need to make for shore immediately."

Caen salutes her and races down the helm's steps toward James at the front harpoon launchers.

Shea returns her focus to Aster, who is smiling rather smugly.

His hands are on his hips and she sees a glimmer of leadership in his strong stance.

"You sure you don't need me?" Aster inquires.

"Of course, I need you," Shea remarks, and places a hand on her son's cheek. "But you're needed here. Triton and I have some plans, and if they succeed or fail, I need the *Duchess* ready to sail. You'll be the last ship out of the harbor. We'll set off a signal if things are going badly. But if we're not there within a half hour after the signal, you have to sail, you have to sail to Erebos."

"How will we get past the siren cliffs? It's a ship graveyard."

"We have a plan," Shea reassures him, and Caen finally arrives at her side.

She hugs Aster and steps away, following Caen into the longboat where Jo and the remaining soldiers are waiting.

"Just wait for the signal," Shea calls out as they're lowered down to the water.

Aster leans over the rail, and she takes a moment to memorize every line, curve, and feature of his face.

He nods, and before she knows it, he's gone. She really hopes this isn't the last time she sees him.

***

"Took you long enough," General Soren greets them with a group of men in the courtyard of the palace near the stables.

The naval soldiers from the *Duchess* retire to their barracks, leaving Beck, Jo, Shea, Caen, Poseidon, and Triton in the square.

The city is thoroughly fortified, from what Shea saw as they made their way to the palace after securing the longboats on the beach, hiding them both out of sight.

The front gates to Arethusa have been closed and the stone wall around the lower town is completely guarded by archers and sentries. The city itself is in chaos.

There are so many people, survivors from Oceanus, refugees from all over Nereid running from the rampage of Perses and Ceto's army.

Shea had held Jo's hand as the queen examined her beautiful capital.

She was proud as they arrived in the higher city, where the mansions and manors of the lords and ladies had opened their doors to their fellow citizens and the Oceanan refugees.

Many Oceanan citizens cheered as well as cried when they saw Beck. All who recognized him regarded him as governor and begged questions of when they would be able to return to Oceanus.

Beck answered the best he could. Upon the first question, he had turned to Shea and Jo with a questioning gaze, but they had no answers, the same as him.

Soren kneels before Jo, but she quickly pulls him to his feet and into a familiar embrace. Soren's face would be comical if Shea weren't just as pleased as Jo to see him. Behind Soren is another familiar face, although Shea can't place his name, but the moment Beck see him, he runs over and gives him a firm hug.

"Caius!"

Shea watches the exchange warmly as Caius accepts the embrace, and her heart stutters as Caius's eyes close and he cups the back of Beck's head in relief.

When they pull away, Caius quickly straightens his clothes and waves Beck off politely, but he has a smile that betrays his true feelings for Beck's return.

A heavy hand lands on her shoulder and she jumps, praying to the gods it's not Poseidon, but when she turns, she finds Caen there instead.

She looks up at him with a heavy sigh and they exchange silent apologies.

Soren greets Shea with a bow as well, which she scoffs at, earning a disapproving glare from him. But they clasp hands, squeezing each other's forearms.

"Great. Now that everyone is happy to see each other, might we retire to the war room to plan for the oncoming invasion in a couple days?" Triton drawls, not rudely, but it is a jarring reminder.

Everyone turns to look at him and Soren warily rests his hand on the hilt of his blade at his waist.

"Tomorrow."

"Tomorrow?" Beck questions.

"We should really start planning tonight, Soren," Shea comments, placing her hands on her hips.

"No. The invasion is tomorrow," Soren explains.

"What?"

Everyone practically screams the word.

Poseidon and Triton look at each other worriedly.

Caen is shouting at Soren along with Jo, while Beck is talking quietly but hurriedly with Caius.

The air is thick with panic.

Shea has to shake her head to clear it, but once she does, she sticks two fingers in her mouth and whistles.

Everyone stops talking, and a yowl breaks through the sudden silence as all eyes land on Shea.

Caeruleus lands on her shoulder.

"Hey, buddy," Shea whispers, nuzzling her face against his.

All eyes are still watching her, and she can feel the royals in the courtyard getting impatient, so she cuts her lovefest with her Lionbird short and focuses on the jarring news they've just received.

"Okay. First, Soren, we're half a week early. How can the invasion be tomorrow?"

"I don't know, Your Highness," he explains, and Shea tries to ignore the title in favor of focusing on what he's saying.

Before he can continue, Jo interrupts him, "It's *Her Majesty* now," she tells Soren, who looks at her, confused.

"Shea and I married on Orena. She'll still need a coronation of course, but considering the circumstances, I think we can just refer to her as queen consort for now."

Soren looks shocked, and Shea takes the small victory. That is until he smirks at her, clearing his throat, "Of course, Your Majesty." Soren nods to Shea and Shea just shakes her head.

It's probably not right to wish him harm at the moment since he really could die soon. Although.

Soren continues, "Scouts report that the Lycon army marched from Oceanus after the scourge. It's like they knew when you'd be back. Soldiers from the eastern part of Arethusa managed to send reports that the Merrow have been ravaging the Arethusian countryside."

"What?" Jo exclaims.

"Yes. We sent units in to retrieve as many civilians as we could. The large estates were hit first."

"Many of our palace staff are from the farmlands in the east," Jo murmurs. "Eione?"

"She traveled with a unit to retrieve her family. They were ambushed, my queen...none survived. I'm sorry, Queen Joana," Soren reports with a heavy heart.

A small choked noise escapes Jo's throat, but she manages to hold it together.

"And my...grandmother," Jo inquires, "Lady Catherine? Did she make it out of Galene?"

Soren doesn't respond, but it's answer enough.

"We lost a lot of good people while you were gone. But we're not going to let them die in vain," Caius tells Jo.

A tear falls from her wife's eye, and Shea watches her wipe it away quickly.

"So, tomorrow? What in Hades are we going to do?" Jo asks, looking around the small group.

"Well," Shea responds, and everyone turns back to her. "First we're going to evacuate the city. And then? We're going to fight."

"Then I take it you found who you were after," Soren asks.

Triton steps forward, and Soren's eyes widen in realization at who he is.

"They found me," Triton states.

"Then there's a chance," Caius sighs.

"Soren," Jo orders, and Soren stands at attention, "take us to the war room. I want Thetis and Venus there when we arrive."

Soren salutes and orders two of his men to find V and Thetis.

Thetis.

Shea pauses as she remembers what she's done. She broke her promise. Triton knows about Proteus. Shea rubs a hand over her face as she follows the group inside the palace, hoping this doesn't go as badly as she predicts it will.

Soren leads them through the airy halls.

Guards stand at every corner, and there's quite a few royals roaming the halls with papers and supplies.

They're taken past the doors leading into the ballroom and throne room, and up a large quantity of stairs to the top of a tower. Slits in the white stone let in a bit of light, but otherwise the steps are not illuminated.

Finally, they all arrive at the top and Shea tries to hide the fact she's out of breath.

Beck, Soren, Caius, and Jo step into the tower room with ease, while Caen leans against the wall with a groan.

Shea takes a moment to catch her breath and she almost bursts out laughing as she sees her brother trying to hide his heavy breathing. Poseidon makes the same attempt, and almost gets away with it, but he leans against the door frame for just a moment.

How are there heavy royals when palaces have so many stairs?

"Don't ask questions you don't want the answers to," Triton's voice tapers into her mind, and she glares at him as she pushes off the wall.

"Will you stop that. My thoughts are private," Shea orders, but her brother merely rolls his eyes.

"Then stop thinking so loud. You're the one who opened the connection in the first place," Triton argues.

"Me? You almost killed me; I needed the advantage!"

"I agree, but then don't start saying your thoughts are private when you invaded mine first!"

"I did not," Shea scoffs.

"Children," Poseidon bellows.

Shea and Triton both turn to their father, looking like scolded kids, and they realize they're the only ones left in the tower halls.

"Considering you both have the plans, might you care

to join us?" Poseidon asks wryly, laughing at both of them.

Triton scowls at him, and stalks into the room, pushing past the old sea god. Shea's about to follow him in when a voice calls her name from behind.

"Shea!"

Shea turns at the familiar tone and smiles when she sees Venus casually run up the last few stairs. Shea shakes her head at the lack of difficulty and almost falls to the ground at the force with which V hugs her.

"I'm so glad you're okay. Look at you," V says as she pulls away, holding both of Shea's hands while she looks her over.

"Your magic is stunning, and you opened a few of your connections. I can feel Triton. I always knew power would look good on you." V laughs, spinning Shea around in a twirl, which almost has Shea falling to the ground again.

"You can see my magic?" Shea asks.

V still looks as beautiful as ever. Her hair is braided back in a warrior style and she's wearing black leather pants and boots with a light chain mail top. A waist belt secures the heavy material, and there are two daggers on either side of the belt in holsters.

"Our kind of magic gives off an aura," V responds. "A specialty of mine, auras. Helps me see love connections…and magic. So, tell me, do you see doors like more of your ocean family or something else? For some reason, mirrors are what I conjure when I enter Olympus mentally to open connections to another's magic. I can't believe you found him."

Shea opens her mouth to respond to V's Olympus explanation about the magical doors, room and halls in her mind, when she sees Thetis over V's shoulder.

She's dressed in the same pants, with similar boots, but her top looks more like a violet robe that falls just above her knees in slits. Gold trim laces the shoulders and a breastplate covers the beautiful material. Her hair is also pulled back from her face in a bun and it exposes a necklace she's wearing made of small shells with a miniature conch as the centerpiece.

It's glowing. But what really catches Shea's attention is the look on Thetis's face—the look of fury.

"We should go in," Shea prompts, but V is one step ahead of her, already making her way to the door.

Shea attempts to follow, but a sharp hand with long nails practically pierces the skin on her shoulder as she's yanked back to face Thetis's wrath.

"Thetis." Shea smiles anxiously.

"What is he doing here?" Thetis grinds out, glaring Shea down.

"Who?"

The nails finally pierce Shea's skin and she covers her cry with a cough.

"Triton! Right. Well, he's here to help."

"Why?" Thetis growls. "Why didn't Poseidon just take the net from him?"

Shea's eyes narrow and she pulls her shoulder out of Thetis's grip.

"You knew."

"Of course I bloody knew. Poseidon created Triton's shell, so obviously he has power over it. What, did you really believe that whole 'child of Poseidon is needed to kill another child'? Because if you did, I may have overestimated your intelligence," Thetis snaps.

"If you knew, why you didn't say anything?" Shea seethes.

Thetis scoffs, "You were going to find out anyway, and besides it's very important that Poseidon returns to Atlantis. I knew he'd need the net in order to regain enough power to open the black gates. You were never supposed to bring Triton back, so I'm asking you why in Hades is he here?"

"We could have prevented so many deaths if we had known," Shea practically roars, but she forces herself to quiet her voice, so the others don't hear. "Why is it so important for him to return?"

"You truly know nothing about your own magic, your heritage," Thetis comments, disapprovingly surprised. She shakes her head, refusing to answer. "It doesn't matter, that's not important now. What is important is that I need to leave."

Shea's eyes widen as Thetis turns her back on her.

"Where the bloody Underdeep do you think you're going? You can't leave! We need you, the invasion is tomorrow," Shea growls, turning Thetis back around to face her.

But when Thetis turns, the small conch shell around her neck is glowing a dark blue, and her eyes are the same shade.

She sees Thetis's lips moving, but she can't hear any words; instead she hears the most beautiful singing voice, it's soft and ethereal. The sound overwhelms her senses and her vision is blacking out.

"Thetis!"

A deep, masculine voice rips through the sound, and Shea gulps, gasping, as she feels her lungs burning for air.

She blinks, trying to clear her vision, and two warm hands cup her face. She focuses on the person in front of her and smiles at Triton, relieved to be breathing.

Movement catches the corner of Shea's eye, and she turns quickly, her hand going to her waterskin as her gaze narrows on Thetis.

Ice blocks her path to the stairs and she's standing there glaring at Triton.

"What the Underdeep was that?" Shea rasps angrily.

"Your brother's magic, enjoy it much?" Thetis drawls.

Shea attempts to lunge at her, but Triton holds her back.

"Chári," Triton attempts, but Thetis recoils at the name.

"You will never call me that again," Thetis hisses in response.

Triton swallows, nodding. He steps away from Shea, gesturing to her to remain calm and he moves toward Thetis until he stands in front of her.

"Okay," he tells her, "I'm sorry."

Thetis chuckles coldly. "What pathetic words leaving your tongue, particularly since you don't know the meaning."

"You don't know him anymore," Shea objects, still catching her breath from Thetis's attack.

"And you do?" Thetis snaps. "Seems his siren magic is powerful enough to overtake even someone like you."

"I'm not under any magic. I just know good when I see it," Shea spits, looking Thetis up and down accusingly.

"I helped you, I saved you, and this is the thanks I get."

"Thetis, there's more important things happening than our bad blood," Triton intervenes. "We need to stop Perses."

"Because you did that so well the first time," Thetis sasses, and Triton winces.

"I know you're angry," he says. "You have every right to be. I hurt you. I lost you your home." Triton steps closer to her and she doesn't step away.

Thetis is watching him warily, and Shea finds herself surprised he's getting so close.

"I was a monster when you met me, but even then, I cared for you, I still care for you. And I want to stop him so we can save Nereid, so I can save you." Triton smiles and Thetis's face looks softer, vulnerable.

"So, I can save our child."

And suddenly Shea can't breathe again. The air is sucked out of the room, and Thetis's features harden. She pushes Triton back and her attention shifts to Shea.

"You," she breathes.

Shea stands her ground.

"Thetis," she warns.

"You," Thetis repeats, storming toward Shea.

She grabs Shea, her hand wrapping around her throat, and throws her back against the wall. She squeezes and Shea chokes on the pressure.

"You promised me, you swore you wouldn't tell him!"

"I...didn't," Shea chokes, "I didn't...have...a...choice..."

"Thetis!" Triton barks.

"What in Hades is going on out here—Shea!"

Shea hears Jo's voice from the war room's door and then there's two sets of hands pulling Thetis off of her. Shea slips down, her ass falling on the ground as she coughs at the inhale of air.

Caen is at her side, checking to see if she's alright while Beck is running interference between Thetis and Jo.

Triton is holding Thetis back while she struggles.

Yelling has broken out in the hall as everyone begins arguing with one another.

Shea's vision seems to be righting itself and as the rest of the voices filter in, she thinks she can hear someone who's not in the room with them.

"Yes...Tear yourselves apart...And you call yourselves the heroes..."

Shea looks around with fear, waiting for her half brother's face to appear, but he doesn't. Then she realizes that she's heard his voice before. She tunes out the screaming and enters what she now realizes is Olympus. She instinctively knows what she's looking for.

The mental link to the Olympian palace has opened up into many more halls and doors with marks on the front.

She passes a lightning bolt and a clam with pink mist spilling from the frame, a scent from the slippery serpent drifting from the door. Shea slips deeper into darkness until she finds what she's looking for.

This one isn't marked. It looks just like her own, similar to Triton's blue wooden door. But this magic is black, with veins of purple lightning striking through the thick mists of power.

The door isn't opened, not all the way, but it is cracked.

Whispers escape from the small sliver of space and Shea throws herself up against it, trying to slam the door closed.

"How?" she whispers to herself.

She tries to close the door again, but when she reaches out and touches it, a memory surfaces of Perses's hand on her throat.

His eyes searching hers, and then he had released her. Like he'd found what he was looking for.

"A connection," Shea gasps.

She's shocked. Connecting with Triton had almost killed her, and Perses had just done it like a snap of his fingers.

"You could be as powerful; you could be a goddess. Join me, sister, open the door and share my power."

Perses's voice escapes from the cracks, and Shea steps away from it.

"So, it can kill me too, no thanks," Shea hisses, turning her back on the dark magic.

"Your choice. Either way, you'll meet your fate tomorrow."

Shea forces herself out of her mind, and she winces as she comes back to the screaming and yelling in the tower hall.

"Enough," Shea coughs.

But no one can hear her over the sound of shouting.

A soft meow catches her attention from the door to the war room and she sees Caeruleus staring at her. He sits down and yowls. No one pays him any mind, but Shea understands.

She turns back to look at her wife, who is shouting at Thetis.

At Caen threatening her and Thetis threatening him back, while Venus holds Caen back.

At Beck arguing with Triton and Jo.

Shea pushes herself up using the wall; she straightens

and squares her jaw.

"Oi!" Shea roars. "Enough!"

She attracts the attention of everyone in the hall.

"We don't have time for this. Perses will be here tomorrow and as he just informed me in my mind, he's prepared for all of us to meet our fates."

That seems to capture everyone's attention.

"Now, we have exactly one night to figure out a way to kill Perses, to hold off a siege of Lycon soldiers and Merrow. And finally, somehow survive this battle. So instead of fighting each other, let's focus on the real enemy."

"Except I don't know who that is anymore," Thetis growls, shaking Triton off.

He lets her go.

"Then I suggest you figure it out, and quickly. Because I have no problem with Soren locking you up, and then regardless of the outcome you can worry about who comes and finds you," Shea bites.

"You would imprison your nephew's mother?" Thetis inquires sarcastically.

"I can't afford to act emotionally right now. Can you?"

Thetis steps back like Shea has struck her and Shea takes it as a win.

She may feel bad for telling Triton about Proteus, but Thetis knew that Poseidon could have stopped Perses before their voyage even if it meant him never returning to Atlantis, and that is unforgivable.

She's the reason Dari and Phoebus are dead. It's enough for the last of her guilt to go away.

"Shall we?" Shea asks, and she leads the group back into the war room.

The tower is impressive; it's completely open to the air except for a white marble railing that goes all the way around. Shea can see the ocean, the harbor, her ship, and even...

Her thoughts narrow down to the view ahead, out

in the distance past the lower town's gates. Past the castle farmlands, along the Trident's Fork Road to the smoke in the distance and the lights. The more Shea studies it, the more she realizes what all those objects are. It's a camp, and more specifically, as she can just barely make out the colors flying, a Lycon camp.

"Oh gods," Shea mutters.

It's happening, they're really here.

Jo comes up beside her; she takes Shea's hand, gripping it tightly as they stare over the marble rail at the army lying in wait.

"How long?"

"Soren said they arrived last night," Jo explains. "Movements suggest they sent scouts, and all the officers agreed they're coming; they attack tomorrow, definitely. At dawn or later, no one knows."

"Then we best make the most of the time we have left," Shea advises her queen.

Jo peers at her and kisses her forehead.

Shea turns, examining the rest of the tower.

The war room is impressive, large enough to fit at least thirty people comfortably. The floor is a large-scale map of Arethusa and the surrounding areas of Nereid. Fake ships and colored wooden pieces are scattered around the map as reference for fleets and army units.

Soren is holding some sort of stick that pushes the pieces into place. It's then that Shea notices Gaea and Rhea are in the tower with them.

The two crones are sitting on cushioned seats with a set of guards standing at attention behind them.

Beck and Caius take a side with two Oceanan advisors with them.

Triton, Venus, and Poseidon stand off to another part of the rail with Thetis standing alone.

Jo keeps her hold on Shea's hand, and she guides her to where the rest of the Arethusians are standing.

Caen surprisingly stands with Poseidon.

They've each broken off into their own factions and hopefully there's enough of them to turn the tide.

Shea thinks about ignoring the two old women, but a voice inside her forces her to say something.

"Ladies," Shea begins with a curtsy, but is promptly cut off by Gaea.

"You are queen consort. You curtsy to no one and you will do well to remember that," Gaea snaps.

Shea huffs, glaring at Caen, who snickers.

"Don't you think we're a little busy for protocol," Shea murmurs, but Rhea glares her down, making Shea feel positively small.

"We are *never* too busy for protocol. Now shoulders back," Rhea orders and Shea finds herself doing what the old woman says. "The general informed us you had a plan. Shall you proceed?"

Shea hears Caeruleus yowl from somewhere nearby and she sees him land on a rail. She missed the old bird.

He's looking worse for wear, his muzzle is almost completely gray now, and his feathers are thinner.

She forgets how old he is. Shea clears her throat, pushing the nostalgia away, and conceals her emotions; what has become the war council is staring at her, and she gestures for Triton to join her on the floor.

"We have a plan," Shea announces.

"Oh good, she can repeat things. How about you explain to the soldiers what exactly they're supposed to do," Gaea drawls.

"Gentle, ladies," V growls.

Shea scowls at the old bats, and she takes a bit of solace when she sees Jo give her ex-handler a sharp look, which seems to cow Gaea.

"As I was saying, we have a plan. First things first, we need to make sure we don't lose any more of our people. They can't stay in the city; the low town, mid-town, and the high city of Thalassa will be the first to be sacked before they reach the castle."

"We're going to allow them in?" Thetis objects.

"We're going to allow them past the first gate," Triton explains, and she shoots him a glare, which he ignores, "so that we can focus all our attention on the palace gate. We use magic to fortify a barrier, and soldiers, lots of soldiers, so that we only let in a few at a time."

"Cuts down casualties, gives the soldiers some reprieve, and takes care of the Merrow and Lycons, but what about Perses?" Caen asks.

Beck steps forward as well. "And where are we evacuating our people?"

Shea nods. "Those are two very good questions. First, for the evacuation, since that's the easier of the two to explain. We have to send them to the last safe place on Nereid."

"There's nowhere left," Soren states, "the Merrow have scourged the continent."

"There's one place, one that's been completely untouched," Triton tells him.

"You're going to take them to Erebos," Venus realizes, announcing their plan.

Jo coughs. "I hate to argue with a goddess, but that's not right, right? There's a barrier around the Eastlands. No one can enter."

"The barrier is only inland," Venus explains.

"And it doesn't extend to the coast," Shea tells her.

Caen sighs. "That's because no one can get through the other side. The cliffs of the Eastlands are siren territory; it's an ocean graveyard on the other side."

"Well luckily"—Shea smiles—"we have the father of sirens on our side."

"You can get our people through," Beck murmurs.

"Yes," Triton confirms. "Easily, but I'll have to be there to do it."

"But what about Perses?" Jo argues. "We need you to

help Shea and Poseidon defeat him."

"I'm not completely useless you know," V interrupts, raising her hand. "I can help, give him a chance to get away."

"Actually, you can't," Triton argues.

"What?"

"We'll need someone powerful protecting the fleet, and our last getaway, it'll be up to you to protect the *Duchess* and the crew until we can get there."

"I'm babysitting." V scowls, folding her arms across her chest.

"I think the refugees and civilians would be most comforted to know a goddess is protecting them, my lady," General Soren notes, blushing when V smiles at him sweetly.

"Well when you put it that way. Fine, when do you want me to go?"

"Now?" Shea asks.

V frowns. "Trying to get rid of me already. Fine, people find out you're the goddess of love and suddenly they don't need you in a fight."

"Wait!" Triton exclaims and Shea turns to him, confused.

"We should give her the backup plan."

Shea's eyes widen. "You're right."

"I'm sorry, what backup plan?" V mutters.

"Triton is the priority for survival in the final fight. But if things start going south, we have to get him out of here to the *Duchess* so he can lead the fleet to Erebos. We'll send a signal to my crew that we're coming, to you V."

"The connection." V nods.

Everyone else looks slightly confused, but the gods and demigod in the room understand.

"And if he doesn't make it? If you don't make it?" Soren inquires.

"Then the refugee ships will sail north to a place called Charis, our backup plan."

"Shea," Caen objects. "We can't send them there."

"There's no choice. At least there, the Oceanans, Arethusians can start over. They can survive even if Nereid is lost."

"I've never heard of this place," Rhea growls.

"That's because it's extremely hard to find," Venus drawls.

"And you'll need this to get there." Shea pulls an amulet from her pocket, a garnet encased in white gold hanging on red silk ribbon.

"What is it?" Soren asks as Shea hands it to V.

"A key," V remarks. "Where did you get this?"

"Nowhere," Shea tells her, quickly trying to change the subject.

Then V's eyes widen as she looks closer at it.

"Shea Lara, you little thief. How did you? When did you? You had it all this time?" V growls.

"Well it was a few years back when we were doing that…thing…" Shea trails off, trying to ignore Jo's piercing gaze.

"What thing?"

"A bit of foreplay," V remembers. "This will get us in alright. I bet you didn't even remember you had it. You must have been quite surprised when you ended up there."

"You have no idea," Shea mutters.

"That's where you went, isn't it? The time Soren couldn't find you," Jo wonders aloud, staring at the amulet.

"It's not important," Shea states, ignoring Jo's question. "If Triton doesn't make it out, you go to Charis, otherwise the fleet follows the *Duchess* to Erebos. The *Duchess* will send the fleet a signal if we don't make it," Shea finishes explaining.

"I can do that," V confirms. "I'll go now."

V disappears with the amulet, heading to the *Duchess*.

"You think Perses will let us go?" Caius inquires.

"I don't know," Shea answers honestly.

"So what happens when Perses shows up?" Thetis

snaps.

Shea rolls her eyes at the other elf's harsh tone and gestures for Triton to take over.

"Perses, with all his power, shouldn't have too much trouble getting past the barrier. He'll only be able to bring an elite team with him, no more than ten men, even mortal magic has its limits paired with my shell, but he'll get through. We have to be ready and waiting for him."

"We've picked a location, one with easy access for escape and with a lot of room."

"The throne room," Jo suspects, and she's correct.

"Yes," Shea states, nodding to her.

"So, you battle Perses there, but how do you intend to defeat him?" Beck asks the next important question.

"He's not immortal," Poseidon pipes up, stepping onto the floor map from the edge.

"He has a lot of power, but the magic inside him is still killing him. And while it may not seem like it, it makes him weak and filled with wild magic, which should he unleash, he might not be able to control."

"You're telling us your plan is to wait him out, tire him out," Thetis notes incredulously.

"Pretty much," Shea chuckles, but there's no humorous edge.

"So how do we help? What can we do?" Jo demands.

"I'm glad you asked because you all have jobs. While we know Perses will be able to get in eventually, we can still make it difficult for him, and we'll need the extra time to prepare for him. When I was first here at Jo's coronation ball, we went out to the gardens," Shea begins, but Rhea cuts her off.

"Where you kidnapped her."

"Right," Shea sighs. "But as we were walking through the gardens, I noticed that the trees were glowing, something only possible with the aid of magic, which means Arethusa has its own magic practitioners."

"We do?" Jo asks, warily turning toward the crones.

"You didn't know?" Beck raises a brow.

"Not exactly."

Jo is glaring at the two old women now.

Gaea breaks first. "We do have certain elves with the ability."

"Free elves," Rhea states, and Shea rolls her eyes at the attempt at a distinction.

"We only allow the use of magic at festivities."

"Why wasn't I told?" Jo interrogates.

"It was on a need to know basis."

"I'm the queen!"

"The military has no knowledge of this either." Soren glares.

"And thank the gods, because Mariner could have been much harder to tame last year," Rhea snaps.

Shea groans. "Look, just tell us if any of the secret magic elves are still at the castle."

"They are," Gaea confirms. "But why do you need them?"

"To feed Triton's barrier, right?" Thetis drawls.

Shea smiles at her harshly.

"Which leads you to your next part of the plan; let me guess, you want me on the front lines," Thetis spits.

"Thetis."

"No. I'm not leaving Proteus."

"We know that," Triton soothes, "that's why, while you're keeping the barrier up, I'll put a barrier around his chambers for protection. That way when you leave the boundary, you can get him and take him to the evacuation point and escape."

"Absolutely not," Thetis screeches. "I'm not letting you near him, you shall never lay eyes on him."

Triton takes a step back at the comment, hurt evident on his features.

Shea, who is not as surprised by her outburst, recovers faster.

"Fine, I'll do it. I can seal the room, and make sure he's protected, but you have to be the one leading the elves. We need you, Thetis—this plan fails without you. We're trusting you."

Thetis is quiet as her eyes scan Shea's features, and Shea almost thinks she'll decline again when she scoffs but nods.

"Good, Rhea, Gaea, show Thetis to the elves. She needs to prepare them. Triton will be along to put up the barrier soon. Once that's done, start the evacuation process, I want both of you on the first ship. Understood?"

Shea doesn't expect a response. Thetis nods and the two old women shuffle from their seat, their guards following behind them.

Thetis walks out without another word, but Rhea and Gaea pause at the door. They turn back to face the war council and stare directly at Shea.

"Yes, Queen Consort," they both reply to Shea's earlier question, curtsying before leaving the tower.

"What's next?" Jo smiles, having watched the whole moment between Shea and her ex-handlers.

Shea is still a bit dazed by the respect, so she doesn't hear Jo's question at first.

Triton takes the lead for her.

"Shea, Poseidon, and I will be laying traps along the halls leading to the throne room. It'll delay, but it won't stop the inevitable; by now Perses should be able to sense when we're near. And unfortunately for all of you, we're what he cares about—somehow I think he believes we can save him from dying."

Shea shakes her head in bewilderment, that's the one thing they hadn't been able to work out.

"And us?" Beck asks.

Shea looks up at him and sees Caius's worried expression.

He quickly schools his features, but Shea understands

how he feels.

"Beck. And Jo," Shea states, catching their attention, "you of course will be on ships leading your people to Erebos or Charis."

There's a moment of silence and then the two of them erupt.

"Absolutely not!"

"Never going to happen!"

Shea sighs; she didn't really expect much different.

"Yes, alright. I figured. Caius and Soren will be there as the leaders of Arethusa and Oceanus."

Now the advisors begin their objections.

"I forbid it!"

"We need them!"

"Yes! I know that," Shea shouts, glaring at Soren and Caius. "But unfortunately, I'm married to that one"—Shea points to Jo—"and that one has seniority," Shea finishes, pointing to Beck.

"So, we three lose," Shea shrugs. "Now, Caius, start the boarding process. We don't have time to wait, go section by section until every civilian in the city is on board one of the ships."

Caius turns to Beck to argue, but Beck beats him to it. "Do as she says."

Caius sighs heavily and nods, bowing to Beck and then briefly to Shea and Jo before leaving the room.

"Soren?"

Soren meets Shea's eyes.

"Before you board, I want you to get the men ready. All the sentries at the lower wall, bring them here. Station them at every point around the castle gates and within. I want this area fortified. But before dawn, I want you on one of those ships. If Jo and I don't make it, we—and I think I can speak for Jo—we trust you to lead…*our* people," Shea orders.

Soren gapes at her, letting her words sink in before he bows to Jo and Shea.

"Yes, Queen Consort," Soren responds, and this time Shea feels like he means it. "Your Majesty." Soren turns to Jo and he awaits her orders.

"Do as she says," Jo confirms, and the next piece of their plan is off and gone to complete his task.

"So, what's our real job?" Beck inquires.

It's just Shea, Triton, Caen, Poseidon, Beck, and Jo left with a handful of guards standing around the room as sentries.

Shea laughs when she sees Caeruleus curled up on the rail sleeping; he's lying on an edge hundreds of feet up in the air. But what does a cat with wings care if he falls?

"While Triton, Poseidon, and I are facing down Perses and whoever else comes with him, I need you clearing our escape path. It'll be your job to get us out, to get Triton out of here."

"We're not leaving without you," all three of them respond.

Triton and Shea laugh at the ferocity, and even Poseidon cracks a smile.

"See, my preservation skills are so high I chose a group of people who wouldn't leave without me," Shea jokes but sobers quickly because she needs them to understand.

"I love all of you." Shea's eyes jump from Caen to Beck, and land finally on Jo. "Deeply. But I am not worth thousands of lives. I wasn't kidding. Charis is the backup plan, because honestly, Erebos, sirens, and a bunch of angry elves is safer than the evils lying north. So, when I say save Triton, I mean it."

Caen is staring at the ground.

Beck is biting his lips hard enough to split them, and Jo looks angry and terrified all at once.

"I need to hear you all say it. Okay?"

Jo and Beck nod sullenly, but Caen keeps his eyes down.

"If I'm lost, you don't come back for me. Say it."

All three of them are staring at the map on the floor—

they won't meet her eyes.

"Say it," Shea rasps. "Please."

Caen is the first to look up. "If there's nothing left to do, I'll get him to the ship."

Beck and Jo repeat exactly what Caen said, and while it's not exactly what Shea wanted to hear, she'll take it.

"What's the exit strategy?"

She grins. "I thought we'd take an old trip down memory lane."

Caen raises a brow and it comes to him quickly. He laughs heartily.

Jo and Beck stare at them both, waiting to be let in on the joke.

"Past the Lover's Fountain, through the barracks, and out the servant's entrance," Caen tells them.

Jo grins, shaking her head. "Here's hoping I'm conscious this time."

Beck still looks confused, so Shea pats his shoulder. "Don't worry, we'll tell you the story sometime."

Eventually, Caen and Beck leave to scout the escape path.

Triton has to head down to meet Thetis and the elves, so he leaves too.

Poseidon lets her know that he's going to survey the throne room for any security risks, and eventually Jo and Shea are left up in the tower all alone.

Their fates decided in a matter of hours.

Shea walks over to the rail where Caeruleus is sleeping and picks him up in her arms. Jo steps up beside her and scratches the top of Caeruleus's head, making him purr.

"We should make the final rounds, confirm everything, and then get some rest. We don't know when they're coming, and we need to be ready."

"Agreed," Shea sighs, staring out at the Lycon camp, wondering if Perses is staring back at her.

Her mind curiously wanders back to his door, but she

forcefully pulls herself away from it. Because even among the darkness there's something familiar about his magic. Something that feels like her own. He's a demigod like her; she thinks of Triton as her brother, but he's a god. He's immortal, but Perses is the same as her. Mortal.

She thinks about the blood that dripped from her nose, and what she did to the Merrow on Orena. There was darkness in that, a need for revenge, a need to kill. She shudders, thinking about Perses's offer. To open the connection between them, but what would that do to her?

"Did you hear me?"

Shea turns to Jo, startled, but covers her thoughts with a smile.

"Sorry, what was that?"

Jo grins, cupping the side of Shea's face.

"You go check on the boundary, I'll check in on the evacuation and Soren, and we'll meet at my chambers. Remember where they are?"

Shea nods, not trusting herself to speak.

"Good. It's going to be okay," Jo tells her.

Shea murmurs a *see you later* before she's left alone in the war room. A couple pinpricks on her hand remind her she's not alone as Caeruleus yawns up at her, waking from his nap.

That's right, she's not alone, she thinks. And maybe that's what holds her back from becoming Perses. Because she has people who will pull her out of her darkness.

CHAPTER 40: THE FOCAL POINT

Shea

Caeruleus flies above her down the hall as she heads to the courtyard once again.

When they had discussed the plan, Triton had told her he'd need to choose a focal point for the boundary—a random point somewhere near the main gate, and since the main gate is off of the stables and courtyard, she figures that's where he'll be.

Some confirmations from fleeing royals and a couple palace guards, and she manages to make it to the door leading out. She's just about to go through when she's stopped by another royal.

"Miss, you should be evacuating," Shea tells her as the beautiful lady with dark skin and curly brown hair comes marching toward her.

"And I will be," the woman answers with a rich tone, similar to Jo's.

She stops in front of Shea, and when the elf attempts to move past her, she's stopped once again.

"Can I help you?"

"Jo should be evacuating too," the woman demands.

Shea raises a brow, examining her once again. Recognition floods her brain, as she thinks of the letters Jo used to write her when they were apart.

"Uh, Berry, right?" Shea attempts, and from the unimpressed look on the lady's face, she guesses wrong.

"Beroe."

"Right!" Shea smiles. "Right. Um…I'm sorry to hear about your, um, co-lady-in-waiting—"

"Then you should understand my concern for Jo's well-being; as her wife, you should tell her to get on the ship."

Shea chuckles awkwardly—news travels fast. "I don't know if you really know Jo, but I can't tell her to do anything. In fact, she's usually the one giving the orders."

"And yet here you are deciding the fate of Arethusa," Beroe bluntly argues.

Shea sighs, getting a little tired of this confrontation. "Jo's made her decision, I suggest you accept it and evacuate."

"Arethusa doesn't need you!" Beroe growls.

Shea stops, and stares at Beroe.

She huffs. "Look. Jo is the queen. She's our leader, by her birthright, she is who belongs with her people. We need her. And let's face it, you're expendable. We can live without you, but we cannot continue without her. Now she's staying because of you! So, I'm asking you to do the right thing for once in your criminal life and tell her to go."

Shea's eyes widen, not because she's insulted, but really because she's impressed. She tries to hide her amusement and instead looks Beroe head-on.

"I like you," Shea states. "You're obviously loyal, smart, courageous, and if we survive, I hope you remain in Jo's service. But I need you to hear me. I don't control my wife, never have, never will. And so as much as I would like to get her on that ship, I'd also like to just accept her wishes, move on, and figure out how to keep her safe with what I've got. You may not like me, but your queen chose me. You're grieving, I get that."

Shea continues, stepping into Beroe's space, and the

woman at least has the decency to look sorry. "But don't ever assume that I do not have my wife's best interests at heart. Get me?"

Beroe's face is like stone, solemn and still, and then her eyebrows start to crinkle. Her nose scrunches up and tears spring from her eyes.

Shea jumps back.

Beroe is sobbing in front of her, and the captain is not entirely sure what to do.

She takes a step toward the woman, placing a hand on her back and then finds her arms full of a lady-in-waiting, sobbing into her shoulder.

"Eione was my best friend! Jo is too, I'm so sorry, I just don't want to lose her."

Shea huffs fondly—she really likes this lady.

"Well then, be there for her. Get to safety so you can help her. There's always a chance I might not live through this."

"Really?" Beroe looks up, and Shea sincerely hopes that's not longing in Beroe's eyes.

But she comforts her anyway. "Yeah. She'll need people she can count on then."

Beroe sniffs and nods. She smiles at Shea and, to Shea's surprise, hugs her.

"Try not to die," she offers before heading back in the direction she came.

Shea shakes her head. Well she knows one thing, if they survive and she actually becomes a real queen consort, this place definitely won't be boring.

Shea steps out of the palace door into the courtyard and quickly avoids a group of soldiers marching toward the gate.

Her mouth drops as she looks in the direction of the palace gate and sees a purple, distorted shield floating around it.

Elves in maid and butler suits have their hands pointed

at the boundary, and the purple shield seems to be pulsing in response.

She approaches them, looking around for Triton and Thetis, but they're not near the entrance to the gate.

Shea asks one of the elves working on the boundary, and the young man points along the gate to the left. She offers her thanks, and as she's sticking close to the gated wall, she smiles when she sees the stable hand that lent her that magnificent stallion at the start of their journey. People always surprise her.

The farther down she goes, the darker the purple boundary turns as it gets stronger.

She runs her hands along the bars, feeling the power of the shield, and it reminds her of a heartbeat. She thinks she might have gone the wrong direction when suddenly she hears shouting from up ahead. She's just about there when she sees a break in the boundary, a tear between one side of the shield and the other. That must be the focal point.

Beside it are Triton and Thetis, arguing so loudly with one another that they don't hear Shea approaching.

"Why did you come back?"

"I had to. For you, for Proteus!"

"Don't say his name," Thetis threatens.

"You shielded yourself. After the banishment, I went looking for you and our child, but I couldn't find you. I came back," Triton explains.

"Too late," Thetis growls, pushing him away. "Too late! You claimed me at sixteen, you seduced me at seventeen, and then when I was old and used up at twenty-one, you threw me away like garbage."

"I was selfish, and horrible. I know, but I never meant to hurt you," Triton soothes, trying to get close to her again, but Thetis slaps him across the face.

"I didn't love you, and you didn't love me…You siren spelled me. I know that now, because after I got picked up by slavers and taken to Lycos, I hated you. And that hate was the truth, not the fake love we shared."

"I didn't—" Triton argues.

"Save it. Proteus is mine! I will not let you take him from me," Thetis cries out, slapping Triton again and again.

Shea's had enough.

She jogs the rest of the way, grabbing Thetis's hand before she can strike again. She pushes the other elf to the ground.

Thetis screams in outrage, quickly standing. Her hand goes to her conch shell necklace and her eyes turn a vibrant red.

She realizes the conch is amplifying her voice into a siren's spell. Shea summons her water from her flask and thrusts it toward Thetis's throat, wrapping around her tan neck and tightening until Thetis chokes on her magic words.

Thetis scratches at the water to release her, but her hand passes through the liquid unable to grasp onto anything.

Shea smiles at the pathetic display. Her hands feel Thetis's neck through the water. She thinks if she just squeezed a bit more, she could snap the fae's neck like a twig.

"Shea!" Triton barks.

His voice snaps her out of whatever strange trance she'd gotten herself into, and she immediately releases Thetis, who falls back to the floor coughing.

Shea stumbles back, and Triton catches her.

"Are you okay?" he whispers into her ear, but before Shea can respond, Thetis looks up at them.

The betrayal is clear in her eyes, but Shea stands by her decision. She stares coldly down at Thetis.

"So, you've made your choice," she mutters.

Thetis gets up from her place on the floor and brushes off her clothes. She sniffs, and gently rubs her neck as she begins to walk away.

"Where are you going?" Shea demands.

"To check on the others," Thetis rasps, "Your Majesty.

I'm beginning to wonder who the real monster is."

Shea flinches at the accusation and opens her mouth to respond, but Thetis is already gone.

Shea walks toward the gate, slamming her fist into it.

"Stupid," she mutters to herself.

"No," Triton argues, "you're not."

"I shouldn't have pissed her off like that, she can be very...unpredictable."

"You don't need to tell me," Triton laughs.

Shea smiles in response.

"Thank you."

Shea raises a brow. "What for?"

"For defending me. She's not entirely wrong, I was horrible to her, but I never knew she thought I siren spelled her." Triton shakes his head.

"What she did to me?" Shea asks.

Triton nods grimly. "That's a very dark version of it, what my true sirens use to lure enemies to their deaths. But what she speaks of is very similar to what Aphrodite can do. Charm speak. She can make a man or woman do anything she says, anything she wants. Sirens on the other hand can only induce feelings, manipulate, persuade decisions but not command. A person technically retains their free will."

"That's horrible," Shea murmurs. "Why did you create something like that?"

"Well...the first siren was a water nymph. She got caught, by pirates," Triton tells her, and Shea sighs, figuring where this probably is going. "They took her against her will. I found her. She was a good friend of mine. She was angry, she felt so powerless. So, I used the shell, to grant her revenge. She lured the pirates to their deaths and crashed their ship on the cliffs of Erebos."

"How long ago was this?" Shea asks, intrigued.

"Eight hundred years." Triton chuckles. "Give or take a hundred."

Shea whistles at the number.

"I tried to turn her back, but she refused, asked if I would grant her the power to make more from other scorned people she found. I granted her the ability, but only the willing can become sirens, and so their voices only work on the willing. They manipulate, sure, but some part of you has to want the manipulation they're offering for it to work."

"I can't imagine," Shea remarks.

Triton gestures for her to step away from the gate and he closes up the focal point with a wave of his hand.

"That should do it."

The sun is setting overhead. Night is falling, and soon the war will be upon them. It's quiet with just the two of them and Shea feels at peace.

The heartbeat from the boundary keeps beating and she relaxes into the sound.

"It's comforting," Shea says, and Triton turns to her.

"What is?"

"The sound from the boundary."

Triton raises a brow.

"It sounds like a heartbeat," she explains.

Triton stares, as if he doesn't understand what she's saying, but then his eyes widen before he squeezes them shut.

She feels a quick probing within her chest and realizes he's touching her door in his mind.

"Can't you hear it?" she asks.

"Yes," Triton breathes and opens his eyes.

There's a beaming smile stretching across his face and Shea has to laugh.

"What?"

Triton is grinning at her like a fool, but then his face freezes and he turns deathly pale.

"Triton?"

He takes a step toward her, placing his hands on her shoulders.

"You need to be careful tomorrow."

Shea cocks her head, grateful for the concern.

"I'm always careful," she teases and with that she excuses herself for the night.

Triton lets her go and she doesn't think about how odd the turn in their conversation was. She doesn't see Thetis when she passes the front gate, and she continues down the halls, making her way to Jo's chambers. It's not long before she arrives at a pair of grand doors. She passes Caen and Beck on their way back from scouting and bids them rest before the battle tomorrow.

Shea enters the doors and is happy to find Jo on the other side. She's smiling at something, staring at her bed, and Shea rolls her eyes as she looks and finds Caeruleus curled in a ball on the blanket.

"How's everything?" Jo whispers, careful not to wake the mangy Lionbird.

"The boundary is up; the guards have retired from the lower gate."

"And the city has been evacuated, all that's left is to wait," Jo finishes Shea's sentence for her, and she nods.

She opens her arms and Jo folds into her. They stand there embracing each other for a moment.

"I ran into your friend Beroe."

"She's okay?" Jo whispers.

"Yes." Shea smiles into Jo's shoulder. "She's okay."

Shea looks out the window and gasps when she sees a shimmer of purple. She breaks the embrace and heads to the open archway, gesturing for Jo to follow. She points out at the air and it takes a moment, but a bird or a leaf, or something disturbs the purple barrier and it shimmers enough for it to be visible.

"Amazing," Jo murmurs.

Shea wraps her arms around her wife and kisses the back of her neck.

"Whatever happens. I'm glad I met you, Joana of Arethusa."

Jo leans into the touch. "I couldn't be more blessed being your wife; it is my greatest achievement."

"Are you saying I was a conquest?" Shea teases.

"Most definitely," Jo remarks, and Shea jokingly huffs, tickling Jo's sides.

Jo shrieks with laughter and they carry on until Jo has managed to turn in Shea's embrace.

She leans down and kisses Shea hard.

Then the queen takes her captain by the hand and leads her to the bed.

They don't take off their clothes, they can't. They have to be ready. So, they lie down, side by side, with Caeruleus at their feet, and pretend to dream until true sleep captures them.

CHAPTER 41: DAWN

Shea

The castle shudders, marble quakes, and Shea and Jo jolt up in bed as the double doors to their chambers slam open.

Caen has his hammer and Beck is carrying a steel sword as they stop in the entry way, breathing heavily. Caen is wearing his normal boots and pants, but he seems to have found a chain mail shirt that fits.

Beck must have changed as well, into new boots, leather pants, and a long-sleeve peasant blouse with a leather vest.

Shea looks out the window and startles as a giant flaming ball comes flying at their room, she tackles Jo to the floor, but it explodes on impact with the purple barrier.

Shea stands quickly, helping Jo up before running to the open window.

The sky is orange and red with a hint of dark blue. She can see the sun rising in the east.

It's dawn and the battle has begun.

Shea can see from here that the Lycon troops have broken through the low town gate. Thalassa is burning, and tiny ant-like soldiers are everywhere.

Catapults have been stationed just inside the city, but the boundary isn't letting the molten iron through.

She needs to get to the throne room.

When she turns back around, she finds Jo dressed in silver armor, as Beck helps her with the cinches.

She pins her hair up in a bun as Beck ties off the last piece. Jo reaches into the chest at the end of the bed and pulls out Shea's gold sword.

Jo looks over at her wife and asks, "You mind?"

Shea uncorks the waterskin at her waist and draws a lasso of water from it. "Not at all."

She pushes the water back into the skin.

Caen throws her some clothes, and she catches them easily.

She smiles gratefully and quickly changes into the leather pants, that'll give her a bit more protection than the clothes she had on before. She keeps her boots and blouse and shrugs on a leather jacket, tying the cords closed.

The flask remains uncorked.

"We should go," Beck warns.

Shea nods in agreement.

They all head for the door. They're a few steps down the hall when another explosion rocks the castle. But this one is different, Shea heads for one of the waterfall windows and looks out. The purple boundary is fading, blinking in the dawning light before it extinguishes.

Screams and battle cries fill the air and Shea has to hold on to the window to keep herself from falling over in shock.

"He broke down the barrier."

CHAPTER 42: HADES'S BARGAIN

Thetis

The gate's warning bells ring, alerting the palace that the war is here. Thetis listens to the sound, rocking her son so he doesn't wake.

Shea placed the room under an illusion. An enchantment much like the one she uses on her brand so that anyone who passes by the door won't see it unless they're looking for it. But for this enchantment, they have to be looking specifically for Proteus for it to work. It's a clever spell and it makes Thetis's blood boil.

She wants to scream. She doesn't want to leave her son. His beautiful black hair is a wavy mess and she desperately wishes he would open his green eyes one last time for her to see.

She's scared, not of this, not of war. But what comes next.

Shea has obviously chosen a side—she believes Triton to be good.

From what Thetis saw earlier, Shea may be no better than he is. What if she tries to take Proteus away from her? What if she believes Triton will be a better parent than she is? Thetis's grip on her son tightens; she won't let that happen.

She lays her son down in his bed, whispering a silence charm that will be disturbed if he's touched, so he doesn't wake.

Thoughts are running rampant in her head, terrible thoughts, horrible ideas, and yet she wonders if she's making a choice, the same way Shea did against her.

Thetis grabs her cloak from the door, wrapping it around herself. She reaches for the door handle, looking back at her sleeping child one last time, and then steps out with her hood veiling her face.

She takes off toward the gate and reaches the courtyard door, stepping out with her hand on her conch shell. Her eyes flash a deep blue and she looks at the world through her siren eyes.

The Merrow are at the gate tearing at the boundary. The pathetic servant elves are holding the line, feeding their magic to the parasite veil.

Thetis keeps her face obscured and hurries to the focal point where she knows she'll find who she's looking for.

The soldiers are hard at work, using Triton's plan, letting in a few fish folk and soldiers before closing the gate again and cutting them down.

If she does this, those men are as good as dead. The thought makes her trip, and her knees slam into the cobbled ground. She's breathing heavily and her head aches.

What is she doing? She's not thinking straight. But a voice from the back of her mind whispers for her to get up. It tells her of course she's not thinking straight, she's protecting her child. She has to protect her child.

Thetis pushes herself off the ground. She focuses her magic again.

A soldier stops her, telling her she needs to go back. She doesn't think twice before enchanting him into believing his sword is food and he's starving. She continues past even as the blade runs through the back of the boy's head and he falls to the ground in a puddle of blood.

Finally, the focal point appears; she can feel the power

CHAPTER 42: HADES'S BARGAIN | 469

emanating off of it. Triton's magic. It's so familiar, it makes her heart unconsciously beat faster. It fuels her rage.

He's there.

On the other side.

In black leather pants, boots, and a black robe top similar to her own that falls in three slits around his legs, making duels easier.

She can see the conch on his hip, the same as the day she first laid eyes on it when Triton blew the shell and a sound more beautiful than anything she ever heard flowed from it, enchanting her. She wants nothing more than to destroy it. She steps up to the barrier and chuckles when she sees Ceto on the other side in full gold armor.

Ceto doesn't have a helmet. Her hair is done up in an elaborate braid with gold spikes sticking out of it. She's carrying a gold sword and is surrounded by five of her men and five Merrow.

Perses is handsome. His features are similar to Shea's and Triton's, but she realizes that his hair is a darker copper and duller. His nose is sharper, like a hawk's beak, whereas theirs is chiseled like a statue. He's noticeably half of what they are. But the power emanating off of him also makes him so much more. His presence stretches even through the barrier.

"Hello again," Perses murmurs and his voice catches her off guard.

It's quiet, solemn, deep, and wise but with a cold tint and lack of emotion. It makes her feel like she's listening to a current at the bottom of the ocean.

"Thetis...come crawling back, have we?" Ceto muses.

Thetis doesn't respond, she doesn't even look at her.

Ceto is a fly in the air behind this magnificent creature.

And if Thetis wants to live, she'll bargain with him.

"What do you want?" Perses asks in the same voice.

He cocks his head like he's trying to understand how she works, what makes her tick.

"My son. I want my son."

"And you know what I want," Perses tells her, lifting his robe and showing her what she knows he already has. What he needs in order to get what he wants.

"Yes," Thetis responds.

"You're willing to help me get it."

"Yes," Thetis repeats, but she knows his last comment wasn't a question.

"Then you know what I need to ask."

"You'll find him in the throne room. I'll delay her."

Perses smiles, and it's like looking into the face of a hungry Lionbird.

"Then let me in," he commands.

Thetis shivers as she reaches her hands up to the focal point.

Perses does the same and she focuses on the magic, disassembling every knot in Triton's framework until the last piece dissolves.

A loud crack echoes across the sky as the barrier lifts. The soldiers at the main gate start screaming, and when Thetis opens her eyes, she finds herself staring into two dark green orbs.

"Go get her," Perses commands.

Thetis obeys.

CHAPTER 43: TOO LATE

Shea

Caen and Beck are held up by a group of Merrow.
Shea wants to stay and help, but they all agree that she's got to get to the throne room before it's too late.

The barrier has fallen, and their plans are in ruins.

Jo's chambers aren't too far from the throne room, but with the halls filled with Merrow and soldiers, it feels like it's miles away.

Shea strengthens her stance and uses her core, thrusting her hands forward, turning her water into ice and stabbing two Lycon soldiers blocking her way with ten different icicles each.

Jo slices through the one that got a jump on them from behind, taking off his sword hand with a particularly nasty blow before slicing his throat.

Her silver armor is more red than gray now.

Shea reaches out into her mind's eyes, stepping inside Olympus to her room of doors. She goes to Poseidon's connection touching the open doorway, and reaches into his magic. And then she just knows. He's in the throne room.

She decides to do the same with Triton but when she

touches his magic, all she feels is pain.

She stumbles onto the ground and Jo shouts in surprise, reaching for her wife.

"Shea!"

"Jo!" Beck yells, as Caen and he catch up to them.

Shea grips her forehead at the splitting agony, before a single word slips into her mind.

Proteus.

"Triton," Shea gasps.

She's quick to stand. She winces as she tries to dissipate the headache.

"What's the matter with him?" Caen questions.

"He's in trouble. We have to find him."

"But what about Poseidon," Caen argues.

"Triton is the only one who can bring the fleet to Erebos. We have to save him. Poseidon can hold his own. I know it," Shea mutters, hoping she's right.

But it really doesn't matter if she isn't because Triton is their only hope.

"So, where is he?" Beck asks, scanning the halls in front and behind them for more attackers.

"Proteus. I think he's going to Thetis's room for some reason."

"Maybe he thought his son was in trouble." Jo's eyes widen in horror.

Shea shakes her head. "We need to go. Come on."

They race down the halls, taking a right instead of a left toward the throne room.

Two Merrow jump them on their way.

Beck blocks an attack with his steel short sword. He parries the Merrow's thrusts, slamming his shoulder into the creature, throwing it off-kilter.

Caen takes his hammer and bashes it into the still oncoming Merrow's skull, while Jo runs it through.

Shea sees a Lycon soldier coming their way, alerted by the noise. So, she whips her water around, flattening it like a knife, imagining a sharp razor as she searches for a weak link in his armor.

When he throws his arm up to block the water with his blade, she maneuvers it around, impaling him through his armpit right into his heart.

The guard crumples to the ground, his mouth open in a cry, but the sound that comes out is not his own.

Shea jumps at the agonized scream. She whips around to find a Merrow who managed to attain the upper hand in his fight—and cut off Beck's right sword arm at the elbow.

Beck collapses to the ground, and the Merrow brings his blade up for the final stab, but he doesn't make it.

Shea's body shakes with rage. Her blood is rushing again like the ocean in her ears, and her hand reaches out. She flings water out toward the Merrow, and it screams as she forces the liquid through the pores of its skin. She imagines tiny balls of lead zipping from one organ to another, ripping the creature up from the inside. It gurgles, and spews blood, as it coughs up its pulverized internal organs before collapsing on the ground.

Shea can't breathe.

She can't see beyond her fury, her magic pulsing, not ready to be put away.

"I can feel you."

Perses's voice breaks the spell, and her heart freezes in her chest.

Jo's and Caen's voices filter through and when she looks up, she almost cries when she sees the frozen spears pointed at them both, about to run them through.

"Oh gods," Shea whispers, falling to her knees, and the ice spears shatter on the ground.

"I'm sorry," she mutters over and over as she crawls to Beck.

He's holding his bloodied stump, his eyes screwed shut and his face extremely pale.

Shea reaches for her belt with shaking hands, knowing

they need to make a tourniquet, but Caen's belt is already there and he's gathering Beck up into his arms while Jo soothes Shea.

"It's okay, it's okay, we knew you'd stop," Jo tells her, but Shea shakes her head.

"I didn't stop me, Jo. He did."

"Who?" Caen mutters, checking Beck's pulse.

Beck gasps and it's like his soul has entered back into his body. He cries out at the pain, and he's breathing so fast he's going to pass out.

"Beck. I know it hurts, man, I know, but I need you to stay with me okay. Stay with me. We need to find Triton and go."

"What about Poseidon?" Shea argues.

"You said he could hold his own," Caen snaps.

"Yes, for now! Not indefinitely! I figured you'd be a bit more concerned, considering."

"Okay, both of you, zip it! We're almost to Thetis's room and we need to hurry," Jo commands, staring at Beck in Caen's arms.

Beck groans in response, and the reality of the situation sinks in.

They're losing. They run the rest of the way down the hall and they're just about to the guest door, when they turn the corner.

Triton is lying on the ground. His shirt is open, and Thetis is standing over him. Her voice is enticing and full of magic as she whispers into his ear. She has a knife in her hand, and she drags the blade across his chest with a grin, enjoying the way Triton cries out.

Shea searches for his bindings, anything to suggest he's being held down, but there's nothing visible.

Nothing *physical* her mind supplies.

Thetis's amulet is glowing brightly, brighter than Shea has seen before, bloodred.

Shea takes a step out into the open, stepping on a piece

of rubble that crumbles under her foot, making noise.

Thetis turns toward her, her eyes dark red. She straightens up with her knife in hand, leaving Triton unseeing on the floor.

"Hello, Shea."

Shea growls, pulling the remaining water out of her flask, wrapping it around her hands and forearms.

"Looks like I chose a different side." Thetis shrugs.

"Traitor," Shea spits.

Thetis laughs, high and familiar.

"That's rich coming from you. I begged you not to tell him, you promised me you wouldn't, and the moment he figured out who could have brought down the barrier, he came to take my son...Just like I warned you he would!"

"He came to protect him from his murderous, cold-hearted mother!"

Thetis scoffs, sneering. "But then who will protect you?"

"Oh, Thetis, I am way out of your league," Shea drawls.

Thetis screams in fury and Shea lets loose a battle cry as they storm toward each other.

Shea swipes her hands down, slicing Thetis across the chest, and she screams out.

She swipes her knife at Shea, and Shea slides back, slipping out of reach from the blade's edge.

Shea flips back, letting her water bending cushion her fall as Thetis comes lunging at her, but she shoots out her hand, blasting Thetis in the chest with a water column.

Thetis hits the ground with a loud thump and before she can get up, Jo is there with a blade to her throat.

"Ah, ah, ah." Jo clicks her tongue in disapproval, forcing Thetis to remain on the ground.

Caen slips out of hiding from around the corner with Beck in his arms. He's holding his stump gingerly but with a lot more presence.

Thetis scowls at Jo, turning her head to watch Caen as

he places Beck down softly so he can look at Triton.

Triton is staring up at the ceiling, with wide horrified eyes, his hands twitching on the floor as he stares unseeing, trapped in his mind.

"Not medical," Caen mutters, looking up at Shea.

Beck looks over at Thetis and she meets his eyes with a coy grin.

"Bad day?" she asks, gesturing to his arm.

Beck huffs, "Fuck you, Thetis."

"Release him," Shea orders.

"No."

Shea gets up from where she made the blast and marches over to her. She straddles her waist, waving Jo away.

But in her miscalculation, Thetis manages to grab her conch.

Shea's caught in that strange tide again, her breath escaping her, Thetis's voice all-encompassing. She thinks she sees Jo fall to the ground, gasping for air, and there's a loud thump, which Shea assumes is Caen as well.

There's a roaring in her ears, and Shea finally hears the voice clearly from the first time Thetis used her siren magic.

"*Shea...*"

Paetre.

His voice is as distinct as a bell, and she can almost make out his form.

"*It's okay, red. You don't have to fight anymore.*"

He's right.

Shea's so very tired. She doesn't want to be hurt anymore.

"*It'll all be okay. Don't fight it, Shea. Don't fight.*"

That roaring noise is getting louder, the sound of an ocean within her veins.

She can feel herself on the cusp, her breaths coming shorter and shorter. But her blood is practically singing in her ears. Drowning out Paetre's whispers.

"*Fight.*"

Her own voice echoes in the darkness.

"*Fight, Shea. Gods damn it all, fight for them!*"

Her eyes open.

Thetis is smiling up at her, and then Shea meets her gaze and Thetis realizes she's still in there.

Shea cocks her head, and a thread of water wraps around Thetis's throat, thin like a cord, and then tightens.

Thetis's eyes bulge as her air supply is cut off.

Shea thinks she can hear Jo and Caen gasp for air, and Beck calls her name, but she pays them no mind. She has to protect them. She has to fight for them.

She reaches for Thetis's necklace and pulls it off with ease, staring at the shell like she's really seeing it for the first time—and sees sand. Millions and millions of pieces of crystallized sand and then suddenly that's what's in her hand.

She pours the sand out onto the ground, and a figure jolts up into a sitting position in her peripheral, shouting.

Caen seems to calm the figure, so she decides he's not a threat.

Instead she focuses on Thetis's red face, slowly turning purple. She runs a finger down the tan neck, feeling the blood rushing under her skin, like a ruby river.

Hands are pulling on her body and she pushes them away with a wave of her hand, the water protecting her from whoever is trying to stop her from exacting justice. And just as she's about to snap Thetis's neck, she feels a hand rooting around inside her chest.

Someone's in her room.

She closes her eyes and finds herself back in her mind filled with doors, and she sees it.

A girl is trying to close her door. A redheaded child; she is pushing on Shea's door trying to take away her magic.

Shea reaches her hand out, drawing her magic from her own door, capturing the thief. She strides toward her enemy, turning the girl around, gripping her by the throat and finding her younger self. Shea frowns, glaring at her struggling twin, wriggling in her grasp.

"Stop," the girl rasps.

Shea shakes her head, confused. "Why?"

"Because…" Shea loosens her grip on her twin so she can speak. "Because the power does not control us, we control it. Don't let it turn us into something we're not. We're the captain, and this is not who we are."

Shea drops her hand; the twin doesn't cough as she lets go. Instead she turns toward the door filled with turquoise and gold magic and walks through it.

Shea gasps as she comes back to herself, the rage fading, the power slinking back, and she allows Caen and Jo to pull her off of Thetis. She releases the water cord and Thetis coughs turbulently.

Her face is practically purple.

Shea pats Jo's white-knuckled hand, letting her know she's back.

Caen has already left her side, checking on Triton, whose chest cuts are healing.

Triton crawls over next to Beck, and Beck gestures at Triton's healing abilities.

"Nice trick," he croaks, and Triton sighs, seeing his arm.

He pulls Beck against him as they all come back down from the fight.

"You could have killed me," Thetis hisses, fuming.

"Yes," Shea huffs, "but I refuse to let power control me. Because I know now what happens when it takes control of you. You're not a bad person, Thetis, and I hope you take back control before you're truly lost."

Shea grabs her old sword from Jo before the queen can stop her and slams the hilt against Thetis's forehead, knocking her out.

Shea drops the sword, leaning over, resting her arms against her knees and breathing heavily.

"Let's not do that again," Shea groans.

Jo laughs tiredly. "Here, here."

"She brought down the barrier," Triton comments.

Shea rolls her eyes and whispers in her mind so only he can hear, *"No shit."*

Triton bursts out giggling, scaring Caen, who startles and smacks Triton on the leg.

Beck, who has no idea what just happened, starts chuckling as well and Jo eventually joins in.

All of them are hysterically laughing, except Caen, who is glaring at them all.

"Fight's not over," Triton sighs, standing up as the laughter dies down.

"It might as well be," Caen notes.

"No," Shea says, agreeing with Triton.

"Caen, Jo, get back to the *Duchess*. We'll meet you there once we have Poseidon."

"We're giving up?" Beck groans.

Jo shakes her head. "I think we should call this a tactical retreat."

"We'll meet you at the ship once we have our father. If we're not there in half an hour…leave without us."

"And go where?" Jo objects.

"Charis," Caen growls.

Shea nods. "Last resort."

"I don't want you to go, we should just leave."

"I can't leave him here alone. He's still my father, Jo."

Jo grits her teeth and instead grabs Shea's jacket, which is cut to shreds, exposing her black peasant blouse underneath. She pulls her in for a hard kiss and Shea gives it back the best she can.

"Okay," Jo states. "We'll see you at the ship."

"One last thing," Shea says, stopping everyone before they leave. "Jo, I need you to go in there and get Proteus and take him to the ship."

"Shea," Triton argues, but Shea glares at him, shutting him down.

"We can't leave him here. Not with Perses and not while Thetis is like this. You take him. Keep my nephew safe."

Jo hesitates but Caen is already walking inside.

He walks out with a small boy in his arms, still asleep.

Triton gasps, seeing his son for the first time. He walks up to Caen and softly, gently runs a hand over his three-year-old boy's head.

"He's beautiful," Triton murmurs.

Shea wants to give him more time, but they have to go.

"Triton."

Triton nods and steps away.

"Here," Caen tells Jo gruffly, and she takes the boy reluctantly.

"Unless you wanna carry him, that's fine." Caen raises a brow, pointing to Beck, who isn't looking too good.

"I can walk," Beck says, trying to get up, but instead he passes out in Caen's arms.

"Like Hades," Caen sighs.

Shea kisses Jo one last time, and then she watches the four of them leave.

Jo carrying Proteus and Caen carrying Beck.

Shea wonders if this really is the last time she ever sees them all again.

CHAPTER 44: INHERITANCE

Shea

"Triton?"

They're standing at the door to the throne room, and they don't need to be told he's inside. They can feel it.

There are shouts of fighting from behind the doors, swords clashing, pained cries. There are dying men inside.

The door is still sealed shut; they must have come through the gardens because Triton tried it and it's still barricaded.

"Yes?"

Shea swallows. She managed to summon some water from one of the rooms they passed on their way here, refilling her waterskin. She also picked up a black Lycon blade off of one of the bodies closest to the ballroom.

Triton summons water from the air, encasing his fists in ice.

"Are you scared?"

Triton turns to her. "Of what?"

"Death," Shea tells him, staring at the doors, focusing on the noises coming from inside.

There's a large crash of what sounds like a wave pounding against a rock.

Poseidon's still alive.

"Yes," Triton tells her.

"Really?" Shea asks.

"I have so much to live for now. I don't want to go yet. But most importantly, even dead gods all go to the same place. The underworld, where the judges decide each fate. We're not just given a pass. There's a reason most dead gods fall to Tartarus."

Shea shivers at the mention of eternal torment.

Could she go to Tartarus?

Shea steals herself, pulling her water from the flask. She leaves her new blade strapped to her back in a stolen sheath.

"Are you ready?" Triton murmurs, the water around his fists turning back to liquid.

"Always," Shea whispers.

She summons her strength and they blast the door at the same moment, throwing everything they've got against it.

The column breaks the door open in an explosion of noise, the left side swinging off its hinges and slamming onto the floor.

The barricade of wood splinters toward the rest of the throne room, and Shea hopes it kills at least a couple enemies.

They summon their weapons back to them, Triton encasing his fists again and Shea summoning her water lasso.

They take one last look at each other before stepping through.

There are dead soldiers everywhere.

Arethusian men who must have retreated back to the throne room to protect themselves and, probably, to protect Poseidon so Shea and Triton could get here.

Perses is standing near the Arethusian queen's throne.

It's been turned over in the chaos. The consort chair

miraculously stands. The marble flooring is stained with dark bits of flesh and blood.

They spot their father standing in the Amphitrite fountain, he has a shield of water encasing him in a circle, keeping Perses from getting to him.

Perses has no weapons. He's standing there calmly, staring, but not at Poseidon—at Shea and Triton entering the room.

All the screaming from before has been silenced except for one Arethusian on his knees, blubbering as Ceto, in a display of power, slits his throat.

Shea sees Lycon men intertwined with the dead, and two Merrow encased in ice, courtesy of Poseidon she assumes.

But that still leaves another two, growling in front of their master, threatening the two new players in the ballroom.

Ceto's armor shines brilliantly against the morning sunlight. It's gawdy next to all this death, but Shea knows she likes it that way.

Poseidon steps away from the fountain, keeping his shield up. He slowly backs toward Shea and Triton until the three of them stand before the other four—Perses, Ceto, and the two Merrow—in a lineup.

Once he's beside Shea, Poseidon drops his shield, swirling the water around his hands.

"Took you long enough," he mutters.

She huffs a quick chuckle.

Ceto looks as if she might say something but Perses holds up his hand, quieting her before she can speak.

To Shea's surprise, the empress listens.

Her half brother clicks his tongue and the Merrow move from their positions, surrounding Shea, Triton, and Poseidon, leaving Ceto and Perses before them.

In comparison to Ceto's gold armor and spiked braided hair, Perses looks relatively plain. He's wearing all black:

boots, leather pants, and a robe similar to Thetis's that falls about his knee slit in three pleats. His hair is cropped, darker than her own, closer to a brown, but the red is still vivid. But his eyes. His eyes are the exact same shade as her own.

"You made it," Perses announces, his voice drawing her in like an undertow.

"Got a bit held up," Shea snaps, clenching her fists, thinking of Thetis.

"Yes, her alliance was quite a surprise."

"No more than yours and the slave queen," Shea argues, and she sees Ceto's eyes widen.

"He's getting me what I want. How could I say no?" Ceto growls, stepping up next to Perses, but Shea's brother pays her no heed.

"Even you must see how insane this is; you ravaged your own lands! Are you truly so desperate for power?"

"I am not desperate," Ceto screeches, lunging at Shea, but Perses holds her back.

She glares at him, reluctantly obeying his commands.

"And along with this deal I made, I get you in the end. Enjoy captivity. You'll be nothing more than a dog at my feet for the rest of your days."

Shea laughs coldly. "The only bitch I see right now is you." Shea looks between Perses and Ceto and the empress's face turns a dark shade of red.

"You insolent little knife ear—"

"Enough," Perses commands, bringing the focus back to himself. "Darling, let me deal with this please."

He phrases it like a suggestion, but Shea knows an order when she hears one and he is definitely in charge.

She can feel Triton practically shaking beside her; she chances a look at his face, and she notices it's not fear, it's anger.

Perses must see her look, because he glances to their brother with a harsh smirk.

"Hello, brother, it's been a while," Perses states, exposing the shell attached at his waist.

Its color has changed since Shea last saw it; once a beautiful white with orange marks running through the curving seams, it's now a dark purple, molted with spots of brown brimming with the same magic Shea saw coming from Perses's door.

He's corrupted it.

Triton's expression wavers when he sees his tether, before his face hardens again.

She notices for the first time he looks younger than Perses, and Shea realizes someday if they survive this, though it seems unlikely, she'll look older than him too.

"How did you survive?" Triton whispers.

But it's loud enough that Perses hears it. He lets go of the conch, his robes falling back over it.

"It wasn't easy," Perses answers, his voice changing, taking on a darker, sinister tone. "I fell into darkness. Cold, harsh, the pressure almost broke me to pieces, squeezing my bones. I was dying, you threw me to the depths, but you all forgot one thing."

"I don't understand," Triton mutters, but Perses cuts him off.

"You forgot what else was down there!" he shouts. "What else lives in the depths with the monsters you keep, what keeps them contained."

Poseidon audibly gasps beside them, a hand rubbing down his face. He ages remarkably as the answer comes to him first.

"Atlantis."

Perses smiles, and Triton's eyes widen, horrified.

"She saved you?"

"Who?" Shea growls.

"Atlantis," Perses answers. "You see, little sister, the city is more than just that. She's an entity, the soul of the ocean. We, as gods, protect her and her domain, and she grants us the power over it. Her core lives in the depths of the black city, she felt me. Felt my fall. And her one drive, her need, her will is to protect what's hers. So, when she felt a child of Poseidon dying, she rescued me. Fed me some of her own power, allowed me to build my strength and return. She has no conception of right or wrong, she only knows survival. She wanted me to survive."

"You are not a god," Poseidon states.

"It is my right!" Perses bellows, spit leaving his lips.

"You fed from the core, the core of all ocean magic," Triton breathes. "No wonder you're insane."

Perses straightens, his face losing all emotion once more and twisting into a semblance of what others could consider a smile.

"Sister. I want to give you a choice."

"Why me?" Shea questions, warily.

"Because for some reason these pathetic people have chosen you to lead them. So, I'm going to give you a choice, a decision to make, a way to save your people."

Shea brings her hands up anxiously, the water surrounding her pulsing as she watches him nervously.

He takes a step forward and Poseidon transforms the water around him into a trident, pointed at his son.

Triton creates two swords of ice, holding both out to the Merrow behind them.

Ceto draws her sword, but Perses stops her again. She growls in response.

"What choice?"

Perses smiles when she asks, but either way, she knows she can't trust him.

But the longer she keeps him talking, maybe the longer she can think of a way out.

"Clever."

Perses's voice whispers from the back of her mind.

Shea growls, "Stay out of my head!"

"As you wish. Now about that choice. I will spare the people of Arethusa; in fact, I'll spare the city. They can resume their lives here. And I'll leave."

"What? Perses!" Ceto cries, but Perses turns to her with a raging expression and she cowers back, afraid.

"In exchange?" Shea prompts.

"In exchange," Perses continues once he's dealt with Ceto, "you let me kill him."

He points to Poseidon, who now at his weakest can be killed by a mortal blade. Shea is waiting to find out why this all matters, so she remains silent and allows Perses to complete his terms.

"And you and Triton come with me to Erebos, to return to Atlantis and claim our rightful places on the thrones of the black city. As gods."

As he says that, a bit of blood begins dripping from his nose. Flowing freely, it runs down his upper lip, into the crease of his mouth. He doesn't bother wiping it away.

"You wouldn't live long enough," Triton barks, glaring at the two Merrow behind them.

"Don't worry, brother, I have my ways. Now do we have a deal?"

Shea stares at her half brother, examining him more closely now.

He's pale, ghastly so, and there are dark circles under his eyes.

She realizes that his powers haven't made him strong, they've made him desperate, and desperate is something she can beat.

Shea smiles at him with a challenging grin. "No. Sorry, I'm just really sick of men who have these ridiculous entitlement issues."

Shea blasts him in the chest.

Perses goes flying back, and the moment Shea does it, Ceto attacks.

She lunges at Shea with her gold broadsword, slashing it down with a screeching cry.

The Merrow behind them attack and Triton blocks

their blows.

They're quicker, smarter than the ones from before, and he's having a hard time keeping up with their attacks, but he manages.

Perses stands, running a hand through his hair. He draws the water from his clothes and turns it into a spear, pointing it at Poseidon.

Ceto blocks each of Shea's water blasts with her sword, cutting through her magic, and it's then that Shea realizes the blade must be enchanted.

Perses gestures for Poseidon to come get him.

Shea fights harder against Ceto so she can join him, but for now he's on his own. She watches from the corner of her eye as Poseidon takes off running with his water trident, jumping up and slamming it against Perses's spear.

Triton is still fighting the Merrow.

Poseidon is now dueling with Perses, their weapons clashing together with the sound of metal instead of splashes of water.

Leaving Shea alone with Ceto.

They find a bit of space away from the obstacles of the dead and circle each other. Shea with her hands encased in ice and Ceto with her gold broadsword dragging beside her making the worst screeching noise.

"You've come a long way from that little girl on the ship I once knew," Ceto smirks.

"I could say the same about you, at least you're wearing clothes this time."

"I'm going to enjoy breaking you," Ceto hisses.

"You haven't done it yet."

Ceto screams with fury.

Shea braces for the hit, blocking the blow with blasts of ice.

The empress keeps swinging and Shea keeps dodging, staying on the defensive. She can hear Triton grunting in effort and turns to see two more Merrow have joined them;

they must have come from the open doorway.

Her distraction costs her as Ceto cuts her side. She masterfully avoids the full blow so it's a shallow scratch, but it's enough. Her waterskin is ripped apart. The last of her water splashes to the ground.

The surprise makes her lose her bending and she quickly draws the black Lycon blade, catching Ceto's second thrust before it kills her. Shea shrugs off her ruined leather jacket, and when she turns back to face Ceto, the empress moans in delight.

Shea sneers in confusion but catches the line of her gaze and looks down to see her brand is exposed through a tear in the black material. She must have forgotten to cast the illusion charm this morning.

"That brand proves you're mine," Ceto laughs.

Shea snarls, thrusting her sword forward, landing a slap across Ceto's face and throwing the empress to the ground.

"Actually, it just proves what a crazy bitch you are," Shea spits.

Ceto glares up from her position on the floor, licking the blood at the side of her mouth. She scurries away, avoiding Shea's lunge as the elf brings her blade down to stab her through.

She's back on her feet again.

Shea makes a quick check of her surroundings.

Triton is back down to two Merrow.

And Poseidon seems to have gained the upper hand—Perses goes flying into the paneled wall behind the thrones, barely missing the secret door.

"I will not rest until my chains hang from your neck and I'm wearing the tips of your ears on my wrists," Ceto shouts, grinning maniacally.

"What in Hades did I ever do to you?" Shea snaps.

"You humiliated me, and that is the worst offense you could have done. I will not be beaten by some knife ear, by some elf!"

"You're about to be," Shea snarls.

She fights harder, swings and slashes her sword down on Ceto's heavy broadsword. She can see the empress tiring; she's skilled, Shea will give her that, but she's chosen the wrong weapon.

After a particularly hard thrust, the golden sword clatters to the ground as Ceto loses her grip.

Shea uses as much of her strength as possible and kicks her square in the chest.

Ceto flies back, landing solidly and groaning in pain as she tries to catch her breath.

Shea stalks toward her with her blade.

Triton is sparring with the last Merrow.

Poseidon is advancing on Perses with his trident.

They're actually winning.

Ceto scrambles back, choking around the pain in her chest, but Shea simply stomps her foot onto the golden breastplate, pinning Ceto down.

The empress looks confused.

She shouts for help, screaming, "Perses!"

But Perses has problems of his own. He too is on his back with Poseidon about to plunge his trident into his chest.

But a cry splits through the throne room.

Shea turns at the sound and she sees the Merrow got the upper hand.

Triton is on his knees his hands over his face. There's yellow liquid on the end of the Merrow's sword, and it's then that Shea realizes the sword it's wielding is made of the same gold metal as the one Ceto has.

Triton pulls his hands away and there's a long cut starting from the left side of his forehead down to the right corner of his jaw. But what makes Shea freeze, turning her back completely on Ceto, is the fact that the cut isn't healing.

Not like with Thetis's cuts. And instead of red blood, golden ichor flows from the wound.

CHAPTER 44: INHERITANCE

Shea studies the blade the Merrow carries, and a single thought shivers down her spine.

The gold sparkles in the morning light, a bit of magic visible to her eyes. But it couldn't be.

The cut still isn't healing, and Shea knows—she doesn't know how, but she knows. If that Merrow stabs his blade through Triton, her brother will die. Because these blades aren't just any enchanted metal.

Celestial steel.

Shea makes her decision. She cocks her arm back and throws her sword as hard as she can. It swings through the air and she summons her magic, pulling water from the atmosphere, and guides the blade, plunging it into the Merrow's back before he can strike again.

The celestial steel sword clatters to the ground next to Triton, who's shaking from the pain of his slashed face.

Shea worriedly turns toward Perses and Poseidon; her father is staring at Triton, his attention distracted, and Perses goes for something under his cloak.

Shea opens her mouth to shout, but a scream comes out instead as Ceto thrusts a celestial steel dagger through her leg. She startles, when she sees golden blood pouring from the penetration. She crumples to the ground, preparing herself for a final blow, but a splatter of water hits her face instead and she looks up to see Poseidon's water trident sticking out of Ceto's chest.

The empress looks stunned, trying to grab the weapon, but the water dissipates, leaving three open stab wounds in its wake. Ceto collapses to the floor and Shea grits her teeth against the agony.

Triton's hands find her side and she feels his touch along her leg, looking at the dagger. He doesn't seem surprised by the ichor flowing from her.

"Triton, get Dad," Shea orders, biting back a wave of pain.

But as they both look up; they find it's too late.

Poseidon is standing behind the thrones, his face strangely calm while Perses stands in front of him, his hand on the hilt of a celestial steel blade run straight through their father.

"No!" Shea cries, trying to get up, but she can't put any weight on her leg.

Triton is by her side, his breath is ragged, while Perses smiles at Poseidon.

He slides his blade further through until he's pressed against him and whispers something, but Poseidon just continues to stare over at Triton and Shea.

Poseidon smiles.

She can see his lips move, but she can't hear what he says.

Triton gasps as he looks down and he finds his conch shell in his grasp.

Poseidon must have used the last of his magic to steal it. His voice echoes through both their heads one last time.

"I love you."

Poseidon starts glowing. A gold light emits from his body and it hurts to watch. The light obscures their view of the two of them, both Poseidon and Perses.

Shea feels like her skin is burning, like she's in the process of getting an extremely painful sunburn.

The sound of rushing water fills the air.

Water from the fountain is being pulled toward the light, surrounding Poseidon and Perses, but it doesn't block the stunning gold rays.

"What's happening?" Shea screams over the tumultuous sound of the ocean crashing around them.

"He had my sword. That was my sword," Triton mutters to himself, attaching the conch to his waist, before explaining, "Poseidon's immortality is being sucked out of him into Perses. That's celestial grace; if we don't get out of here, it'll burn us to dust."

Triton tries to help Shea up, but she can't put any

weight on her leg, and his strength is weak as well.

They hobble toward the entrance to the garden; the light is scorching their skin. They both look sunburnt and their lips are chapped and dry. It feels like all the moisture in the air is being sucked away.

"I can't," Shea yells. "You have to go, I'm slowing you down."

"I'm not leaving you," Triton shouts back.

Shea pushes him away and he stumbles back.

"Damnit, Triton, think about your family!"

"I am!"

He pulls her close and keeps dragging her away from the throne room.

The light is still raging and the pain on their skin is growing more intense.

Triton collapses, and she falls beside him.

"I'm sorry, I'm so sorry," he tells her.

But it's okay, she wants to tell him, they both failed.

Shea holds on to Triton, their eyes closing as they wait for Hades to take them, but a strong hand wraps around her bicep and pulls her to her feet.

"Sorry I'm late!"

Caen pulls Shea off the ground and into his arms, then grabs Triton, pushing him back onto his feet.

"Caen!"

"Yeah, I know, yell at me later, now we gotta go. Where's Poseidon?"

Triton points toward the light, and Caen nods, not looking back.

He takes off running with Shea in his arms.

Triton remains a few feet behind them, but they keep going. They pass the Lover's Fountain, and Shea absently wonders if it'll survive this day.

Caen leads them through the barracks door, through the hall that's crumbling with dust around them, past the kitchens and servants' hall, and finally out the last door.

A yowl echoes as they exit the palace, and Shea smiles up at her lucky Lionbird. There's a horse waiting and Caen places Shea on first, before hopping behind her and helping Triton onto the back.

Caeruleus flies ahead, scouting. The farther they get from the palace, the more they can see the bright golden light reaching into the sky—it rivals the sun. Caeruleus clears them a path to the harbor, using his claws to scratch out the eyes of any enemy soldiers who dare to stand in their path.

Shea cries as the horse ride jostles her leg.

The light seems contained to the palace, though it shines like a beacon, a golden city on the cliffs.

Caen hurriedly dismounts the steed, and Shea can see the *Duchess* out at sea. He practically throws her and Triton into one of the hidden longboats that remain and rows them out to the ship.

They're about halfway there when the light from the palace seems to expand just a bit more and then clashes like a bolt of lightning, shrinking back into the castle. A loud crack, like the sound of a whip, echoes across the water, and Shea cries out in pain as does Triton.

Their magic snaps in their chests, taking their breath away.

Shea is pulled into her mind, back into her room of doors. She sees Poseidon's door, gold cracks creaking through the frame, and then it shatters. The blast pulls her out of Olympus, and Caen is screaming at her to snap out of it.

A rush of wind settles over the ocean, pushing the boat closer out to the *Duchess* and pressing the ship toward the rest of the sea.

"He's dead," Triton announces.

Shea is breathing heavily. Her magic feels distant, but she notices the shell on Triton's waist is losing the purple shine, returning to the color she first saw it as.

They make it to the ship.

They have to bring up the longboat because Shea can't

CHAPTER 44: INHERITANCE | 495

climb the wooden steps on the side of the *Duchess*.

They pull her onto the deck, Triton following behind with Caen.

Jo is there, holding her, embracing her tightly. She doesn't see Beck but suspects he's down below with Nol.

James is giving orders, and Aster is steering the ship away from Arethusa; they're getting ready to sail her away to the fleet, to Erebos.

Because they lost.

The crew breaks off running in different directions, manning their stations, the gunners finding their places at the harpoon launchers and cannons.

Because they lost.

Jo is examining Triton's cut.

Shea can hear her ordering them both below, but there's something about the ocean wind. Something untamed and wrong.

"We need to go," Caen orders, and the ship lurches forward as it catches the strange breeze.

V is watching Shea and Triton with a miserable expression; Shea's sure she can feel it too.

"V, send notice to the fleet to sail to Erebos," Caen commands, and V nods. She walks away toward the bow.

When she gets there, she holds her hands up to her mouth, speaks softly, and then releases a light. Soft pink rays fly into the air and race ahead out to the horizon.

Shea's watching the palace as the *Duchess* sails away, and she can feel Triton right beside her.

She doesn't know what's happening. She can't feel Perses at all, and it scares her. She wants to know what's happening.

So, she makes a decision.

She enters Olympus, closing her eyes. She journeys down the massive hall to the door where she knows it'll be waiting. The hairs on the back of her neck stand at attention like maybe she's not so alone in this mental palace.

The door is still cracked like before, but the power seems contained, possibly by distance or his new immortality.

She's not sure what will happen when she does this, but she doesn't have a choice.

"Shea, what are you doing?" she hears Triton ask.

"Shea?" Jo's voice joins in too.

But she ignores them in favor of walking closer to the door. Maybe it didn't work, maybe he's dead, and Poseidon's grace killed him. But then she has to know for sure, right? She places her hand on the doorknob, turning it gently; she thinks she can hear Triton shouting at her, but she doesn't listen. Instead, she opens the door, completing the connection between her and Perses.

Power floods her core. Memories split her mind. The Underdeep, the black city, Triton's smiling face while sparring, the despair, the betrayal of their father's rejection to save him from his own magic killing him.

She sees it all, everything, rising in Erebos, her mother...She sees her mother, she's alive!

She sees herself when Perses first formed the connection, she feels a sick sense of pride, of family.

And then Poseidon, his dying face all-encompassing in her vison, the feeling of triumph wrought with pleasure.

Someone's screaming, she can hear it even while trapped in her mind. Then she realizes—it's her.

Her chest aches, and the power is burning through her body. She collapses, falling on her bad leg, letting loose another scream.

"Were you concerned, sister?"

A voice echoes in her head.

"I'm alive. And I won."

Shea shakes her head, gathering her courage.

"Not while I still breathe," she responds.

A cold chuckle lilts through the air.

"Then you best run, Captain, as quickly as you can, be-

cause if that is all that stands in my way, your breath can be easily extinguished."

Shea is brought back to the land of the living when Jo slaps her across the face, breaking the conversation with her now immortal brother.

"I'm sorry," Jo gasps when she sees Shea's awake.

She's on the ground, looking up at Triton, V, Caen, and Jo beside her. The knife, she notes, is still in her leg; she'll need to get that out.

"It's okay. We need to hurry. Where's Proteus?"

"Down below. He's coming?" Caen asks.

Shea nods, and her quartermaster curses, taking off running to talk to James.

"What did you see?" Triton asks.

"Everything. He's alive," Shea tells them and all their faces fall. "But my mother is alive too."

Triton's head snaps up at that.

"Ami?"

"Yes," Shea chuckles.

"She's alive?" Triton bursts out laughing, hollering with delight.

"I didn't know you were so close," Shea murmurs.

Jo is staring at his reaction as well.

V starts laughing too; she's shaking her head, and Shea asks Jo to help her stand so she can look at the goddess of love properly.

"What?"

"You don't know? You still don't know?"

"Know what?" Shea growls.

V looks over at Triton, who's bent over at the waist. His shoulders are shaking, and Shea can't tell if he's laughing or crying with relief.

"Of course they're close. She's his mother too."

"What?" Jo questions, grabbing ahold of Shea so her wife doesn't fall over.

And she just might.

"Ami? Her true name is Amphitrite, goddess of the sea, queen of the oceans, wife of Poseidon, and mother of Triton," V states. "And you."

"But I'm not a god," Shea croaks.

"You sure about that? Because I'll tell you, no demigod I've met has ever been as powerful as you without a price."

"Is it true?" Shea gasps, turning to Triton with Jo's help.

He looks up at her with a tired grin and points to the golden ichor pouring from her leg. "Yes. The knife wouldn't have affected you. You'd be bleeding like normal. But you're a god and therefore vulnerable to celestial steel."

"He has celestial steel? We need to get you two to Erebos," V murmurs, horrified, noting the blade in Shea's leg.

Triton nods, sobering up.

"Why?"

"Because. The king is dead, and Atlantis will need a new ruler; it'll have to be one of you. You'll need to travel to the black city, into the Underdeep, and restore order to the ocean."

"What? I—I can't do that. I don't understand," Shea whispers.

She feels like she's asking this question for the millionth time. "Why?"

"Because if someone doesn't claim the throne, Nereid will have a lot more to deal with than just a pissed off immortal. It'll have the ocean against it, and we don't want the ocean ruling itself. Plus, if it's not one of you who claims the throne, then it could be Perses, and I'd prefer if he wasn't the king of the sea," V mutters.

"This war isn't over," Triton states. "We could still beat him, if we can make it to Atlantis first."

"So not only do we need to get our entire fleet to Erebos before Perses sends someone after us or comes himself, we have to travel into the realm of the gods and enter Atlantis to replace Poseidon to stop the entire ocean from possibly killing us all," Jo says, with an anxious expression. "Is that all?"

"Perses now has the power of the sea god. So he can also bring down Ami's boundary. We should probably expect another army, not to mention convincing the elves to help a bunch of humans," V tacks on to the list.

There's silence around the group.

Shea feels despair trying to settle, but the words inside of herself come back to her.

Fight, Shea. Gods damn it all, fight for them.

"We'll do it," Shea says.

"How?" Jo argues, looking completely overwhelmed.

Shea turns, looking back out at Arethusa, falling away in the distance.

"I don't know," Shea chuckles. "But I refuse to let him win. We'll get Triton to the throne. We have to fight, because I have people worth fighting for."

Shea looks back at Jo, who is smiling at her widely.

She pulls her into a kiss, and she can tell Triton and V are still watching.

"As long as I have all of you, I can do anything. We'll beat him. He's not just dealing with one demigod now, right? It's two gods against one."

Shea holds Jo, and they watch their city fading in the distance.

Jo orders V to help get Triton and Shea below to the medical quarters.

Shea laughs when Caen runs over after seeing her limping toward the deck doors and scoops her up into his arms so she doesn't have to walk.

They're going to make it to Erebos, and she's going to find her mom. She's going to make Perses pay for everything he's taken.

But for now, she rests her head against Caen's chest and lets the voices of those she loves to lull her into a moment of hope.

CHAPTER 45: EPILOGUE ONE

Perses

The light fades from around him, and the next thing Perses knows, he's holding a blade out in thin air.

Poseidon is gone, but he can feel his father's power running through his veins. He feels stronger—and *alive*. He looks over at where Shea and Triton were before and notes their absence.

The woman known as Thetis comes limping into the room. The bodies on the floor are steaming, smoking, burned from the celestial light.

His magic is running wild through his entire system, so that he almost doesn't notice when one of the corpses twitches.

He walks around the remaining throne, and down the steps onto the scorched floor.

Thetis limps toward him and then Coral Fang and a group of Merrow enter the throne room as well. He gestures for them to secure the perimeters and they get to work.

Perses stops in front of the burned body.

The creature is shaking, shivering in pain.

He coldly examines Ceto's bloodied form, her body covered in burns, pieces of her hair missing—and the gold spikes that adorned her once regal head seem to have melted to her scalp.

He can't quite believe she's still alive as he takes note of the three stab wounds on her chest. But then again, serpents have always had a way of surviving even the worst of events.

He squats down beside her, running a finger along her face, and she can barely squeak out a moan.

He cocks his head, smiling at her predicament.

Her burned lips move, and her eyes glisten at the effort.

"Help me," she rasps.

Perses grins. "Oh I will, my love. I know just how to help."

There's relief in her eyes and he shakes his head at the blind trust.

"There's only one way to finish off a serpent," he tells her, standing.

He strolls over to her abandoned broadsword, enjoying the weight in his hands, and then walks back to her.

"You cut off its head," he finishes.

Thetis stands still, watching, hoping she isn't next.

Ceto's eyes widen when she sees the sword, and she uses all her strength to shake her head.

He swings the sword up over his head and brings it down on her neck, severing her marred face from the rest of her disgusting body.

There's a shocked expression on Ceto's decapitated head, and Perses laughs at it.

He turns to Thetis with the blade still in his grip and she takes a step back, stumbling right into Coral Fang, who secures her arms behind her.

"No. Please, I did as you asked, I still want to help you," Thetis pleads as Perses comes closer, until he's standing right in front of her. "They have my son! He's your nephew!"

Perses pauses, then lifts her face from under her chin as he examines her expression, forcing her eyes to meet his.

"Triton's boy?"

She nods, confirming.

"I had no plans of killing you before. You're an elf after all. One of the gods' children, so you were safe from me, but now..." Perses drawls, he leans in and kisses her cheek. "Now...you're family. Release her, Coral Fang, there is much to do."

"What do you want to do about the Lycons?" Coral Fang hisses, releasing Thetis from his grip.

Perses brings his hands up and a dark blue energy, like little sparks of underwater lightning, courses over his fingers. He peers up at them, his green eyes swirling with pieces of gold in them now. His immortal power on display.

"Bring them to me, for they shall receive an eternal reward. We'll need more Merrow anyway if we're to attack Erebos."

Coral Fang smiles in delight and he orders two of his fellow creatures to begin rounding up the remaining Lycons.

"The king is dead," Perses crows, walking back to the thrones.

He gathers some water from the fountain and uses it to right the knocked over throne. He takes a seat and Thetis and Coral Fang follow, kneeling before him.

Perses opens his mouth to continue, when he feels a disturbance within his mind. He closes his eyes, venturing to his room of mirrors inside Olympus. He looks around, nodding with satisfaction when he sees Poseidon's mirror shattered. Triton's swirling looking glass is where it's been since they trained together in the Underdeep. They formed their connection long ago, but a new mirror is now in his inner circle.

One he unveiled but couldn't access without her permission. He strolls over to the magic mirror, placing his hands through the surface, and he can see her standing there on her ship, staring out at Arethusa.

So, they made it.

"Were you concerned, sister?" he teases.

And she doesn't like that. Her turquoise magic bursts with sparks of gold. She doesn't like that at all.

He boasts of his success and laughs at her predictable counter, but a seed of doubt plants itself in his gut as he tests her magic.

He examines it and compares it to his own. They're almost identical.

But not to his mortal magic, no, to his now immortal magic.

She's a mortal god, somehow, not a demigod like he once was. She's like Triton. Suddenly there's cause for concern, indeed, particularly since she's not on his side at the moment.

But she could be, a voice whispers from his mind's shadows.

He recalls the memories that he saw when he opened the connection, the man who wished to be king, the empress of slaves, her fears, yes. But also, those she loves. The queen, the governor's boy, the cropped elfling, the giant, the one-armed Tauri, and the half man.

There's power, and darkness in her. He just needs to expose it.

He threatens her life as casually as advice, and then she fades away. But he needs to deal with this, quickly.

"Sire?" Coral Fang asks, and it seems as if they've been trying to get his attention for a while as they're no longer kneeling.

"Gather a group. Swim out to the *Duchess* and their fleet of refugees, and sink them. All of them."

"Survivors?" Coral Fang inquires wickedly.

Perses smiles. "Those strong enough to survive the siren cliffs, you can let those go, but the ships, I want them all sent to the Underdeep."

"Yes, Master," Coral Fang replies, bowing and stepping away. He whistles for the remaining Merrow to follow him and they do, out the garden.

Thetis steps closer to Perses with a harried expression.

"Please...my lord," she struggles to find the right title before continuing her request, "I believe my son is on the *Duchess*, you can't sink it."

Perses stands, storming closer to her until their faces are inches apart. "I will do as I please," he hisses.

Thetis looks down at the ground, cowering in fear.

"Besides," Perses tells her sweetly, and she looks up reluctantly, meeting his gaze, "he's with his father, and I'm sure Triton won't let anything happen to him."

Perses pushes past her and heads for the broken-down doors.

"Follow me," Perses shouts back to the other elf, and he can hear her high-heeled boots clicking on the marble as she runs to catch up.

"Where are we going?" Thetis asks.

"To make an army," Perses answers. "We'll need one, if I'm going to become the king of the sea."

And with that, they continue the rest of their way in silence.

Perses smiles to himself. *Let's see how powerful my dear sister is...when she loses everyone she loves.*

CHAPTER 46: EPILOGUE TWO

Atlantis

Deep within the Underdeep, away from the monster's trench, past the shipwreck graveyard, and the merfolk's lair...

Black gates rise from the ocean floor.

Sentinels stand along each iron spike, and their electric spears stomp the seafloor in a steady pace, a funeral rite for their beloved king.

Through the gates, the black city awaits.

Atlantis.

Her stunning buildings made of black pearl shimmers from the blue lights trapped within streetlamps along the paths and corners. The towers and mansions reach high toward the surface. Coral trees lay scattered throughout the magnificent city, once home to the old gods of all the oceans.

All of them, the mother of water nymphs, the father of tides, the son of a king, and the old king himself. How Atlantis yearns for the days of old, the days she could taste the power with every step her gods took.

She's waited dormant, longing for her king's return. She mourns the loss of the old sea king. But the throne of power has been empty too long.

Atlantis is alive.

She was here long before Poseidon won her in a game of chance as a guardian of the seas, mistress to the titan Oceanus.

She feels her king's death like the loss of a child.

Her core burns, and her existence tortures her to find the oceans' new master.

Through the city to the palace, to the twin towers, and the royal hall, deep within the immortal rooms, and waiting in the throne room of the gods—the trident pulses, brimming with power, calling to its next master.

The throne is empty; the king is dead; Atlantis cries for her guardian.

Cracks and earthquakes shatter the seafloor.

She extends her power to the surface, past the merfolk, and graveyard of ships, away from the monsters of the deep, and the Merrow hiding in the shadows.

She extends her call to the portal.

The portal leading into Erebos, into Nereid.

She makes the vines surrounding it glow a pale white, and once she feels them in her grasp, she forces them to grow. She imagines the vines crawling toward the elven city, ripping apart the buildings and the earth, swallowing it back into the depths.

It's begun.

She can feel her master's heirs.

Her children above the sea.

She'll bring them down, and back home to take their rightful place in her underwater city, and then, she'll never let them go again.

The thrones of the ocean kingdom groan.

They need a successor.

Without one, the sea will grow untamable, and the world will fall to chaos.

There must always be a king.

Or queen, Atlantis muses, feeling the female child

near.

And if they won't come to her, then she'll bring Nereid down with them.

For the ocean must have a master, and Atlantis looks forward to seeing which one that will be.

The Story Continues In Book Three Of The Veiled Duchess Series, The Veiled Throne.

GLOSSARY

Achelous the white cliffs of Achelous; The crying god cliffs; where elves claimed by Triton go to claim their conch shells from the sirens; the siren cliffs that protect the ocean side the Eastlands.

Achelous Gulf Siren territory, a graveyard of ships in shallow water that protects the ocean coast of the Eastlands.

Acheron Capital city of Lycos, translates in elvish to the City of Pain.

Aiolos reef the reef that used to serve as a barrier between the Old Sea and the Nereidan waters created by Poseidon to expel monsters from the inland waters.

Aphrodite Greek goddess associated with love, beauty, pleasure, passion, and procreation.

Amphitrite Greek goddess of the sea, wife of the god Poseidon, and one of the fifty (or one hundred) daughters (the Nereids) of Nereus and Doris (the daughter of Oceanus). Poseidon chose Amphitrite from among her sisters as the Nereids performed a dance on the isle of Naxos.

Amidship The middle of the ship.

Arethusa Northern queendom on Nereid ruled by a matriarchal line.

Arethusian Rose The official flower of Arethusa; white with blue on the petals.

Aurai Wind spirits that live over the Aiolos reef.

Aquarian Elves who can use water elemental magic.

Aquarius Magic A common gift of the elves and one that solidifies a bond with Water

Azulean Lionbird A creature with the body of a cat and the wings and neck of an owl. It has both vibrant fur and feathers on its body varying in shades of greens, blues, purples, and reds. It has razor sharp talons on its paws and eats small creatures like mice and bugs. They are loyal creatures and will often bond with one being for either it or their entire life. They live an average of 40 years.

Azulshade A plant that grows in the Underdeep and the shores of Tenaro; it has healing properties if turned into a salve, but is deadly if ingested. A black plant with blue veins.

Atlantis The black city and kingdom of Poseidon in the Underdeep; an entity that grants the gods their power (she/her); mistress to the titan Oceanus.

Bos'n A warrant officer or petty officer in charge of a ship's rigging, anchors, cables, and deck crew.

Bow Front of a ship.

Bowsprit The slanted spar at a ship's prow jutting out in front of the ship. It is usually used as a lead connection for a small navigational sail.

Brizo River   The run off river through Oceanus that stems from the Nereus River.

Broadside   A general term for the vantage on another ship of absolute perpendicular to the direction it is going. To get along broadside a ship was to take it at a very vulnerable angle.

Charis   Hidden country to the north of Nereid.

Cabin boy/girl   A child employed to wait on a ship's captain or passengers.

Captain   Captains were selected because they were respected, not because they were feared. When electing a captain, the crew looked for someone who was capable of commanding and navigating a ship. Also, it was crucial that captain had courage and skill in sword fighting and leadership.

Celestial Steel   The only material that can kill an immortal god or titan. If used by a mortal to kill a god it can transfer the essence of that being, turning the mortal immortal. It was created by Hephaestus after the Titan War to keep the Titans at bay.

Claiming   When elves are claimed by the old gods and trained in their specialty of magic, they are claimed priests and priestesses. Some elves come into their magic without being claimed due to many elven children being born outside of Erebos in slavery.

Cocytus   Elven province in Lycos.

Crow's Nest A small platform, sometimes enclosed, near the top of a mast, where a lookout could have a better view when watching for sails or for land.

Council of Nobles The advisory council of elected nobles selected by the Queen of Arethusa to advise and counsel alongside her supreme rule.

Eastlands Elven country on the east coast of Nereid, home to the last of the free elves and guarded entrance to the Underdeep.

Elder Council The high council of elves that lead the separate tribes of the Eastlands and reside in Erebos, the elven capital city that protects the portal to the Underdeep.

Elvish The language of the elves.

Elysium The afterlife for the virtuous souls and heroes of the mortal world. A underworld realm of peace.

Erebos Capital city of the Eastlands where elven clans and tribes gather for the Elder Council meetings, claimings, and other events.

Fates Three women who weave the fate of mortals.

Fire Daisy's Tavern Tavern in Port Town on Orena.

First Mate First mate had rank just below the captain. He would take control of the ship if the captain could not perform his duties any longer. However, pirate ships usually did not have first mates; quartermasters performed their duties.

Forecastle The section of the upper deck of a ship located at the bow forward of the foremast.

Galene Eastern city in Arethusa near the borders of the The Eastlands. Where Lady Catherine, Joana's grandmother lives.

Galleon A large three-masted sailing ship with a square rig and usually two or more decks.

Gangplank A board or ramp used as a removable footway between a ship and a pier.

Grace A Charis or Grace is one of three or more minor goddesses of charm, beauty, nature, human creativity, and fertility, together known as the Charites or Graces.

Gunner Gunners were leaders of small groups who operated on the artillery. They watched for the safety of their men and usually aimed the cannons themselves.

Gunwale The elevated side edges of a boat, which strengthen its structure and act as a railing around the gun deck. In warships the gunwale has openings where heavy arms or guns are positioned.

Helm The steering wheel of a ship, which controls the rudder.

Helios Island to the east of Nereid. Was once a massive slave port and it's where Captain Shea Lara found Aster.

Hippokampos General Soren of Arethusa's naval ship; a mythological creature with the head and body of a horse but bottom half and back legs of a fish. Often refered to as a Seahorse.

Hold A large area for storing cargo in the lower part of a ship.

Hull The body of a ship.

Hypnus Eastern port of Lycos, near the volcano.

Hydra of the Sea The Hydra was a Lycon royal vessel that carried the Pearl of Lycos before it was sunk by Shea.

Iron Serpent The Oceanan naval ship that was sailing Beck and his people to Arethusa before it was sank by Perses.

Knowman's Canyon Apart of the Pieria Islands, south of Nereid.

Libras Elves who can use air elemental magic.

Libra Magic A common gift of the elves and one that solidifies a bond with the Air.

Longboat The largest boat carried by a ship, which is used to move large loads such as anchors, chains, or ropes. Pirates use the boats to transport the bulk of heavier treasures.

Lycos Southern empire on Nereid ruled by emperors or empresses who come into power either by force or birth. Capital of the elven slave trade.

Mainmast The longest mast located in the middle of a ship.

Megathirio Elven word for water dragon; a giant water dragon with red scales that lives in the monster's trench of the Underdeep and breathes boiling water.

Melinoe River Major river in Lycos.

Merrow Former elves who were either banished or never escaped the Underdeep during their claiming and turned into horrid fish beings left in the depths. They fell under Perses command when he freed them from the ocean realm.

Metis Capital city of Oceanus.

Nereid Island continent home to four countries: Arethusa, Oceanus, Lycos, and the Eastlands.

Nereus River Largest river in Nereid, runs from the ocean through Arethusa and ends right before the border to the Eastlands.

Nereidan Ocean The ocean on the east side of Aiolos reef that spans past Nereid and around many of the neighboring islands.

Oceanus Free state, which won its independence from Lycos over a hundred years ago. Ruled by a lineal position called the governor and a senate.

Oceanus Senate Elected officials that rule the free state of Oceanus alongside the Governor, who inherits their position.

Old Sea Name for the Ocean between Tenaro and the Aiolos-Reef.

Orena Merchant island in the Old Sea that is the halfway point between Nereid and Tenaro. Known for its exotic markets and for being outside the law. Its a safe haven for outcasts, criminals, and runaways looking to escape their countries.

Pearl of Lycos A black pearl the size of a child's fist, surrounded by gold and silver tentacles inlaid with precious gems; passed from Lycon ruler to ruler until Captain Shea

Lara stole it and sold it on the black market.

Pinnace A light boat propelled by sails or oars, used as a go between for merchant and war vessels; a boat for communication between ship and shore.

Pieria Islands South of Nereid, where Knowman's Canyon is located.

Poop Deck The highest deck at the stern of a large ship, usually above the captain's quarters.

Port The left side of the ship when you are facing toward her prow (opposite of starboard).

Port Town The city on the shores of Orena.

Poseidon God of the sea, earthquakes, storms, horses, and ruler of the Underdeep, the underwater realm of the sea gods.

Quarterdeck The after part of the upper deck of a ship.

Quartermaster After captain, the quartermaster has most authority on a pirate ship. As a captain's right hand, he was in charge when the captain was not around. He had the authority, and he could punish men for not obeying commands. Quartermaster was also in charge of food and water supplies.

Queendom A queendom is when all power is concentrated in a central female figure. A matriarchal monarchy ruled by a strong queen.

Rigging The system of ropes, chains, and tackle used to support and control the masts, sails, and yards of a sailing vessel.

Rivren Western province in Arethusa.

Sagittarian Elves who can use fire elemental magic.

Sagittarius Magic A common gift of the elves and one that solidifies a bond with Fire

Scuttle A small opening or hatch with a movable lid in the deck or hull of a ship.

Scylla A legendary monster that lived on one side of a narrow channel of water, opposite her counterpart Charybdis.

Seams The slums and underground of Lycos.

Slaver's Bay The largest slaves port in Nereid located on the shores of the Lycon capital, Acheron.

Slippery Serpent The pub and inn in low town of Arethusa; Venus's establishment.

Spyglass A telescope.

Starboard The right side of the ship when you are facing toward her prow (opposite of port).

Starfish Cross The road on Orena that leads to the near center of island.

Tartarus Realm in the underworld of eternal torment for immortals.

Tauri Elves who can use earth elemental magic.

Taurus magic A common gift of the elves and one that solidifies a bond with the Earth.

Tenaro Islands The westernmost islands hundreds of miles off the coast of Nereid; aka World's End.

Thalassa Capital city of Arethusa.

Titan War War between the gods and the titans fought long ago.

Trident's Fork Road Often referred to as the Trident; it runs up and down Nereid as the main road.

Triton A Greek god, the messenger of the sea. He is the son of Poseidon and Amphitrite, god and goddess of the sea respectively, and is herald for his father. He is usually represented as a merman, which has the upper body of a human and the tail and fins of a fish.

Underdeep The underwater realm of the gods.

Vault of Secrets The Lycos Vault of secrets passed down through each emperor and empress currently in the possession of Empress Ceto of Lycos. The largest archive of information in Nereid.

Veiled Duchess the Duchess; Shea's ship, passed down to her from Paetre Lara and passed down to him from Captain Phoebus of Orena; dark cherry wood planks, almost black; burgundy sails; three masts galleon.

ACKNOWLEDGEMENT

First, I want to thank all of my supporters and the fans of these characters and books. You have been such an excellent source of light in my life, and I am so happy to share these crazy characters and stories with all of you.

Thank you to my editor Kelley Frodel. Your comments keep me going, and your edits make my story possible. I've loved working with you, and I'm so glad to share this fantastic journey with your incredible talents.

This year I was able to get the audiobook for The Veiled Threat, the first book in the series done, and it was because I found the woman who was able to bring all of my characters to life. To the real-life Shea Lara, Jess Nahikian, thank you for all of your hard work, and I can't wait to start on The Veiled Descendants with you!

To my husband, James, you're my biggest supporter, and none of this would be possible without you. Thank you for helping me achieve my dreams and always encouraging me to reach for the stars.

To my parents, Mom and Dad, another book down. I love you both so much and thank you for instilling in me the drive to persevere even when it seems impossible.

To my little sister, you little monster, I'm so proud of the work you've achieved this year, and now I'm going to have to write another book just to show you up. I love you, pumpkin head.

To my girls, Lauren and Julia, you lot keep me sane and make me feel valued. Thank you. I could not have asked for better friends, even if I created them myself. You are both inspirations to me, and your futures are stories I refuse to miss out on. Thank you both for all your support.

Lauren, you were able to recreate the world in my head on paper and I am so in love with the new map. Thank you for encouraging my work. You've always been one of my biggest supporters. None of this would be possible without you.

And finally, once again to all my readers, thank you. Thank you for reading, for laughing, for crying, for loving, and hating along with me. Shea Lara is a character I hold very dear, and her story has changed my life. Thank you for joining me on this incredible voyage, and I can't wait to show you what happens next in the final book of the first trilogy, The Veiled Throne.

ABOUT THE AUTHOR

Sophia Menesini

Sophia Menesini lives in Martinez, CA, with her husband and their three dogs, Ziggy, Zeppelin, and Tali. The Veiled Threat was her debut novel, and The Veiled Descendants is the sequel in The Veiled Duchess Series. She has an Associates in History and currently attends UC Davis to finish her BA. Sophia is an avid tea connoisseur and lover of Scotland with an unconventional memory for obscure Disney and Broadway song lyrics.

BOOKS BY THIS AUTHOR

The Veiled Threat

Captain Shea Lara is the leader of The Veiled Duchess, the most feared pirate ship in all of Nereid. And now, after completing her former mentor's final score, she's retiring. Everything she's known seems to be coming to an end. Until a night in her favorite tavern, when a mysterious stranger drags her back into the fold with an offer for a score, she can't refuse. All she has to do is kidnap the crowned princess of the northern Queendom, Joana of Arethusa. The prize is just within reach. But sparks fly as the two women collide. And a veiled threat that could upturn Shea's entire world storms on the horizon. Join the crew of Captain Shea Lara as they battle their way through dangerous court intrigue, rebellion against slavery, an unlikely romance, and ultimately face villains who masks conceal them till the very end. Something's brewing on the horizon and the Veiled Threat is just the beginning.